SARAH MAY

The Rise and Fall of the Queen of Suburbia

A black-hearted soap opera

HARPER

Harper
An imprint of HarperCollins*Publishers*
77–85 Fulham Palace Road,
Hammersmith, London W6 8JB

www.harpercollins.co.uk

A paperback original 2006
6

A catalogue record for this book
is available from the British Library

ISBN-13 978-0-00-723232-1
ISBN-10 0-00-723232-2

Set in Meridien by Palimpsest Book Production Ltd,
Grangemouth, Stirlingshire

Printed and bound in Great Britain by
Clays Ltd, St Ives plc

THE RISE AND FALL OF THE QUEEN OF SUBURBIA

Sarah May lives in London with her theatre director husband Benjamin May and their sons. She is the author of three previous novels: *The Nudist Colony*, which was shortlisted for the Guardian First Book Award, *Spanish City* and *The Internationals*. She is currently writing her next novel for HarperCollins.

Visit www.AuthorTracker.co.uk for exclusive information about Sarah May.

Praise for *The Rise and Fall of the Queen of Suburbia*:

'May's shrewd sideways glance makes this a novel moving and menacing by turns. Her ensemble – aerobics-obsessed Linda, rebellious Dominique, the creepy Niemans – are often gruesome, but all too convincing.'

Observer

'The narrative is beautifully observed, with the subtle touch of a writer who makes every action and mannerism feel plausible. Sarah May has a rare talent for melding the farcical with the tragic, and has produced a novel which – but for an ending worthy of Tom Sharpe – is a scathingly successful piece of social commentary.'

Daily Mail

By the same author

The Nudist Colony

Spanish City

The Internationals

This book is dedicated to all parents who dream of bringing their children up in a better world, out of harm's way . . . and to all children who dream of escaping and getting in harm's way. *Que Sera Sera.*

My overwhelming thanks go to all the extraordinary women who made this book possible, in particular – Katie Espiner at HarperCollins, for her enthusiasm, commitment and understanding of the darker side of life; Clare Alexander at Gillon Aitken Associates for her beyond-the-call-of-duty support, demonic tenacity and unflinching ability to respond to e-mails written in the early hours of the morning, and last but not least . . . Jennifer Hutchinson and Sarah Weedon, for providing the sort of childcare you can't pay for.

I would also like to thank my husband for keeping our marriage going during Linda Palmer's reign of terror . . . there were more dark days and long nights than I'd ever want to have to account for.

PROLOGUE

ELECTORAL ROLL

LITTLEHAVEN DISTRICT

POLLARDS CLOSE

Cont RH12 9NA

1260	YOUNG, BRIAN	02
1261	YOUNG, SHEILA	02
1262	SAUNDERS, MICK	04
1263	SAUNDERS, DOMINIQUE	04
1264	25 Jan 84 SAUNDERS, DELTA	04
1265	NASSAM, OSMAN	06
1266	NASSAM, SANDRA	06
1267	PALMER, JOE	08
1268	PALMER, LINDA	08
1269	NAME REMOVED	10
1270	KLINE, VALERIE	10
1271	KLINE, BRENDAN	10
1272	NIEMAN, WINKE	12
1273	NIEMAN, DAPHNE	12
1274	NIEMAN, PAUL	12
1275	BROWNE, ANTHONY	14
1276	KLUSCZYNSKI, MARGO	16

9 DECEMBER 1983

8

It had been snowing in Littlehaven for what seemed like forty days and forty nights, and everyone over four feet tall was tired of having to keep Christmas tree lights on all day long so that flickering neon could counteract a numb and unanimous sense of foreboding. The real world and snow didn't go.

Then on 9 December, which was a Friday, it stopped.

Inside No. 8 Pollards Close the heating was pumping and the blinds in the master bedroom were still on tilt. Linda Palmer was naked, bent over the open drawer of her vanity unit. When she straightened up, a pair of clean bikini briefs in her hand, she was able to see not only herself, but the reflection of the TV screen and Selina Scott's face just left of her hips, at pussy-level.

She put the bikinis on and turned the TV off. Since the show's first airing in January she had done Diana Moran's workout faithfully every morning, but now they were nearly at the end of the calendar year, her body had clocked up over eighty hours of workout since then and the Green Goddess just didn't do it for her any more. The Green Goddess was for people who wanted to be like Linda Palmer, so what did she want with the Green Goddess when she already *was* Linda Palmer.

She turned back to the vanity unit, changed the Barry Manilow cassette in the stereo for a Bruce Springsteen compilation, then climbed onto the mail-order exercise bike she'd had long enough for the rubber stoppers on the legs to leave imprints in the carpet. With the switch on *dead flat* she started to pedal. If she didn't do twenty minutes before the aerobics class, sweat formed on the back of her pink and grey striped leotard, and at the end of class Dominique Saunders would ask her if she was okay; tell her she looked tired.

A slow track came on, something about Vietnam, and she switched to *gradient*. She was just getting into the uphill rhythm when the phoned started to ring. After counting six rings, she flicked the switch from *gradient* to *dead flat* to *off*, and dismounted.

'Is that you, Joe? Joe?'

'Hello? Mrs Palmer?'

'Joe – is that you?'

'Mrs Palmer?'

The voice sounded foreign, and she didn't feel like being spoken to by a foreign-sounding voice right then. 'Who is this?'

'Mrs Palmer, it's Mrs Klusczynski.'

'Who?'

'Jessica's advanced physics teacher.'

Linda backed away from the vanity unit, put the phone on the floor and jammed the receiver between her right ear and shoulder. The only word she caught the foreign voice saying was 'advanced'. 'Listen, if you're trying to sell me anything . . .'

'It's Mrs Klusczynski, from Jessica's school.'

'. . . anything at all, I'm just not . . .' she stopped herself.

8

A long time ago, she had trained herself to keep the unfamiliar in the background, and this is what she did now. The foreign woman faded out and all she could hear was Bruce, still singing about Vietnam, and she couldn't work out if he'd actually been or not or whether this even mattered. Maybe she was just missing the point. 'It's who?'

'M-r-s K-l-u-s-c-z-y-n-s-k-i,' the foreign woman yelled down the phone.

Linda held the receiver away for a moment as forty years of Poland in exile made its way through the barricade of redneck vocals on the stereo. She had a sudden image of a woman who wore cardigans and the sort of slip-on shoes that were more prescription than high-street, emerging from one of the two-bedroom terraces at the top of Pollards Close with her severely epileptic son. 'Wait. Mrs Klusczynski, top-of-the-Close Mrs Klusczynski?'

'That's right. I'm also your daughter's advanced physics teacher here at school.'

'Her physics teacher. Right. I knew that. Sorry. I'm with you now.'

Looking at her alarm clock, she saw that there was less than an hour to go before class. The phone line fell in a coil between her breasts as she got back onto the bike. 'I'm with you now,' she said again, sideways through the receiver as she started to pedal.

'Mrs Palmer, are you still there?'

'I'm here.' She flicked the switch to *gradient*, and breathed out hard.

'I'm afraid there's a problem with Jessica.'

'A problem?'

'It's an interesting problem.'

Linda had never found problems interesting and didn't like the fact that Mrs Klushwhatever was enjoying this conversation more than she was. 'Yes?' she said harshly, switching from *gradient* to *gradient: steep*.

'She refuses to complete – no – even to look at the module on nuclear physics, which is a compulsory part of the A Level examination.'

'What d'you mean "refuses"?'

'I mean she walked out of my classroom just now on ethical grounds.'

Mrs Klusczynski paused. She sounded pleased and this confused Linda, who had begun to swing her head slightly in an attempt to regulate her breathing. 'You're sure?' She couldn't imagine Jessica walking out of class.

'I'm sure. It's never happened to me before.'

This was too intimate – more of a confession than a comment. Linda arched her back and tried to relax her shoulders.

'But the school said to put her in for early-entry A Level Physics. They said she was a straight "A" – no doubt.' Linda was having trouble finding enough oxygen to speak, think and cycle at the same time.

'There is no doubt. All we have to do is get her to overcome her reaction to "nuclear" in the syllabus. I respect it. I respect Jessica and her decision,' Mrs Klusczynski added, 'but she doesn't fully understand the physics of it. Once she understands the physics, or begins to understand, she will be able to see – or she will be a lot closer to seeing, anyway, that it's not the physics that are corrupt.'

Linda became suddenly, acutely aware of her thigh muscles.

'. . . She can't study physics and turn a blind eye to the splitting of the atom. That's not wanting to know the whole truth . . . that's fanaticism –' Mrs Klusczynski said, carried away, '– and ignorance.' The art block was being refurbished

10

and they were holding art classes in the science block this term. She reached out for the plastic cup full of mixing water that Miss West had been using during the last period and drank it like coffee. 'I urge you and your husband to talk to her.'

'We'll talk,' Linda said, with a hungry intake of breath.

'Tell her – tell her not to throw her strength away on morality; that's not the path for Jessica. Tell her –'

'If she does the work she's meant to do on this . . . this . . . module, she'll still be in line for an 'A'?' Linda cut in, breathless, thinking about the number of times she'd told Dominique Saunders and others that Jessica was going to get an 'A' in A Level Physics – and Mathematics – at the age of fifteen. Trevor Jameson at the *County Times* was going to run a whole feature on her when she did – and here was some foreign woman whose garage wasn't even an integral part of her house talking to her about nuclear bombs; about Jessica and nuclear bombs. Why was this all anyone ever talked about any more? She lunged forward as her lungs collapsed, her entire weight on the edge of the saddle . . . fuck the bomb.

'Mrs Palmer? So . . . you'll talk to Jessica, Mrs Palmer?' Mrs Klusczynski no longer sounded convinced. 'I had to give her a detention, I'm afraid. Whatever I think of what she did, I have to make it clear to the rest of the class that walking out in the middle of a lesson is unacceptable behaviour, and . . .'

'You gave her a detention?'

'Don't worry, an hour's supervision in the special needs room is all it really amounts to.'

'Tonight?'

'Tonight, yes, between four and five.'

'But I'm having a dinner party tonight. The Niemans are coming to dinner, and . . . Jesus, that's enough.' She

11

flicked the switch down and changed gear, at last finding some sort of karma between the balls of her feet and the pedals. 'Jessica was meant to be helping with the canapés . . .'

16

Mrs Klusczynski put the phone down, pulling a tissue out of her cardigan sleeve and wiping her mouth, which was tingling. She had phoned Mrs Palmer to talk to her about her daughter, and Mrs Palmer was having sex. She was sure of it. She looked at her watch – it was ten a.m. – and carried on dabbing at her mouth. There had been music in the background as well. Mrs Palmer had taken a phone call concerning her only child while having sex to music. She stared at the tissue, which was stained black – why was that? – then through the windows in their chipped, cream-painted metal frames. Standing up on the rungs of the stool, she could see the entire school playing field. It had stopped snowing.

8

Linda pressed the phone against her chest and rested her chin on it as she recalled what it was she had been trying to remember about Mrs Klusczynski, who lived at No. 16. It had happened the summer they moved in. Mrs Klusczynski had been to meet the local-authority bus that used to drop off her son, who was prone to, on average, seven fits an hour, and Linda was watching mother and son walk back up the street, when it happened: Peter had one of his fits and collapsed onto tarmac that was melting in the heat. She remembered Joe, who was coming home early from work, leaving the car in the middle of the road and breaking into a run – she'd never seen Joe run before. He took off his suit jacket and put it under Peter Klusczynski's head, and she watched from behind the blinds in the lounge as he carried the boy indoors, into their kitchen, sat him at the old dining-room table – the one they used to have before the glass-topped one – and gave him water to drink. Mrs Klusczynski hovered at the front door in a canary yellow sundress and Linda stayed in the lounge because she didn't know what to say to her. At that moment she didn't understand Joe bringing the boy into their house like that.

'You all right?' she heard Joe say.

'Peter?' Mrs Klusczynski's voice came through the front door.

Afterwards Joe walked mother and son up the street. Linda saw him and the Polish woman talking together and the car still parked in the middle of the road with the door open. For a moment, the world felt as if it had suddenly emptied and she was the only one standing there, watching, only there was nothing left to watch, and someone somewhere was laughing at her.

4

By the end of the aerobics class, Dominique Saunders' leotard
was wet and the 'D' pendant on her necklace was stuck to
her collarbone. She crouched down at the side of the hall
where some orange plastic chairs were stacked, rocking back
on the heels of her Reeboks while trying to regulate her
breathing and not worry about the fact that Linda Palmer
still wasn't sweating.

Mrs Kline from No. 10 sat slumped beneath the Union
Jack the Guides used for church parade, in a well-worn
peach and turquoise tracksuit. The sort of tracksuit you put
on, Dominique thought, to gorge and cry in. The sort of
tracksuit she didn't possess; not even as a secret. Mrs Kline
was sitting with her legs stretched out across the brown
carpet tiles that covered the floor of the Methodist Church
hall, wiping sweat off her forehead and studying the palm
of her hand.

Dominique wondered what had made Mrs Kline, who
weighed sixteen stone and who had done the class barefoot, decide to take up aerobics. She didn't strike her as the
sort of woman losing weight meant anything to.

Linda knelt down next to her, her blonde perm letting

off hairdresser-fresh aromas, and they watched as Mrs Kline put a pair of summer sandals on over some socks. It took her a while to get to her feet and when she did she walked unevenly towards where Dominique and Linda were sitting. Dominique realised, too late, that she was coming to speak to them, and that she should have said something before now anyway, given that they were all neighbours.

'Haven't seen you here before,' Dominique said.

'No. Well.' Mrs Kline smiled shyly.

'Thought you'd come along and give us a try-out?'

'Well. Yes.'

'Well. Great.' Dominique hung back on her heels.

'Well,' Mrs Kline said, clutching the empty carrier-bag her sandals had been in. 'Bye.'

'What was she thinking of coming here?' Linda said, realising that the story of Mrs Kline at Izzy's aerobics class – that she could try out first on Joe when he got home – would go well with the gazpacho tonight. 'Does somebody who's murdered her husband and buried him at the end of the garden have the right to come to an aerobics class?'

'That's only rumour,' Dominique said.

'Well, I thought we were going to have to resuscitate her after the high kicks and that's not fair on Izzy – having someone in the class she might have to administer first aid to.'

They watched the Reverend Macaulay talking to Izzy as she stacked the blue aerobics mats away.

'What's he doing?' Linda said.

'Telling her about the design for the new stained-glass window behind the altar.'

'How d'you know that?'

'There was something in the local paper about it.'

'But how d'you know that's what they're talking about?'

'That piece of paper he's showing her.' Dominique

17

watched Izzy in her rainbow-coloured head and wrist bands, smiling at the Reverend Macaulay.

'Is stained glass something she's into?' Linda asked.

Dominique shrugged. Mrs Kline was more of a problem for her. As much of a problem as the rapport between Izzy and the Reverend Macaulay and their mutual interest in stained glass was to Linda. Things that didn't fit; things that broke up the rhythm they lived their lives to. 'Right. That's me. Everything.'

'You off?' Linda asked.

'Mick's taking me out to lunch.'

Linda didn't want to think about lunch – she'd been on a liquid shake diet for the past fortnight. 'Where's he taking you?'

'Gatwick Manor – and the snow's stopped so we might actually make it.'

'The snow's stopped?' Linda said, then called out, 'See you tonight,' as Dominique left the church hall in her new sheepskin hat. 'Around seven thirty. Don't forget.'

Through the windscreen of her two-seater green Triumph that was an anniversary gift from Mick, Dominique saw Mrs Kline, in sandals, waiting at the bus stop, which was banked in grey slush. She slowed down, trying to imagine Mrs Kline in the seat next to her with her empty carrier-bag and having to talk to her for the ten minutes it would take them to reach Pollards Close.

Mrs Kline watched the green Triumph pass, not bothering to back away from the kerb when the car's acceleration sprayed the pavement with more slush as it sped up again.

Dominique told herself that Mrs Kline probably had shopping to do or friends to meet for lunch, but she knew this wasn't true: Valerie Kline had an armchair lunch every day in front of *Dr Kildare* repeats. She'd seen her through the windows of No. 10 with her legs rolled up under her, a plate of food balanced on the arm of the chair and Richard Chamberlain on the screen.

She'd probably watched the series as a teenager when it first came out, Dominique thought, suddenly able to see – clearly – an immaculate room with antique rugs and cut flowers that somebody had been taught how to arrange, and an overweight girl sitting in it, alone with Dr Kildare. And into this room walked a young man . . . or rather arrangements had been made for a young man to walk into this room and turn the overweight, lonely young girl into Mrs Kline.

Five years into the marriage, Mr Kline had bought No. 10 Pollards Close, a four-bedroom executive house on Phase III of the Greenfields development, and moved Mrs Kline and their adopted son into it. Then he left for work one morning and never came back. He hadn't been seen since, and nobody in Pollards Close really remembered him. Dominique had heard rumours during waxes at Sinead's that Mrs Kline waited a fortnight before informing the police. Without really knowing why, she had a sense that the marriage had been brutal. She thought about Valerie Kline at aerobics that morning in her peach and turquoise track-suit, and the way she looked standing at the bus stop in socks and sandals with an empty carrier-bag in her hands. Then she thought about the table in the bay window that Mick always booked when he took her to Gatwick Manor because it overlooked the gardens. She couldn't have lived Valerie Kline's life; she couldn't have lived a single second of life as Valerie Kline.

8

It was three o'clock in the afternoon and Linda was standing in the lounge of No. 8 Pollards Close tilting the blinds so that she could see out into the street. The blinds were part of an over-order for Quantum Kitchens that Joe had brought home and put up at the lounge windows and all the bedroom windows at the front of the house as well because Linda liked things to match. They were made of strips of stiffened fabric connected by chains that clattered when you tilted them. They were clattering now and it was making her nervous. The snow had eased off again and she'd just got in from the new Tesco superstore on the other side of Littlehaven that had launched an inflatable elephant for its opening week. She saw them launching it from the roof while she was there, and men in suits had been wrestling with guide ropes. When she got home she realised she could see it from the window in the spare room, but what had she been doing in the spare room anyway? She couldn't remember. Now here she was looking out into the street from behind the same blinds Joe had in his office, chewing her nails and wondering why Dominique and Mick weren't back from Gatwick Manor yet; eaten away by the fact that they were probably in one of the hotel's rooms together right now having sex in the afternoon on linen sheets. A married couple having extra-marital sex with each other.

The only thing that managed to distract her was a purple Granada turning into the Close and parking outside her house. She watched as a man in a ski jacket with what looked like oil stains on it got out of the car and started to walk down her drive. She went outside.

'Hello?'

'Wayne Spalding,' he said, flipping up the sunglasses lenses attached to his spectacles. 'Local council.' He paused. 'Were you going out?'

'No, I was –' She looked down and realised that she still had her coat on – a grey fake fur one that an anti-vivisectionist once spat on. 'Did you say local council?'

'Environment department.'

'The tree. Of course.'

'We tried telephoning this morning, but there was no answer.'

'I was at an aerobics class,' she said automatically.

This seemed to please him, and the way he looked at her made her feel as though she had done something worthy; something moral even, and this confused her momentarily: a) because she didn't like him very much, and b) she'd never really thought of aerobics as either moral or immoral. 'D'you want to come through?'

She led Wayne Spalding through the garage and he held the door open for her as they went into the back garden.

'You've got a lot of snow here,' he said.

'Hasn't everyone?' Linda smiled, and walked into the middle of the garden, trying not to notice the trail of dog turds dotted across it. 'There she is. The bane of my life.'

Wayne Spalding turned his flat stare to a four-hundred-year-old Turkey oak. Half the tree overhung the back fence of No. 8 Pollards Close, its lower branches disappearing into the snow piled on the lawn.

'You should see it in autumn.' Linda crossed the snow with Wayne following her like a prospective buyer, his basket-weave grey loafers sinking twenty centimetres deep. 'The leaves make me really frantic. Really, really frantic.' The idea of a rogue tree was gaining momentum with her; it helped keep her mind off the fact that the Niemans were coming to dinner that night; that Joe hadn't called yet; that Jessica was in her first ever detention; and that there were still no lights on in the Saunders' house. 'The leaves get – just – everywhere. All round here. Everywhere. My husband,' she sighed, 'well, he's a busy man and it would take him all weekend – all of an entire weekend in something like October, November – to clear this lawn.' She faded out, less sure. Wayne Spalding was still staring flatly, his bovine gaze on the spot where the lowest branches disappeared into snow like they were about to start growing downwards into the lawn. Linda felt a sudden panic. The tree had intentions. It wanted to ruin things for her.

'You see what I mean?' she said, pointing to the branches. She glanced at the dandruff in Wayne's hair. 'The council should be doing something about it.'

'I'm here, aren't I?' Wayne said, without turning round. He walked over to the fence at the end of the garden where some honeysuckle had been dying ever since Linda planted it two summers ago. 'It's nearly four hundred years old. Healthy,' he said, looking up into the tree then reaching out for a lower branch and running his hand along its underside.

The garden at No. 8 was the same as all the other gardens on the executive side of Pollards Close: approximately one hundred and forty-four squares of turf that had grown into 144m² of lawn infested with a strain of clover that not even

Flymos were able to eradicate (Linda was convinced the clover was Irish), and bald patches where paddling pools stood during photogenic summers. The whole thing was framed with puddles of buddleia, lilac, viburnum and hebe. The gardens arrived on the back of contractors' trucks and were left pretty much as they were delivered. The world in which people who moved there found themselves was too new for them to contemplate changing.

Wayne Spalding counted the paces between the spot where the branch touched the lawn and the house. He walked past Linda, his flat eyes on the patio doors.

'What are you doing?'

'Just checking something.' He paused, watching the TV through the double glazing. 'Anyone in there? Anyone watching that?'

'My dog, Ferdinand. He likes TV.'

'You've got the TV on for your dog?'

'He's a dachshund.'

He turned and stared at Linda for a moment then walked back up the lawn, counting his paces again. 'Waste of electricity.'

Linda didn't say anything. She wanted to, but couldn't think of anything, so she put her hands in her coat pockets instead.

'You've got a lot of space between the house and the tree. A lot of space,' he said to her, adding, 'This is a big garden' – making it sound like excess rather than achievement.

Linda began to get the feeling that her time was being wasted. 'So what are you saying?'

'I mean, even if there was a storm and the tree got hit by lightning – even if that happened and we determined that the tree would fall into your garden and not into the field, even then –'

'Even then, what?'

'Well, it wouldn't hit the house.'

'Hit the house?' Linda shouted. 'I was just talking about leaves.'

Wayne stared at her.

'So I'd have four hundred years' worth of oak lying across my lawn, but it wouldn't hit the house? What then?'

'You'd have to call a tree surgeon.'

'And how much would that cost?'

'Look,' Wayne moved his hands slowly up and down, pressing the thick, cold air downwards with his palms. 'Look,' he said again, louder, as if Linda was already hysterical and not just showing signs of it, 'I've done the risk assessment.'

'You've done it? That's it? That's your risk assessment?'

'That's my risk assessment, and I can safely say that there is no risk. That tree poses no threat to your property, none whatsoever – not even in the event of an act of God.'

'Wait. Wait. Wait.' Despite the heavy cold, she could feel angel wings of sweat growing across her back. 'That's all there is to it? You walk across my lawn and that's it? What if . . . what if we're out here in the garden in the summer having a barbecue . . . and the tree falls down? What about that?'

Wayne thought about this, his face going grey now with the cold. 'The wind would have to be gale force to bring that tree down – why would you be barbecuing in the middle of a storm like that?'

'Listen, I phoned your department and talked to some-body about leaves, not lightning and . . . and storms, and oh, for Christ's sake.'

'Do *not* take the Saviour's name in vain. I won't have that,' Wayne said quietly, pointing his thick mitten at her.

'I'm not having this,' Linda said after a while. 'You walk across my lawn . . . you've got no equipment with you or anything, no tape measure or . . . or machinery. You don't even have a clipboard. I want a second opinion.'

'I can put it in writing.'

'I don't want *your* opinion. I want someone more senior.'

'You want someone older or someone more important?'

Linda swung nervously from side to side not knowing what to say again, and this wasn't like her. She had to be herself tonight; she had to be wholly herself because the Niemans were coming to dinner.

'We can't just go round cutting down all deciduous trees on the estate,' he said.

'I don't follow.'

'Deciduous means that a tree sheds its leaves in autumn.'

'I know that,' Linda snapped.

'No you didn't.'

'I did.'

'You didn't. You should be more honest.'

'I don't accept this,' she said loudly, trying to fold her arms, which was difficult with so much fake fur encasing them.

Linda followed Wayne Spalding back across *her* lawn, through *her* garage, and onto the road outside *her* house where he'd parked his car. 'I really don't accept this.'

Wayne got into the car and wound his window down. His trousers were wet to the knee. He flipped the sun lenses down over his spectacles again and two discs of tinted glass stared up at her so that she was looking back at herself, twice over.

'Do you get hot in the summer?' he asked her suddenly.

She checked to see if there was anybody around who might have heard this: only Mrs Kline, lumbering down the pavement towards them in the tracksuit she'd worn to aerobics that morning. 'Do you get hot in the summer?' he asked her again, his voice as flat as his eyes. She stared at his hands, loosely gripping the steering wheel. The oversize mittens were on the seat next to him and the backs of his hands were covered in freckles. She didn't like freckles on men. Was Wayne Spalding hitting on her?

'He planted trees to provide shelter from the heat.'

Linda hung back, lost. 'Who did?'

The streetlights came on, making everything seem much darker.

'God did – and you should think about that. You should think about that a lot.' He turned the ignition on. 'Do you have children?'

'Just one daughter.' Why was she telling him this?

'Then you should think hard about trying not to take the Lord's name in vain. For your own sake. For the sake of your daughter.' He looked up at her. 'I can help you, Mrs Palmer.'

'I don't need your help.'

'People say that. Then things change. People change.'

'I don't know what the hell you're talking about.'

She stood on the drive and watched the purple Granada pull away, thinking about phoning the council's environment department and speaking to Wayne Spalding's boss – if he had one – before he got back to the office, but she didn't move.

The Granada disappeared round the corner into Merrifield Drive and the next thing she was aware of was Mrs Kline standing at the top of the drive.

'Hi,' Linda waved and turned abruptly towards the garage.

'I didn't know you knew the minister.'

She spoke so quietly, Linda half considered pretending she hadn't heard. There were a couple of gateaux she needed to get out of the chest freezer in the garage for the party that night. 'Knew who?'

'The minister,' Valerie said, more loudly this time, still smiling.

'What minister?'

'Minister Spalding. Our minister.'

Valerie Kline waited at the top of the drive.

'The man in the car?' Linda called out. 'The man who was just here?'

Valerie nodded.

Linda hesitated then walked to the top of the drive. Valerie, she noticed, was still wearing sandals. 'He was from the local council. He came about the tree. You know, the one that hangs over most of our back garden?'

Valerie didn't know because she'd never been invited to No. 8 and didn't ever expect to be.

Linda was becoming increasingly unnerved by Valerie Kline's silent, comprehending nods. 'We have a huge problem with the leaves. In autumn. A really huge problem.' Behind her, through the open garage door, she heard Ferdinand whining. 'So what's this about a minister?' she said impatiently.

Valerie stopped nodding, suddenly. 'Oh, I'm sorry, I forgot he worked for the council as well – the environment department, isn't it?'

'So – he's Minister Spalding?'

Valerie started nodding again. 'At the Free Church. We hold a service up at the school on Sunday mornings, and I thought . . .' she batted her hand quickly in front of her face, '. . . anyway, it doesn't matter.'

Linda thought of Wayne Spalding as he'd been dressed today. 'The Free Church? What's that then – evangelical or something?'

'It's non-denominational, that's why it's called the Free Church.'

Linda couldn't be certain, but wondered if Valerie might be laughing at her. 'And Minister Spalding,' she said hurriedly, 'does he do that healing stuff?'

27

'The healing stuff? He does the laying on of hands. Faith healing.'

'What – like making cripples walk? Blind men see? Cancer disappear? Infertile women pregnant?' She forgot, too late, that Mrs Kline's son was adopted. 'That kind of stuff?'

'Sometimes,' Valerie said, quietly.

It was starting to snow again.

'He does that? What – like – miracles?'

Valerie shrugged.

Linda couldn't shake the impression that Valerie was laughing at her, and it didn't seem right that they should be standing here talking about miracles in the middle of a snowstorm.

'I should go, we've got people coming to dinner tonight,' she said.

'Well . . . give my regards to your husband, and to Jessica,' Mrs Kline replied, disappearing into the snow in her track-suit and sandals.

Linda went into the garage and lifted the lid of the chest freezer, on the brink of remembering what it was she needed to get out for dinner that night when she heard the phone ring. She dropped the lid, letting it bang shut.

'Where are you?'

'Brighton,' Joe said.

'Still? It's nearly quarter to four. I thought you said you were leaving at three?'

'It took longer to pack away the stall than I thought – then I called in to see your mum.'

'My mum?'

'Just a cup of tea. I'm leaving now.'

'Well, if it's of any interest to you, I'm going out of my mind over here,' Linda exploded. 'There's a blizzard you're probably going to get stuck in if you stay there any longer drinking tea; Jessica – who's meant to be coming home to help me – is in detention because of something nuclear; and this man from the council came round to talk about the tree, you know – the tree – and I thought we would just talk about the leaves, but he didn't want to talk about the leaves, he came to do a risk assessment – with no warning or anything – and then when he got into his car to go, some end-of-the-line Granada – he had freckles, Joe, all over his hands – he started talking to me about God – the man from the council – and Mrs Kline says he's a minister or something, and . . .' She stopped suddenly.

'Linda?' Joe prompted her.

'Gateaux.'

'What?'

'The freezer. Triple chocolate mousse cake and Black Forest gateau – that's what I was looking for in the freezer.'

Down the line from Littlehaven to Brighton, faster than the speed of light, came a profound sigh of relief.

Tired, Joe Palmer had made a deal with Steve, his business manager. If Steve agreed to oversee packing up the two showroom kitchens and stand into the van, Quantum would pay for him to stay in the Metropole that night and he could drive the van back to Littlehaven on Saturday morning.

'I could do that,' Steve had said, off-hand but sincere at the same time. Neither of these were qualities Joe liked on their own, but Steve managed to run them simultaneously and it had always made Joe trust his business manager.

He'd left the Brighton Centre, where Britannia Kitchens roadshow had been running for the past three days, and crossed the road onto the promenade. As he walked it had started snowing again and the headlights of late-afternoon traffic picked people out, making them look more interesting than they did in daylight. Above and beyond the traffic was an uneven December night, and the sea, which he couldn't see but knew was there. Something that was true of a lot of things in life, he supposed. He'd heard it dragging itself backwards and forwards across the pebbles on the beach, distant and impartial.

The pier had been open, sending out its multi-layered stench of fish and chips, waffles, candyfloss and donuts: smells he found less easy to stomach the older he got. He'd thought about the penny slot machines in the amusement arcade, but it was too cold and anyway he'd promised to drop in on Belle, Linda's mum.

The Pavilion Hotel on the corner opposite the entrance to the pier hadn't drawn its curtains yet and passers-by were treated to a panorama of geriatric diners eating in sync. Foreign waiters stood poised against green fleur-de-lys wallpaper as the diners stared out the window, past the SAGA TOURS coach, looking for someone or something they might recognise.

Joe had passed the Aquarium where he used to take Jessica when she was small, then carried on up Roedean Road that rose with the cliff. No. 26 still had its stained-glass hotel fanlight: a rising sun with LYNTON HOTEL written underneath. It used to belong to Jim, Linda's stepfather, and after his death it had been bought by a trust that built sheltered accommodation for the elderly. It was flats now – he didn't know how many. There were six buzzers by the door and he was sure there had only been four the last time he came.

How could they say the world was getting bigger when all the time they just kept on dividing it up like this. What was it Jessica said? Something about matter being continuous, that you could divide up one piece over and over again and never stop. He didn't understand what Jessica said half the time – hadn't understood what she'd been saying, in fact, since she was about nine. But then children, he discovered, were the one thing in life you could love without understanding.

He rang the bell for Flat Three, which used to be the upstairs residents' lounge, and about four minutes later a young woman in jeans opened the door, a pair of scissors in her hand.

'Hi,' he said.

'Hi.' She stared at him. 'Belle said it would be you.'

'Who's me?'

'You're Joe, aren't you? Her son-in-law, Joe? There's a photograph of you on the sideboard upstairs. You on your wedding day,' she said slowly.

'Ah.' Joe didn't want to think about his wedding day right then, and his prick – which had gone from belonging to Joe Palmer to belonging to a munchkin to belonging to a Lego man – was about to drop off with the cold.

'Only you're old now.'

'Older,' he corrected her, shoving his way into the hallway. 'But then that's only natural.'

The girl nodded, unconvinced, and led the way upstairs past the badly maintained stairlift tracks.

'I sent Lenny down to get the door. She's younger than me,' Belle said as he walked into the flat.

She was sitting in her wheelchair with a Chanel towel wrapped round her shoulders, which Linda had got free with some perfume and given to her mum as a Christmas present. The girl, Lenny, went and stood behind her and carried on cutting Belle's hair. The toes of her boots were covered in grey curls and a halo of them had formed on the carpet around the chair.

When Joe thought about it later, it was what he remembered most about that afternoon in December: the sound of the scissors and Belle's grey curls on Lenny's boots.

'Don't mind, do you, Joe?' Belle asked. 'We was right in the middle.'

'You go ahead. Wouldn't want to get between a woman and her hair.'

He went over to the window, pulling the nets to one side. A seagull on the ledge eyed him and let out a shriek then flew away. In summertime you got a bird's-eye view of the nudist beach from here.

'Not such a good view in December, is it?' Belle said, smiling.

He looked to see if Lenny was smiling as well, but she wasn't.

The room was lit by the gas fire and a couple of heavily tasselled standard lamps with shawls draped over them. The lack of overhead light combined with net curtains, snow and twilight made it difficult to see anything but shadows in the room, and the flat suddenly felt as though it was waiting for somebody long overdue.

'Your eyes all right?' Joe asked Lenny.

She nodded, tucking the scissors into her belt as she started setting fat pink curlers in the old woman's hair.

'D'you want tea?' Belle asked Lenny, her eyes closed. Then, without waiting for an answer, 'Go and make us some tea, Joe, and don't forget the biscuits.' Her eyes opened and followed her son-in-law into the kitchenette in the corner. 'And you can take your coat off – the flat's got central heating.'

The light in the kitchenette was orange and unsteady, and speckled with the corpses of flies. It made his eyes hurt. Belle's cupboards were full and it took him a while to find the tea caddy – the one with elephants on that he remembered from his courting days – behind the rows of sugar, flour and canned fruit and vegetables that she always had in, never having recovered from rationing and the urge to

32

stockpile. The whistling kettle had been replaced by an electric one, and as he plugged it in he wondered when the overhaul had happened and why Lenny, the hairdresser, didn't like him. Animals and children liked him, which meant that most men and women did as well. Why didn't the hairdresser? He looked down at his black suit and dark purple tie and thought about her standing in the hallway with the scissors.

In the room next door the hairdryer went on, and when he took the tea in neither of the women looked up. Belle still had her eyes closed and he hoped she hadn't fallen asleep. He put the Coronation tray on the coffee table and walked past the photographs on the sideboard, as alarmed as he always was at how prolific they made his life seem. They were nearly all of him, Linda and Jessica. The only one Belle had of herself was of her and her first husband, Linda's father, who had drowned in the sea while home on leave at the end of the war. This was the first thing Belle ever told him. Then she said that Eric had never been able to make her laugh while he was alive, but talking about his death always set her off.

There were no photographs of her and Jim, her second husband, or even just of Jim. When he died all the money from the sale of the hotel went to Brighton Cricket Club, who got a new clubhouse and practice wickets built with it.

Joe looked at a photograph of himself as a grown man then looked away. The hairdryer cut out.

Belle's hand went up to her hair and Lenny unhooked the mirror from the chimney breast.

'Isn't it nice? Won't last, but isn't it nice?'

'Won't last if you keep touching it and messing it up. Here.' Lenny took a can of spray out of the case on the table and covered Belle's head in it.

The spray hung heavily in the heated air.

'You staying for tea?' Belle asked her.

'I should go. I've got Mrs Jenkins in Flat Four to do, and she's going out tonight.'

'Jenkins is always going out,' Belle grumbled. 'Probably goes out more than you do, and she's not "Mrs". Never got married – whatever she says. Pour her a cup, Joe.'

'Milk? Sugar?' he asked.

'Both,' Lenny said, packing away the hairdryer, scissors, spray and rollers into the case.

'How many?'

'How many what?'

'Sugars.'

'Three. Please.'

'How many sugars'll you have, Joe, now she's not here to tell you off?'

He smiled, but didn't put any in his cup.

'Go on, just have one.' Belle turned to Lenny. 'He used to have sugar with some tea in it when I first knew him. Won't let you have sugar no more, will she?'

'Linda's just looking after me.'

'That's what she calls it, is it?'

Joe paused then dropped a spoonful of sugar into his tea. 'Look what you made me do, Belle.'

Belle smiled, pleased at her son-in-law's dissent.

Lenny, moving about rhythmically in the corner of the room, didn't look up.

'Joe's been at the Britannia Kitchens roadshow at the Brighton Centre. His company had a stand there.'

Lenny looked up, taking in the suit. 'That's what you do, then?'

'Course it's what he does, I told you.'

'What?' Joe said to Lenny, over Belle's head.

'Build kitchens?'

34

'He doesn't build kitchens, he sells them, but that isn't what Joe does.' Belle slurped her tea and started on the biscuits. A flake of chocolate melted in the corner of her mouth and ran in a rivulet down one of the wrinkles there. 'Joe makes money.'

'I'm a carpenter,' he cut in. 'By trade, I'm a carpenter.' Why did he think this sounded better than making money?

'Was a carpenter.' Belle wasn't having any of it. 'Now you just make money. Got a whole office full of people working for you. Joe's got his own company.'

'I'm a carpenter by trade. My dad was a carpenter.' If Lenny didn't look up or say something soon, he thought he was going to explode. 'I'm from Brighton,' he yelled. 'Brighton born and bred.'

Lenny turned her back on him and clicked the clasps on the case shut.

'Cassidy Street. Right there on Cassidy Street.' He gestured blindly at the net curtains as if his entire past lay just beyond them.

'Calm down, Joe,' Belle said, leaning forward to pour herself another cup of tea and farting. 'You've earned the money. No need to be ashamed of it.'

Lenny drank her tea in one go and at last turned to look at him. 'What makes you think I'm from Brighton?'

'I don't know, I . . .'

'You think I'm from Brighton?'

Belle started rattling the biscuit tin. 'These'll melt if we don't eat them. What'd you put them so near the fire for, Joe? Look at this!' She held up her hands, covered in chocolate, for him to look at. 'Look at this, Joe. Why'd you get the chocolate ones out? It's a bloody sauna in here with the gas on and you know what I'm like with the chocolate ones.' She let out another fart. 'I'll sit here and eat them all. Why'd you get these ones out?'

'I don't know.'

Belle was disappearing out of earshot.

'Turn the heating down, Joe. Have a fiddle with the thermo-stat or something, there's bloody chocolate everywhere.'

'Skirton Street,' Lenny said.

'What?' Joe couldn't hear. The flat was suddenly made of chocolate and it was melting.

'I grew up on Skirton Street. The one after Cassidy.' She was smiling.

Lenny the hairdresser was smiling.

'The thermostat, Joe. Just behind the microwave.'

'Skirton Street. I know Skirton Street,' he said to Lenny.

'There you go then,' she said, walking past him into the kitchenette and re-emerging with the carpet sweeper.

'Don't know why you put the microwave there,' Belle said to Joe, 'I can't get to the thermostat.'

'All right, Belle, I'll sort it out.'

'It's just behind the microwave.'

He went into the kitchenette and found the thermostat, which was above the sink. When he went back into the living room, Lenny was gone. 'Where did the hairdresser go?'

'Don't know why you put the microwave there.' Belle shook her head. 'Didn't you get me any tissue, then? I'm covered in bloody chocolate.'

Joe went back into the kitchenette and pressed his knuckles into the sink rim, letting his head drop between his shoulders. After a few minutes he grabbed the kitchen roll off the windowsill and went back into the living room.

'Pass me that.' Belle flicked her eyes over him, her hands full of kitchen roll. 'You should phone Linda or I'll be getting into trouble for keeping you here.'

He stood there watching the kitchen roll moving in her hands, the rings and liver spots suddenly intensely familiar.

'I'll be getting into trouble,' she said again.

He sat down in the armchair that matched the lamp-shades on the standard lamps and dialled home.

After a struggle, Belle dragged the small leather pouf across the rug towards her. She heard 'Brighton', and 'I called in to see your mum', and 'Just a cup of tea. I'm leaving now', then settled her head back against the cover she'd crocheted for the wheelchair, put her feet up on the pouf and let out a small, silent fart. Joe was going to do something stupid, she was suddenly convinced of it – and Joe wasn't the kind of man who could get away with doing stupid things and not suffer the consequences. What had she done?

Linda went into the shed to look for a bucket. She couldn't remember whether they had a bucket or not, but she hadn't been able to find one in the house or the garage so if they did turn out to have a bucket, this is where it would be. The torch-beam swung across the red-tiled roof and upper-storey windows of the doll's house Joe built Jessica for her fourth birthday that was put into storage by the time she was six, after the incident with the Sindy dolls. Linda had been cleaning Jessica's room one day and opened up the doll's house to find a scene inside worthy of a Turkish prison. Jessica had a penchant, it turned out, not only for cutting off her dolls' hair, but for holding bits of them – usually the forehead or breasts – against light bulbs until the plastic melted. There wasn't a doll with nipples intact or a complete forehead left.

The light hit a Classic Cars calendar for 1979, hung on a rusting nail, the page turned to May. The girl in the picture was wearing a white cowboy hat and looked happy. She didn't know why Joe had put the calendar up. The off-cut from the lounge carpet at Whateley Road that he had put down on the shed floor was much more Joe than the Classic Cars calendar; much more the Joe she knew anyway. She looked down at the orange swirls, remembering Whateley Road as clearly as if it was a place she could walk into. They'd had a bucket at Whateley Road – Jessica's old nappy bucket – that she used to mop the kitchen and bathroom floors with twice a week, and that Joe used to wash his car and the windows with. Whateley Road had been immaculate – bacteria free.

Then she moved to Pollards Close and met Dominique, who didn't mop floors or put magazines at right angles on the coffee table, or iron the family's underwear. Once a week an elderly woman with facial hair and arthritis came and cleaned No. 4 Pollards Close. She did the ironing as well, and in between her weekly visits Dominique just let the fallout gather. When they ran out of dishes she bought Findus ready meals and they ate them out of the cartons; clothes were worn un-ironed, and dirty underwear was left stranded on the bedroom floor. Linda remembered on only her second visit to No. 4 – while drinking coffee from a cup with rings of stains inside – the cleaner coming downstairs with a pair of lace knickers in her hand.

'What d'you want me to do with these?' She held them up in a crabbed hand to show where the lace panel at the front had been ripped.

The three women stared at the ripped knickers. Linda tried to take a sip of her coffee and burnt her mouth.

'Bin them,' Dominique said.

The cleaner nodded, her yellow eyes watering, and left the room.

'No initiative,' Dominique apologised.

Linda soon realised that Dominique and her cleaner were playing games with each other. War was going on; a war that had never been declared, which was what games were, she supposed: war without the declaration, and people played them whether they loved each other or hated each other. Not because life was too short, but because for most people life was too long. Even people like Dominique, who got their underwear ripped during marital sex. All Linda saw for months afterwards, every time she shut her eyes, was the pair of knickers held aloft in the cleaner's arthritic hand. What kind of animal was Dominique married to? An animal who knew how to fly planes, and who looked like an anarchic version of Cliff Richard: Captain Saunders.

No. 4 was a pigsty whose pigs were having sex, and its slovenly glamour was something Linda spent a lot of her early months in Pollards Close trying to emulate, until Joe complained. Then, when she finally persuaded him to take on the Saunders' arthritic cleaner themselves, she got embarrassed about the state of the house and ended up cleaning the day before the cleaner arrived. The thought of a stranger finding pubic hairs in her bath made her wince, and this was something she just couldn't change about herself. After ten months the arthritic cleaner handed her notice in. She stood there in a badly felting jumper with a row of snowflakes knitted across it and told Linda that her conscience wouldn't let her carry on taking money from her every Thursday. Linda handed her an envelope with her last week's wages in and the yellow watering eyes nodded their thanks. No. 8 Pollards Close became immaculate once more, and that month Linda ordered over fifty pounds' worth of home-improvement gadgets from the *Bettaware* catalogue, including a hands-free can opener, a vacuum packer for storing summer clothes under the bed during the winter and vice versa, and a stone frog with a hollow stomach to hide spare sets of keys in. She especially loved the frog that came lying on a lily pad – until Dominique pointed out that it looked like it was masturbating.

After a while she found a bucket shaped like a castle that they must have bought for Jessica on one of the Dorset holidays. Ever since the company had taken off she'd tried to persuade Joe to take them somewhere they'd need suntan lotion, but he didn't like it abroad – wherever that was. The white plastic bucket handle had rust notched into it from where it had been hanging on a nail in the shed wall. Inside there was a web, but no spider. Linda went back into the garden. When did snow fall so hard and fast it technically became a blizzard? She swung round, the bucket in her hand, and tried to pick out the lights at the back of the house while wondering if anybody had ever died in a blizzard in their own back garden before, but was too preoccupied by the Niemans coming to dinner that night to imagine her funeral properly, and Joe's grief over her tragic death.

Trying not to look at the tree, whose branches stood out clearly, she ploughed through the snow to where she'd seen the dog shit earlier. If this blizzard carried on the turds would be buried, but she needed to make sure because she wanted to put the garden floodlights on later, the ones Joe put in last weekend, and leave the curtains in the lounge open, and she didn't want Mrs Nieman staring out through the patio doors at a trail of turds. She stumbled around for a while, her nose streaming and the bucket banging against her thighs, but the turds were buried without trace.

Just to make sure, she went back into the garage and flicked on the switch for the garden lights. Peering through the kitchen window, she could see floodlit snow and, if she concentrated, the pond Joe put in last summer for his fish. Joe loved fish; he loved sitting in his deckchair watching them, and he'd made a good job of the pond. She was proud of it as well because theirs was the only back garden in Pollards Close with a pond, but was it worth putting the lights on tonight if the guests had to concentrate in order to see it? Was concentrating something you should expect guests to do?

She carried on staring through the window, becoming slowly more aware of the kitchen behind her, reflected in the glass, than the floodlit garden on the other side of it. There were two empty plates on the breakfast bar where there had been a triple chocolate mousse cake and Black Forest gateau before she went into the shed. She turned slowly away from the reflection in the window to stare at the real plates on the real breakfast bar. For the next two minutes, she swung between reflection and reality, her life pivoting on the fact that the gateaux were no longer there. She'd been on the Slimshake diet for over a fortnight now. Was she so desperate for solids she'd eaten the gateaux herself – without even realising?

Still in Jessica's old Wellingtons, she ran into the garage, yanked open the lid of the chest freezer and pushed her arms through a month's worth of freezer food the Ice Man lorry had delivered only yesterday, but there were no more gateaux: cheesecakes, but no gateaux; ice cream, but no gateaux. She'd spent hours over the Ice Man catalogue preparing the order, and the gateaux had a whole centre spread to themselves. She could see that centre spread now as she walked in from the garage.

'Ferdie! FERDIE!' she yelled.

A dog's collar bell tinkled in the living room.

She went through. The dachshund she'd asked Joe for last Christmas stood up on the sofa, but looked as though he was still sitting.

An oasis of brown and pink vomit lay underneath the coffee table, caught between spasmodic festive light from the tree and the aura from the TV.

Ferdinand was panting expectantly.

41

Linda went over to the patio doors and slid them open. 'FERDIE, OUT!' She gave a nasal yelp, trying not to breathe the stench in.

The dachshund jumped off the sofa and went over to the vomit, nosing his way round it.

'FERDIE, OUT!' Linda grabbed hold of his blue-studded collar, dragging him through the carpet and the open patio doors. 'OUT, YOU FUCK.' She slammed them shut before he managed to get fully outside and his tail, which was trapped inside, went stiff. Ferdinand screamed.

She slid the door open then shut it on the dog's tail again. 'You fuck, Ferdie, you fucking, fucking dog.'

Ferdinand was trying to turn round and reach the part of him that hurt, but his head kept smashing into glass. Linda didn't hear the front door open. 'Those were centre-spread gateaux, you fucking, fucking fuck of a fucking –'

'Mum!'

'What?'

Jessica came running into the lounge, covered in snow, her school bag still over her shoulder and her keys in her hand.

'Mum – what's going on?'

Linda turned round, but could hardly make out her daughter standing there. 'What?'

'Let Ferdie go.'

'Why should I?'

The dog started to howl.

'Let him go,' Jessica shouted, trying to pull Linda's arm off the door. 'Come on, Mum.'

Ferdinand pulled himself suddenly out from between door and doorframe and shot across the garden leaving a thin trail of blood specks across the snow.

'He's bleeding. You made Ferdie bleed.'

Linda slammed the door shut and tried to regulate her

42

breathing just like she'd tried to regulate it on the bike that morning and then at class, but failed because she was so wound up about the Niemans coming.

'He ate the gateaux. Both gateaux,' she said.

'What gateaux?'

'The centre-spread gateaux. The gateaux for tonight.'

'He wasn't to know.'

Linda surfaced from her rage, gasping for air. 'And Mrs Klushky rang me today,' she said, trying not to let the fact that Jessica hadn't taken her shoes off in the hallway bother her.

'Klusczynski,' Jessica corrected her.

'Klushwhatever. She gave you a detention.'

'Did she tell you why?'

'She told me, and we need to talk about this.'

'I don't want to talk about it, and anyway the teacher who was meant to be giving it never showed.'

'But it's five o'clock now – what have you been doing?'

Jessica was watching Ferdinand in the garden. 'I was with Peter Klusczynski. He was in detention as well. He had a fit during period two and Miss Witt sent him to special needs.'

'You were in special needs?'

'It's where detentions are held.'

'With Peter Klush . . .?' Linda didn't want to think of her daughter holed up for an hour alone with Peter Klushky. It would be just like her to fall for an epileptic. 'But what did you do?'

'We talked,' Jessica said, staring through the patio doors. 'It doesn't matter – I think Ferdie needs to see a vet.'

'It does matter. I need to phone the school about this.'

'Since when have you ever phoned the school?' Jessica said, rounding on her.

'Jessica . . .'

'I don't want to talk about it, Mum.'

'Well, we are going to talk about it. Maybe not tonight, but we are going to talk, and now I need you to clear that up,' she said, pointing to the vomit underneath the coffee table. 'There's a blue jug under the sink, and some carpet shampoo. Use the floral bouquet room spray when you've finished. Leave no trace.'

'Where are you going?' Jessica asked.

'Out.'

'Out where?'

'To find dessert. We have no dessert. I need to find dessert.'

Jessica let her miner's bag, which had badges pinned all over it, slip off her shoulder onto the carpet. 'But what about Ferdie? Ferdie's bleeding, Mum.'

Linda ignored her. 'When I get back we need to sort out the canapés. And,' she stared past her daughter, suddenly realising that the blinds at the front window were still open, 'shut those bloody blinds.'

She put the fake fur coat back on over her sweatshirt and jogged through the blizzard across the road to the Saunders'. Stephanie, who was six, answered the door dressed in a fluorescent emergency services outfit. Her feet, in rollerboots, were moving backwards and forwards across the parquet in the Saunders' hallway.

'Hi.'

Stephanie took an orange ice-pop out of her mouth and stared at Linda's Wellingtons. 'Hi.' She put the ice-pop back in.

'Is your mum in?'

Stephanie shook her head then took the ice-pop out of her mouth again. 'My sister's been crimping my hair. She's going to do my whole head.'

'Who's there, Steph?'

'Delta? Are you in there?' Linda called out.

'Who is that?'

Stephanie skated off down the hallway.

Linda hadn't slept for a week when Dominique told her she was having her fitted carpets ripped up and parquet flooring laid down. Then Dominique told her how much it was costing – and she let Stephanie skate indoors? On the parquet flooring? She'd tried telling Joe at the time that Dominique would never get the asking price if they sold the house without fitted carpets, and Joe had said, 'not these days'. 'Not these days'? Joe wasn't a cryptic man – she was used to understanding him. So what did he mean by that? She felt she was missing something that Joe was on to – that everybody but her was on to.

Delta appeared in a kimono that belonged to Dominique. Linda recognised it immediately. It was the one Mick had brought back with him from a trip to Kyoto, and she was struck – as she always was – by how much more attractive Delta was than her own daughter. Especially in Dominique's kimono. She couldn't imagine Jessica wearing any of her clothes.

'How are you, Linda?'

Delta always called her Linda – never Mrs Palmer – and even though the smile was frank, for the second time that day Linda got the feeling she was being laughed at. 'I don't suppose your mum's in, is she?'

'Nope.' Delta shook her head, then trod in the puddle of melted orange pop. 'Shit – what's this?'

'I think it might be Stephanie's ice-pop.'

Delta looked down. 'Shit.' She hooked her feet up one after the other and wiped them on the end of the kimono.

'So – your mum's not in?'

'Sandra dropped Steph off after school – Mum and Dad were having lunch or something.'

'Lunch? It's nearly five p.m.'

'Shit,' Delta said again, still trying to wipe her feet.

45

A bedroom window opened and Stephanie hung her head out. 'Delta, you promised you'd do my whole head.'

'Just coming, Steph. Don't touch the machine, it's hot.'

'You promised.'

'And I'm coming.'

Linda caught Delta looking at her fur coat and her Wellingtons. She forgot she still had Wellingtons on. She straightened up.

'Did your mum get her Ice Man delivery this week?'

'What – the freezer stuff? I guess she did.'

'And do you know if she got the triple chocolate mousse cake and Black Forest gateau? They're difficult to describe – there was a centre spread in –'

'I don't do catalogues,' Delta said.

'No, of course not. Neither do I, really, but the Ice Man one . . .'

'Have you got your mother-in-law to dinner tonight or something?'

'My mother-in-law?'

Didn't everybody know they had the Niemans coming tonight? And didn't Delta know that mother-in-law jokes were for women who had them?

'I mean,' Delta said, dragging the words out, impatient at Linda for not getting it, 'that freezer stuff isn't something you give to people – it's something you inflict on them. Have you read the back of the packet? Have you read what's in that stuff?'

Linda read the front of the box where it gave you the maximum freezer storage time and – if it was microwave-able – how many minutes it took to defrost. 'But does your mother still get the Ice Man?' she said, coming back to her original point.

'I guess it's what Steph's been eating all week. I mean, it's Friday and she's climbing the walls. She's toxic. I'm probably toxic as well, but it's too late, and Mum *can* cook, that's what really pisses me off.'

Linda tried to be offended that Delta was swearing in front of her, but she was too busy worrying about Dominique and the Ice Man, and the fact that Delta's nipples were pushing their way through the branches printed on the kimono because of the cold.

'We have people round and she's doing soufflé.'

'She does soufflé?'

'That's what I mean. She only cooks for dinner parties.' Delta paused. 'So . . . d'you want me to go and look in the freezer and see if she's got a triple mousse . . . mousse . . . what was it?'

'It doesn't matter.'

'What's it for anyway?'

'It doesn't matter. Honestly.'

'You sure?'

'Honestly.' Linda turned and sniffed the air. 'What's that?'

Stephanie skated up the hallway, screaming.

'Steph? Oh shit, Steph. I told you to wait.'

'You told me it was hot,' Stephanie cried, clumps of burnt hair falling onto the shoulders of her cardigan.

'Where's the crimper now? Is it still on?'

'I dropped it on the carpet,' Stephanie sniffed.

The girls disappeared indoors and, turning away from the smell of burnt hair, Linda crossed back over the road to No. 8, temporarily caught in the headlights of a car. She stopped at the top of the drive thinking it might be Joe, but it wasn't. It looked like Dominique's green Triumph. Without waiting to find out, she went back indoors, took the Wellingtons off then went into the kitchen to attack the collection of cookery books she and Joe had been given as newlyweds. She left the cordon bleu one where it was because it had never been opened, and grabbed *Good Housekeeping's Quick Guide to Dinner*

Parties that she often used the beef bourguignon recipe from. Turning to Contents, she saw that there was a whole chapter on soufflés. A whole chapter, and no pictures – apart from a series of diagrams showing you how to prepare the soufflé dish. A hot soufflé had to make an impressive entrance at the end of the meal and TIMING IS CRUCIAL.

After reading the page through three times she finally digested the fact that soufflés had to be prepared in advance but served *immediately*. 'Finishing Touches' had a section to themselves. And what was everybody else doing while she was standing there making her way through 'Finishing Touches'? Who was preventing Joe from roaming freely through his repertoire of flatulence jokes, then his record collection, and putting Pink Floyd on? Who was taking care of all that? How did Dominique Saunders manage to serve immediately. Come to think of it – had they ever eaten soufflé at No. 4? Linda couldn't remember. The times Dominique must have served soufflé were the times she and Joe weren't there – the dinner parties she and Joe weren't invited to – and how many of those had there been?

She slammed the book shut. Who were these people? TIMING IS CRUCIAL. What did they know about her life? SERVE IMMEDIATELY. They didn't know anything about the early years of her marriage and the house on Whateley Road; or what she and Joe had been through.

Whimpering with the effort of trying not to cry, she pushed *Good Housekeeping's Quick Guide* into the bin, then went into the garage, the cement floor freezing the soles of her feet in their thin socks.

She pulled up the freezer lid and saw the box with the picture of the mandarin cheesecake on it.

'Jessica!' she shouted up into the house when she was back in the kitchen.

A bedroom door opened and she heard music, then feet on the stairs.

'What's wrong with your face?' she said as her daughter walked in.

'Ferdie's bleeding.'

'You've been crying?'

'Ferdie's bleeding, Mum.' Then Jessica saw the dog's water bowl on the floor by Linda's feet and started crying again.

Linda stared at her. She hardly ever cried herself and didn't know what to do when other people did – especially when those other people were her own daughter. She'd never picked Jessica up when she was small and started crying – grief left its marks on the shoulders of jumpers and blouses, and some of them were dry clean only. So now they stood in the kitchen and did what they usually did: Jessica sobbed and Linda stood staring at her, and after a while she got the mandarin cheesecake out of its box and put it on the cake stand to defrost.

'I told you to go and change,' Linda said, her back turned. Jessica sniffed.

'Did you clean the lounge carpet?'

'Yes.' Jessica sniffed again.

'There's a pineapple over there in the fruit bowl – why don't you cut it up and mix it with some cottage cheese?'

Linda watched her daughter move round the kitchen in silence and start to deftly slice up the pineapple, still sniffing.

'Ferdie ate all the desserts I'd organised for tonight. All of them.' Linda paused.

Jessica didn't say anything. She put the mixing bowl with the cottage cheese and pineapple chunks in to one side.

'Then he sicked them up.' She stared at her daughter's back in its school pullover.

'D'you want me to make dessert for tonight?' Jessica said, turning round at last.

'I've got dessert for tonight. I sorted it.'

'I could make something,' Jessica said, looking at the mandarin cheesecake.

'Like what?'

'Like – syllabub.'

'Syllabub?'

'We did it in home economics last Thursday, all you need is some double cream and some wine and some –'

'I don't like syllabub,' Linda cut in.

'It's dead simple.'

'I don't like syllabub,' Linda said again.

'You've never even tasted it.'

'I have tasted it.'

'Haven't.'

Linda began drying the knife Jessica had used to cut up the pineapple with. 'Where's Ferdie?' she said suddenly.

'Upstairs.'

'Upstairs, where?'

'On my bed.'

'On your bed?' Linda yelled, throwing the knife and the tea towel down on the draining board.

'He needs to see a vet,' Jessica yelled back. 'You made him bleed.'

'I want him off your bed and outside – now!'

'We can't put him outside in this – look – there's a blizzard going on out there.'

Linda's mind flicked briefly to Joe, who she hoped had the sense to take the new bypass home from Brighton and not the road over the Dyke, then turned back to Jessica, who was crying again and pulling the cuffs of her school jumper over her hands.

'He's a bloody dog,' Linda shouted at her.

'He's *your* bloody dog. Dad bought him for you.'

'Upstairs. Now. Get upstairs.'

'I hate you.'

Linda turned away and picked the tea towel up off the draining board. 'Yeah, well . . .'

'And that cheesecake's disgusting – me and Dad have jokes about that cheesecake.'

She swung round, but Jessica was already out of the room. The clock on the kitchen wall shook as she banged up the stairs and slammed her bedroom door shut.

Linda went to the foot of the stairs. 'Dad and I,' she shouted up into the darkness. 'Dad and I.'

She went back into the kitchen and there was Joe standing in the doorway to the garage.

'What's all that about?'

'I don't know. You're late,' she said, looking at him.

'I phoned. I was at your mum's – you know what it's like: tea, biscuits, amnesia, more tea, more biscuits.' He paused, but didn't mention that Belle had been getting her hair cut while he was there. 'She looked well,' he said after a while, then walked past Linda into the hallway.

'Joe? Where're you going?'

'Upstairs. See Jess. Change.'

She followed him to the foot of the stairs. 'When you've changed I could do with some help down here. We've got people coming tonight.'

Joe stopped, his hand on the banister. 'I forgot.'

'You forgot? For Christ's sake, Joe.'

She went back into the kitchen and opened Jessica's lunch box, which was lying by the sink, automatically shoving a handful of uneaten crusts and half a packet of crisps into her mouth. The only serving plate she had big enough for the canapés had a crack running across it, but she covered this with some green paper napkins then put cling film over the bowl with the cottage cheese and pineapple in it. From upstairs she heard running water,

51

and a few minutes later Joe came back downstairs in old jeans and a sweatshirt.

'I thought you might have worn your new polo shirt.'

'I couldn't find it.'

'That's because it's still in the bag.'

'Oh.'

Joe sniffed and disappeared into the garage. He came back with a can of beer.

'So – who've we got coming tonight?' he asked, watching her open a sachet of Hollandaise sauce.

'Mick and Dominique – if they show.'

'Why wouldn't they?'

'I went over there a while ago and they weren't even back from lunch.'

'Who were they having lunch with?'

'Each other.' Linda looked at him then poured the contents of the sachet into a pan of boiling water. 'They went to Gatwick Manor.'

'It's expensive there.'

She looked at him again.

'So – anyone else coming?'

'I invited the Niemans – the new people at number twelve.'

'The Niemans?'

'Yes, the Niemans, Joe. The double-glazing people two doors up.'

'The Belgians?'

'I thought they were Dutch.'

'It doesn't matter – they all speak English.'

Linda stopped stirring the sauce. 'I'm sure they're Dutch.'

'Well, why don't we ask them?'

'We can't just ask them. Don't you dare ask them.'

Joe started drinking the beer.

'D'you want a glass for that?'

'Jess seems upset,' he said, ignoring her. 'She's lying on

52

her bed upstairs with Ferd, and Ferd's bleeding or something. She wouldn't say what happened.'

'Has she changed out of her school uniform yet?'

'I don't know.'

'You were only just up there.'

'I didn't notice.' He finished the beer. 'I said Ferd's bleeding.'

She started to stir the sauce again. 'Ferdie ate a triple chocolate mousse cake and a Black Forest gateau this afternoon.'

'He did?' Joe started to laugh. 'Is pudding gone then?'

She felt him behind her. 'Dessert – it's dessert gone.'

'So why don't you make one of your steamed puddings?' he said softly. 'What about one of them treacle ones?'

'I can't give the Niemans steamed pudding.'

'I love your treacle puddings. Best thing, they are.' She felt his hair brushing her ear. 'I'll do the custard,' he said.

'Custard?' Gravity gave her a short sharp pull. 'We've got gazpacho for starters, Joe. After the gazpacho, we've got salmon en croute with Hollandaise sauce. Do you really think the Niemans are going to want to finish with treacle pudding? And custard? Why don't we just throw a brick at them while we're at it.'

'I like treacle pudding.'

'We've got mandarin cheesecake,' she said.

'But I bloody hate mandarin cheesecake.'

'What's wrong with everyone tonight?'

Joe disappeared into the garage again.

Linda stopped stirring to watch some lumps the size of Atlantic icebergs forming in the sauce. 'Joe,' she called into the garage. 'Are you coming back in? Joe?'

Silence.

'I could do with some company in here. It's been a long day.'

Silence.

'You know sometimes I wish I was a bloody schizophrenic – at least I'd have my other self to talk to.'

Joe appeared in the garage doorway, a second can of beer in his hand.

'So what d'you want to talk about?'

She watched him drinking his beer, one hand in his trouser pocket, and one bare foot on the kitchen step. She didn't know. 'Aren't you cold? You should go and put some socks and shoes on.'

'I'm going into the garden.'

'You can't go out like that.'

He picked up some rubber clogs Linda had ordered from the back of a *Sunday Times* supplement, which was the only part of the paper she read.

Pouring the sauce down the sink, she watched through the window and falling snow as he went into the shed and came out with a deckchair, planting it in the snow next to where the fishpond was just about still visible. He had his back to the house and his feet in their rubber clogs stretched out over the frozen pond. What was he thinking?

She made a second batch of Hollandaise sauce then laid the table before going upstairs to shower. Jessica's bedroom door was shut but the music had been turned down. She would have gone in – to make sure Jessica had changed and Ferdie hadn't marked the bed – but she was afraid. Were other women afraid of their daughters?

So instead she showered, put on the new dress she'd bought at Debenhams the other weekend, where they'd also bought Joe's polo shirt, then went into Jessica's bedroom, wearing heels and fully made up. Jessica was lying on the bed with Ferdie stretched out beside her. She was still in her school uniform.

Over the summer they'd painted and refurnished Jessica's

54

room so that it was better suited to the needs of a fifteen-year-old girl taking A Levels three years early. That was at least four months ago and it still smelt of freshly unpacked MDF. The new furniture was dwarfed by a black and white CND poster Jessica had insisted on putting back up, alongside an even larger floor-to-ceiling poster of Snoopy. Without ever knowing why, Snoopy had always depressed Linda – even now, when she was on the antidepressants that came with the Slimshake starter pack to help overcome any emotional instability likely to be encountered switching to a liquids-only diet. On the wall above the stereo, the Advent calendar Jessica was still adamant about buying had nine open doors. Linda looked through the black sugar-paper snowflakes stuck to the bedroom window, down at the garden. Joe was still out there, and beyond him was the oak tree, which she'd started to feel inexplicably threatened by since Wayne Spalding's visit that afternoon. She drew the curtains then turned to face the bed again.

'Jessica?'

Jessica didn't move.

On the pinboard above the desk there was a photograph of Jessica aged eight on the beach at Brighton, with Belle. They were both smiling. The photograph next to it was of an even younger Jessica on Joe's shoulders; her hair was almost covering her face and she was yelling something at the camera. There was a river and castle behind them, in the distance. Linda tried to remember where they might have been that day, but couldn't. She remembered the sandals Jessica was wearing – and the dress – but she couldn't remember the day. Above the photographs were a series of images she'd first noticed a week ago when she came into the room to dust, and that she'd since asked Jessica to take down – of a captured Iranian soldier with ropes attached to his wrists and ankles, spread-eagled in the dust, about to be quartered by Iraqi-driven Jeeps. Jessica had to explain all that to her – and that American Indians used to torture prisoners in the same way, using horses. Why had Jessica told her this? Did she expect her to have an opinion on it or was she just giving her some sort of chance? Jessica's German teacher had torn the pictures out of *Das Spiegel* for her. 'She knows this is the kind of thing I'm into,' Jessica had said – implying that she, Linda, didn't.

'Jessica,' she said again, resisting the urge to pick up the can of Impulse body spray on the corner of the desk and shake it to see if it was being used. She watched her daughter roll onto her back, one arm resting protectively over Ferdie's flank. 'I told you to get changed.'

Jessica rolled back onto her side again and watched Ferdie blinking at her, wondering if he was trying to send her a message in Morse or something. Was it possible to blink in Morse? Probably – with either dedication or desperation.

Not wanting to push it any further, Linda went downstairs and arranged some Ritz crackers on the serving plate then took the cottage cheese and pineapple out of the fridge and started spooning it onto them in bite-size dollops. Joe was still in the garden, sitting on the deckchair by the frozen fishpond. Maybe he'd fallen asleep. Was it possible to fall asleep in a shirt and rubber clogs when it was minus five degrees Celsius? Didn't people die if they fell asleep in the snow? Then she started laughing, thinking how funny it would be if she was in here putting cottage cheese and pineapple on Ritz crackers while Joe was out there dying.

Joe, hearing laughter, looked up and turned towards the kitchen window.

The Niemans arrived at seven forty, before the Saunders, which meant that even though there were two Niemans to two Palmers, Linda felt outnumbered. They arrived in coats, hats, scarves and gloves, looking like identical (European) twins with their matching spectacles and matching haircuts.

Joe had forgotten to close the door to the downstairs loo and the smell of bleach was hanging heavily between them as they all stood awkwardly in the hallway.

'I'm sorry we're late,' Daphne said. 'Winke was in Brighton today.'

'Brighton?' Linda echoed, excited. 'Joe was in Brighton today as well.'

Winke gave Joe a slow, almost suspicious look, but didn't say anything.

'What were you doing in Brighton?' Daphne asked sharply.

Joe had a brief but strong memory of Belle's hairdresser stood in front of him with a pair of scissors in her hand, and forgot to reply.

'He was at the Britannia Kitchens roadshow – at the Brighton Centre,' Linda said. She waited for some sort of reaction to this, but there wasn't any. 'Quantum Kitchens – our company – had a stand.'

'I wasn't at the Britannia Kitchens roadshow,' Winke said at last.

'So.' Linda laughed. 'The coats, Joe?'

'What? Oh, right.'

Daphne handed her coat to Joe and they all watched as he tried to get it onto the hallstand, which was already full.

As Daphne's coat fell onto the floor for a third time, Linda said, 'Upstairs maybe, Joe?'

'Upstairs, where?'

'The bed,' she said awkwardly.

'Nice coat,' Joe said as he took Winke's from him.

'Thank you. Wait a moment, please.' He pulled a spectacle case out of his coat pocket, waving it briefly in the air. 'I might need these. My reading glasses.'

Linda tried not to panic. What had Winke anticipated doing that would require his reading glasses?

Joe disappeared upstairs with the coats while Linda stood smiling enthusiastically at Daphne and Winke, unable to believe that Littlehaven's renowned entrepreneur was here in her hallway. She tried not to stare at Daphne's grey knitted dress, which reached nearly to her ankles and looked like it was made of cashmere. Her jewellery was large, tribal; the sort of jewellery Linda would never have conceived of buying.

'You have a nice hallway,' Winke said, leaning towards her.

She was immediately suspicious. Was he laughing at her? 'Well, I suppose they're all the same. The hallways. In these houses, I mean.'

Daphne shook her head. 'No, actually.'

'So,' Joe said, coming back downstairs, 'what can I get you people to drink?'

'I'll just take a mineral water, please,' Daphne said.

'Do you have whisky?' Winke asked.

Joe nodded.

'Let me help you,' Daphne said, sliding into the kitchen after him.

'Would you like to come through?' Linda led Winke into the lounge.

In spite of viewing No. 8 Pollards Close three times before buying it, it wasn't until they moved in that Linda realised the lounge wasn't wide enough to fit two sofas in facing each other, which meant that they had to go side by side, with the armchair near the patio doors. The effect, when both sofas were occupied, wasn't unlike a row of seating at the theatre. Only there was no stage. Opposite the sofas there was a coffee table with a fish tank on top, and a TV cabinet. Winke and Linda sat on the sofa opposite the fish tank.

Linda had been preoccupied by thoughts of the Niemans for as long as she could remember. She had watched their comings and goings from behind the lounge blinds for so long, and the virtual Niemans had become so familiar, that it struck her now as odd – how unfamiliar the real ones were. Total strangers, in fact.

They heard laughter from the kitchen.

'Your fish is dead,' Winke said.

Linda sprang up and went over to the tank, peering through Perspex and algae to see if anything was moving in there. She could just make out bubbles coming from the statue of a diver standing over an open treasure chest. Maybe that was the fish. Maybe? What else was it going to be – the diver?

'I think it's breathing,' she said, tapping on the side of the tank.

'Fish don't breathe.'

'Yes, I read that somewhere,' she said, trying to keep her voice level.

The reflection of Winke on the side of the tank didn't look convinced.

'Maybe you should clean the tank.' He folded his hands on his lap. 'Or buy a filter.'

'I know, I know,' Linda said, keeping it light. 'I'm terrible. Jessica's always telling me to clean out the tank, but I just get so busy the day runs away with me, then it's time for that first glass of wine and everything just goes down the chute.'

Winke didn't react to this, he just sat there with his hands in his lap.

Linda was thinking, simultaneously, fuck the fish and thank God for the fish. If it wasn't for the dead or dying fish they'd both be sat there listening to Daphne and Joe laughing in the kitchen. And how long did it take Joe to ask Daphne if she minded tap water because they didn't have Perrier, and to pour Winke a whisky? Did he realise that she was alone in here with Winke trying to find some common ground.

'Is the fish your daughter's?' he said, after what seemed like ages.

'Sort of.' She tapped the Perspex again, smiling vaguely. Her tapping produced small shockwaves across the surface of the water; waves that pulled the fish out from behind the diver, on its side. There were clumps of white stuff that looked like cotton wool bulging from its body, and she might have cared more if the creature wasn't so genderless. She hoped Winke couldn't see as she started tapping on the other side of the tank, trying to send out waves that would pull the fish back behind the diver. She didn't have the stamina to face the fish's death right then, and once Winke knew it was definitely dead he might expect some kind of reaction on her part: like grief or resuscitation or burial even, and she hadn't prepared gazpacho and salmon with Hollandaise sauce just so that the Niemans and the Saunders (if they ever stopped fucking in order to show up) could stand out in a blizzard and bury a fish.

The fish had a spasm.

'Do fish dream?' she asked Winke hopefully.

Winke didn't answer. A sudden thought occurred to her – maybe Winke was vegetarian. Did vegetarians eat fish?

Then, after a while he said, 'It's a terrible thing when a child's pet dies. When anybody's pet dies, but especially a child's. They have a connection to animals we just don't understand, don't you think?'

'Jessica's fifteen.'

'I hope, for Jessica's sake, the fish lives.'

'So do I.' Linda wondered how much longer she was

expected to carry on kneeling in front of the tank waiting for the fish to either live or die.

'What's its name?'

That was enough. Linda couldn't do the fish any longer – she'd done the fish. After dinner they'd either stay in the dining room for coffee or make sure, if they did come in here, that Winke was put on the sofa opposite the TV cabinet.

'Valerie,' she said off the top of her head, because she'd been thinking how like Mrs Kline Winke was. In fact, they could almost be related. She could see quite clearly, without making her mind stretch at all, Winke dressed as Mrs Kline and Mrs Kline dressed as Winke.

'So,' Winke said, nodding, 'the fish is a she.'

'What?' Linda was by the door, trying to exit so that she could get Winke his whisky. She needed Winke to drink his whisky.

'The fish – Valerie. Valerie's a she.'

Linda looked at him closely, suddenly suspicious again. Was he laughing at her?

'Unless you mean Valéry, which is a masculine name in both France and Russia.'

What was he doing bringing France and Russia into her lounge?

There was the doorbell.

'Excuse me.' She went into the hallway. 'Joe! Winke needs his whisky. Joe?'

She opened the front door. Mick kissed her first, then Dominique.

'Where d'you want us?' Mick asked, tripping up over the step.

The hallway smelt suddenly of alcohol.

'In there.' She tried to guide them into the lounge, but Daphne was waving at them from a bar stool in the kitchen, food in her mouth.

Linda moved over to the breakfast bar. What was Daphne eating? How could Daphne be eating when nothing had been served yet?

Joe and Mick nodded at each other.

There were about five canapés left on the serving dish and a pile of pineapple on the paper napkin she'd lined the plate with. She watched Daphne take the fifth remaining canapé, pick the pineapple off and push the cracker into her mouth.

'So – you found the canapés,' Linda said.

'You know Joe,' Mick said, 'you've got to lock him up.' He stretched past Daphne and grabbed remaining canapés numbers four and three. There were two left. Linda tried to laugh, but couldn't.

'I hope you don't mind, but I'm allergic to pineapple,' Daphne said.

'Maybe somebody wants to offer Dominique a canapé,' Linda said, looking at Joe. 'And Winke's still waiting for his whisky.'

'Poor Winke,' Daphne said, smiling and watching Joe pour the whisky.

'What can I get you two?' Joe asked the Saunders.

'No more wine,' Dominique said.

'Two glasses of red wine it is then,' Mick said, pulling the other bar stool up next to Daphne.

'We've been talking about beer,' Joe told them.

'Belgian beer,' Daphne said proudly. 'I'm going to send Winke home to fetch some Belgian beer.'

'Please. Don't. Really. You don't have to,' Linda pleaded.

'Joe must taste some Belgian beer,' Daphne said, banging her hand down on the breakfast bar with each word.

Linda handed Mick and Dominique their wine then went to take Winke his whisky.

Winke was kneeling in front of the fish tank with his

reading glasses on and his face pressed up against the Perspex.

'Your whisky.'

'It is very strange, but I smell something like vomit here – and your fish is definitely dead,' he said, shaking his head.

'Maybe,' Linda conceded.

'Maybe? Definitely.'

'Winke,' Daphne said from the doorway. 'Winke, I want you to go home and fetch some Belgian beer.'

Winke got slowly to his feet, his eyes still on the tank.

'Don't worry,' he said to Linda, 'we'll sort this out when I get back.'

Linda, who was still holding his whisky, tried to nod as mournfully as she could, and sighed.

The front door shut and Daphne disappeared back into the kitchen, her tribal jewellery clinking as she moved.

Linda put the whisky down on the coffee table and stared into the tank. The fish was lying on its side just by the diver's feet. It made the diver look guilty.

She turned the dimmer switch by the door so that the lighting level in the room went down, and hoped that a combination of flashing tree lights, low overhead lighting and algae would make it difficult for Winke to pick up where he left off.

Five minutes later the doorbell rang and she went to answer it. The porch light illuminated Winke, a crate of Belgian beer, and a younger, slimmer, taller version of Winke with blond blow-dried hair.

'Paul carried the beer for me,' he said, stepping back into the house and leaving his son and the beer on the doorstep.

'Everyone's in the kitchen,' Linda said. 'Straight ahead. Just there.' She put her hands on Winke's back and pushed him in the direction of the kitchen.

63

Paul was stamping his feet loudly on the doormat. 'Mind if I come in?'

'Oh, I'm sorry.'

She stood to one side and watched as the Niemans' son carried the beer into the kitchen, treading snow laced with mud from the soles of his shoes into the hallway carpet, which was beige. Resisting the urge to get down on her hands and knees and start removing the stains, she followed Paul into the kitchen.

The crate, which had been put on the dining-room table, was being unpacked by Daphne. The cutlery and fantailed napkins were pushed to one side, and two of the candles had fallen over.

'Linda – we need glasses here,' Daphne called out.

Linda squeezed past Mick, who was staring at the wooden gazelle he'd just picked up from the sideboard, and got to the cupboard where she kept her glasses. She made a show of moving around some tumblers and a couple of Jessica's old baby beakers. 'No beer glasses,' she said, hoping it sounded as though they'd once had some.

'Any cognac glasses?' Daphne persisted.

'I've got these.' Linda held up a couple of tumblers.

'Make it wine glasses. The bigger the better.'

'Joe,' Linda said, 'we need glasses from the drinks cabinet.'

Joe unlocked the door in the sideboard behind him.

'These'll do,' Daphne said, pushing past Mick who was still contemplating the gazelle, and taking the glasses out of Joe's hands.

Everybody had a glass. Everybody had to drink. Daphne had taken over.

Linda tried to catch Dominique's eye, but Dominique wasn't seeing straight. Why weren't they sitting on the sofas in the lounge with their pre-dinner drinks like she'd planned? Why were they all crowded round the dining table instead with an empty crate of Belgian beer on it and Joe and the Niemans – all the Niemans – pressed up against the frosted glass that acted as a divider between the kitchen-diner and the hall.

'You'll stay and eat with us?' Daphne asked Paul.

Paul shrugged.

'He doesn't have to if he doesn't want to,' Linda said. Repeating, 'Really, he doesn't have to.' There was enough gazpacho for six people. There were six pieces of salmon and six dining-room chairs. Paul would make them seven, and she didn't have the stamina to pull off the 'fish and loaves on the shores of Galilee' stunt tonight.

'He'll stay,' Daphne said.

Linda stood smiling back at her. 'So – will he eat fish fingers?'

Daphne laughed. In fact, she didn't stop laughing for a long time after the fish-finger joke. Only Linda wasn't joking. Fish fingers were the only thing she could think of to remedy the disaster of turning an evening for six into an evening for seven, and she was working on the premise that all children like fish fingers. Only Paul wasn't a child. He was the tallest person in the room, and he was drinking beer. In fact, there were no children here tonight. Linda felt her hormones take a quick dive. She had to stop thinking about Paul Nieman.

'I'll get Jessica down,' she said. Then, 'Maybe she and Paul could eat before us?'

'Yes, I'd like to meet Jessica,' Winke said sadly.

'Jessica,' Joe yelled up the stairs.

'Why don't we just all eat together?' Daphne asked.

'I'll get her, Joe.' Linda went upstairs and knocked on Jessica's door. When she went in, her daughter was sitting at her desk. 'Jessica?'

'I'm busy.'

'What are you doing? Homework?'

'No. Just something.'

'I need you to come downstairs.'

'I don't want to.'

'You have to come and have something to eat.'

'I already ate. You told me to get something earlier.'

'Well, now you have to eat something with us. Downstairs.'

'I'm busy.'

There was an A4 pad on the desk with the words 'Biological Hazards' written across it. Then a list underneath: *Anthrax/splenic fever/murrain/malignant* – she couldn't see the rest. 'Paul Nieman's here, that's why I need you to come downstairs. You know Paul, don't you?'

'He's in my physics class.'

'Well, then – downstairs. Now.'

Jessica stood up. She had a pair of washed-out jeans on and an oversize black T-shirt with the word 'Kontagion' printed across it in white.

'For God's sake, Jessica. I told you to get changed.'

'Well, I got changed.'

Linda grabbed hold of her daughter's arm, and kept hold of it as she pushed her down the stairs in front of her.

The crockery didn't match and nobody commented on the gazpacho. There wasn't enough elbow space, and Paul and Jessica, who Linda had hoped to sit together, were on opposite sides of the table in deckchairs from the garage – ones she hadn't been able to wash the mildew off. She hadn't even got round to lighting the candles.

'Computers'll never take off,' Joe said.

'You're not tempted to get one for the office?'

Joe shook his head and Winke put his reading glasses on. 'In two years' time you won't be able to avoid them.'

Then, waving his spoon at Joe, 'The school's ordered thirty-five BBC computers.'

'When?'

'Last week.'

'How d'you know?'

'I ordered them.'

'At the last Governors' meeting, we appointed Winke Information Technology Liaison Officer.'

Linda started to clap then saw the look Jessica was giving her.

'We were thinking of starting up a distribution company – when the time's right,' Daphne added.

'As well as double glazing?' Linda asked.

'For a while.' Winke turned to Jessica. 'You'll get to use them maybe . . . learn some basic programming skills.'

'You've got daughters, haven't you? You should bring them over,' Daphne was saying to Dominique.

'Steph's too young and Delta's looking after her.'

'Delta – that's a beautiful name.'

Linda stood up and started to clear away the gazpacho bowls so that she wouldn't have to listen to the story of how Delta was conceived in Egypt at the mouth of the Nile when Mick and Dominique used to fly together.

'I read in the *FT* that Laker Air's in trouble,' Winke said to Mick.

Linda looked at Dominique to see if this was something she knew about.

'Difficulty. Not trouble,' Mick said. Then, seeing Winke smile, he added, 'It's weathered worse.'

'Do you miss flying?' Daphne whispered to Dominique, who was sitting next to her.

Dominique stared at the Belgian woman whose hand was on her arm. 'I don't know – it was a long time ago – yes,' she added unexpectedly.

The two women smiled at each other.

Something in the way Daphne was resting her hand on her arm made Dominique run on, way beyond the usual confines of her 'Mick and I got it together at fifty thousand feet' speech. 'I mean, I miss the flying, but not the job. The trolley, the foreign hotels between coming and going – I don't miss that, but the flying itself . . .'

'Was it what you always wanted to do?'

'I didn't know what I wanted to do – the only O Level I passed was Home Economics. Then I got accepted on this training programme, and –'

'Do you ever think about going back to it?'

'I don't know – no – I've changed so much.' This sounded indefinite, more like she was looking for reassurance than making a statement. 'I've changed so much,' she said again. Then, turning to Winke, 'What were you saying about Laker Air?'

'That it's in trouble,' Winke said, pleased to repeat this.

'It's fine, Dom.' Mick, who had overheard, watched his wife's face as it turned towards him, settling fully on him and resting there.

'I hope so.' Winke started shaking his head, and he was still shaking it when conversation moved on, and Joe was telling everybody his favourite story.

'Believe it or not, it was one of the first jobs I took on after starting up the company,' Joe's voice was saying, 'and it came my way through one of the estate agents in town – can't remember which one. They'd been renting out a house for some people who'd gone to America short term then decided to sell, as renting it out was too much hassle and the last tenants had disappeared without a trace. The agents reckoned they'd get a better price if they had the kitchen re-done. So . . . I went in on a Tuesday, I think it was, yeah, a Tuesday. One of the first things I did was turn

the freezer off so that I could move it out the way, and –
bloody hell . . .' He turned to Mick. 'I know you've heard
it already – don't you dare say anything.'

Linda wanted Joe to finish his story and start making an
effort with Winke so that in, say, two weeks' time, Joe could
ring him to talk about the possibility of offering Nieman
double glazing at a reduced price to people who were getting
kitchens designed and fitted by Quantum. She also wanted
to ask Daphne whether they'd considered getting their original Laing kitchen replaced? The Nassams at No. 6 and the
Saunders all had Quantum kitchens.

Joe let his chair fall forward, forcing his belly into the
edge of the table.

'Guess what I found when I opened the freezer? The
missing tenant. Well, one of them.'

'Oh, come on,' Daphne looked cross. 'Not in the freezer,
surely.'

'Seriously – I'm not kidding you.'

'He's not,' Mick added.

Here was Joe talking about dead people, Linda thought.
Dead people here in Littlehaven, where the only thing people
should have to worry about was whether they ought to take
advantage of the new offer by Quantum Kitchens and have
Nieman glazing – at a reduced price – put in at the same
time. Why was Joe the one rocking back on his chair legs,
laughing, when she was the one who got to open the letter
from the bank telling them they'd missed a mortgage
payment.

'It was in the papers and everything,' Joe carried on. 'The
head was in the bottom drawer and everything else was in
those freezer bags with labels and dates written on them.
Each bag had a different date on it – never worked that one
out. Must have been something personal; a private joke or
something between the killer and her victim.'

'Wait,' Daphne said, 'it was the wife who killed the husband?'

'Well – according to the estate agent it was a husband and wife who left without paying their last month's rent, only, technically speaking, I suppose the husband never vacated the property after all because he was in the freezer the whole time.'

'Why don't you two go and watch some TV?' Linda whispered to Jessica.

'Who's "you two"?' Jessica asked, staring back at her.

'You and Paul.'

'I need to go and see if Ferdie's okay.'

Linda saw this as her last opportunity to reclaim the evening for six people. She'd managed with the gazpacho, but she just didn't know how to make six salmon steaks into eight.

'Ferdie's fine.'

'Who's Ferdie?' Paul asked.

'Ferdie's our dog,' Linda said, then to Jessica, 'and Ferdie's fine.'

'How do you know – have you been upstairs?'

'Jessica!'

'I'm going.' Jessica shunted her deckchair back into the breakfast bar.

'So what is this Kontagion thing?' Winke said, looking at her T-shirt as she stood up.

'Last year's Glastonbury T-shirt for Youth CND,' she mumbled.

'You went?'

Jessica looked at Linda. 'I wasn't allowed to go – a friend brought it back for me.'

'I think Paul should go to Glastonbury,' Winke said, his mind on neither Paul, who was sitting opposite him, nor Glastonbury.

70

'That was very good gazpacho, Mrs Palmer,' Paul said as Jessica left the room.

'What the hell's gazpacho?' Joe asked Mick.

Linda wondered briefly if anyone was checking Paul's alcohol intake. Then whether anybody needed to – how old was he, anyway? 'Teenagers,' she said nervously.

'You're okay, you escape all this with a boy,' Dominique said to Daphne. Then, turning to Linda, 'I mean, when did you last get to use your own phone?'

Linda gave what she hoped was a sympathetic shrug. Jessica didn't seem to phone anybody, and nobody phoned Jessica – apart from Mr Browne, who lived at No. 14.

'And all the cupboard space taken up with cheap make-up – Delta doesn't seem to stick to one brand, she just gets bored and moves on to the next one.'

'Tell me about it,' Linda said, hoping Dominique would leave it at that.

'And that's just the ongoing stuff. This afternoon – while we were out – the girls nearly set fire to the house.'

Linda tried to look surprised.

'Some accident with a crimper – you should see Steph's hair.'

'Will Jessica be going to university next year?' Daphne asked, turning to Linda. 'I mean, what's the procedure for someone her age, in her position?'

Linda didn't know. She hadn't thought about anything much beyond the feature Trevor Jameson was going to run in the *County Times*, and now she came to think of it – what was going to happen with Jessica next year?

'You should think about an American university for Jessica – maybe wait four years, let her mature . . . specialise . . . get her head round the direction she'd like her research to take. I've got a good friend at Berkeley you and Joe should speak to.'

'Anyway, you got your picture in the paper, didn't you?' Mick was saying to Joe.

'I did.' Joe looked pleased. 'Yeah, I did.'

Linda put the mandarin cheesecake on the table and tried not to look at Daphne's face. She had a feeling that Daphne would have an opinion on frozen mandarin cheesecake.

'Well, it's not soufflé,' she said, because nobody else was saying anything.

'Since when has anyone here made soufflé?' Dominique asked.

'Oh, come on, Dom, I know you make soufflé . . .'

'I've never made soufflé in my life before. Have I ever made soufflé before, Mick? Mick?'

Mick looked up. 'What's that?'

'I said, have I ever made soufflé before?'

'You and soufflé? Never. Dom doesn't cook, she – well, she just doesn't cook.'

'So you've never made soufflé?' Linda persisted, thinking of Delta in the kimono; Delta who had lied to her. Why?

'Linda, I'm telling you . . .'

'Well,' Linda lifted up the cake slice, her stomach vibrating with nausea, 'this is mandarin cheesecake.'

'I love mandarin cheesecake,' Paul said.

4

Taking one last look at herself in the mirror, Dominique turned off the light in the en suite and went through to the bedroom where Mick lay with his head propped in his hand and *A History of Winemaking* open on the pillow.

'You're tired,' he said, looking up at her.

She nodded, still yawning. 'I don't know how you can read – aren't you drunk?'

'I'm not drunk.'

'You looked drunk tonight.'

'Just doing a good impression – to make it look as though I was enjoying myself. For your sake.'

'You weren't enjoying yourself, then?'

'Come on, Dom.' He paused. 'We had mandarin cheese-cake.'

'You shouldn't pretend for my sake.'

'I should.' He shut the book and sat up, pushing the dressing gown off her left shoulder.

'I can't sleep,' Stephanie said, walking into the room and bringing the smell of burnt hair with her.

'Steph –' Mick fell back onto the bed.

'Come on, baby, it's sleep time. And you can't sleep in

73

this,' Dominique said, lifting the yellow hard hat off her daughter's head. Stephanie was dressed in the full emergency services outfit she'd insisted on wearing to bed earlier and in the end Dominique had given in.

'What time is it?' Steph pulled the hard hat sharply back down onto her head.

'It's after midnight.'

'Then it's tomorrow. That's late.'

'It is late and you should be in bed now.'

'I want to see Dad.'

'Dad's trying to sleep.'

'But he just waved at me.'

Dominique turned round to see Mick lying with the pillow over his head and his right hand in the air, waving.

Stephanie squealed and jumped onto the bed as Mick pulled the pillow off his head and threw it at her. 'I made up some new jokes,' she said, bouncing up and down.

'Like . . .'

'Like – what d'you call a one-legged horse?'

'I don't know, what d'you call a one-legged horse?'

'A unicycle,' Stephanie said, still bouncing. 'And – what d'you call a one-legged cow?'

'I don't know, what d'you call a one-legged cow?'

'A unicycle. And – what d'you call a one-legged pig?'

'A unicycle?'

'Noooo.'

'Why not?'

'Just because. I haven't thought of a joke for a one-legged pig yet.'

'But why can't a one-legged pig just be a unicycle like a one-legged horse and a one-legged cow?'

'Mick,' Dominique interceded.

Stephanie jumped off the bed and went running back to her room.

Dominique followed her.

'Don't worry,' her daughter said from under the duvet, 'I'm asleep.'

A china toadstool with a china mouse family inside illuminated the room with a dull red light.

'Steph – you can't sleep in that hat.' She paused. 'We'll get an appointment at the hairdresser's tomorrow morning – first thing.' Dominique waited a few minutes. 'Night,' she said from the doorway.

'Ssh, I'm asleep.'

When she got back to the bedroom, Mick was lying on his back, staring up at the ceiling.

Taking her dressing gown off, she got into bed next to him.

'What's this?' Dominique said, as something sharp dug into her left ear.

'I was looking at it tonight.'

She picked up the wooden gazelle from the pillow and put it on her bedside table. 'This is Linda's, Mick.'

'I got attached to it.'

'You stole it?'

'I put it in my pocket – they won't notice.'

They lay there not talking and neither of them made a move to turn out the light.

'I didn't realise Laker was going bust,' she said after a while.

Mick rolled over and looked at her, but didn't say anything.

'They're going to make you redundant, aren't they?'

'Maybe – I'm over forty anyway, Dom.'

'That's what lunch was about.'

'That's not what lunch was about.'

'How soon?'

'I don't know – nobody knows – I've probably got another month.'

75

'Another month? When were you going to tell me?'

'There's nothing to worry about, Dom – the terms of the package we're starting to discuss are very generous.'

'You're not going to look for another job as a pilot?'

'We should go away,' he said.

She didn't say anything.

'We should. We should go away.'

'Where would we go?'

'New Zealand.'

'And what would we do in New Zealand?'

Mick raised himself up on his elbow. 'We'd have a vineyard.'

'A vineyard?'

'I'd call it *Dominique's*, and even though it would take a few years to set up and those first few years would be tight – difficult – after that we wouldn't look back – award-winning wines – a huge export business – the girls helping – acres of land.'

'My God, Mick.'

'What?'

'You've been thinking about this?'

'I've been thinking.'

'But – why? I mean, New Zealand – why?'

'Space. You. The girls. You.'

'But, New Zealand, Mick. D'you know what you're talking about? Do you know what it is you're actually saying?'

'No. But think about it.'

'It's the other side of the world.'

'So we'd take our world with us – Delta and Steph. What would be left behind?'

She shook her head hard. 'But – you fly, Mick. That's what you do. You fly.'

Mick stared hard at her then slumped back onto the pillow, deflated. 'I fly.'

'You love flying.'

'I love flying.'

'And you don't know the first thing about growing grapes.'
Mick sat up again and smiled.

Why did he see this as a positive thing?

'I know, but I'm learning. I bought shares in a vineyard.'

'You did what?' Dominique sat up now as well.

'And I thought we could go and visit – maybe at Easter-
time. We could rent a villa for a fortnight or something over
Delta and Steph's Easter holidays.'

'You bought shares in a vineyard, Mick?' Dominique was
trying to think and not to think all at the same time.

He passed his hand lazily over her breasts as he sank back
onto the pillow and fell quickly asleep, leaving her alone
with the night, and the vineyard in New Zealand.

8

Above the sound of Pink Floyd, Linda heard the flush of the downstairs loo and stood watching herself in the mirror as she held her breath and waited to see if Joe was going to turn off the music and come upstairs to bed. She'd already been down to see him once and she didn't want to have to go down again. The music carried on. She watched herself exhale then pick up a cleansing pad from the pack by the sink and start to wipe off her make-up, rubbing at her cheeks, eyes and mouth much harder than she needed to.

She spent a long time doing everything in the bathroom – even giving her nails a brush and polish before going through to the bedroom. Then she sat on the end of the bed and listened to Pink Floyd coming up through fitted carpet. Forty minutes must have passed since she'd been downstairs and asked Joe if he was coming up and he'd mouthed the words 'five minutes' at her.

She got up from the bed and went downstairs.

Joe was on the sofa, watching TV with the sound off. He didn't look up.

'What are you watching?'

'I don't know.'

'How can you hear it?'

'Subtitles.'

'What?' She moved closer to the TV.

He pointed to the screen where there was a band of black with words across it. 'Subtitles.'

'The people look Japanese. In the film. They look like Japs, Joe.'

'Yeah.'

The fact that they were Japanese made her feel like she had a case – that and the fact that it was past midnight.

'So – you're coming to bed soon?'

'Yeah.'

'You are?'

'No – I mean, I don't know.'

'Right.' She stood there staring at the screen for another minute. 'I'll be upstairs.' She stopped again by the lounge door, picking up the ends of her dressing-gown belt and letting them slip through her fingers. 'I thought it went well tonight.'

'Tonight?' he said, thinking about this. Then, 'Oh, tonight. Yeah.'

Back upstairs, she stood at the end of the bed, breathing hard, then took off her dressing gown and put a T-shirt on instead. She climbed onto the exercise bike and after a couple of minutes flicked *straight* to *gradient*. At some point the music went off and she thought she heard Joe climbing the stairs, but he didn't come into the bedroom. She was so angry that she'd been cycling uphill for five minutes now without realising it, and her heart was starting to let out a strange metallic click.

Joe knocked three times then went in. At first he thought Jessica was asleep, but after a while she opened her eyes and took off the headphones.

'I was nearly asleep.'

'You should be. It's one a.m.'

She leant over and turned off the stereo, trying not to disturb Ferdinand, who had his head on her stomach. 'How was the film?'

'I don't know. Everyone died, apart from this one man at the end who was crawling around in the grass. Then he died too.' He sighed and went over to pull the curtains shut.

'They're already shut, Dad.'

'There was a gap.'

'Does it matter? There's nothing out there but fields and trees.'

'Well, they're shut now.' He looked down at the desk. 'Homework?'

'No – just something I'm working on.'

'Looks complicated.'

'Not really.'

Joe switched the desk light on.

'Dad, you don't have to – you're not interested.'

Joe looked more closely. 'What is this, Jess?' He read out, '"Botulism poisoning is very rare, but an ounce could kill close on forty-three million people. There is no immunity to it and no effective treatment."'

Jessica rolled onto her side. 'It's part of a chapter on biological hazards.'

'A chapter? What – you're writing a book?'

'On how to survive a nuclear attack.'

'Since when?'

'The summer holidays.'

Joe didn't know what to say. He looked down and read again silently to himself the line he'd just read out loud. Then, glancing up at Jessica's pinboard, he saw her aged four, sitting on top of his shoulders, and could almost feel the weight of her again. The castle in the photograph was

Arundel. They'd walked – his parents and him and Jessica – along the river from Amberley to Arundel. That must have been before his dad got ill. Linda hadn't come that day; he couldn't remember why.

'It's more of a manual than a book, really.' Jessica paused. 'I'm writing it with Mr Browne – well, I'm doing the research anyway.'

'And who's Mr Browne?'

'He lives at number fourteen – the end of the Close.'

'The end of the Close? Our Close? What does he do?'

'He was in the army.'

'And why isn't he in the army any more?'

'He retired.'

'How old is he?'

'Thirty-seven, I think.'

'He retired at thirty-seven?'

'Or left, or something. I don't know. It's to do with his leg. Sometimes he uses a walking stick.'

'How did you meet him?'

'Youth CND – he came to give a talk.'

Joe sat down on the end of the bed, looking at the blue seashells on the duvet cover.

Jessica sat up on her elbow. 'What?'

'Nothing.'

He felt for her legs under the duvet and gave her ankle a squeeze.

'This book's really important, Dad. It talks about how not to die. How to survive.'

'And what if this bomb of yours never goes off, Jess, and you have to do more than just survive?'

Jessica fell back onto the pillow. 'You're drunk.'

Joe stood up, trying to hide his disappointment. 'Probably.' He turned the desk light off and heard her turn over in bed. 'How's Ferdinand?'

81

She didn't say anything.

'We can take him to the vet tomorrow, if you like.' What did he want? He wanted to tell her about meeting a hairdresser called Lenny today. What was wrong with him? Jessica was the one person he wanted to tell and he couldn't, because she was his daughter. 'Night, Jess.' He stood there waiting for her to say something.

Then, at last, 'Night, Dad.'

He left the room, shutting the door behind him, and crossed the hallway.

In the master bedroom, Linda was going full tilt up a virtual hill thinking about the muddy footprints Paul Nieman had left in the hallway when he came in with the beer, and how much she'd wanted to clean the carpet. Then she pictured the scene again with herself naked, scrubbing at the mud in a pair of black marigolds, and Paul standing over her, angry.

'Shit, Joe,' she said, catching sight of him in the vanity-unit mirror. 'What are you creeping up on me for?'

He shrugged and watched as she flicked the dials on the handlebars until it looked like a cartoonist was running her in slow motion.

'Jessica's writing a book.'

'Seven miles. I just did seven miles,' she said, breathless and preoccupied.

'On how not to die – with a Mr Browne – Jessica says he lives at the end of the Close, but I've never seen him. Who is he?'

'I don't know, Joe, and I didn't know she was writing a book.' Linda got off the bike and picked up the dressing gown from the bed. 'Mr Browne?'

'She said she met him at Youth CND.'

'I think I met him once.'

'He was giving a talk.'

'He seemed okay.' Linda paused. 'And anyway, she needs to be around other people more.'

'She's fifteen years old, Linda!'

'That's what I'm talking about – she never goes out.' Linda threw the dressing gown back down on the bed. 'Did you see her tonight, Joe? She doesn't speak – she doesn't eat . . . the way she talked to me in front of everybody.'

Joe ignored this. 'She's got things she needs to work through.'

'Like what – the end of the world?'

'Well, that's one of them.'

'Jessica never leaves her room – she needs professional help, Joe.'

'For what?'

'For just about fucking everything.'

'What – like the time she had to see that educational psychologist – what was her name?'

'Penelope – but she told us to call her Penny.'

'She spent eight sessions with Jessica – alone – filling her mind with fuck knows what, only to tell us Jessica had a fear of dolls.'

'I don't want to start talking about Penny again – you refused the further counselling she recommended.' The nausea she'd experienced earlier while stood over the mandarin cheesecake rose up again.

'For fuck's sake, Linda, this is our daughter we're talking about . . . where are you going?' he said, watching her. The T-shirt she was wearing had dark sweat patches on it.

'The bathroom.'

'It's nearly one thirty in the morning.'

The door slammed shut, and a minute later he heard retching sounds. 'Linda?'

'It's okay.'

'Are you sick?'

'It's the solids.'

'The what?'

'The solids – dinner tonight. I'm not used to it.'

He listened at the door, but didn't hear any other sounds, and after a while he went back into the hallway towards the other bathroom, stopping by the window like he used to when they first moved in. That was two years ago, and everything had been so new then that the contractors hadn't even got round to putting tarmac on the roads and pavements. It was a new world they hadn't finished building yet, and he would stand at the hall window in the early hours of the morning, half expecting to see virgin forest carpeting the horizon.

Now all he could see was the glow of Gatwick and, in the distance, beyond the Surrey Hills, the monochrome aurora borealis that hung over London. How had he ever felt himself capable of imagining that the world – his world – was still unfinished?

He went into the bathroom, looked into the macramé basket hanging from the ceiling and failed to work out what he was doing there, then went back to the bedroom and undressed in the semi-dark because Linda was already in bed, and the light on her side was off.

He took off everything apart from his vest, then got into bed and lay looking up at the ceiling where it had been pricked by Artex.

'Your mum was having her hair cut today,' he said, turning his head to face Linda, who had her eyes closed.

'I don't want to talk about my mother,' she said, her breath smelling faintly of vomit. Then, after a while, 'And I don't know why she has that hairdresser – she can't afford her.'

'Well, it's difficult for her to get out and about.'

The chains on the blinds started to rattle as the extractor fan in the en suite cut out, blowing a draught through the bedroom. Joe felt himself drifting off. 'The soup you made tonight was good.'

'Gazpacho, it was gazpacho,' she said, 'and before you say anything, it was meant to be cold.'

'Why's that, then?'

She didn't answer, and Joe was almost asleep when Linda said, 'She used to be in the army.'

'You never said.'

'Not my mother – the hairdresser. She was in the Falklands or something.'

He didn't say anything, and after a while leant over to switch off the light on his side of the bed.

When he woke up it was still dark, and he didn't know what time it was because the alarm clock was on the other side of the bed. Linda was lying on her back with her head turned away from him and her left hand curled into a fist.

He drifted off to sleep again.

23 DECEMBER 1983

4

The dark was still deep when Dominique left the house at five a.m. Mick's flight from Florida – his last flight – was due to land in half an hour.

The road from Littlehaven to Gatwick was all new bypass, cutting across land with small strips of forest that deer used to graze in. She remembered pointing out the deer to Delta when she was small, but now there were no deer left to point out to Steph. They'd hit a deer once, in the red Renault, and Mick had wanted to stop and pull the animal off the road, but she hadn't let him; she'd told him to keep driving. Then it started raining and they had to pull over anyway because the ton of running deer that had hit the windscreen had snapped both wipers clean off and they couldn't see a thing. She'd tried to remind Mick about that deer a couple of years ago, but he couldn't remember and this had shocked her. There was no way she could have forgotten a thing like that, but Mick told her, smiling, that he had no memory of it, no memory at all. As if he'd never been there in the car while they waited in the dark for the rain to stop, the dead deer and forest somewhere to their left, and Delta crying uncontrollably in the back. It was a shame the deer were gone, she thought, looking at the early-morning darkness and the way it hid the land's details.

Leaving behind the patch of countryside the bypass intersected, she entered Gatwick's network of roundabouts, Jacuzzi showrooms, electronics factories, out-of-town warehouses, hotels and – finally – the airport itself.

She had been a first-class air hostess working long-haul flights when she and Mick met. The first-class bit mattered, and 'we got it together at fifty thousand feet' was a conversation opener she still used. Most of the passengers in first class then were men, and she got on with men – even growing up without a father. It was women she didn't like. Mick once called her a misogynist and it was true. She knew how to make men happy. How did you make a woman happy?

As soon as the plane wheels used to leave the tarmac – wherever she was in the world – she not only felt herself breathing again, but felt pleased to be breathing again. She never got claustrophobic in the pressurised cabin's few cubic feet of reconditioned air and she never worried about dying. It was being on the ground she was afraid of: gravity. Anything that sucked you in or down or tried to anchor you in any way. She started taking as little time off between flights as regulation allowed and spending more and more time in hotel rooms in foreign cities with curtains shut and phials of sleeping pills, trying to defy gravity. As long as she had movement, as long as she had altitude, she was fine. It was her ground life that was going all autistic on her. Then Mick came along, and he changed all of that. Mick changed all of her.

When she told her mother, who was a scientist researching food dyes, that she was thinking of becoming an air hostess, Monica had just smiled at this new fatality in her life and said, 'I suppose everybody's got to do something.'

Then, two weeks later, Dominique got a phone call from her on a busy Friday night at the pub she was working in, and Monica told her she had an interview with someone running training sessions for Laker Air the next day. Which made Dominique feel, when she got accepted on the training programme, that the whole air-hostess thing had been her mother's idea in the first place; that her whole life so far had been her mother's idea. Even Mick; even Mick's love for her; even her happiness – and Dominique being happy or not was the last thing on earth her mother cared about. It was just that happiness was part of the plan Monica had formulated for her daughter in the absence of academic success, because that's what normal people were: happy. So she presumed.

Dominique stood for a while at the Arrivals barrier watching passengers from the Florida flight, jetlagged, walk through the automatic doors, thinking she should have done what Mick wanted and taken the girls on this last flight with him. Why hadn't she just gone? She was about to leave her post by the barrier and get a coffee when she saw Laura, whom she used to fly with on Laker Air in the late Sixties.

Laura had always had long hair, but now it was cut short, close to the scalp. Her legs looked long and brittle and her knees too pronounced, but Laura was still flying. Dominique felt herself pause, trying to decide whether she wanted to talk to Laura, who was still flying, or not. Whether she'd ever liked Laura, who was still flying, or not.

'Dominique. My God. Dominique.'

'Hey, Laura.' Up close, Laura felt taller than her, slimmer, and better smelling. The short haircut pronounced her cheek-bones and shoulders. Dominique wondered how she was looking under airport strip lighting. 'Just landed?'

Laura sighed. 'Just landed.' She parked the small suitcase

on wheels by her side and kept hold of the two duty-free bags.

'They've changed the uniform,' Dominique said.

'The uniform?'

She nodded at Laura's navy suit and Laura looked down. 'Oh – I'm with BA now.'

'Since when?'

'This was my first flight with them. To Delhi.' She looked down at her suit again. 'You don't think it's too dowdy?'

'Dowdy? No.'

The two women looked at each other, trying to simultaneously absorb and keep at arm's length their different lives.

'God – isn't it awful what's happening to Laker?'

'Well – you got out in time.'

'Just. It's the people with families I feel sorry for. God,' Laura said again, suddenly exhaling. 'It's been a long time, hasn't it?'

'It has – can't remember how long exactly, but – yes.'

'Yeah, ages. God. So. You're here waiting for Mick?'

Dominique laughed without knowing why. 'He should be around somewhere – the screen says his flight's in Baggage Reclaim and people are already starting to come through.' She wished she didn't sound so vague. It made it seem like her and Mick didn't really speak any more, like one didn't really know where the other one was; like they often missed each other.

And sure enough there was Laura laughing and saying, 'It sounds like you lose your husband a lot.'

'Not too often.' Vague.

Laura nodded with her lips partly open. 'I was in Mick's cabin crew on the Barbados flight a month ago. One of my last flights on Laker Air.'

Dominique didn't know what to say to this. Why were

92

they talking about Mick? Laura gave the sleeves of her sheepskin coat a couple of tugs. 'Where were you?'

'Where was I when?'

'Barbados – you should have been in Barbados.'

'Well, I wasn't.'

Laura paused. 'Have you ever been?'

'No.'

'You've never been?'

'No.'

'Well, the next time he flies to Barbados, you get him to book you a seat on the plane,' Laura said sympathetically. 'I know it's difficult with the kids and everything . . . how many have you got?'

'Two.'

'. . . But you should go. You really should. Barbados is . . .'

'Laura!'

They were standing in the shadow of a second air hostess, who Laura didn't introduce.

'This is Mick's wife. Mick Saunders.'

The other girl nodded.

'I used to fly too,' Dominique put in, 'a long time ago.'

The girl nodded again.

'When did you give up?' Laura asked.

'Well – I didn't really give up – I got married,' Dominique said, looking for the first time at Laura's left hand, which was ring-less. She held on to this, and the fact that up close there was a food stain on the lapel of Laura's jacket.

'So,' Laura said heavily, 'there you go.'

'There you go.'

'Well. I'll probably see you again. Give my best to Mick.'

'I will,' Dominique said, hands in pockets. 'Bye.'

'Bye,' Laura replied, steering her friend away.

Dominique was thinking of going to the Laker Air desk

93

and getting them to phone through and find out where Mick was when Laura parked her case and came running back.

'I meant to say – I saw Mick go up to the observation deck.'

'The observation deck?'

'About ten minutes ago.' Laura shrugged. 'And I heard about him being laid off – I'm sorry.'

'Well –' The way Laura said it made Dominique want to defend, not Mick, but herself. 'I think he's pretty pleased about it. The package was good.' She paused. 'So good, in fact, that we're thinking of emigrating to New Zealand and –'

'New Zealand? When?'

'I don't know, I –'

Laura turned abruptly away, tripped over a suitcase somebody had parked in her path, then broke into a run.

Dominique watched her go, feeling unsettled. Something about the way Laura was running made her think she was crying at the same time. She rejoined her friend and the two women in uniform disappeared through the sliding doors that led to the car parks, the friend taking one last look at Dominique before the doors shut again. Dominique stood there wondering what either of them had to show for all those air miles they'd clocked up between them – after how many years of service? And even if there *was* anything to show – who was there to show it to? She started to make her way to the observation deck, thinking about the food stain on Laura's lapel. Was Laura happy? Were women like Laura happy? 'Women like' – had she really thought that? There were no other women like Laura. There was only one Laura: Laura was unique. Just as she, Dominique, was unique.

She got into the lift, and a few seconds later the doors opened onto a lobby whose floor was covered in rubber matting. Through the lobby doors she saw Mick standing outside in the persistent dark in his overcoat and a pair of gloves. The gloves were thick woollen ones that made his hands look disproportionate to the rest of him, and his pilot's cap was on the wall beside him.

When the automatic doors opened the wind nearly blew if off. A plane flew over and Mick turned his head to follow its undercarriage.

'Your hat'll blow off the wall,' she said, stepping outside.

He turned round and smiled at her. 'Hey, you.'

They stood looking at each other.

'How'd you find me?' he said at last.

'Just did. Aren't you cold?'

'Maybe.'

They stayed where they were, not moving any closer.

'Sad?'

'Maybe.'

She wished she hadn't said that. It sounded as though she was attacking him in some way. Her clearest, most instinctive thoughts always came across as aggressive when she articulated them.

'I was waiting for you downstairs in Arrivals.' She thought about mentioning Laura. 'I didn't know where you were.'

'I was watching the planes.' He broke off.

For some reason this seemed like a stupid thing for a pilot to say.

'Was the flight okay?'

'The flight was fine. How are the girls?'

'The girls are fine. I left them both asleep. They missed you, but they're fine.'

'So everything's fine.' He reassured her with a smile, but it wasn't enough to make her want to cross to him. 'You know what I was thinking up there? I was thinking – I can't remember the last time a child asked to come into the cockpit. We never get children up front any more and I was trying

95

to work out why that was; why the fact that aeroplanes stay up in the sky at all doesn't interest them any more. So I came up here.'

'To watch the planes?' she said.

He smiled at her. 'To watch the planes.'

'You look tired.'

'Maybe I am.

'You sure you're okay? Nothing happened on the trip, did it?'

'The trip happened. The flight happened, and the thing I'm still waiting to happen hasn't yet – so I'm waiting.'

'What's meant to be happening?'

'I'm meant to have some sort of feeling – definitive feeling – about the fact that I've just flown a plane for the last time. I don't seem to be having that feeling.' He paused. 'I called you from . . .' another plane went over '. . . Florida,' he shouted. Adding, 'Don't worry – everything's fine.'

'It's probably the jetlag.'

'The jetlag. Probably. It always makes me maudlin.'

'Well don't be maudlin – when you're maudlin you make other people sad,' Dominique said.

'So.' Mick smiled then grabbed hold of her hand, pulling him towards her. 'Come here.'

'I am here.'

'No. Come here.' He kissed her. 'I missed you.'

'I missed you.'

'I mean I really missed you.'

Dominique laughed. 'There's a lot of kissing going on here.'

'I kissed you once.' Mick put his arms round her, picking his cap up from the wall.

'Why aren't you wearing that?' she asked.

'No idea.' He kissed her again, on the forehead this time. 'Come on, let's go home.'

96

They left the observation deck and got into the lift, walking out a minute later into high-voltage airport lighting. They were holding hands and the world around them was moving rapidly.

The green Triumph made its way down the layers of multi-storey, through the barrier at the bottom and out into the morning.

Mick spoke to the woman in the car-park kiosk, calling her Barbara and asking her when her shift ended. Dominique knew that if she asked him in an hour or even three hours' time when Barbara's shift ended, he would be able to say three o'clock without any hesitation. Mick wasn't just talk, he took people to heart. He listened to them, and they trusted him. Dominique didn't ask – because the subject bored her – but she was pretty certain Mick had all the data on Barbara: husbands, lovers, children, other jobs. Mick would have the whole Barbara panorama at his fingertips because Mick understood that although Barbara's life and death meant nothing to him personally, there were a lot of other people to whom it did. This was a leap of faith she herself had never been able to make. She didn't give a shit about Barbara or how long her shift was, but Mick did.

For a while the road followed a metal fence with runway the other side, then turned off at right angles. She stared at the web of runway and lights and couldn't ever imagine knowing what they meant.

'I missed you,' Mick said, turning to look at her.

'You said. I missed you too. I think I already said that as well.'

'One hundred and forty-four hours is a lot of hours to spend away from you.'

'You were counting?'

'I always count.'

She smiled and rested her head on the seatbelt. 'You'll never have to count again.'

By the time they parked the car outside No. 4, dawn was at last streaking highlights through the remains of night, diluting it with an early-morning grey. Stephanie answered the door in her gymnastics leotard, preoccupied.

'Hi, Dad – can you make pancakes?' she said to Mick. Then, turning to Dominique, 'And can I take the mirror off the wall in the downstairs toilet?'

'If you want –'

As they walked into the house the phone started to ring. 'I'll get that.' Mick disappeared into the study and Dominique wandered into the kitchen where Delta was sitting drawing at the table.

'Where's Dad?' she said.

'On the phone.'

'Somebody called for him a few minutes ago.'

'Who was it?'

'I don't know – they wouldn't leave their name. How is Dad?'

'Jetlagged.'

'No – I mean, how is he?' Delta lowered her voice, anticipating a searing insight into the state of her father's mind.

'I don't know.'

'It must be weird,' she persisted, 'to suddenly stop doing something like that – after all these years – especially something like flying.'

She was floundering. They'd told her, but not Steph, that Mick had been made redundant. They'd told her that Florida would be his last flight, but they hadn't told her what to think about this. Whether it was a good or a bad thing; whether it was something they were meant to be celebrating or not talking about. She'd been given facts without guidelines and wasn't that interested anyway, so she was floundering.

'Yes, it must be,' Dominique trailed off.

She opened the fridge then shut it, staring at the magnetic letters on the door's white surface for a while, trying to make out a pattern. Then, yawning, she went over to the kitchen table and sat down.

'What are you doing?' she said, watching her older daughter.

'A sketch for a mural.' Delta turned the sketch pad round and carried on adding details with a pencil.

'What is it?'

'A matador delivering the *coup de grâce*. I thought I could paint it on the wall opposite my bookshelves.'

'Well, I don't mind you painting there, but . . .'

Delta wasn't listening. She turned the sketch pad back round to face her.

'Won't it give you nightmares?'

Dominique sat staring at the Great Wall of China, which was December's picture on the calendar they got free every year from Mr Li's Chinese takeaway. Then she went to find Mick in the study.

'That was Station Pets,' he said when she went in, signalling to her to shut the door. 'They've got two hamsters left: a boy and a girl.'

'Well, we only want one.'

'Why don't we just buy them both – she won't be expecting two.'

'But they'll breed, Mick.'

'So they'll breed . . . we'll buy a bigger cage or sell them or drown them or something.'

'Don't hamsters eat their young?'

'Not these ones – they're Russian hamsters. I told him we'd take them both.'

'So why did you even ask me?'

He smiled at her. 'He's got a cage with a wheel, and because we're taking two hamsters he recommended buying an extension with plastic tubing so they've got more to do . . . some kind of hamster gym. He'll throw in the exercise ball for free.'

'Hamsters need exercise?'

'That's what he said.'

'Well, if we're buying the hamsters we should buy whatever goes with them, you know, whatever makes them happy.' She watched him run his finger along the edge of the desk. 'What about the Sindy House?'

'We'd better keep it – she might change her mind again. We could just give her both anyway.'

'The Sindy House and the hamsters? I don't know, Mick.'

She looked at him standing there in his uniform. How did he do it? How did he walk off a plane and into No. 4 Pollards Close and just pick up all the threads like that as soon as he crossed the threshold? She couldn't have done that. He'd just landed a plane that had been in the air for over eleven hours and here he was talking about hamsters and Sindy Houses like he'd never been anywhere but here all the time. Maybe that's why she stopped flying when she had Delta. Why they both decided she should stop when Delta arrived, because they both knew that if she carried on, one day she'd get onto a plane and never come back. Whereas Mick never had to come back because he'd never left in the first place.

'Stephanie wants pancakes for breakfast,' she said, as the phone started ringing again.

'Hello?' Mick sank onto the corner of the desk, his hand resting in his groin while staring at Dominique. 'Hello? Monica? No – I just got back from Florida. Didn't hear about any tornadoes – what? She's just here,' he said, passing the receiver over.

100

'Stephanie wants pancakes,' Dominique whispered, in a sudden panic.

'You said.'

'Don't make Scotch ones, I want normal ones – lemon – sugar.'

'Don't worry, I'll sort it out.' Mick blew her a kiss then left the room.

Sitting down at the desk, Dominique watched the door shut behind him. She was alone in the study with her mother.

'Dominique?' The voice was impatient, almost angry.

The first of her mother's boyfriends she remembered was Clive, a child-development researcher, who specialised in Early Years. His arrival in their lives coincided with her own early attempts at speech, and on his advice the 'mumumuh' she was beginning to stutter was encouraged to become 'Monica' rather than 'mummy' because Clive believed that the great universals 'mother' and 'father' should be unleashed from their biological fetters and given spiritual status instead. They even managed to get the Danish au pair to go along with this. Clive stayed in their lives for only nine joss-stick-filled months, but two of his legacies remained (because they suited Monica): a belief that yoga was necessary to civilisation, and that Dominique should never have recourse to use the word 'mother' or any of its diminutives.

When she'd had Delta, she'd asked Monica if her daughter could call her 'grandma', but Monica said there was no way she could do 'grandmother' when she hadn't even done 'mother'.

'Dominique?'

'Sorry, sorry – we just got back from the airport. Where are you, anyway? Minnesota?'

'Minnesota? Who told you I was in Minnesota?'

'Mick did, I think. Anyway – I thought you were in Minnesota.'

'I was in Montréal. Montréal's got nothing to do with Minnesota. Are you sure he said Minnesota?'

Dominique wasn't sure any more.

'You probably heard him wrong.'

'Probably. I don't remember.'

'That's your problem, Dominique, there's very little you do remember.'

'I remember things,' Dominique said slowly.

'What would I be doing in Minnesota anyway?' Monica cut in.

'I don't know, but weren't you meant to be spending Christmas there?'

'Where?'

'Minnesota.'

'I wasn't in Minnesota,' Monica exploded, 'I was in Montréal. Montréal, Canada.'

'Sorry,' Dominique said. Then again, 'Sorry.'

'And no, I wasn't meant to be spending Christmas in Montréal – I was running tests on healthy animals with the help of some people there so that we can get this new red food dye approved.'

'So . . .' Dominique said, unwilling to follow any of this. 'Where are you now?'

'Gatwick.'

'Gatwick?' Dominique sat up and looked out the study window at the side passage where there was mint growing between the paving slabs and the fence. 'We were just at Gatwick.'

'I've got some other people to see at Ciba Pharmaceuticals about the new dye, which is why I flew back.'

'Ciba? How long are you at Ciba for?'

'Oh – just a few days.'

'But it's Christmas Eve tomorrow.'

'Yes.' Monica paused. 'So – how are all of you?'

'We're all fine – Stephanie's excited. About Christmas. Stephanie's excited about Christmas.'

'And is Mick off flying again soon?'

'Mick never flies over Christmas.'

'Right. So. You're all pretty busy then.'

'Not really. Just getting ready for Christmas.' She wished she could stop saying the word 'Christmas'.

Monica paused again. 'I did phone last week – I spoke to Mick.'

'Mick? He didn't say.'

'I phoned right after I heard about the Harrods bomb. I was in Canada and I saw it on the TV, and I had this sudden feeling you might be up in London shopping, so I rang . . .'

'When was the bomb?'

'The seventeenth.'

She could hear Monica trying not to become angry with her again for not knowing the date of the Harrods bomb when it only happened six days ago. 'I wasn't up in London then.'

'I know – Mick said.' Monica paused. 'I was thinking . . .'

'What?' Dominique laughed nervously. 'You want to spend Christmas here?'

Monica breathed out. 'I suppose I could do, couldn't I?'

Dominique stared at Linda Palmer's gazelle that Mick had brought downstairs and put on his desk. What was it he'd said about the gazelle? He'd said that it confronted him – that the gazelle confronted him. There was something going on between Mick and the gazelle that she didn't understand, and it wasn't even his – it belonged to Linda. She picked it up then put it down. How exactly did a wooden animal that fitted in the palm of your hand get confrontational anyway? She didn't like it.

'But you've probably made arrangements,' Monica was saying. What else had Monica said that she hadn't heard?

This was something she'd always been able to do – fade people out. When she was a child she used to be able to make them invisible as well. Something that had prompted Monica to have her tested for epilepsy.

'No arrangements – no. We're having a small party on Christmas Eve, and Christmas Day – just family.'

'Well, I'm family . . .' Monica said.

Dominique heard the airport down the phone, and the Tannoy announcing a delay to the Dubai flight had more clarity for her right then than anything she and Monica were saying.

'If you're sure that's what you want to do,' she said. 'Christmas here, I mean.'

'And if *you're* sure you could put up with me for three to four days,' Monica said. Now it was her turn to laugh nervously.

Dominique didn't say anything. She'd never heard Monica laugh nervously before. 'So – do you want to come straight here or are you going to Ciba first?'

'No, I'll come to you.'

'You're sure? I can get Delta to come and pick you up?'

'Delta drives?'

'She was eighteen on her last birthday.'

'I'll get a cab.'

'I would come myself but we've just got back from the airport.'

Why was Monica doing this? She'd never spent Christmas with them before – maybe once when Delta was small, but never more than once. Dominique couldn't work out Monica's motive – and life, for Monica, had to have motive.

'I'll get a cab.'

'Okay – fine.'

'You're sure about this?'

'Of course.'

'You don't sound sure.'

'It's unexpected, that's all.' Dominique paused. 'Impulsive; and I'm not used to that in you. You're not a very impulsive person.'

'Well, I was here, and I thought . . . well, it's Christmas.'

'It is Christmas.'

The Tannoy was updating people about the Dubai flight, then the phone flatlined.

She stared out the window at the mint again, wondering where it came from. She'd gone through a stage of reading gardening books and they all warned against mint; mint and bamboo. There were others she couldn't remember, but they were all difficult to control, and she never could work out why this was seen as a bad thing.

Out in the hallway, Stephanie was doing a headstand over the bathroom mirror, which was on the floor between her hands. 'What are you doing, Steph?'

There were flecks of spittle on the mirror.

'Watching the blood in my head,' she said with difficulty.

'Well, stop it – you'll make yourself sick.'

'It's Christmas Eve tomorrow.'

'What's that got to do with anything?'

'Steph – pancakes,' Mick's voice called out from the kitchen.

Steph was leaning against the hallway wall looking at her Mickey Mouse watch. 'Four minutes and twenty seconds that time,' she said, walking unevenly into the kitchen where there was a plate of immaculate pancakes on the bench next to the hob.

Dominique followed her in. 'Monica's coming for Christmas.'

Mick, still in his pilot's uniform, put the pancakes on the table. 'You're sure?'

'I've just spoken to her.'

105

He got the maple syrup out of the cupboard and didn't say anything.

'Who's Monica?' Stephanie asked.

'She's your grandmother,' Mick said.

'Mick – you know we don't call her that.'

'OK. She's Mummy's mummy, which makes her your grandmother, only we call her Monica because she suffers from a disorder called babushkaphobia.'

'What's babushkaphobia?' Delta asked.

'A woman's aversion to her grandchildren.'

'But we don't know a Monica, do we?' Stephanie insisted.

'She was here about a year ago – maybe longer,' Delta said, without looking up from her matador.

'Is she the one with the short hair and dragonfly earrings?' Stephanie asked.

'I don't remember dragonfly earrings,' Dominique said, sitting down at the table. Mick made his way round everybody, sprinkling chocolate drops from a packet over their shoulders and onto their plates.

'Well, I do,' Stephanie said.

'Why's she coming now?' Delta asked.

Dominique shrugged, looking up at Mick. 'She said she phoned last week?'

'Last week?' He thought about this. 'She did phone last week – to make sure none of us got blown up in the Harrods bomb.'

'That's what she said.' Dominique looked down at her pancakes. Mick had sprinkled chocolate drops in the shape of a heart.

'Why's she coming now?' Stephanie repeated. 'I hate Monica.'

8

Joe went into the lounge and shut the door behind him. 'Where's Mum, Jess? Jess?'

'In the garage – doing a stock-take of the freezer.'

He moved over and stood in front of the TV.

'Dad, I'm watching this.'

He looked down towards the screen at a newsreader standing in a field outside some barracks. 'What is this?'

'A documentary on para psychological training for soldiers.'

'You didn't feel like watching something more seasonal?'

The newsreader started to interview a couple of soldiers.

'They did the same thing in America,' Jessica said. 'The Army Research Institute ran a programme to enhance the para psychological abilities of a few select soldiers.'

'Meaning what?'

'Meaning they were trying to train them to use a range of non-weapon-dependent techniques not readily available to the average soldier.'

'Like what?'

'Like walking through walls – being able to leave their bodies.'

'How d'you know all this?'

'I read.'

'Oh, you read.'

'They were trying to develop a First Earth Battalion.'

'To fight what?'

'I don't know – intergalactic wars?'

'Yeah, right.' Joe sat down next to her. 'I need your help with something.'

'What?'

'Mum's Christmas present.'

'You haven't got her anything?'

'Not yet, no.'

'Nothing?'

'Nothing.'

'It's Christmas Eve tomorrow.'

He leant forward, watching the screen.

'That's just so depressing, Dad – Dad?'

'I was thinking of maybe underwear.' He turned towards her and paused. 'Jess?'

'What?'

'Well, what do you think?'

'What's it got to do with me?'

'Well, you're a woman, and . . .'

'I'm not a woman – I'm your daughter.'

'But I don't know about size and stuff.'

'You don't know her size?'

'Well, do you?'

'Why the hell would I? This is really depressing, Dad.'

Joe watched the screen as a man in uniform started to levitate, then got up and changed channels.

'Dad – I'm watching that.'

'There's got to be something else on.' BBC2 was showing *The Wizard of Oz*. He watched Judy Garland get surrounded by munchkins – Jessica didn't say anything – then sat back down on the sofa.

Why did men buy women underwear? To buy them the sort they imagined fucking them in or taking off then fucking them without. What did he imagine fucking Linda without? Without black? No. Without white? In fact, what colour underwear did Linda usually wear? He couldn't remember. He saw her either fully clothed or naked, but never in between. In between was for people who didn't make it to the bedroom; people with sex drives still intact; people like Mick and Dominique, according to Linda. He could imagine Mick buying underwear. Mick would have a place he went to regularly in Brighton or London where they knew his name and where all the assistants imagined being the woman he was buying the underwear for. Did Linda ever wonder what it would be like to be Mick's wife? Why didn't he have any drive for this kind of thing? Was he dead? Maybe he'd died and Jessica and Linda were just too polite to point it out.

'Perfume,' Jessica said, watching the screen intently now. 'Get her perfume.'

'She said if she got one more bottle of perfume or one more pair of earrings she'd . . .'

'She'd what?'

'I don't know, she was too angry to finish.' He felt a sudden, intense pity for Linda and, turning to Jessica, was about to say something cutting when a huge smile started spreading across her face as she watched the film, which meant that any minute now she was going to start laughing, and Jessica laughing was something he wanted to see.

Then the phone rang.

Joe was standing in the lingerie department at Farrington's, Littlehaven's only department store, listening to a woman with backcombed hair on the Windsmoor counter confessing loudly to another assistant that she always washed her face in her bathwater. He scanned the rails of mostly white under-wear, broken by a single block of purple and more beige than seemed necessary. It was all wrong. He wasn't going to find Linda here, and he definitely wasn't going to find him and Linda here.

'Can I help you?'

It was the woman from the Windsmoor counter who, up close, was much taller than him and had mostly grey teeth.

'Well . . . yeah . . . I was looking for something for my wife. For Christmas. For my wife. For . . .'

'. . . Christmas,' the woman finished, then nodded as if she was thinking about this. 'Let me show you our new range – Lissière.' She headed towards the purple. 'The lace is French,' she said, and paused as if this should mean something to him, or maybe she'd just been trained to say the word 'French' a lot because everybody knew that the French were the only nation who had post-marital sex. 'The sequin detail really is quite unique – of course it means it has to be hand-washed, but then I always hand-wash underwired bras anyway. My washing machine broke down once and when the engineer came out to fix it he found wire from one of my bras jammed behind the drum.' She stared down at the purple Lissière bra. 'I nearly died.'

Joe, who had been staring at the bra as well, looked up. 'I don't know,' he said slowly.

They glanced quickly at each other, both suddenly aware that neither of them was going to enjoy this.

'The range is entirely new. Very French.'

Joe nodded rhythmically in time to her patter. What was this – did you have to be French to fuck these days?

'And look at the detail.' She flicked up the single sequin sewn between the cups then flicked it down again. 'You can tell it's French.' She held the bra out towards him. Unsure

110

what he was meant to do, he rubbed the lace trim between his thumb and forefinger. 'Very nice.'

'Isn't it wonderful?' She looked down, contemplating the bra again.

'The only thing is . . . I'm not sure about the purple.'

'It isn't purple.'

'It isn't?'

She shook her head. 'It's lilac – you don't like lilac?'

'I don't think my wife would.'

'The bra's very feminine. Very . . .'

'French, yeah, I know. Would you wear it?'

The Windsmoor woman was staring at him.

'You're a woman – would you wear this bra?' He held it up against himself.

She stared back, suddenly afraid. 'All briefs are half-price when purchased with a bra. We're running a promotional offer at the moment because the range is new.'

'Not a bad offer,' Joe said. 'Only the thing is, see, I was looking for something in black.'

'Everything all right?' It was Mr Farrington, the third son of the third generation of the Farrington dynasty, unmarried still at fifty-two with hair and teeth the same tobacco-yellow as his eyes, hidden behind smoked-glass lenses. 'All briefs are half-price when purchased with any bra from the Lissière range.'

'Thanks very much, but I think I'll leave it.'

'Well don't leave it too long – we've had to re-order twice on this range.'

The strip lighting caught the chain round Mr Farrington's neck and Joe sniggered as he handed the Lissière bra back to the assistant. He couldn't help himself.

Mr Farrington and the Windsmoor woman watched Joe leave the shop because they didn't have anything else to do.

'That man . . .' Mr Farrington said, his eyes still on Joe's retreating back, '. . . I see men like that up at the golf club . . . the car pulls into the car park with some girl in the passenger seat who's so young her chin's knocking on the dashboard.'

The Windsmoor woman was staring at Mr Farrington's neck where it rolled over his shirt collar and gravity was opening the red, greasy pores.

'They're out of the car and straight into the steam room quicker than you can say . . . and you walk into the steam room with a couple like that in there and you wish . . . you wish . . . then as soon as it gets dark they're screwing in the car in the lane behind the club.' The jewellery of the Farrington dynasty clattered against the glass counter as his hand gripped it. 'And these days they don't even have to cover it up. People just go ahead and do exactly what they want – have you noticed that? I can't even tell the difference between girls and boys any more – girls dressing as boys and boys dressing as girls.' He grunted as he hauled the torso mannequin off its stand, his hands on its tanned tits as he tried to replace the white bra it was wearing with the lilac Lissière one.

The Windsmoor woman was thinking that it was only fifteen minutes until her coffee break, and she couldn't work out why Mr Farrington was getting worked up about trans-vestites.

'The world isn't made up of males and females any more . . . it's the young and the old.'

'He was looking for a Christmas present for his wife,' she said, thinking about Joe. 'He wanted something black.'

Mr Farrington turned to look at her. 'Women don't want black.' He ran his hand through his hair. 'And after Christmas, I want you to do a stock-take of the Lissière range. If nothing's sold, you can put the whole lot in the January sale.'

The Windsmoor woman wasn't listening. 'I like black.'
'You're not a woman, you're a sales assistant.'

Joe got the donut he had been eating earlier, before Winke
Nieman arrived, out of his desk drawer and started eating
it again while staring at the three double-glazing samples
propped against the filing cabinet. When he'd finished, he
brushed the sugar out of his groin, screwed the bag into a
ball, aimed for the wastepaper basket and missed.

'He seemed keen – Winke Nieman,' Steve said, coming
into the office.

'It's business for him . . .' Joe was temporarily distracted
by Steve's Tom and Jerry tie, '. . . and it's no skin off his
nose – cut-price double glazing with a Quantum kitchen.
We're the ones doing the selling.'

Steve took this in. 'You don't like him?'

'I don't know. You know each other?'

'Who?' Steve said.

'You – you and Winke Nieman.'

Steve shook his head. 'No – why?'

'I thought Winke recognised you – looked like he was
surprised to see you here.'

Steve shook his head again.

They both stared at the samples.

'I went to Farrington's on my way in this morning,' Joe
said after a while.

'I thought it was meant to be closing down?'

'In about a month's time. I was looking for something
special for Linda for Christmas, you know . . .'

'Something special?'

'I don't know, some underwear maybe or something.'

'And you went to Farrington's?'

Joe looked up.

'How special's special?'

113

'Well – she's my wife.'

Steve thought about this. 'You should go to Leroy's in Brighton,' he said after a while.

'Never heard of it.'

'Well, it's not really just underwear, but if you're looking for something special . . . it's on North Lane.'

'You're a dark horse, you are, Steve,' Joe said, getting up. He took his suit jacket from the hanger on the back of the door. 'Why don't we shut up shop now; call it a day. Ease yourself into Christmas nice and gentle.'

'I could do.' Steve didn't sound convinced.

'Go on, I'm off down to Brighton to find Linda something in this . . .'

'Leroy's.'

'Leroy's. Right.'

'You're sure?'

'Course I'm sure – it's bloody Christmas Eve tomorrow. Go on – make the most of it. You can tell Maureen she can go as well.'

'Maureen's not in today.'

'She's not?'

'You gave her the day off so she could fly to Geneva to see her son.'

'I did?' Joe smiled kindly at him. 'You look bloody knackered. And thin – you're getting too thin, Steve.'

He stood back against the glass partition that separated his office from the showroom, crushing the blinds. He was still standing there watching through the window as Steve got into his car and drove off so that the only cars left in the car park for Foundry Lane Industrial Estate, where Quantum Kitchens was based, were his own and an 'X' registration BMW. Then the only things he was staring at were a couple of conifers, which he hated. Conifers had always depressed him. He scratched at the corner of his mouth where some donut sugar had got trapped, then picked up the phone and dialled home.

'Linda? I was thinking . . . what? No, Winke's already been – he left about half an hour ago.' He paused. 'Anyway, I was thinking maybe I'd go down to Brighton this afternoon and pick up your mum today instead of tomorrow – I can get there and back this afternoon if I leave now.' He paused again. 'I know she's not expecting me – I'm just about to phone. What's that? What was Winke wearing? I don't know – I can't remember. So – it's okay if I go to Brighton this afternoon? Linda, I really can't remember – a suit, I think. Why does it matter?' He put the phone down and stared out the window at the car park again.

The BMW had gone. Now Joe's was the only car left. He took one last look round his office at the cards and tinsel tree on top of the filing cabinet, and the paper chains Maureen had spent an afternoon stapling into the ceiling panels, then he set the alarm and left, getting into the only remaining car – the Ford with the Quantum logos on the side.

He took the A23 down to Brighton, and by the time he reached the cricket club he was so hungry he stopped and bought himself a bacon roll from a roadside café. He ate the roll in the lay-by, grease running down his wrists as he watched lights go on in the tower blocks opposite. It was only three o'clock. A jagged edge of orange made a rift in the darkening sky that a flock of birds – starlings, he didn't know, all birds looked black from a distance – made their way along. Then he got back into the car, wiping his hands on the passenger seat, and drove into town where people were out spending money they didn't have, goaded on by the optimism of too much electricity. Electricity that kept the darkness at bay – at a price.

Linda waited until the line went dead, then put the phone down and went back over to the ironing board where she finished the last of Joe's shirts. Why was it that he found it so difficult to remember what Winke Nieman was wearing when he dropped off the double-glazing samples? Situations hung on things like this, and no matter how many times she told Joe he just didn't seem to take it on board.

She switched off the iron and left it to cool on the draining board, staring absently at the garden. Then, just as absently, she got a can of tuna out of the cupboard, opened it and ate the whole can, listening to her stomach rumble. Opening the fridge door, she pushed a tablespoon of the butterscotch Angel Delight she'd made for Joe and Jessica the night before into her mouth, felt guilty, thought about punishing herself then stared around the kitchen at the hour's worth of ironing she'd just finished. Yawning, she tried to imagine Daphne Nieman in the same situation, but couldn't. The cleaner did Dominique's ironing for her, and the Nassams at No. 6 used the same cleaner now as well. Daphne Nieman didn't, but Linda couldn't imagine her doing her own ironing either. She yawned again. She'd woken up at four o'clock that morning to find herself sitting propped up against the pillows with her bedside light still on and the magazine she'd been reading the night before still open on the duvet. The forecast for Scorpio, which wasn't even her star sign, had imprinted itself on the palm of her hand while she slept, and when she woke up she'd been worried about something, only now she couldn't remember what it was. She'd dozed on and off until six, when she heard the milk float, then Joe woke up and said she'd been talking in her sleep.

Carrying the ironing upstairs, she went into Jessica's room and put her clothes away. The notepad was gone from her desk – the notepad and Jessica were at Mr Browne's. Did middle-aged men really write books about the end of the world with fifteen-year-old girls? Maybe they did. She didn't know any more. Ferdie jumped off Jessica's bed to come

116

and sniff at her feet as she closed the wardrobe door, and she was about to push him away when she had a sudden vision of herself jogging up the steps of The Haven Golf Club – where she was going now – with Ferdie under her arm, her coat undone and smelling strongly of something vicious by Christian Dior: her life a magazine spread waiting to happen. The vision's only blemish was the splint and bandage Ferdie had at the base of his tail that he had to wear for another ten days. Sighing, she turned her back on the dog and went into the master bedroom, where she changed out of the tracksuit she was wearing into striped leggings and a white blouse whose waist she pulled in with a red patent leather belt. She could always take Ferdie to the golf club with her and leave him in the car, she supposed, watching him claw at the valance around her and Joe's bed in an attempt to mount it. It was easier to discard Ferdie than it was to pull him out of thin air, and she might decide when she got there that Ferdie was, after all, the thing to set her off.

She looked at herself in the mirror, pleased with the fusion of *Country Diary of an Edwardian Lady* and Olivia Newton-John. Then, putting on her new suede boots and coat to match – which was as close to Dominique's as she could find – she went downstairs and briefly took up her position by the blinds in the lounge, but there was nothing going on in the Close. She turned round, sure there was somebody else in the room with her, but it was only the TV. She'd nearly gone out and left the TV on. What was it? *The Wizard of Oz* – why hadn't she noticed earlier? Jessica must have been watching this and forgotten to switch it off.

Linda stood chewing her nails, watching the screen as Judy Garland clicked the heels of her red shoes together. 'I want to go home. I want to go home. I want to go home.' As she squeezed Toto, Linda heard Ferdie barking upstairs and remembered that she'd been about to get into the car and go up to the golf club, only now she was crying; sobbing, in fact. How long had she been stood there in her coat and boots doing that for? Running back upstairs, she rubbed her hands over her face to remove any traces of snot and tears, took the last of her antidepressants, grabbed Ferdie, then left the house, forgetting to switch off the TV.

She was just opening the garage door when a Fairways minicab pulled up outside No. 4. She stood on her drive, gripping the handle of the half-raised garage door as a woman in a man's hat got out. Who was she? Linda got into her car, but the garage wall jutted out too far for her to see anything other than the puddle of pampas grass in the Saunders' front garden buckle in the wind, and the minicab leaving. She thought about how Jessica said it had been planted to cover up the marks left behind by space-ships that landed to take the blueprint of Pollards Close back to their home planet. Then Linda wondered why she spent so much time worrying about Jessica not speaking to her when these were the kind of things she said when she did. Did she and Mr Browne talk about spaceships and pampas grass?

Linda put the car into gear and within ten minutes was driving through countryside that was dry with cold, and empty. Ferdie, sitting panting on the passenger seat next to her, was staring out the window streaked with de-icer and blinking like he knew where they were going as the car passed through prehistoric woods where humans used to hide from animals that outnumbered them. Linda was unaware, as she changed gear, that the trees they passed were once looked on by the eyes of a species that came before her, with feeling. She was unaware that the first humans who lived among them were too far down the food chain to contemplate life out in the open, or that the ponds on either side of the road were used by them to extract iron ore from. She was also unaware that dragons used to live in the woods until a man called Leonard – later canonised – killed them all. When Jessica was two she used to be terrified of St Leonard's Woods and would scream herself blue trying to tell Joe and Linda about the dragons she saw between the trees. She still didn't like the woods, only now she no longer knew why, because now she was too old to see dragons.

Leaving the woods behind, Linda came to a clearing that was home to The Haven Golf Club. She found a space in the car park, which was virtually full, turned off the engine and sprayed herself – including her hair – with some perfume she kept in the glove compartment. She looked down at Ferdie but was beginning to find his sense of expectancy off-putting, and anyway, something yellow was leaking through the bandage on his tail, so she crossed the car park, skirted the edge of the indoor swimming pool where two children were fighting over a rubber ring and a lifeguard was staring out into the trees, and jogged up the steps into reception without Ferdie.

The automatic doors slid open. She was in, and only slightly disconcerted to find that the hallowed golf club smelt of damp carpet – damp carpet undercut with chlorine – when the doors to the swimming pool suddenly opened and one of the two children who'd been fighting over the rubber ring came running into reception. It was Jamie Nassam, the doctor's son, from No. 6 Pollards Close.

'I'm running fast,' Jamie said as he flew past, his teeth chattering and his breath hissing through the gaps between them.

The receptionist smiled at Linda. 'Lovely boy,' she said, her eyes on Jamie's retreating back. 'Half-caste, of course, but a lovely boy. Half-Egyptian, I think, and if you look closely there is something quite Arabic about his eyes.' The receptionist's chin sank into her neck as she contemplated the child's wet footprints trailing across the carpet.

'I think he's only a quarter-caste,' Linda said, 'because his father's only half Egyptian. He's a Junior Tennis Champion,' she added.

'He is? Well I never. Well-I-never.' The receptionist thought about this. 'Lovely family – you know the family? Lovely family.'

Linda put her car keys on the desk. 'I've come about a new membership.'

The receptionist eventually tore her eyes away from Jamie's rapidly drying footprints and focused on Linda. 'You telephoned last week, didn't you? I remember the voice. It's Mrs Palmer – it is Mrs Palmer, isn't it?' She looked up at Linda, still smiling. 'New joint membership as a gift for Mr Palmer.'

'That's right.'

'Will you be playing golf as well or do you just want club membership? Club membership entitles you to unlimited use of all facilities in the health and fitness suite, and the members' bar, and . . .'

Once the forms were filled in the Palmers officially became members of The Haven Golf Club, and Linda was given a guided tour of the premises by the receptionist. Leaving reception behind, with its green carpet, green wall trellis and fake ivy, they passed through the Mahogany Bar with its Regency-stripe club chairs and choir singing traditional carols through the loud speakers, but it was in the health and fitness suite down by the sauna that Linda became suddenly aware of just how profoundly happy she was; a happiness that wet, quarter-caste children could run through and not spoil.

By the time the door to the steam room opened and Winke

and Paul Nieman emerged from the miasma of eucalyptus steam with matching, monogrammed white towels round their waists, she was no longer thinking coherently. She was deranged with a happiness that was verging on clinical and she'd probably only been this happy twice before in her life.

'How European,' she said when she saw them, throwing her head back wildly.

They both had chains round their necks, only Winke's chain – like his nipples – was lost in hair, and Paul's chain – like his nipples – wasn't.

'I did not know you were a member here, Mrs Palmer,' Winke said.

'Just now.' Linda paused then had to say it again. 'Just now.'

Winke nodded. 'And tell me – why European?' he asked, genuinely interested.

Somewhere in the building they heard a child crying.

'Will you excuse me,' the receptionist said, running towards the doors.

Linda waved the receptionist away and let her body slouch. 'Well . . . father and son in the steam room together . . . it's just so European,' she said again, loudly.

Winke was nodding slowly. He put his hands on his hips. 'Not really.'

Linda laughed and put her hand on her throat, smiling happily at Paul as if they both knew that nobody but Winke made her laugh so much.

'And the way you say it, Mrs Palmer . . . it sounds more pornographic than European.'

Paul Nieman scratched the back of his head and Linda stared at the hair under his arms, which was much darker than the hair on his head. Did he dye his hair? Was Winke waiting for her to speak? Was she meant to add something to this?

121

'You make it sound as though my son and I were engaged in sodomy.'

'Only,' Paul said, turning to Winke, 'if we *had* been sodomising each other it wouldn't – strictly speaking – be sodomy: it would be incest.'

Winke clapped his son on the back and said something to him that Linda didn't catch because she was too busy wondering when one of them – all of them – would start laughing. So this was civilisation, and now she really was ready to believe that she'd arrived at its epicentre when semi-naked people could joke with fully dressed people in broad daylight, and while fully sober, about Belgian sodomites. The world felt suddenly sophisticated, profane and unbelievably light to the touch.

Then something popped inside her head and the next minute she felt blood trickling out of her right nostril. When she tipped her head back she could taste it; in fact it was all she could taste: warm blood.

Winke was standing next to her – shoulder high – his hand on her back. 'This is a common error,' he said, trying to push her forwards. 'You must never lean back with a nosebleed.'

'Tissue. I need tissue,' Linda said.

'Just lean forwards.' Winke put his hand on the back of her neck, gently forcing her head.

She parted her legs just in time to avoid blood hitting her suede boots. 'The carpet,' she said, blood flowing over her upper lip into her mouth. 'There's blood on the carpet.' Her hands went instinctively to her face.

'This way the flow will be stemmed naturally,' Winke continued, 'and you won't get a headache afterwards.'

'The carpet,' she said again, breathing through her teeth and trying not to swallow any more blood.

A hand with painted nails and rings, full of tissue, crossed her line of vision, which consisted of nothing but blood-stained carpet and toes: Winke's fat toes, Paul's curled toes and her own suede toes.

'This really is not necessary,' Winke said. 'The flow is nearly . . .'

Linda passed out.

When she came round she was sprawled in one of the Regency-stripe club chairs in the Mahogany Bar, which had featured on the cover of the brochure for The Haven Golf Club. The only thing she could see clearly were the dog hairs clinging to the front of her suede coat. She'd had dog hairs on her during the guided tour; dog hairs on her when the Niemans stepped out of the steam room; dog hairs on her when she started to bleed; and dog hairs on her when she passed out. Fucking Ferdie.

'How are you, Mrs Palmer?' Paul Nieman was standing in front of her, holding a snooker cue. He was dressed, but his hair was still wet.

Reminding herself that she'd just blacked out in the epicentre of civilisation, she tried to sit up straight, but the thudding in her head started again. In the background she heard glasses being handled at the bar and the soft knocking of balls as they rolled across baize. Digging her elbows into the side of the chair, she slid into an upright position and breathed out. Somebody had put a glass of whisky on the table in front of her, and Winke Nieman was in the chair opposite dressed in the V-neck Lacoste she'd tried to buy for Joe.

'You need to eat more,' he said.

Winke clearly dressed himself. He probably cooked as well – she could imagine him in an apron standing over a hob full of pans. His way with clothes and his way with food would have been turned into deviances by her mother, the sum total of which was . . . what? Her hand went to her throbbing right temple. She took a sip of the whisky and started coughing. 'What's the time?'

'The time?' Paul said. 'Around two.'

The back of her neck hurt as she shook her head. 'How long was I out for?'

'Not long.' He paused. 'Five minutes.'

'Five minutes,' Winke agreed, sticking out his lower lip.

She looked at them both, now fully dressed. 'I was out for more than five minutes.'

Paul blew some excess chalk dust off the cue. 'Maybe.'

She had another sip of whisky then got to her feet. 'Well . . .'

'Mrs Palmer – don't get up,' Paul said.

'I've got things to do.'

'It isn't safe for you to drive – let me take you home – you are going home, aren't you?'

'I'm fine,' she said to Paul. 'I can drive.'

'It really isn't safe for you to drive.'

'It's just a bruise,' she said, her hand going automatically to her right temple. 'Please – don't let me keep you from your game.'

Paul Nieman made no move to return to the snooker table.

'You should let Paul drive you home – the car's just outside,' Winke insisted.

'Honestly, I'm fine.' The back of her neck was hurting badly now and she had a feeling she might start crying if she didn't make it to her car soon.

Somehow sensing this, Winke changed the subject. 'We dropped the samples off at Quantum this morning – offering discount double glazing with a new kitchen is a good idea,' he said.

Paul started to slowly chalk the end of his cue again. 'It was your idea, wasn't it, Mrs Palmer?'

She shook her head. 'It was Joe who came up with it – offering the double glazing – that was Joe's idea.'

'It was your idea, I know it was.' Paul Nieman was smiling.

'Why would I come up with something like that?' She tried to laugh.

'Because you're clever,' he said, staring at her over the snooker cue.

'You should go into business,' Winke added.

She did up the buttons on her coat and tried to ignore the dog hairs. 'I really do have things to do.'

'Then let me drive you,' Paul insisted.

'I don't want you to drive me anywhere – I can drive myself.' Why was she shouting?

'But you blacked out, Mrs Palmer.'

'So I blacked out.' She picked up her bag.

'But it isn't safe to drive, Mrs Palmer.'

'Will you please stop calling me "Mrs Palmer".'

'Okay,' Paul said, watching her, 'so what should I call you?'

She stared back at him, gripping the car keys in her hand while Winke took stabs at the whisky with his mouth and said nothing.

She left The Haven – trying not to break into a run as she crossed the car park – narrowly missing a collision with an Audi. The Audi was driven by a Financial Adviser called Nathan, and Daphne Nieman was sitting in the passenger seat. This would have interested Linda if she'd realised, but she was too preoccupied by the thought that Paul Nieman had made her want to cry, and that she might have blood on her face. When she got to her car and pulled the mirror down she saw that she did have blood on her face and spat into a tissue to wipe it off, only able to hold her head at one angle because the back of her neck hurt so much now.

Ferdie stood up on the passenger seat and tried to vault over the gear-stick onto her lap, but she knocked him down among the pedals, yelling at him, 'Who the fuck do you think you are, just who the fuck?' Ferdie panted happily, and the wind, which gave the day's temperature a wind-chill factor of zero, blew the two conifers on the other side of the windscreen from side to side. The air was full of freezing rain that didn't seem to reach the ground, she could feel the bruises growing on her forehead, elbow and hip, and she was no longer profoundly happy.

It suddenly occurred to her that she didn't want to be sitting alone in her white Toyota at The Haven Golf Club – she wanted to be with Joe; somewhere with Joe; anywhere with Joe: even a council flat. She pictured an intense renegade romance lived out on the welfare state with her and Joe as outlaws from all their achievements. The more she sat staring through the windscreen at the freezing rain, the more the romance became a lovers-against-the-world epic where they did nothing but smoke and fuck all day long. There was no room for detail in the epic because when they weren't smoking or fucking, they'd be talking about suicide . . . sometimes they'd do all three. Then she remembered what it was she'd been so worried about when she woke up at four o'clock that morning – she'd lost the gazelle Joe made her when they were first married, and that's what had woken her up. At the thought of the gazelle she'd never liked – the gazelle she'd nearly thrown away when they moved to Pollards Close – something inside her head popped again and another nosebleed started. She found some tissue with lipstick prints on it in the glove compartment – what had made her choose a shade like that? – and filled her right nostril with it. How much blood had she lost already today? She turned the keys in the ignition, the engine drowning out Ferdie's happy panting, suddenly bored shitless with herself. Then it passed.

When Linda got home there was a letter on the doormat, addressed to Jessica. Taking it into the kitchen, she put it on the dining-room table, moved it to the breakfast bar, propped it against the fruit bowl, then opened it:

> Jessica –
> *There is no evil in the atom, only in men's souls.*
> Adlai Stevenson

Who the fuck was Adlai Stevenson, and which number did he live at?

The windows at Leroy's were blacked out, but white lettering told any pedestrian passing that the shop sold ADULT FILMS, ADULT MAGS, SEX AIDS and SEX TOYS. The beaded curtain hanging across the entrance had the Mona Lisa painted on it and Joe walked through her smile into the shop, wondering briefly what the difference between a sex aid and a sex toy was – deciding that it had something to do with proficiency.

Nobody looked up when he went in. The goth behind the counter was writing on an A4 pad and there was a pregnant woman browsing through the magazines. Was this how Steve interpreted 'something special'? How did Steve know about Leroy's anyway – and what did Steve buy here? He passed the shelves of videos, getting an overall picture of reclining women with their hands disappearing up their crotches. The only one that looked vaguely interesting was *One Hundred Things You Should Know About Your Neighbours*. Next to this were a couple of seasonal titles, which confused him because he'd never thought of Christmas as having much of an impact on pornography before – in terms of content.

'Excuse me,' he said as he reached the counter.

The goth looked up slowly.

'Hi – excuse me – but d'you do underwear?'

'Men's or women's?'

'Right, well, women's.'

'Through there. With equipment.'

She pulled back the beaded curtain behind the counter. This one didn't have the Mona Lisa on it, this one had the Rio Jesus printed across it. Joe went in. The light was better because of a skylight, and there were no joss sticks. A table in the middle of the room had a bowl of dog biscuits on it and a vase of roses. Confused again, Joe bypassed this and the racks of harnesses and suits to where the bras were. Leroy's could lay claim to being the antithesis of Farrington's, but Joe wasn't sure he wanted the antithesis – a rich relation would do. He thought about leaving it, going back to Farrington's tomorrow and buying the lilac Lissière bra, but the thought of the Windsmoor woman flicking the single sequin between the cups depressed him all over again. Then he looked at the rack in front of him and couldn't imagine buying any of the stuff here for anyone – least of all Linda.

Sighing, he picked out the least complicated bra he could – black with a red satin ribbon running round the top. He was just checking the label when a couple walked in, laughing loudly. They seemed to know what they were doing, and were soon rattling their way through the harness selection. Joe didn't know what he was doing and this wasn't just a passing thought, it was a profound realisation: none of this stuff meant anything to him. He looked up at the winter dark through the skylight and watched a pigeon scratch across the glass. He'd buy the bra and not give it to her or he'd buy it and maybe give it to her – either way he'd buy the bra. The bra and these – what were they? Edible pants – strawberry flavour.

He turned round to look at the laughing couple and there she was: Belle's hairdresser, Lenny, and a man in a raincoat and leather beret, who was looking at Lenny and the two sets of harnesses she was holding up for him.

Joe turned quickly round, trying to get the bra back onto the railing, but Lenny was already standing beside him, smiling and tugging at the arm of his coat.

'Don't get strawberry.'

'Strawberry?'

'It gives you a rash.'

'They're not for me.'

'Well – they'll give whoever they're for a rash.' She was still smiling at him. 'How old is she?'

'My wife?'

'That's who you're buying them for?'

He nodded. She smelt of smoke and looked younger than the last time – the first time – he'd seen her at Belle's flat. No, that wasn't right – she didn't look younger, she looked happier. Women had to be either happy or unhappy, and men either employed or unemployed. He turned round to look at the man she'd come in with. It was an instinctive thing; he tried to stop himself, but couldn't.

'Forty-one – she's forty-one.' He didn't have to tell Lenny that, but he just did.

'Too old.'

'For what?'

'For the edibles.'

He looked down at the box, trying to read the words – any words – printed there.

'They're more for teenagers.'

'Teenagers? Where does it say that?' he asked, still trying to read the box.

'It doesn't say – it's just one of those things – you know, gimmicky; for kids.'

He nodded, taking this in. 'I've got a teenage daughter and . . .' he swung round and took another look at the man Lenny came in with, '. . . she's not into anything like this.'

'So what is she into?'

'Jessica? Well – nuclear disarmament, CND – all that stuff.'

'Lenny,' the man called over, 'I think I'm going for this one here.' He held up a red studded harness and walked through the Rio Jesus back into the main shop.

They heard the harness clattering against the counter as the goth wrapped it.

'How's Belle?' Lenny asked.

'I'm here to pick her up – she's coming to us for Christmas.' Joe paused. 'Aren't you meant to be cutting her hair today – it's a Friday.'

'I went yesterday instead. Today I had to see some premises I'm thinking of renting.'

'You're starting up your own business?'

'I'm thinking about it.'

'If you need any advice, you know . . . feel free to speak to me.'

'The carpenter turned entrepreneur.'

Joe stared at the underwear rack in front of him, but apart from patches of colour he didn't really see anything.

'You remembered I cut Belle's hair on Fridays?' she asked, watching him.

The man she'd come in with put his head through the bead curtain. 'Lenny – I'm off now.'

'Already?'

'It's three thirty – I'm meant to be there at four.' He blew her a kiss and waved at Joe then disappeared. Joe enjoyed the fact that the man's face was covered in pock marks – he hadn't seen this when they first came in.

They watched the bead curtain fall still and the Rio Jesus become intact again.

130

'You're not buying anything?' he asked her.

'No – I just came in with Ray.'

Joe thought she was going to say that she had to go, but she didn't. She just stood there fiddling with the buckle on her handbag. The pigeon scratched its way back across the skylight and he tried not to think about her and Ray laughing or Ray buying the harness.

'Who told you about Leroy's?' she said at last.

'Why did somebody have to tell me about it?'

'Somebody told you.'

'How d'you know?'

'Somebody told you.'

'Okay – it was my business manager. I said I was looking for something special and he told me to come here.'

'Leroy's *is* special,' she said, pleased. 'It's not like other sex shops – you know – taking the piss out of sex. I hate that. Leroy's takes sex seriously.' She paused. 'Are you buying that?'

'What?'

'Whatever it is you've got in your hand that you don't want me seeing.'

'Well, after your judgement on the edibles . . .' he said, putting them back on the shelf.

'I wasn't judging – I don't do that – I was being helpful, and anyway it doesn't matter what I say, does it, because you're not buying them for me.' She was smiling at him again.

Then she walked through the Rio Jesus back into the main shop and he thought she'd left Leroy's altogether, but when he went through to pay for the bra there she was, standing next to the pregnant woman, looking at a magazine.

They stepped outside onto the pavement.

'All done?' She shivered.

131

'Cold?'

'Just goose bumps.'

He looked up and down the street in either direction for no reason then back at Lenny. 'Where are you going now?'

She pushed her hands into her jeans. 'To see my mum.'

'Skirton Street?'

'That's right.' She tried not to look surprised.

'I grew up on Cassidy,' Joe said, 'remember?'

'No.'

'You do,' he insisted.

'I don't.'

They stared at each other.

'D'you want a lift?' Joe asked.

'Won't Belle be waiting?'

'She can wait a bit longer.'

'It's out of your way.'

'I could go and see my mum – haven't seen her for months.'

'You don't get on?'

'Oh, we get on, it's just complicated.'

'It always is.'

They drove for fifteen minutes through heavy traffic and familiar streets.

Lenny lit her third cigarette. 'We were in the army together,' she said. 'Me and Ray – the man in the shop.'

Joe turned to look at her and nearly went into the tail lights of the car in front.

'You knew I was in the army?'

'No,' Joe lied.

'We're not together or anything,' she said after a while. 'I mean, we spend time together – now and then – but we're not together or anything.'

They were on the outskirts of the Downside Estate and the only thing that had changed since he was last here, in the summer, was the greengrocer's on the corner of Cassidy Street and Thurrock Road that was now a kebab shop with fluorescent lights and a queue.

'You can drop me here.'

He pulled up outside the new kebab shop, wondering briefly what had happened to Mr Carsons, who used to run the greengrocer's. Evolution had made mincemeat out of the Carsons.

'Well – see you,' he said.

'Yeah, see you.'

She got out of the car, was about to shut the door, then leant back inside again.

'Ray works for an escort agency – women pay to get fucked by him – you know, housewives and stuff. He wouldn't mind me telling you that.' She paused, shivering. 'I was helping him choose some equipment so that the women feel they get their money's worth.'

'I thought he was your boyfriend,' Joe said, looking up at her standing in the road.

'Ray's a good man, but he'll do anything for money. Anyway – I hope your wife enjoys her present.'

After a while she shut the door and he watched her join the queue in the kebab shop. He waited, but she didn't turn round. She acted like he'd already driven the car away so he put it into gear and drove round the corner, pulling up in front of No. 24 Cassidy Street.

Turning the engine off, he stared through the window at the house he grew up in. The curtains in his parents' room had been roughly drawn, and the window in his brother's old room was crowded with marijuana plants clamouring for light. The house, like all the others on Cassidy Street, was in a permanent state of civil unrest. Downstairs, the heavy velvet curtains hadn't yet been drawn and through the nets he saw his mother sitting smoking at the dining-room table, surrounded by what looked like miniature windmills.

After five minutes – during which he debated whether to get out of the car or switch the engine back on – he got out of the car. His brother Darren's Raleigh was still propped against the wall in the front garden, and in the corner there was an old oil drum with a couple of monkey wrenches balanced on it. Tilting the wrought-iron '24' so that it was straight, he rang the bell.

There was movement inside the house, but nobody answered the door. He rang again. The second ring brought his mother to the window where she stood with a handful of net, staring out at him. A minute later the outside light came on, but even then it took her a while to recognise him. Her hands went to her face and she started to cry.

At last, wiping her eyes with the nets, she answered the door and grabbed him by the neck, pulling him towards her. Her face was still wet and streaked with dirt from the nets, which hadn't been washed since – he didn't want to think when.

'Joe,' she said, starting to cry again.

'All right, Mum, let's move inside.' He pushed her gently into the hallway.

'I thought it was you, but I couldn't believe it. What are you doing here?'

'Passing by – thought I'd drop in.'

She nodded, taking him in again, knowing that he'd be in Brighton to pick up Belle for Christmas.

'How'd you get here?'

'I drove.'

'Let's see the car then.' She pushed him to one side, smiling. 'Quality Kitchens – that's you?'

'Quantum, Mum, it says Quantum,' he said, immediately wishing he hadn't.

'You should have rung.'

'It was a spur of the minute thing.'

'But you knew you'd be in Brighton.'

'I wasn't sure how much time I'd have.'

She caught at her lower lip with her teeth. 'It's good to see you, Joe.'

They went through to the lounge diner, walking into a wall of marijuana fumes.

'Are you smoking again, Mum? Well – are you?'

She gave him a slow, breathless look. 'Just now I had one. It calms me down.'

It was so cold in the room, he could see his own breath.

'You want me to light it?' she said, seeing him look at the gas fire.

'I'm fine.'

'You're not fine, you're bloody shaking with the cold.' She found the matches and lit the fire, which let off dust. 'Tea?'

She disappeared into the kitchen, leaving him alone with the TV, two armchairs whose foam stuffing was now showing, and the sofa, which had blankets and a pillow at one end. There were no Christmas decorations – not even any cards. No. 24 Cassidy Street used to do the full battery-operated offensive at Christmas and he remembered not being able to take a step in any direction – not even being able to take a piss – without something singing or flashing at him. She put her head round the door. 'Milk and sugar?'

He didn't want sugar, but said 'yes' to both because accepting sugar would cause her a disproportionate amount of joy; the sort of joy nobody should have to justify.

'Make it two sugars,' he called out, looking at the blankets and pillow on the sofa again. Then he remembered Lenny at Belle's that day, asking for three. 'Make it three,' he called out.

135

She put her head round the door again, smiling openly at him as he crossed back through the years to her. 'Three?' She wanted to hear him say it again. Sugar was their secret; sugar was what lay between them.

'Three,' he repeated.

In the kitchen, she started humming, and upstairs, through the ceiling, he heard someone turning over in bed.

He went across to the dining-room table where there was a copy of the *Brighton Advertiser* and a magazine: *Hunks of Humankind*. He was sure he'd seen it on the shelves at Leroy's – only here it was open at a centre spread of full frontals and, disconcertingly, he was sure he recognised one of the centre-spread hunks. Wasn't that Ray, the man who'd been with Lenny at Leroy's? The joint in the Bonnie Scotland ashtray was still smoking and he stubbed it out, trying not to breathe in the fumes.

'Clear yourself some space on the table,' she said, watching him through the door. 'I'll be through in a minute.'

'What's with the windmills?' he asked, closing *Hunks* and going through to the kitchen.

'The windmills? Oh, that's Dad – he's been making them for a brother of someone he used to fish with who reckons he can sell them to the garden centre.' She thought about this. 'Something like that anyway, only he hasn't showed up yet, the brother of the friend.'

'It's quiet out the back,' Joe said, wanting to move on from the windmills. 'What happened to the dog?' He looked out through the kitchen window at the weed-infested soil where rows of dahlias used to grow, remembering how he and Darren would be woken up night after night before a show and told to go out into the garden with their torches to pick off slugs and anything else they found from the prize dahlias.

'I told Darren he couldn't keep the dog here – there was

136

no one to exercise it, and it was going for people. I was frightened of going out there with the washing even, and then it went for Tara and I said to him . . . I said . . .'

How old was his niece, Tara? Joe couldn't remember.

'. . . You either get rid of that dog or I'm having it put down.' She paused, reliving the scene. 'I wasn't putting up with that. There are some things you don't mind, but . . . not that.'

Joe stared at her, unsure whether she was even talking about the dog any more. 'How is Darren?'

'Working.'

'Oh?'

'Down at the new marina. It's just casual, but he's been there for three months now.' Throughout their childhood it was always Darren who was talked about; Darren who was praised; Darren who'd make his fortune. So when it turned out to be Joe – and not Darren – who made good with his marriage and work, it made her uneasy talking about his brother – like she'd dealt him, Joe, an unfair blow somewhere along the way, and she wasn't an unfair person. 'Come on, let's go through.'

She carried the tea through on the tray Linda had bought for her birthday from a National Trust property a few years ago.

'And how are him and Charlene?'

'On and off; off and on – I can't keep up with them. All I know is that between the both of them Tara ends up on my doorstep more often than not . . .' She faded out, staring at the chimney breast. 'The world's a terrible place, Joe, a terrible place. I was reading in the local paper earlier about a disabled woman who got her leg jammed in her car and ended up dying of exposure.'

Joe, watching her lift the tea carefully off the tray onto the table, was unsure what this had to do with Charlene and Darren's marriage.

137

'You remember Pete, don't you? Two doors up? Big foreign Pete? He's lived here as long as us – used to work on the railways. The police came and got him Guy Fawkes night.'

'They did? What for?'

'Led him out of his house handcuffed and everything. Nobody knew what was going on, then a week later there was this picture of him on the front of the *Advertiser*. He was in one of them Nazi death camps and he killed more people than . . . he killed people, Joe. Pete did. Two-doors-up Pete. They deported him to Israel to stand trial, and I don't even know if it's right after all these years.'

'Well . . . if he did those things.' Joe was thinking. 'His name wasn't Pete though, was it? He was Polish or something.'

'Ukrainian. He was Ukrainian, and we called him Pete because that was the only part of his name anyone could understand. Your dad and him were close. He was the only one – your dad – who went down to the station and tried to see him. Then there was that picture in the *Advertiser* – front page. You just never know with people, do you? Your dad misses him – even if it's true what they said in the papers about him, and they said some terrible things, Joe.' Her hand went briefly to her back as she straightened up.

'You should see somebody about your back.'

'It's nothing.'

'You can hardly stand up straight,' he said, watching her fingertips pressing into the edge of the table.

'I can stand, and . . . it's not worth it.'

'It is worth it.'

'Says who?' She sat down. 'How's Linda?'

'Linda's fine.'

'Still trim?'

'She keeps in shape,' he said, wondering whether to allude

138

to *Hunks of Humankind*, which was on the table in front of them, or not.

'Hard work that, keeping in shape.'

'She enjoys it.'

His mother was looking at him, nodding, her hand on the locket she always wore; the one with photos of him and Darren inside.

'And Jessica – tell me about Jessica.'

'Jessica's writing a book,' he said, looking around for somewhere to put the tea bag that was still floating around in his cup.

'About what?'

'How to survive the end of the world.'

'That's nice,' she said absently. Then, 'I'm sorry I haven't got her a present or anything, but I didn't know if I'd see you and . . .'

'It's fine – really – it's okay.'

'No, it's not fine, none of this is fine, but I didn't know if I'd see you – like I said – and the thing is, well, we spent the money on Tara this year, and . . .' she broke off, 'd'you want a cigarette? Sorry – you gave up – I forgot you gave up.'

'Linda got sick of having to get the ceiling in the lounge whitewashed every six months, and the curtains dry-cleaned.' Joe paused, listening to himself talking about the incompatibility of smoke and décor. His mother was staring and nodding at him again, making him feel like he hadn't quite finished his sentence. Then, suddenly defensive of Linda, he pushed out his wrist to show her the watch Linda had bought him for giving up, but she didn't say anything; she just blew smoke sideways out of her mouth over the cover of *Hunks*. 'How's Dad?'

'The same.'

'He should go and see somebody.'

'He doesn't know anybody round here any more. He goes out drinking with strangers.'

'I didn't mean that – I was talking about somebody professional. Somebody who can write prescriptions.'

'I see you looking around,' she cut in, 'and it was wrong of you to come here and start judging us, Joe.'

'I'm not judging you, Mum.'

'You are. The way you're moving your eyes – see – there – like that.' She pulled a loose piece of tobacco out from between her teeth. 'So what are you going to do about it?'

'About what?'

'About this – what you're looking at.'

'I don't know.'

'You don't know?'

'I don't know, no. I said.'

'So – you just came to have a look?'

'I came to see you. Jesus.' He swung his head away from her towards the TV – feeling suddenly vindictive towards it for its persistent impartiality – and had to stop himself from putting his foot through it. 'Can we turn that off?'

'Your dad likes it on.'

'Dad's not here.'

'He's upstairs.'

'That's what I mean; he's not exactly watching it, is he?'

'It's the sound he likes – if he wakes up and he can't hear it he gets nervous. So I leave it on.'

He looked at her in the green cardigan she'd knitted for herself years ago, the sleeves rolled up to the elbow while sitting drinking tea among the debris of broken family and the shadow of a man who'd once taken her out to sea in a boat at night and proposed to her. It was his dad who told him the story of the boat at night, not her.

She leant forward and took hold of his hand, her voice suddenly soft. 'It's all right, Joe, I don't need anything from you, and don't ask me if I need money because money isn't currency in the place I'm in right now. It's nice to see you like this, what with Christmas and everything, but I don't need anything from you – I don't need you.'

'Mum – everybody needs someone.'

She stubbed out her cigarette and looked up at the ceiling. 'If I need anyone, I need him, Joe, and don't go telling me he's upstairs because he's not. I go up there and I see a man lying in my bed, and it's not him. It isn't him, Joe, and I don't know where to find him.'

'Mum,' he said again, but he wasn't listening any more, he was suddenly terrified of his dad waking up and coming downstairs.

'You want to go now?' she said after a while.

'I should be getting back.'

She stood up. 'He beat up a blind man last week.'

'Who did?'

'Dad did,' she yelled at him, as if he hadn't been listening to a word she'd been saying. 'Outside the pub – beat the shit out of a blind man for asking to be put on a bus up to London Road. He goes out drinking with strangers – not with people who know him, and you shouldn't drink with strangers, Joe.'

They stood staring at each other across the windmills on the dining-room table waiting to be deported to the garden centre. Did men who laboured over things like these – right down to the carved wooden miller carrying a sack of flour over his shoulder on one, and a dog biting the fleas off his haunches on another – also beat the shit out of blind men? He looked up at his mother again, but was too frightened of stepping into her marriage in case his feet didn't touch the bottom.

They went out to the hallway.

'Got any plans for Christmas?'

141

'Not really.'

The front door was stiff to open where the heat of summer had swollen the wood and winter's cold had warped it, and in the end he had to pull on it so hard a strip of foam insulation came away.

His eyes stared out over the cement that was the front garden. Over by the fence somebody had painted it blue then gone back and painted a starfish as well as a couple of other fishes to make it look like the sea. Tara, he guessed.

He felt his mum standing in the hallway just behind him, her green shadow stretching through his legs and over the threshold into the front garden.

'Where are the chimney pots? The ones you and Dad brought with you from the old house? What happened to them?'

'I sold them.'

'You sold them?'

'Two men drove past here in a Jaguar one day – asked me how much I'd take for them.'

'For the chimney pots?'

'For the chimney pots. I was sorry to see the primulas go – remember how I always planted them with yellow primulas in the spring?'

'They took the primulas as well?'

'Oh, they didn't want them, but they were in a hurry, see, so they got the chimney pots and the primulas.'

'How much for?'

'I can't remember, but a lot – not as much as they'd be selling them for, though – architectural salvation, that's what they did.'

'Salvage. It's architectural salvage.'

'Oh?'

'Picking up people's old stuff and selling it as antiques.'

'So – buying off people like me to sell to . . . to sell to people like you, Joe.'

Mother and son considered each other for a moment.

'I put something in your pocket – for you and Linda for Christmas – I found something after all.'

By the time he got back into the car the front door had already been shut and the velvet curtains drawn.

He put the key in the ignition and turned on the engine. In his coat pocket he found a freezer bag with about two grams of marijuana in it. He opened the car door and looked up at the house thinking he'd put it back through the letterbox, but then he saw the curtains moving at his parents' bedroom window so he quickly shut the door again and pushed the bag into the glove compartment.

He left Cassidy Street, thought about cruising up Skirton, and was still thinking about it as he turned the car back towards the seafront. When he got to Roedean Road, he was cut up twice trying to find a place to park, and in the end had to use a bay marked 'disabled' because he'd said he'd pick up Belle at five, and it was now six. He went running up the steps into Lynton Flats, brushing harshly against the tree in the lobby – a donation from St Mary's Church of England Primary School – which hadn't been there last time. It was hung with decorations made by children, and he had a brief memory of Jessica, aged five, dressed as an angel, then Belle's voice was yelling down the stairwell.

'Joe? What's taken you so long, Joe?'

'Just a second, Belle.'

'Joe?'

'Just coming.'

Belle was waiting for him on the landing outside her flat, both hands gripping the banister.

'Why aren't you in your chair, Belle?'

'I'm having a good day today – thought I'd just have a toddle out here and see where you were. I've been ready since five – you said five to me on the phone, Joe. The door downstairs went at five and I came out here thinking it was you and it was this man who said he'd come looking for someone only he couldn't remember who and I thought he was probably calling for Jenkins, and then I thought she must be bloody desperate, picking them up with Alzheimer's. Mind you, it could have its advantages. Think about it, Joe . . .' She trailed off.

He stood there, too busy catching his breath to realise how relieved Belle was to see him, even though she knew she wasn't going to enjoy Christmas at her daughter's. The point was she had somewhere other than Lynton Flats to go, and this had given her a temporary ascendancy over the other residents that she badly needed since refusing to go to carols round the tree with the children of St Mary's.

'Then I thought, maybe he's not here for Jenkins,' Belle said slowly, 'maybe he's a rapist, and he could have been – could have been a rapist for all I knew, but his lips were moving like he was chewing on a piece of meat he'd had stuck in there for at least a decade. He had no hair either, so I guessed he was having chemo.'

Joe got his breath back. 'It's okay, Belle. I'm here now.'

'. . . And I didn't know whether chemo affects their drive or not.'

'Whose drive?'

'The rapists.'

'Let's just move on from this rapist thing,' Joe said, pushing her into the flat.

'I thought you said you'd be here at five,' Belle said, in a panic again. 'I've been all packed since five.'

Joe felt suddenly exhausted. Too exhausted right then to try to imagine what the anticipation of spending Christmas

144

at Pollards Close must be like for Belle. 'Well, I'm here now,' he said again.

They went into the flat, which had been decorated since he was last here, and he recognised the clockwork wooden tree from the first Christmas he came here when it was still a hotel and he spent Boxing Day with Linda, Belle and Jim. He remembered Linda and Belle having an argument after the meal while Jim slept in his chair.

'So?' Belle accosted him.

'So, what?'

'So, where've you been, Joe? What's been keeping you?'

'My mum.'

'Your mum?'

'I went to see my mum.'

'But you haven't seen her in months, have you?'

'It was a spur of the moment thing.'

He felt Belle eyeing him. This was something he wasn't meant to do, and it was the one thing Belle and Linda were complicit about because ever since he got married, Joe had belonged to them. 'She was in good spirits – you know – looking forward to Christmas,' he lied, but then he wasn't going to tell her about the dope and the windmills and *Hunks of Humankind*, or the light above the dining-room table swaying as his dad turned over in bed. He wasn't going to tell anybody about those things – not even himself. So, to change the subject and get Belle to stop eyeing him, he added, 'I had something to pick up for Linda for Christmas as well.'

Belle smiled. 'A secret something?'

He nodded.

'I'll just go and sort out my jewellery then I'll be done,' she said.

He watched her shuffle slowly through to the bedroom. 'Don't let me forget those grapes on the sideboard – I

145

only bought them yesterday and they'll be off by the time I get back if I don't take them with me,' Belle shouted from the bedroom. 'Have some if you want.'

Joe went over to the sideboard and, ignoring the grapes, picked up a Christmas card with a coach and horses on it, making their way across a winter sunset. It was from him and Linda. That's what it said: *from Joe, Linda and Jessica*. Not *love from*, just *from*. He stared at Linda's handwriting for a while then put the card back on the sideboard next to the bowl of grapes Belle wanted to take with her.

He watched her through the bedroom door, standing at her dresser picking brooches out of a jewellery box that played a tune.

'Spoilt for choice,' she said, turning round and smiling at him. 'Might give this one to Jessica,' she added, holding up a brooch in the shape of the Eiffel Tower.

'She'd like that,' Joe said, not really thinking about it.

'Right – I'm done. Ready when you are.'

He moved the suitcase to one side and helped her ease herself into a powder blue anorak, matching powder blue headscarf, then into her wheelchair where she sat staring at the brooch she said she'd give to Jessica.

Joe took hold of the wheelchair's rubber handles, staring at the two ridges of bone running under Belle's skin at the back of her neck beneath her hair, suddenly remembering the grey curls covering the toes of Lenny's boots that day – the first day he saw her.

14

Jessica put down her pen and stared at Mr Browne on the other side of the dining-room table. He was running his hands along the sides of his notebook and she could see his right leg through the glass table-top – jogging up and down.

'There's no room for theories here,' he said after a while. 'It's not *if*, it's *when* . . . *when* the West comes under nuclear or chemical attack. *When* is the point of this book, which is why it won't be something to put on the shelves or balance against the Teasmade . . .'

The idea of the Teasmade distracted Jessica and she hoped – profoundly – that Mr Browne didn't have one.

'This book is something people will reach out for in their hour of need. This isn't some discourse berating the atom – it's a survival manual.' He paused. 'A manual for survivors . . . and there *will be* survivors.' He paused again. '*I* intend to survive.'

'So do I,' Jessica said.

Mr Browne nodded absently. 'And for those of us who *do* survive, survival will be the beginning of the *real* nightmare.' He leant forward over the table. 'In terms of writing this guide/handbook/manual – because it's all these things,

147

Jessica, all these things and more,' he said, '– we need to make the contents as concise as possible. We need to deal with the explosion itself: the light, heat, blast . . . radiation.'

'Fallout – and how to seek refuge from fallout.'

He pointed his pen at her. 'Good.'

'Symptoms of radiation sickness, and decontamination procedures.'

'Good girl.' He wrote it all down. 'We have to be completely specific about shelters as well – private shelters, conversion shelters, purpose-built shelters . . .' He looked up at her. 'What are the two most important things you need to remember about shelters?'

Jessica was struggling to think, but was too busy experiencing wave after wave of elation at the thought of sharing not just a nuclear shelter but the end of the world with Mr Browne.

'Come on, think,' he urged her. 'You're not thinking. Picture it: we've got the under-floor shelter sorted – concrete, sandbags, reinforced mesh. What two things have you forgotten?' He was staring at her across the table. 'Don't die on me, Jessica. We've survived the blast, we've made it to the shelter – what do we need when we get there? What have human beings always needed? They'll need the same things after the bomb that they needed before it.'

'Love,' Jessica wanted to scream, 'human beings need love,' and she had enough unmolested ideals to believe that love had a better chance of survival following a nuclear attack than it did signing a mortgage agreement.

Mr Browne banged his hand down on his pad. 'YOU'RE DEAD,' he shouted. Then, more calmly, 'Okay, let's think about this. You've just survived an attack from a ten megaton weapon, which produced a temperature equivalent to that inside the sun – a temperature of up to eighteen million degrees Fahrenheit – in a millionth of a second. You survived this, okay?'

Jessica nodded.

'You then survived the radiation, heat, light, sound and blast released in all directions, and you survived this because you were prepared – you got to your shelter. So, you're in your shelter and yet you just died. Why did you die in your shelter?'

'I don't know.'

'Why did you just die, Jessica?' he insisted, but didn't wait for her to reply. 'You died because you forgot to think about VENTILATION and LIGHT. You died because you're thinking – deep down you're thinking – *if* and not *when*.'

'I'm not,' she said, suddenly anxious to defend herself.

'This book not only serves as a manual to those who intend to survive – it's an indictment to those who won't.' He broke off. 'Now, we've made a start here, but there's still a lot of work to do. I'm willing to take you with me, Jessica. I'm willing to take you to the end of the world, but you have to keep up.'

'I will keep up.'

'And not die on me in the shelter.'

'I won't die on you.' She couldn't stop herself looking at him in the way she did when she said this. She couldn't help the fact that she no longer heard the carriage clock on the mantelpiece or saw the framed Highland cattle on the wall behind him, herded into the bottom of a glen by a thunderstorm. She no longer saw the shelves of Len Deighton, the framed photographs of Mr Browne in uniform somewhere cold, or the small wooden Nativity Scene, which was the only concession to Christmas at No. 14. All she saw was his mouth and his Adam's apple, rhythmically jostling the slightly frayed collar of his check shirt. She was in love with the end of the world; it was her biggest secret, and she was full of it.

149

He smiled at her and lowered his voice. 'When we come out of the shelter . . . are you listening to me, Jessica? When we come out of the shelter our nostrils will be full of the smell of smoke . . . rotten food . . . excreta . . . decomposing corpses. The only sounds will be cries for help from the injured and diseased.'

The phone started to ring. 'Will you excuse me?'

He stood with his back to her, staring out through the patio doors at his back garden: an immaculate lawn surrounded on three sides by a screen of semi-mature conifers. The only thing to cast a shadow over his world right then was an overhanging branch from No. 16 – what was it? A cherry tree? He'd have to speak to the Polish woman next door about pruning it – he didn't want cherry trees overhanging his property. 'No, I'm sorry. No, that's not something I'm interested in. This is a new property and I don't have any requirements of that sort.' He raised his voice. 'I said I'm not interested.' Slamming the receiver down, he turned to Jessica. 'Somebody trying to sell me double glazing – where were we?'

He sat back down at the table, preoccupied.

'After the bomb.'

'What's that?'

'We were talking about life after the bomb.'

'Life after the bomb?' He put his hands together and started to suck on his knuckles. 'Danger, privation, and . . . other people.'

'Other people?'

'The after-effect of the bomb will be like a bonanza for criminals, the insane . . . those carrying lethal diseases. Other survivors might not necessarily be good people. Think about it – on 13 July 1977 the electricity supply failed in New York. We're talking about one day here, and 3,481 people were arrested for looting, arson and sniping – and those were the ones they caught. Only some of those people arrested were criminals; the rest were ordinary citizens behaving like criminals and all it took was one day without electricity – one day – to reduce the population to that. The same thing happened in flooded Wisbech, Cambridgeshire on 13 January 1978, and it happened in Lewisham and Ladywell in 1977. Imagine emerging from confinement in a shelter, hungry, thirsty, shocked, bereaved and, most of all, afraid – the normal stabilising influences of society utterly suspended. You're no longer a person, you're a survivor. A person is something you have to learn how to become all over again.' He looked up at her. 'How will you know what sort of person you'll become, Jessica?'

They stared at each other.

'I won't.'

'You won't.' Mr Browne looked pleased. 'And neither will anybody else. That's exactly the right way to think. Now, how's work on Zoological Hazards going?'

'I've done a rough outline for the chapter here,' she said, handing him the manuscript.

He stood up, suddenly preoccupied. 'Is that the time? I've got to go.'

'I thought we were going to start putting some ideas together for the introduction,' she said, looking up at him and not even bothering to hide her disappointment.

'Another time. I really have got to go,' he said.

Jessica couldn't leave things like this. 'Another time – when?'

'Well,' he said, scratching his arm, 'it's Christmas Eve tomorrow, I'm going away, and I've got to get packed.'

'You're going away?'

'I'll be back in the New Year.'

'We won't see each other until next year?'

'Look,' he said, 'I got you this – it's a sort of early Christmas

151

present.' He handed her a copy of *Surviving Doomsday* by Colin Bruce Sibley.

'This is for me?' She tried not to sniff it in front of him.

'Might be a good starting point – for the introduction.'

'You've read it?' She was only interested if he'd read it.

'When it first came out. It made a huge impression on me. Anyway, listen . . . have a good Christmas.'

8

When Jessica got home she stood in the kitchen and opened *Surviving Doomsday* at random, running her nose up and down the spine. It smelt of Mr Browne's house and – faintly – of Mr Browne. She opened her eyes and started flicking through the book looking for inscriptions, notes, messages . . . anything, but there was nothing. Nothing? Nothing. She headed upstairs towards her room.

'Jessica?' Linda called out. 'Jessica – come here a minute.'

'Where are you?'

'The bedroom.'

Jessica went into her parents' bedroom and saw Linda crawling round the fringes of the bed, lifting up the valance.

'Where've you been?' she said as her daughter walked in, but Jessica was too busy staring at the tissue paper in her right nostril.

'What's wrong?'

'My nose won't stop bleeding.'

'You should lie down.'

'No, you've got to keep your head forward. That's the thing to do with a nosebleed – keep your head forward.'

'But it'll never stop bleeding. D'you want me to get you some ice?'

'I want you to come and help me find the gazelle.'

'The what?'

'The gazelle – the wooden gazelle. The one from downstairs on the sideboard.'

'Well – isn't it downstairs?'

'No, it's not downstairs, I already looked. It never gets moved – there's no reason for it to get moved – and now I can't find it.'

'What does it look like?'

'A gazelle – you know, four legs and horns?'

Jessica shook her head.

'Dad made it before you were born and it's been downstairs on the sideboard since we moved here. Well don't just stand there, help me look for it.'

'Okay, okay.' Jessica put *Surviving Doomsday* down on the bed and started to walk round the room, stopping every now and then to peer vaguely into a corner as if dark corners were more likely to reveal something than open spaces and broad daylight.

'Dad made it.'

'You said.'

'He carved it all himself; the whole thing.'

Jessica wasn't listening. 'Who for?' she said, without thinking.

Linda sat back on her haunches. 'For me,' she answered, watching her daughter check behind the unit on Joe's side of the bed. 'Are you listening? You couldn't care less, could you?'

'I'm helping, aren't I?'

'You don't even know what you're looking for.'

'Fine, I'll stop then.'

Linda stood up. 'Have you got any idea how much that

gazelle means to me? He made it with his own hands and I've been looking everywhere and now your man's coming tonight instead of tomorrow and I've got to make up the sofa bed downstairs because she can't manage the stairs – there's no way she'll manage those stairs.'

'Nan's coming tonight?'

'That's what I'm talking about.' Linda dropped with a thud back onto all fours and started to work her way round the valance again. 'Well, help me.'

Jessica went over to the en suite and turned on the light, wondering how much longer they were going to carry on with this.

'What are you doing?' Linda yelled at her.

'Helping you.'

'Well, you're not helping me. I already looked in there.'

'How was I meant to know?'

'Just get out, Jessica, I don't have time for this.'

'I don't know what you're getting so frantic about anyway – Dad won't notice.'

Linda stared at her daughter, breathing heavily, the creases in her jeans cutting into the tops of her thighs and the skin behind her knees.

'And your nose is bleeding again.'

She scrambled to her feet and went running into the en suite, cupping her hands under her nose to save the carpet. Even above the sound of the extractor fan, she heard Jessica's bedroom door slamming and Jimi Hendrix going on.

'Stop slamming your bloody door,' she screamed into the bellowing fan, then sat down on the loo, shoulders sagging and a handful of toilet paper plugged up her nose. After a few minutes she leant her head over to one side so that it was resting against the tiles.

The curtains at Whateley Road used to be unlined and she would wake up early in the summer because of the light and the milk floats from the Unigate dairy opposite starting their rounds. The morning Joe gave her the gazelle they'd both woken up at first light and been unable to get back to sleep. She'd lain there watching the big hand on the clock moving round as Joe started kissing her back between the shoulder blades. After a while he'd lifted up her nightdress and gone into her from behind and by the time they'd finished the sun had moved round the room onto the wardrobe, they'd broken a chair, and the carpet was wet. In bed, listening to Joe in the kitchen, she remembered that they'd slept with the window open the night before and anyone passing by on the pavement outside would have heard them, and this bothered her. The gazelle came in on the same tray as breakfast, which they ate in bed. Joe had been so proud of the gazelle, watching her turn it over in her hands for a while then taking hold of it himself again.

'See the grain here – I worked with it along the flank.'

He gave it back to her and she carried on turning it over in her hands and telling him how beautiful it was until at last she felt that it was safe to put it down on the bedside table.

'Why a gazelle?' she asked when Joe came back into the bedroom after shaving, running his hand over his chin.

The hand dropped. 'South Africa. We saw gazelles when we were in South Africa, and you had this thing about them.'

She remembered South Africa, but she didn't remember the gazelles. She remembered Joe's second cousin who'd worked for an insurance firm just outside Johannesburg and whose wife came from Basingstoke, but she didn't remember the gazelles. She remembered that Joe's second cousin had a housekeeper, a cook and a cleaner; that was three people they had working for them – black people, admittedly, but still people – but she didn't remember the gazelles. They'd half thought of emigrating themselves, but hadn't in the end. Why hadn't they? She couldn't remember.

She could see him so clearly standing in the bedroom at Whateley Road that morning, looking at her and knowing that she didn't remember the gazelles. She asked him to take the day off work, knowing that he wouldn't, and he didn't. Work was going well and he was half thinking of setting up his own company, but that wasn't the reason why he wouldn't take the day off work: it was because she couldn't remember the gazelles in South Africa or how much she'd liked them.

Now the gazelle was lost and it was lost because she hadn't realised at the time what it meant. She hadn't realised that Joe had loved her in the beginning. He'd once spent weeks carving, sanding and oiling a gazelle for her and he'd never do that again. The gazelle had been Joe's Taj Mahal to her and she hadn't even had to die for it; it had been sitting downstairs on the sideboard for fifteen years and she'd nearly thrown it away when they moved to Pollards Close. 'And now you've gone and fucking lost it,' she said to herself, getting up and walking slowly over to the sink. Planting her hands on its rim, she stepped onto the cork Hanson scales and looked down, then looked up, watching herself in the mirror. 'You fucking bitch, you fat fucking bitch . . .'

Jessica switched the record player on then threw herself face down on the bed, burying her head under the pillow so that all she could hear through the filter of polyester hollow fibres was Hendrix, and her own breathing. With the smell of unwashed hair in her nostrils, she tried to think herself into a fallout shelter, managing to create a vague picture of candlelight, fear and Mr Browne as he explained to her in gentle but firm tones that it was their duty to repopulate the earth. Would he use a word like that? Repopulate? No, he wouldn't. He would say that they had an evolutionary duty and make a few unnecessary biblical references because a) it would be silent and b) he'd think she needed persuading. She tried to get further into the daydream, but what happened next? – and, more to the point, what did 'what happened next' feel like? How many Sunday afternoons watching rain through her bedroom window did she have to get through before she finally laid eyes on the mushroom cloud?

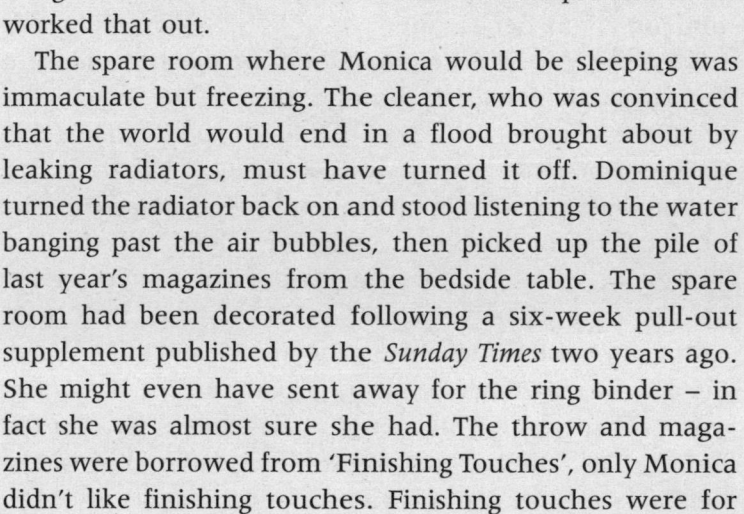

4

Dominique moved down through the house, trying to tidy it before Monica arrived, in an attempt to pre-empt her and make sure there was no evidence left lying around because that's what Monica did when she came to her daughter's house, she looked for evidence, and she always found something – but to convict her of what? Dominique had never worked that out.

The spare room where Monica would be sleeping was immaculate but freezing. The cleaner, who was convinced that the world would end in a flood brought about by leaking radiators, must have turned it off. Dominique turned the radiator back on and stood listening to the water banging past the air bubbles, then picked up the pile of last year's magazines from the bedside table. The spare room had been decorated following a six-week pull-out supplement published by the *Sunday Times* two years ago. She might even have sent away for the ring binder – in fact she was almost sure she had. The throw and magazines were borrowed from 'Finishing Touches', only Monica didn't like finishing touches. Finishing touches were for people who watched daytime TV, which was – as Monica had pointed out in one of their biggest rows of 1983 – the beginning of the end. According to Monica, daytime TV was in Revelations. Dominique had said she didn't know Monica read the Bible or that she had such evangelical leanings, and this had provoked Monica into saying the sort of things Dominique wanted to forget – by watching more daytime TV.

She put the magazines and throw into the airing cupboard because she didn't know right then what else to do with them, and went through into her and Mick's room to look out the window and check on Stephanie, who was in the back garden. There she was in her snow-suit and rollerboots, trying to do cartwheels across the patio. She must have known she was being watched because she turned round instinctively and squinted up at the house, then waved. Stephanie was a natural smiler, whereas Delta – you had to make sure you'd proved that a smile would be worthwhile before you got one out of Delta. Dominique ran her hands down the curtains, thinking about her children.

Then she left the bedroom and its unmade bed and went onto the landing, looking through the panel of frosted glass into Delta's room. Delta was painting – Dominique could see her silhouette moving against the wall, which meant that at some point today there would be a matador in the room delivering the *coup de grâce* to a bull, who had no choice. She went into the family bathroom, retouching her lips with one of Delta's lipsticks – pink soda – and stood staring at herself in the mirror, the lipstick still in her hand. She'd worn this shade before to a party at The Haven last year – when was it? She couldn't remember. She put the lipstick back on the windowsill and went downstairs. Stephanie was pressed up against the patio doors, trying to get in.

160

'Sorry, honey, I thought you could let yourself in,' she said.

'It's too stiff – maybe it needs oiling or something,' Stephanie grunted as she pulled her rollerboots off. The sun moved round the house and shone down on the crown of her head.

Dominique's hand went out automatically to her daughter's new, much shorter hair, and she stood there stroking it, staring out into the garden.

'Where's Dad?' Stephanie asked after a while.

'He had to get something in town.'

'Can we get some lunch?'

Dominique's hand slid off her daughter's head as Stephanie got to her feet and crossed the lounge, her legs, still in the snowsuit, brushing loudly against each other.

'Can we have toasties?'

'Of course we can have toasties. There's only cheese to put in them, though.'

'Can I make them?'

'If you want, but don't switch the toaster on – I'll do that. Are toasties okay for lunch?' she called upstairs.

'Anything – I'm easy,' Delta shouted back down.

They went into the kitchen.

'D'you want to take your suit off, Steph?'

'I'm fine.'

'What are you looking for in the fridge?'

'Tomatoes.'

'I thought you didn't like tomatoes.'

'I only like them in toasties because they burn your mouth,' Stephanie said with satisfaction.

Dominique sat down on one of the bar stools and tried not to say anything as she watched Stephanie use a knife and fork to cut up the tomatoes until their insides popped out, running down the front of the unit and collecting in a

161

puddle on the floor that Stephanie walked through as she carried the sandwiches over to the toasting machine. 'I'm ready – make the light go on.'

Dominique pressed the lid down and turned on the switch. As the hot plates began to heat up they let off the smell of previous lunches.

Stephanie climbed up onto the other bar stool, her eyes fixed on the machine. 'Delta says Monica experiments on animals.'

Dominique stared at her, wondering when her daughters had been speaking about Monica.

'Sometimes – fruit flies mostly.'

'How does she catch the fruit flies?'

'I don't know, Steph, you'll have to ask her.' She heard Delta on the stairs, and the next minute she walked into the kitchen, her hands covered in paint, wearing one of Mick's old shirts – one they'd bought on holiday in Tunisia years ago.

'How d'you catch fruit flies?' Stephanie asked her sister.

'The same way you catch other flies.'

'How's that?'

'No idea.'

Dominique went back into the lounge to retrieve Stephanie's muddy rollerboots, because if she didn't do it now, while she was thinking about it, she'd forget. Her head was filling up with fruit flies, tomatoes and toasting machines.

Picking up the boots, she stared through the patio window at the sun lounger tipped on its side in the middle of the garden. She spent hours lying on that in the summer; whole days. In fact she spent most of the summer asleep – the heat made her narcoleptic. Then, cutting across all of this, was the thought that Mick had stopped flying. Forever.

In the background she heard Delta's voice:

'Flies can lay eggs on a body even before its death and

then maggots will hatch in under twenty-four hours. Maggots can jump all over a corpse – they can leap as high as eighteen inches into the air . . .'

Then Stephanie's voice:

'How high's that?'

Then Delta's:

'Like this – this high – and they attack in packs. You wouldn't think it, would you, looking at a maggot, but that's what they do, they attack in packs and sometimes there's such a fight over a corpse that they knock out its false teeth.'

She heard them laughing and started to walk back towards the kitchen to tell Delta that this was the sort of information a six-year-old didn't need in their life, that nobody – as far as she could see – needed in their life, when the door-bell rang.

She froze en route, staring at the two Advent calendars pinned to the door of the cupboard under the stairs, suddenly intensely aware of the smell of hyacinths that had been in there for over three weeks now.

'D'you want me to go?' Delta said, watching her from the kitchen door.

Dominique stared back, unable to speak. A second ago she'd been about to tell her off for talking about maggots and false teeth, and here was the same daughter offering her a salvation of sorts – even though it would only be temporary. She shook her head.

The outline beyond the frosted glass in the front door looked too big to be Monica's, and for a moment Dominique thought there were two people standing there, but when she opened the door there was Monica in a raincoat and man's hat, looking too foreign for the backdrop of Pollards Close. There was Monica looking too preoccupied – despite the expensive haircut and expensive make-up – to be really glamorous; there was Monica not looking any older than the last time they'd seen her a year ago; there was Monica not looking like anybody's mother.

Dominique saw her glance at the rollerboots still in her hand, then they hesitated, staring at each other and trying to decide whether to kiss or not.

The Christmas tree lights flashed colours over Belle that Linda remembered her mother wearing as a child.

'Now, have you got everything you need, Mum?'

'You'll have to bring one of the side lights over next to the bed for me.'

Linda moved the nest of tables over.

'I don't need all of them.'

'Well, it's easier to bring all three over,' she said, putting the side light on top. 'Can you reach that?'

'I'll be fine.'

'Well have a go while I'm still here – I don't want to get upstairs and you can't manage it.'

'I'll be fine.' Belle stretched over, put her large-print copy of *Lucky* on the side table and let out a belch. 'Sorry, that's the pork that is. Pork always does that to me.'

'It was chicken,' Linda said.

'It was?'

'Chicken kiev.'

Belle thought about this. 'If it was frozen I wouldn't of been able to tell. Pork and chicken always taste the same to me if they've been frozen.' She paused, belching again. 'All frozen meat tastes the same.'

'I thought you liked chicken kiev.'

'What's that?'

'What we had tonight.'

'I've never had that before.'

'You have – with the garlic and herbs.'

'Garlic? I never eat garlic. I hate garlic.'

'Well you had it last time you came.'

'I won't remember that, though, will I? That was a long time ago.' Belle let this hang in the air between them while Linda pushed her big toe through the shag pile. 'What happened to the fish tank? The one that used to be over there on the coffee table?'

'The fish died.'

'Well, at least it won't be buzzing all night long.'

'It would have been the filter that made the buzzing sound – not the fish. We put the filter in so we wouldn't have to clean the tank out every week.'

'I don't know what it was, but it kept me awake.'

'There's the spare room upstairs – bed all made up and everything.'

'I won't manage the stairs.'

'Not even with me and Joe helping you?'

'I prefer it down here.'

'I'm worried about your back on the sofa.'

'My back's buggered anyway.' Belle sighed. 'You're tired, you get to bed.'

'I'm not tired.'

'Well, you look it. It's the menopause – got me terrible when I was about your age. It's no good you covering it up.'

'I'm not covering anything up – and I'm not tired.'

'It got me terrible,' Belle said again, staring at the cover

166

of *Lucky*, which she'd had her name down for at the mobile library for two months because Jenkins had kept renewing it. 'Not that there were pills or anything in my day.'

'I don't need pills – or anything.'

'It's only nature taking its course, Linda.'

'Why are we even talking about this?' Linda hauled her arms rapidly up and down as if sending out a signal in semaphore through the patio doors.

'And why have you stopped eating?'

'I eat.'

'Well, you weren't eating tonight.'

'I had my shake.'

'Don't tell me you've lost your appetite – you always used to have such an appetite. I remember Jim saying you put away more than a packhorse.'

Linda didn't say anything. Her stepfather was the last person she wanted to think about.

'Anyway, it's off-putting,' Belle said, watching her daughter move into the corner of the room.

'What's off-putting?'

'You sitting there staring at everybody while they're eating – with big hungry eyes.'

'My eyes don't look hungry.'

'I thought you were going to rip the pork out of my mouth.'

'It was chicken,' Linda said automatically, turning out the tree lights. 'D'you want anything else? I'm going to bed.'

'My grapes – what have you done with my grapes?'

'I don't remember any grapes.'

'I asked Joe to bring them with us.'

'He probably put them in the fruit bowl.'

'I hope he remembered them – I did say. I only bought them a few days ago and I told him, I said to him they'd go off if I didn't bring them with me. What's wrong with Joe anyway?'

Linda, who was about to leave the room, stopped. 'What's that?'

'I said, what's wrong with Joe?'

'With Joe? Nothing.'

'Oh.'

'What?'

'He just doesn't seem quite himself at the moment.'

Linda waited at the door and didn't say anything. After another few seconds she closed it gently and went into the kitchen. Belle's grapes were in the fruit bowl. She picked them up and walked over to the bench next to the sink. Dropping the grapes onto the draining board behind the frozen turkey, she pulled open the cupboard door and filled the palm of her hand with peanuts from one of the tubs she'd bought for Christmas. After the second handful she realised she was grunting. Slamming the cupboard door shut, she made herself the fourth and final Slimshake of the day that you were meant to drink just before going to bed to get you through the night. Linda liked the wording on the package – which assumed that a Slimshake was all you were going to need to get you through the night. Walking over to the drinks cabinet, she added some Campari to it and went upstairs.

Joe was already asleep, his clothes in a pile by the side of the bed; one shoe lying on its side.

She stood with her head to one side, watching him, then she went over to turn out his night light and saw the brochure for pond fountains and mist-makers he must have been reading before he fell asleep. Picking it up, she started to flick through pictures of water features with stainless-steel pipes, named after rivers of the world. The Euphrates and Tigris were the biggest with 4,000 Iph pumps, and the smallest was The Trent. The Hudson, which came complete with a 3,000 Iph pump and was made from mirror polished stainless steel, had been ringed in black biro. At the back of the brochure, where the pond misters promised to add a touch of mystery to any water feature or garden, Joe had written – in the same black biro that he'd circled The Hudson – *phone to check that mister includes low water level cut-out.* Why – when she asked him what he wanted for Christmas – hadn't he told her about this? She leant down to switch out the bedside light and there was Joe, wide awake, staring back up at her.

'How's your mum?'

'Convinced we had pork tonight and not chicken because all frozen meat tastes the same to her. God knows what she'll make of the turkey – there's sixteen pounds' worth of frozen bird on the draining board downstairs defrosting itself into an identity crisis. I'll be glad when Christmas is over.' She thought about sitting down on the side of the bed, but when Joe didn't say anything to this, she went through to the bathroom and started to get undressed. She watched herself drink the Slimshake, waiting for her stomach muscles to stop contracting. Did she look hungry? What did hungry people look like? She dug around in the bathroom cabinet, looking for the anti-depressants, then remembered that she'd already taken the last of them.

'Your lips,' Joe said as she walked back into the bedroom.

'My what?' The fan didn't cut out for another five minutes after turning off the bathroom light and she couldn't hear Joe because it was drumming in her ear.

'Your lips – they're blue.'

Linda wiped her mouth. 'It's the shake – it stains.' She sat down on the side of the bed. 'That better?'

Joe nodded, even though her lips were still blue.

'Do I look hungry?'

'Hungry?'

'Belle said I looked hungry. My eyes –'

They stared at each other, then, suddenly uncomfortable, looked away.

'I wouldn't say hungry.' Joe watched her get into bed, moving himself instinctively away as his knee brushed her thigh. 'Who was the note from?'

'The what?'

'The note on the vanity unit – the one addressed to Jessica.' He paused. 'Has Jessica seen it yet?'

'I didn't want to show her – it was on the doormat when I got back this afternoon. Who is Adlai Stevenson, anyway?' she said, staring up at the ceiling and trying not to notice him moving his leg. 'Do you know any Adlai Stevenson?'

Joe yawned. 'Not personally.'

'Maybe it's somebody on Sycamore Avenue or Merrifield Drive.'

'He's an American statesman,' Joe said.

'Living on Sycamore Avenue?'

'For Christ's sake, Linda.' He rolled over.

'What?'

'Any time any politician wants to back something nuclear they use Adlai Stevenson – it's a famous quote.'

Linda lay there, staring at Joe's back, wondering when exactly he listened to politicians speaking. 'So who sent Jessica the note?'

'I don't know – why don't you just show it to her?'

'I can't show it to Jessica.'

'Why not?'

'Because – she frightens me. I'm frightened of her.'

'Frightened of Jess? She's your daughter.'

'She hates me.'

'She doesn't hate you. Anyway – all girls go through this stage – with their mothers,' he added.

'Only with Jessica it isn't a stage,' Linda said quietly,

170

wanting him to turn round, knowing he wouldn't. 'What if the note's from Mr Browne?'

'Why would it be from Mr Browne?'

'I think it's a love letter.'

'Some love letter,' Joe mumbled. Then, 'Why would he post it through our letterbox – why not just give it to her?' He paused. 'Know what I think? I think it's from that Polish woman – Jessica's physics teacher – trying to persuade Jessica to go ahead with this module on nuclear physics.'

'But that's weird, Joe.'

Joe didn't respond.

'Really weird. Should we speak to the school about this?' When Joe still didn't respond, she shut her eyes, opened them, then shut them again.

CHRISTMAS EVE, 1983

4

Dominique was sitting with Delta underneath a plastic tree with pink leaves inside Fontana's coffee shop. They had one of the tables by the window so that Dominique could keep an eye on Mick and Stephanie, in the queue for Santa's Grotto. Stephanie, in her red ear muffs and duffle coat, kept appearing between automated elves waving signs – *Santa's Grotto this way (sponsored by Wrights Insurance)* – as the queue shuffled forwards.

'So what are we going to get Monica, Mum? Mum?'

Dominique, who had been thinking about the party they were throwing that night and how they'd thrown a Christmas Eve party every year since they first came to Littlehaven – would this be the last? – swung her head round slowly to face Delta. 'I don't know,' she said.

'Well, we've got to get her something.'

'D'you think she's got us anything?'

'I don't know. Probably.'

Dominique stared at her daughter for a while, wondering where this faith in Monica came from, then peered through the green lettering of the Fontana's menu painted on the window. Beyond prawn cocktail open sandwich, she saw Stephanie waving wildly.

'She's next,' Dominique said, waving back, as Stephanie and Mick disappeared inside the grotto.

'D'you think she still believes in him?'

'Of course she does – she's only six.'

Delta didn't say anything.

'What?' Dominique said after a while, drawing another cigarette out of the pack in front of her.

'I didn't believe in Father Christmas by the time I was six.'

'How can you remember?'

'It's going to school – you get those things taken away from you. It's a question of survival.'

'That's terrible.' Dominique watched Delta turn the coffee cup round in her hands.

'And anyway, isn't the whole thing ludicrous – adults insisting children believe in something that they themselves don't? I think it is.'

'But they believed in it once.'

'That makes it even worse.' Delta shook her head and stared out the window. 'It's about manipulation – control; nothing else.'

'Is it really that sinister?' Dominique said, wondering if Delta wasn't just jealous of Stephanie for being enough of a child still to want to queue to see Santa in his Grotto, and not know that the whole thing – Santa, his elves and the Arctic snow – had been paid for by Wrights Insurance.

She was just turning to look through the window, her cigarette and lighter still in her hand, when Stephanie ran screaming out of Santa's Grotto, pushing her way through the queue and the row of elves and running blindly towards the wicket fence, her red coat and screams stark against the artificial snow as she started wrenching at the fence, too upset to find the gate.

The cigarette and lighter clattered onto Formica as

Dominique ran out of Fontana's and across the precinct. 'Steph,' she yelled.

'Let me out, let me out,' Steph carried on screaming, even as Mick's arms went out for her, flying her over the wicket fence and onto Dominique who was standing on the other side.

'Father Christmas . . .' she said, trying to get the air back into her lungs. 'Father Christmas . . .'

The people in the queue pulled their children towards them, uncertain as Mick stalked past.

'Okay, calm down, Steph. It's okay,' Dominique said, crouching down beside her and feeling her tights rip on the precinct's brown tile floor.

Stephanie shook her head.

'It's okay,' Dominique said again, staring up into her daughter's face, made blotchy by grief or fear or both.

'Father Christmas is a woman; he's a woman,' Stephanie said through tears. 'I was sitting on his lap and I was just getting my present and he had tits,' she finished, still through tears.

'Stephanie,' Dominique said automatically, already aware that it was no good reprimanding her for her loss of innocence. Father Christmas had gone from their lives and was never coming back. No currency in the world existed to pay Stephanie compensation for that.

By the time Mick made his way to them, Stephanie was standing beside Dominique, wiping her nose with the sleeve of her duffle coat and asking for milkshake.

Ten minutes later, halfway through her second banana milkshake and already aware that nobody had told her to take off her ear muffs, Stephanie was telling anyone who'd listen how much she hated Father Christmas.

'I'm writing to the council about this,' Dominique said to Mick.

'Good idea.' He watched her, the cigarette she was holding brushing against her lips as she stared fixedly out the window of Fontana's at Santa's Grotto as if Charles Manson was in residence there, sponsored by Wrights Insurance.

'Forget Santa,' Delta said harshly, 'let's go and see Darth Vader.' The magnanimous gesture only half distracted her mother, but had the right effect on Stephanie.

'Where is he? Where is he?' Stephanie yelled, nearly knocking her milkshake over.

'Good idea,' Mick said again.

'Are you sure?' Dominique wasn't convinced. 'Where is this Darth Vader person?'

'Outside Goodies Toy Shop.'

Stephanie had hold of her sister's hand. 'Come on, he might leave any minute,' she said. Then, turning to Dominique, 'And he's not a person.'

Dominique watched her daughters disappear into the precinct. 'It's not right, Mick,' she said. 'You can't mess with Father Christmas's gender – I'm writing to the council about this.' She finished her cigarette, pushed the cold coffee to one side and started drinking the remains of Stephanie's milkshake. 'Was it obvious – the tits, I mean?'

'I thought it was just a paunch then realised it was too far up to be a paunch. Nobody else seemed bothered,' he said, looking at the queue still stretching across the North Pole enclosure. 'I blame it on equal opportunities,' he added, ignoring the looks they were getting from people waiting for tables.

'Mick, I'm serious.'

'So am I. Next year Father Christmas will be female and from an ethnic minority – not that we have any ethnic minorities in Littlehaven.'

'Mick . . .'

'The year after that she'll be a female amputee from an

178

ethnic minority, and the year after that she'll be a Down's Syndrome female amputee from an ethnic minority – with a terminal disease. In fact, by focusing so exclusively on bipeds here, aren't we discriminating against quadrupeds?'

'Mick, have you got any idea what's just happened to Stephanie?' Dominique lit another cigarette.

'She had a shock – she had a milkshake – now she's got Darth Vader.'

'It's not the same,' Dominique said, vaguely aware of a hand in a rubber glove wiping coffee rings off the table with a cloth. 'I was sitting here watching her in the queue and she kept appearing – this patch of red – between the elves. Within the space of a few minutes that child has ceased to exist. She's been taken away from us, Mick.'

'Come on, Dom.'

'I mean it.'

'We've been through this with Delta – the child doesn't go, another one comes along – they're like Russian dolls. Look at Delta – she's eighteen and she's still got all those other children she's been inside her. So have we. We're great big fat Russian dolls and one of those dolls still believes in Father Christmas. Stephanie's going to go to bed tonight so excited, she'll have forgotten she doesn't believe in him any more.' He sat watching her, waiting for some response, and after a while she gave him a nod, dropping her lighter into her handbag.

They stood outside Fontana's checking they had all their shopping, and Dominique was about to remind him that they still needed candles when she saw Monica. Actually, she saw a tall woman in a trench coat and a man's hat walking down the centre of the precinct then she recognised her as Monica. Monica was laughing and carrying a lot of bags, and there was somebody with her – Brendan Kline, Valerie Kline's son, and Brendan Kline had a lot of bags as well, which could only mean they'd been shopping together. Brendan Kline was also laughing.

'Dom?' Mick said.

'Look at that.'

'What am I meant to be looking at?'

'Monica.'

'Monica? Where?'

'Over there.' Dominique watched them walk, laughing, down the length of the precinct, past the white wicket fence running round the North Pole and Santa's Grotto.

'Who's she with?' Mick asked.

'Brendan Kline – he works for Ciba Pharmaceuticals.'

They watched them walk past Boots, Dixons and Barratts as the world carried on with its festive shuffling, oblivious to the passing of Monica and Brendan. 'Monica's out shopping.'

'I can see.'

'Monica never goes out shopping – that's something Monica just doesn't do.'

'So –' Mick didn't know what he was meant to say to this, he was only aware that he didn't want to aggravate Dominique any more after the incident with Father Christmas.

'What would you think – looking at them – if you didn't know them?'

Mick shrugged.

'Come on . . .'

They watched them disappear through the exit to the car park, out of sight.

'Wouldn't you think, looking at them,' she said, turning to Mick, 'that they were mother and son out shopping together?'

8

Linda walked out of the hairdresser's, where she'd been getting her hair highlighted, and into the town square, which the council had recently pedestrianised and were trying to rename The Piazza. They were also planning to install Victorian lampposts and a memorial to famous local poet Percy Bysshe Shelley, but due to an overspend the year before they didn't have enough money for both. The *County Times* had recently run a readers' survey, the response to which was overwhelmingly in favour of Victorian lampposts. The memorial to Shelley – Littlehaven's immortal son, a pamphlet published by the Shelley Society claimed – would have to wait. His birthplace, anyway, had just been bought by a couple who bred Dalmatians and who were convinced that the Shelley Society was a smokescreen created by competitors trying to gain access to their kennels.

It had stopped raining and Linda paused for a moment in the sunlight, her eyes partially closed, shaking off the last of the irritation caused by her hairdresser, Louise, who'd spent the entire two hours it had taken her to do her highlights talking about the spiritual bonding she'd experienced with orangutans in Sri Lanka or Indonesia or wherever orangutans lived. Linda wouldn't have minded so much if the same thing hadn't happened to her a month ago at the butcher's when she was buying stewing steak. She had the money in her hand, about to pay, when the butcher leant over the counter and told her he'd seen Christ in the abattoir that morning at 5.24 and Christ had told him to go into the desert. Not knowing what else to say, Linda had asked him which desert, and he said, 'Christ wasn't specific, but there are plenty to choose from.' She stood there waiting for him to bag up the steak while he told her that he'd seen Him over by the racks of pork, which was strange because he'd always thought that Jews, who were God's chosen people, were forbidden pig – so what was Christ doing appearing to him by the racks of pork? Orangutans, Christ . . . what was happening to people, and how did they find the time? At least when the butcher closed down his shop and disappeared into the desert in search of Christ she could buy her meat from Tesco, but where would she get her highlights done if Louise went back to Sri Lanka or wherever, searching for more spiritual encounters with orangutans?

She could hear people singing and, opening her eyes, saw the congregation of Littlehaven's Free Church in yellow sweatshirts, holding guitars and singing seasonal songs that didn't sound like carols. Wayne Spalding was trying to collect money with a blue bucket, and as he swung round to corner a passer-by she saw *Jesus is for Life – not just for Christmas* printed across the back of his yellow sweatshirt. Valerie Kline from No. 10 was there as well, her arms raised above her head, clapping in time to the music and lurching from side to side. There were even children.

Forsaking the sunshine, orangutans and Christ, Linda went running into the precinct towards Marks and Spencer, where she bought a silk top with a butterfly appliqué on it that she hoped her biceps were toned enough to carry off

182

at the Saunders' Christmas Eve party. Was a black top with a butterfly appliqué the sort of thing Joe liked?

Distracted, she picked up some room spray and bubble bath as stocking fillers for Belle. She'd given up buying her expensive perfume because all she did was save it and save it until it went off. Linda left Marks and Spencer, heading out of the precinct back towards the town square, and as the automatic doors opened, she failed to notice Wayne Spalding break away from his evangelical revels – then when she did it was too late. She thought of running, but what if he broke into a run and followed her? Worse still, what if he caught up with her?

'Mrs Palmer,' he called out, 'Mrs Palmer,' getting closer and closer until she was able to home in on the Littlehaven Free Church logo on the front of the yellow sweatshirt.

She looked down at the black nylon trousers he was wearing with their broken creases and the grey loafers he'd had on the day he came to look at the tree, then she tried smiling, but couldn't. She was a member of The Haven Golf Club and had unlimited access to the health and fitness suite and members' bar, and just didn't want to be seen talking to Wayne Spalding, who was bent over smiling at her as he got his breath back.

'Good to see you again, Mrs Palmer.'

It hadn't been good the first time she thought, staring at him, so how could it be good again?

He winced, clapped his left hand to his heart, exhaled then stood up straight.

'Seasonal greetings,' he said, trying to make it sound as upbeat as the songs the congregation were singing. 'What d'you think of the music?' he added, grinning and briefly gyrating his body.

Linda, who hadn't spoken yet, was still staring at him. 'What music?'

He spun round to face his congregation. 'Our singing.'
'Oh, the singing.'

This wasn't the flat, bovine man who'd counted the paces between the oak tree and her patio doors, narrowly avoiding Ferdie's turds. This Wayne Spalding – the amateur Christian Wayne Spalding – was another version, who had so much excess energy that he was standing there clapping in time to music he'd probably written, making the other Wayne Spalding – the professional environmentalist – seem more like a Gollum sent out to make money for him.

There was something thuggish about this Wayne's happiness, as if it was an element of himself he couldn't control, and Linda wondered – looking at him and trying not to look at him – if he was on some sort of medication; lithium maybe. She wished that he wouldn't keep swinging between her and his congregation so that she didn't have to keep reading the slogan on his back over and over again.

'I tried to phone you,' he said suddenly. Then, without warning, the professional environmentalist took over. 'They're building houses in the field behind your house,' he said, his eyes flattening and his shoulders rounding.

'They're what?'

'They're building houses. The field's been acquired for development by Laing. There used to be a chalk quarry on that site, and it was badly backfilled about two hundred years ago.'

'Two hundred years ago?' Two hundred years ago didn't exist for Linda.

Wayne nodded, thinking she was interested. 'The land belonged to the council and we didn't want to sell because we were worried that there might be illegal chalk mines beneath the quarry.' He coughed. 'I'm a member of the British Industrial Archaeological Society, so I do have some understanding of this sort of thing – not that anyone listened to me, of course. Not that I was even in the meeting,' he said, raising his voice then suddenly breaking off. 'We sold it to Laing to prevent Plymouth Brethren from building a church there.'

'Plymouth Brethren? I didn't know there were cults in Littlehaven.'

Half Linda's mind filled with images from the Dennis Wheatley novels her stepfather used to read and pass on to her without Belle knowing, and the other half was reliving a conversation she'd had with Sandra Nassam – how long ago? When Sandra, wearing the kind of suit and jewellery you had to have a career to wear, had told her that houses on their side of the Close always got the asking price – at premium – because they didn't back onto anything; they overlooked fields. Now the fields and any hope of getting the asking price were gone because Laing were building more houses there. Maybe they should put the house on the market before they started building, but where would they move to – Phase IV?

Just then the loud-speakers outside Goodies Toy Shop started to play the *Star Wars* theme tune and a smoke machine positioned outside the front of the shop started to send out stage smoke that was supposed to drift into the square, but ended up obscuring the Free Church choir instead so that all Linda could see of Valerie Kline now was her hands, severed from the rest of her, but still waving in time to the song the choir was still singing.

'So if you want to take the matter of your tree up,' Wayne carried on, 'you should contact Laing, because soon it'll be in someone else's back garden.' He turned away from her, scratching his stomach. 'That's what I meant to say to you on the phone – is that smoke?' he said, breaking off.

The Free Church choir reappeared, their ranks and voices broken by the smoke, which had almost completely disappeared by the time Darth Vader walked unsteadily through the door of Goodies and out into the square, where he stood in his helmet looking from side to side.

'The inspiration behind the new Phase IV development is Tudor England – that's what I heard anyway,' Wayne laughed, as if he'd said something funny, then took off his glasses and started to wipe them.

Over his shoulder the choir were talking among themselves and Darth Vader was pulling a large white cage full of lightsabers out of the toy shop, stumbling over the step. The *Star Wars* music was still going and there were Tudor mansions growing in the field behind No. 8 Pollards Close. How could a tree – a single tree – mean anything to her right then?

'I just wanted you to know that the tree's no longer in my jurisdiction. I tried to get a preservation order out on it, but . . .' He turned round, suddenly aware that his congregation had stopped singing, and watched as Darth Vader gave a demonstration of the lightsaber he was holding with both hands while trying to execute a 360-degree turn. 'Will you excuse me,' he said. 'That music – it's too loud, and it's . . . offensive.'

Linda watched Wayne Spalding make his way across the square to Darth Vader. At that distance she could still read *Jesus is for Life – not just for Christmas*, and make out Delta and Stephanie Saunders in the crowd outside Goodies. Darth Vader clearly wasn't co-operating and after a while Wayne disappeared inside the toy shop.

Looking around the square, she saw Paul Nieman sitting with his legs outstretched on the replica stocks the Littlehaven Historical Society had erected last year. There was a replica pillory just beside it and a bronze plaque that always shone.

Wayne Spalding reappeared and made his way over to

186

the congregation, shouting at them to regroup. The guitars and singing started again and the *Star Wars* music carried on. After a while the *Star Wars* music got louder, then the choir got louder, and this went on for a while until the crowd, who'd been laughing at the Littlehaven Free Church choir, suddenly switched allegiance when they realised that Darth Vader, who had seemed so much more likeable than the Free Church minister, was becoming abusive enough for them to move their children away.

Linda was so busy watching all of this, she failed to see Wayne Spalding pushing his way through the crowds now gathered round the choir and making his way towards her again.

'I'm sorry about that,' he said. 'The people in the shop were very unreasonable, and their employee – the one in the black suit and helmet – was drunk.'

'How could you tell?'

'I used to drink, Mrs Palmer,' he said.

Feeling suddenly helpless, Linda clutched onto her handbag strap and checked to see if Paul Nieman was still sitting on the stocks. Why did this always happen to her? Why did people end up confessing when they should keep their confessions to themselves and not expect other people – especially strangers – to share the weight of them. It was as if they knew her childhood had been spent in the dark corners of her stepfather's hotel absorbing adult secrets, first unknowingly, then unwillingly, until it got to the point where she'd digested so many secrets and put on so much physical weight because of it that Belle had to take her to the doctor, who put her on a special diet.

She was back to nine stone the morning Joe walked into the hotel with his father. They'd come to repair the banister on the hotel's first floor – she'd taken them two cups of tea and Joe hadn't even looked up. Then, when she left the room, she'd turned round and caught him smiling at her and known, immediately, that if there was another flood, there was a man who could build an ark. So they got married; she left the dark corners and bedrooms of Lynton Hotel behind and finally thought she was sailing out into open water, only to find that the ark Joe built them wasn't watertight and the weather wasn't always fair, and it was almost impossible to skim the surface when people insisted on penetrating it with such ferocity there was nearly always a squall. Like now – caught out when she was least expecting it, while out shopping on Christmas Eve, by an Evangelist in a yellow sweatshirt confessing that he used to be an alcoholic. How dare Wayne Spalding think she gave a fuck – how dare he? Were people no longer capable of having a simple conversation without a storm blowing up?

'I used to drink, Mrs Palmer,' he said again.

Not knowing where else to look, Linda looked up at the sky, willing the clouds to let something loose – rain, snow, hail, the hairdresser's orangutans, the butcher's Christ; anything.

Then, as if in answer, the clouds parted and there was the inflatable Tesco's elephant. She focused on it with the tenacity of a lost traveller on the Pole Star.

'I can't tell you how many years of my life I drank away.'

Alarmed, Linda realised that Wayne was raising his voice.

'Everybody's lost hours, days . . . maybe weeks and sometimes even months,' he said loudly, leaning in so that his words rebounded off her face, 'but I lost years,' he shouted. 'I lost years.'

She looked around. People were staring; people like her, out shopping on Christmas Eve – innocent people.

Even Paul Nieman turned his head in their direction – and the stocks were at least eight hundred yards away.

'Oh, well,' she said, trying to keep it light. 'Life goes on.'

'Not even God can give those years back to me – even though I walk with Him now. Those people you hear singing . . . they've all lost something. We've all lost something. Everybody you see in this square here has lost something.' He turned round to look at his congregation then turned back to her. 'I sense you've lost something, Mrs Palmer.'

'I haven't lost anything.'

What was this? She believed that if you made money, you were entitled to the privileges money could buy, and she believed in those privileges. She believed in the four-bedroom detached house they lived in. She believed that this privilege and others they enjoyed made her and Joe smell good. She believed that if they ever got washed up on a desert island inhabited by cannibals and those cannibals ate them, they'd taste good.

'Maybe – but I see how hungry you look, and that's good: hunger will be your salvation.'

'I just came out to do some shopping,' Linda yelled.

'The more replaceable things we buy, the more irreplaceable ones we lose. We're at the dawn of a new age, Mrs Palmer, and in this new age there won't be any mothers or fathers, sons or daughters, sisters or brothers. Mothers will be something you have to rent and brothers something you have to buy. I see soul banks where you'll be able to walk in and buy a soul. How much would you be willing to pay, Mrs Palmer, to buy the Pope's? The Dalai Lama's? I see all these things so clearly,' Wayne said, putting his glasses back on. 'So clearly,' he said again, his voice still insistent, but lower at last. 'Don't you?'

'Paul,' Linda yelled at Paul Nieman, who was only a couple of feet away now.

'Are you okay, Mrs Palmer?' he said, his eyes on Wayne Spalding.

Without thinking, Linda grabbed hold of him because he

smelt of aftershave and, like her, was carrying a Marks and Spencer carrier-bag. She steered him towards the stocks, not daring to look back.

'Hunger will be your salvation,' Wayne Spalding called out after them, 'I can already feel you among us, Mrs Palmer.'

'Are you okay?' Paul said again.

'I think so.'

They sat down on the stocks and watched Wayne Spalding make his way back over to the choir.

'Who was that?'

'I don't know.'

'There's a whole group of them in yellow sweatshirts – Littlehaven Free Church or something.'

Linda was nodding, the corners of her eyes full of yellow sweatshirts, trying to empty her head of Wayne's visions of the future with its agencies where you could rent a mother by the hour. He'd mentioned the Dalai Lama, but she'd already forgotten what he said about him so that was good. She didn't want to remember a single thing he'd said – especially the bit about her looking hungry.

'You've had your hair cut – it looks nice,' Paul said.

Linda passed her hand over the back of her hair.

'And I'm glad to see your nose has stopped bleeding.'

'My nose?'

'Yesterday – up at The Haven.'

'Oh, my nose.' She looked sideways at him to see if he was laughing at her.

'Paul!'

It was Delta Saunders, carrying the packaging from Stephanie's lightsaber as Stephanie trailed behind with Mick, who was trying to make it work.

'What did you think of the showdown between Darth Vader and the evangelist?'

'Showdown?' Linda said.

Delta turned to face her. 'I saw you talking to him.'

'Talking to who?'

'The evangelist.'

'It won't work,' Stephanie was saying, as she and Mick reached the stocks.

'Are you coming tonight?' Delta said, turning to Paul.

'Coming where?' Paul asked.

'The Christmas Eve party – our house?'

'It will work,' Mick said to Stephanie. 'It just needs batteries.'

'It won't work,' she moaned, ignoring him.

'It needs batteries, Steph,' he said, trying to keep his patience. 'Hello, Linda. We were coming over to commit a charitable act and rescue you from the evangelist, but Paul got there first.'

'Only we weren't sure if you needed rescuing,' Delta put in.

'Tonight? I don't know.'

'I want batteries,' Stephanie started to cry.

'Why have you got two lightsabers, Stephanie?' Linda asked, trying to distract her.

'One's for Monica,' Mick said. 'It was Steph's idea.'

'Batteries,' Stephanie wailed.

'Bloody hell, Steph,' Delta snapped. 'Will you just shut up!'

'I'd better go,' Linda said. 'See you tonight.'

Mick watched Paul Nieman with interest as he tracked Linda Palmer's arse in its red jeans until it was swallowed by shoppers. An aerobics queen's arse was the last thing he expected the writer of facetious poetry and editor of the school magazine to be interested in, but that's definitely what he'd been looking at.

Paul looked over to where the Free Church choir had started singing again now the *Star Wars* music had cut out.

He spotted Wayne Spalding moving from side to side in front of his ranks like a fairground target shot. 'I'd better be off as well,' he said, above Stephanie's wailing, which had got louder since she was told to shut up. 'See you tonight.'

Then Mick saw the way Delta was looking at Paul as she watched him walk across the square towards Goodies Toy Shop and the basket of lightsabers, and thought how much she reminded him of himself.

'So you're coming then,' she called out, but Paul didn't hear.

Mick stood in the middle of the town square with his two daughters and thought about what he'd seen going on between Delta and Paul and Linda Palmer as clearly as if it was a landscape he was flying over. Then Delta turned round and asked him what he was frowning at.

By the time Linda got back to Pollards Close, the last clouds had disappeared and a winter sun was hitting the wind-screen rendering her blind as she drove into the garage, nearly running over Joe as he stood by the chest freezer at the back, wondering whether he'd bought the right pot for his mum at the garden centre.

'For Christ's sake, Joe,' Linda said, fractious, as she got out of the car and slammed the door, then realised her coat was still shut in it so opened it and slammed it again – even louder this time. She was walking round the bonnet to tell him that they were building Tudor houses in the field behind them and that this was the beginning of Phase IV, when she saw the pot and was immediately distracted. 'How much did that cost?'

Joe looked up. 'I got stone in the end,' he said. 'I had a look at the terracotta and these big oak barrels like you see planted up outside the pub, but in the end I went for stone.'

'How much, Joe?'

Joe looked back down at the pot then up at Linda again. 'Fifteen pounds.'

'Fifteen pounds?' she yelled, banging Belle's stocking fillers onto the bonnet of the car.

'They were running a promotional offer – all stone pots half price.'

Linda laughed. 'They've been running that promotion forever – the stone pots are always half price; half price is full price, Joe, and we never talked about fifteen pounds.'

'I thought you weren't interested.'

'I didn't know I was meant to be interested in your mother's pot,' she said watching him, wondering why he'd never been up to the garden centre and bought a pot like that for their garden, and when exactly he'd notice that she'd had her hair cut and highlighted for the Saunders' party that night.

Joe shrugged, turning his attention back to the pot, which had Dionysus's head and some wreaths of grapes on either side. 'Have you seen this?' he said. 'It's Dionysus.'

'Dionysus?' Linda said, staring at it. 'Looks more like Terry Wogan to me.'

The pot was the first thing he'd enjoyed buying in a long time, but he didn't tell her this. 'It's meant to be Dionysus,' Joe insisted, determined not to let her spoil it for him, but Dionysus was rapidly disappearing, to be replaced by Terry Wogan. 'Guess who I saw up at the garden centre?' he said, willing Dionysus back into being and trying to keep a grip on the morning, which he'd enjoyed. 'This old boy who used to grow dahlias with Dad.'

Linda stared at him smiling at the memory of the meeting. This was Joe all over. It took him a day to remember the news that Mick Saunders had been made redundant by Laker Air and yet here he was after a trip to the garden centre barely able to contain himself because he'd seen someone his dad used to grow dahlias with – whose name he couldn't even remember.

'I was looking at the ponds and I heard someone call out "Joe", clear as day. He said he recognised me straight off – no doubt – Derek Palmer's boy. He won't have seen me since I was thirteen either.' Joe gave his head a light shake and touched the pot gently with the toe of his shoe. 'It brought back all those times we used to go to the shows on Saturdays: in the car by eight with three flasks and a picnic, and Dad shouting at everyone. Sometimes it was earlier – depending on how far away the show was. We went some-where north of London once – can't remember where, but I remember sitting in the back of the car and it being dark and me and Darren shining torches into the boot.' Joe broke off. 'Al – that was his name.' He paused. 'And if Dad won . . . well. Al remembered exactly how many times Dad won first prize. Exactly.'

Linda didn't realise that Joe was telling her a story – or that it was the first story Joe had told her for a decade, in fact – which probably made it the most important thing he'd said to her in a decade – because Linda wasn't listening. Her mind was too busy reaching out for the chest freezer behind him as she made a mental note of the things she needed to get out and defrost for tomorrow. Joe had already told her the story – when they first met. Only trust had been implicit between them then because they had nothing to fear from each other, and Linda hadn't been wondering whether to keep the two bags of mixed vegetables she'd bought in the fridge or whether to freeze one of them. What would people's appetite for vegetables be like tomorrow? Had she bought the standard or family-pack size? They'd probably only need one bag – it wasn't like there was going to be more than four of them sat round the table, she thought, feeling suddenly depressed.

'I'm going to make some tea,' she said, not moving.

'Al's got involved with the National Auricula and Primula Society to keep himself busy in spring, before the dahlias. I told him about Mum's old chimney pots and her primulas and he's going to give me some alpine auriculas in a few months' time so I thought I'd just give her the pot now – as it is – then after I've been to see Al in February/March, she could plant it up then. I was thinking maybe the auriculas are something Dad might get interested in – the way Al was talking about them.'

Linda didn't say anything. She wasn't getting drawn into another conversation about Derek Palmer, who had persistently refused professional help – or even lithium – for his manic depression and seemed oblivious to the fact that his younger son had a criminal record. She'd never forget that afternoon two years ago, when he came wandering downstairs to tell them that all the manhole covers in the street had been opened and that there were thousands of people pouring out of them. Of course they'd all gone to the window to look – just in case – and they'd all seen nothing. The only way she got through that afternoon was by looking at the tea tray they'd bought Audrey from Stourhead, in the summer.

She never had been able to work out why Joe was so hung up on a man whose life had failed. It was as if Joe was forever trying to catch up with his dad when everybody but Joe knew that he'd already outstripped him.

Derek Palmer's depression started when property developers moved in and bought up most of Brighton between them, dividing it up and converting the old Regency houses into flats. Carpenters Palmer & Son began to take on more and more work and that's when the fitted-kitchen business started up. It was Joe who took the calls, went to the meetings and then turned up to do the work, and Joe who started

195

to blame himself for what was happening to Derek Palmer, who couldn't keep up or didn't want to keep up. Linda hadn't cared then and didn't care now. You either kept up with the world or dropped off the edge of it. They were a young married couple with their whole future ahead of them – why should they turn their future down for the sake of one man and his nostalgia. Nostalgia for what, anyway? Odd jobs, being home in time for tea, scraping by – and a car full of prize dahlias, a family of four, three flasks and a picnic, making its way through the dawn, headlamps switched on, to another village hall. Nostalgia had driven Derek Palmer mad.

'I thought the alpine auriculas might spark something off in Dad – who knows? I might even get Al to give him a call – or go round and see him.'

Becoming slowly aware of Joe again, Linda realised that he was standing with his hands in his pockets, staring at her like he'd just asked her a question and was waiting for the answer.

'What?' she said. It had suddenly occurred to her that she had no intention of letting Joe take the pot to Cassidy Street; it was staying here in the garden at Pollards Close – the front garden, maybe. Nobody else had a pot like that in their front garden. Not even the Niemans. Derek and Audrey Palmer and the National Auricula and Primula Society were gaining the upper hand here and Linda wasn't having it. The pot was staying here; she was staying on top of the situation and on top of Joe. She was going to triumph; she was going to prevail.

Joe thought about Linda's 'What?' for a long time then said, 'Nothing.'

She pulled the Marks and Spencer bag off the bonnet of the car. 'When were you thinking of taking the pot to your mum?'

196

'I thought I might drop it off when I take Belle back.'

'I'm taking her back.'

'You are?'

Linda nodded, and while Joe carried on standing there, looking confused, said, 'And you'll have to move it into the garden – I need to get to the freezer.'

'I can't leave it outside.'

'It was outside at the garden centre. Put it in the shed,' she said, disappearing into the kitchen. 'Are cheese sandwiches all right for lunch? I'm just doing something light because we're going out tonight.'

'Where are we going?'

She reappeared in the kitchen doorway, still in her coat. 'We're going to the Saunders', Joe.' She waited for him to acknowledge this. 'It's Christmas Eve – we always go to the Saunders' on Christmas Eve,' she shouted, remembering the way Derek Palmer looked that afternoon when he came downstairs to tell them people were crawling out of manhole covers, and Dominique saying that mental illness was genetic, and Linda getting her head round the idea of something being genetic – and what that implied.

'Is your mum coming?' he said after a while.

'Keep your voice down,' Linda hissed, stepping down into the garage. 'How can she come? We can't go pushing her around in a wheelchair at the Saunders', can we?'

'She could use her sticks.'

'Just keep your voice down,' she said again to Joe, who was standing watching her in silence. 'Who's she going to talk to?'

'I thought Dominique's mum was staying with them – what's her name?'

'Monica; her name's Monica, and Monica's one of the world's most renowned food-dye researchers, Joe – what exactly is it you think they've got in common?'

Joe shrugged. 'We can't just leave her here, Linda. It's Christmas Eve.'

'I've spent all morning convincing her that we won't be gone long and that it would be best if she stayed here and watched a film on TV, so don't you go and say anything, Joe. I've got it all sorted.'

'All right,' Joe sighed. 'All right.'

Linda waited until she was convinced he'd accepted defeat then disappeared back into the kitchen.

'Put some onion in the sandwiches with the cheese,' he called out.

Linda was standing with the loaf of bread in her hand, wondering whether to allow Joe his onion or not, when Belle manoeuvred herself and her two sticks into the kitchen, followed by Ferdie, who'd been on her heels all morning.

'What was all that then?' she said.

'Nothing, Mum,' Linda said, turning her back on her and bearing her full weight down on the knife as she cut through an onion.

'I thought I heard shouting.'

'It's nothing.'

'What's wrong?'

'Nothing's wrong.'

'And what's lunch – self-service? You can starve yourself to death, if you want, but the rest of us need to eat.'

'Lunch is just coming and there's nothing wrong,' Linda said, rubbing her arms across her eyes.

'Is that onion I can smell – are we having onion?' Belle said, staring at her daughter's back.

'I was doing some cheese sandwiches and Joe wanted a bit of onion in his.'

'Is that what we're having – sandwiches?'

'Well, we're out tonight.'

'But I'm not, am I?'

198

'I'm getting you something sorted before we go – I told you that.'

Belle grunted. 'Well, you can put some onion in mine as well,' she said. 'I don't know what's wrong with everyone today.'

'There's nothing wrong, Mum,' Linda said loudly.

Joe put his head round the door. 'D'you want me to make that tea?'

'No, I don't want you to make that tea, I want you to move that bloody pot out of the garage so I can get to the freezer.'

Joe disappeared and a second later she heard the hollow grinding of stone against the cement garage floor as he moved the pot, grunting and swearing. He carried on grunting and swearing until he managed to lever it over the step into the garden. Then it went silent and she watched through the kitchen window as Joe rolled the pot up to the shed.

'What's wrong with Joe?' Belle said.

'Nothing's wrong with Joe – there's nothing wrong with him.' Linda got some plates out of the cupboard and stayed crouched behind the breakfast bar longer than she needed because Belle couldn't see her down there so she could take the draughts of air she suddenly wanted, coming from the garden through the garage to the kitchen.

'Linda?' Belle's voice said. 'What are you doing down there?'

Linda stood up, the plates in her hand, and realised that she'd left the bag with Belle's stocking fillers in on the breakfast bar.

'Are those sandwiches ready? It's nearly two o'clock.'

Linda cut them in half and put them on the plates.

'Where's Joe?' Belle said.

'Joe? He went into the shed.'

199

'I know he went into the shed – I saw him go in – I just haven't seen him come back out again.'

They stood staring through the kitchen window.

'Well, he's still in there, then.'

'I hope so,' Belle said, lowering herself into the nearest chair and propping her sticks against the table.

'Where else would he be?' Linda said, starting to raise her voice again. 'It's a shed – not a bloody Tardis.'

'I don't know,' Belle replied thoughtfully, as if there might be options.

Linda stared out the window, saw that the shed door was open and felt relieved.

'Where's Jessica?' Belle asked.

'Up in her room, I suppose.'

'Isn't she coming down to eat?' Belle sniffed at her plate. 'There's not onion in this, is there?'

'You said you wanted onion.'

'I didn't – onion gives me wind – why would I say I wanted onion?'

'Well just put it to one side, I'm not making any more.' Trying to regulate her breathing, Linda went into the hallway. 'Jessica,' she called upstairs, 'lunch is on the table.'

Upstairs the bedroom door opened.

'I don't want any.'

'What's that?'

'I said I don't want any.'

'Well, it's all I'm doing until we go out to the party tonight.'

'I'm not coming to the party.'

'You're coming, Jessica.'

'I'm not.'

Upstairs the bedroom door shut.

'What are you doing still in your coat?' Belle said as Linda walked back into the kitchen.

Looking down, she saw that she was – as Belle pointed

out – still in her coat, and that there were breadcrumbs and grated cheese caught in the fake fur. Ignoring her, she went into the garage and through to the garden. 'Joe?' she said, when she got to the shed. From her vantage point at the open door, she stood looking round the interior as if there was a reason – other than the stone pot – for him being in there. 'Joe?' she said again.

He turned round slowly to face her and she saw that he'd been crying.

'Lunch is ready – I put onion in yours.'

She stood there waiting for him.

14

Tony Browne took in the packed holdall on the sofa, half-empty and sagging, and went to stand at the patio windows. It wouldn't take more than two hours to drive to his sister's and it was only three in the afternoon now. He stood there with his fingers pressed against the glass and the sun on his face, which was tilted slightly, his eyes closed as he concentrated on the light filtering through the lids: blue and red then more red. The sun shifted and his face went cold. He turned round to check that the presents he'd bought for his three nephews were on the sofa beside the holdall – if he hadn't already put them there or didn't do it now while he was thinking about it, he'd forget. They were there: three copies of *A Pictorial History of the Olympic Games* because Abigail said they were interested in sport.

He turned back to the garden, which he'd made sure winter would have no effect on by planting conifers. The conifers also hid the railway line – even though nothing he could plant would keep out the noise – and when he got back from Rory and Abigail's he really did have to speak to the Pole next door about her cherry tree. He looked at his watch – why not go and talk to her about the tree now? It was winter flowering and he hated the sight of his conifers in February with pink blossom all caught up in them. If it wasn't for the overhanging cherry tree he could pretend that she didn't exist at all; that nobody existed outside the barricade of conifers.

Leaning his forehead against the glass, he closed his eyes again. He really did have to get rid of those overhanging branches – even if it meant taking his stepladder and pruning shears round and doing it himself. If she refused, he'd have to do it from his side of the fence, and if this meant paying for special pruning shears with longer handles, he'd post the receipt through the door making it clear that he expected her to recompense him for them. If she didn't respond, he'd seek legal advice from his solicitor down in Brighton.

He stood there until every possible scenario he could conceive of regarding the Pole and her cherry tree had passed through his head – why did she even have a cherry tree? Nobody else did. She wasn't going to get away with it. He went to the front door and unhooked the house keys from the brass key rack he'd put up when he had the new security system installed. Putting them into his pocket, he left the house, shutting the front door gently behind him.

When he moved in there was only a narrow strip of gravel separating the paths leading up to the front doors of No. 14 and No. 16. He'd written a letter to the Pole asking her if she minded him planting three dwarf conifers between the properties, and when he didn't hear anything from her, he went ahead and planted them anyway. They were still only forty centimetres high and he could have just stepped over them, but he didn't; he walked to the end of his path, then up the Pole's, the house keys ringing in his pocket.

The door to No. 16 was wide open and two Tesco carrier-bags lay in the path. Some celery had fallen out of one of them, and, stepping over this, he rang on the doorbell. There was no answer, and there were carrier-bags abandoned in the hallway as well, only these weren't from Tesco and they smelt of fish. The entire hallway smelt of fish as he leant in. 'Hello?' What was the woman's name? He couldn't remember.

'Hello,' he called out again, stepping into the hallway of No. 16, whose walls and ceiling were festooned with tinsel, convinced he could hear sounds coming from the back of the house. 'It's Mr Browne from next door.' He'd never seen so much tinsel concentrated in a single space before.

Through the kitchen doorway, he saw legs in a pair of jeans lying across the floor. The Pole, still in her coat with the strap of her handbag caught round her wrist, was crouched over her son, who was having an epileptic fit on the kitchen floor. The boy was making the chattering, moaning sound Tony Browne associated with hypothermia.

She turned round to see him standing in her kitchen doorway and before he had time to apologise or explain, said, 'A cushion – I need a cushion.' The layout of the Pole's house was the same as his own, in reverse. He went through to the lounge, picked up the nearest cushion and took it back to the kitchen, watching as the Pole lifted up her son's head and put the cushion under him, trying not to get any hair caught in her watchstrap.

After quickly wiping her nose, she knelt back, her knuckles still clenched, waiting for the epilepsy to finish rattling through her son, and ignoring Mr Browne, who didn't know whether to stay or go because now wasn't the time to mention the cherry tree. The Pole was panting and there were streaks of mud from her boots across the lino.

At last the boy went still and lay there with his feet in

their oversize trainers turned outwards and his head to one side. The Pole stayed kneeling on the floor, her head hanging down, and it felt as though somebody who nobody wanted to see had just left the room.

A few seconds later she got awkwardly to her feet. 'Thank you,' she said, unwinding the strap of her handbag from her wrist and putting it on the kitchen table. 'For the cushion,' she added when Tony didn't say anything. 'Thank you for the cushion.'

They both looked down as Peter Klusczynski rolled slowly onto his side.

'You've got shopping out in the hallway,' Tony said.

She pushed her hair off her forehead, staring at him with grey eyes.

'There's shopping on the path outside as well.' He looked down the hallway through the open front door to where he could see the two Tesco carrier-bags and the celery on the path still.

'The fish,' she said, after a while. 'The fish needs to go in the fridge.'

'I'll get it in for you.' He walked down the hallway and out onto the front path, picking up the celery and the two Tesco bags and collecting the bags with the fish in on the way back, instinctively shutting the front door behind him with his foot. 'Where d'you want it all?'

'The table,' she said, watching him walk sideways through the kitchen door with all the bags.

He saw Peter Klusczynski, who was now sitting in a chair, look at him then look away.

'What about the fish?'

'The fish? Oh, the fish should go in the fridge,' she said, making no effort to move.

He put the bags on the table, repositioning the more precarious ones until he was convinced none of them were going to fall off, then placed the bags with the fish in by the fridge. 'Should these go in now?' he said when she carried on standing there.

'Now would be good,' she replied, still without moving.

After a moment's hesitation he opened the fridge door, which had memo notes stuck to it that had been written on then crossed through. Inside it was almost empty and he quickly pushed the fish in – seeing the inside of her fridge felt more intimate than seeing her son in the throes of an epileptic fit. 'That's a lot of fish you've got there,' he said, standing up again.

'Traditionally we eat fish on Christmas Eve. You want something to drink?' she said, taking her coat off and hanging it on the back of a chair.

'To drink?' he repeated, aware of Peter Klusczynski staring at him, making him feel uncomfortable.

'Yes – to drink,' the Pole was saying, smiling at him.

'Oh, right, well . . . tea?'

'You want tea?'

'Is that okay?'

'Of course.' She turned away and started to fill up the kettle at the sink. 'I'm having brandy,' she said, putting the lid on the kettle. 'You want some brandy?'

'No – tea's fine, honestly.'

'I don't doubt your honesty, Mr Browne. Maybe you don't drink brandy?' she said, smiling again. 'Try some of this.' She took a Coca-Cola bottle full of pink liquid out of one of the cupboards. 'Peter?'

'No, I'm . . .' He stood up, scraping his chair back and, pushing past Tony, disappeared upstairs.

'Will you excuse me?' the woman said.

He heard her call out, 'Peter? Do you want something to eat?'

There was no reply.

206

When she walked back into the kitchen she looked preoccupied, but was still smiling.

'You don't have children, do you, Mr Browne?'

'No – no, I don't.'

She shrugged as she carried the bottle and two glasses to the table. 'Thank you for your help. Most people – they would see the door open and they'd walk past. So – thank you.'

'I didn't do anything,' he said, sitting in the chair she pulled out for him and thinking about the cherry tree again.

'You came in.'

He watched her pour the brandy, which was pink, into the two glasses. 'I'm sorry – about your son.'

She nodded, but didn't say anything for a while. 'He wants to look like the lead singer from that band – The Cure? Is that what they're called? The man with all that black hair and the make-up.' She paused. 'I suppose it's his age – I don't remember. I mean, I remember wanting to be somewhere else, but not someone else.' She broke off and handed him his glass. 'Now you have to look at me, like this,' she said. 'Then we have to drink immediately.' They fixed each other with a stare, toasted and downed the shots.

'So . . .' she said, putting the empty glass on the table, 'what do you think of my brandy?' Without waiting for an answer, she poured them both another glass. 'It's cherry brandy.'

'Cherry?'

He stared through the kitchen window at the garden, which was the same size as his only it looked bigger, and the train running across the end of it looked like it had a different destination to the one it had when it passed the end of his garden.

'From the tree in the garden,' she said, watching him. 'Peter helps me.' Then, 'We bought the house because of the tree.'

207

She looked at him, wanting him to have an opinion on this, but he didn't. He couldn't imagine anybody buying a house because of a tree, but here was someone who had and he was sitting next to her, drinking her brandy.

'You can see it from my garden,' he said, wondering if he was going to mention the overhanging branches now.

'I'm surprised you can see anything from behind those conifers.' She paused. 'But then maybe you don't want to see anything.'

Unsure what he was meant to make of her comment on the conifers, he looked around the kitchen, noticing for the first time how untidy it was and that there were purple marks – that looked like beetroot stains – on the tiles behind the cooker.

'You want more brandy?'

'No,' he said quickly, 'but it was very good.'

She rubbed her hands over her face and sighed. 'One of my students – I see her coming to your house.'

Mr Browne stared at her. The word 'student' struck him as archaic and it took him a while to realise who she was talking about, and to remember that Mrs Klusczynski was a teacher.

'Jessica – Jessica Palmer?'

'Oh, Jessica.' He felt he had to add something to this. 'She's helping me with something I'm working on right now – something to do with Youth CND.'

'Ah, CND.' She nodded, but didn't ask any more questions. 'Jessica's going to be extraordinary when she grows up,' she said after a while. 'And my son – he's going to be extraordinary. I believe in children, Mr Browne.'

'Of course,' he said, without really knowing what he was saying any more and unclear where all this was going. 'We're writing a book – Jessica's helping me write a book on survival following nuclear attack.'

The air had cleared, and even though it was the first time he'd been in the kitchen at No. 16, it felt suddenly familiar. 'It's more of a manual, really – something people can actually use.'

She was smiling at him again now and he had the same impression he'd had earlier – that she wasn't really interested.

'Maybe you'd like to come and eat something with us tonight? As you saw – we're having fish,' she said after a while.

'No, I'm sorry.'

'You don't eat fish?'

'No, I eat fish, but I'm going to my sister's for Christmas.' He realised, looking at her, that she didn't believe him. 'She lives in Hampshire – I've got three nephews.' He didn't know why he was bringing the nephews into this – to make it sound more plausible? But then why did he need to make the truth sound plausible?

'So – not too far to drive then.'

'Not too far, no.'

They smiled at each other, instinctively standing up at the same time.

She saw him to the door. 'Merry Christmas, Mr Browne.'

'Tony,' he said. 'My name's Tony.'

'I'm Margo.' She folded her arms and watched him walk down her path and up his own.

Tony shut the front door, hung the keys back on the rack and went through to the lounge. He'd left the lights on, which was unlike him, and saw the reflection of his holdall in the patio doors, floating in the garden just above the lawn. He sometimes thought that this was the hardest part of living alone – things not moving.

He stood there, staring at the cherry tree again, suddenly angry with himself for not mentioning it when he had the chance. Then he thought of his sister, plastered to her Aga and unable to sustain a conversation – even a basic exchange of words – without breaking off to yell at someone. He thought about how loud Abigail was, how loud his three nephews were, how loud the house was and how every time he came away he had overriding memories of noise and mud – noise that never stopped and mud that never seemed to dry. His nephews – when they bothered to acknowledge his existence at all – got together to bait him (usually about the Falklands) until he ended up exploding and saying things that sent them into hysterics; things that made their father, Rory, snigger and Abigail stare vaguely at whatever food was left on the table. There was that time he'd found *Uncle Tony's a prick* written across Tim's Etch-a-Sketch and the bathroom mirror, and every time condensation covered the mirror the phrase kept reappearing – *Uncle Tony's a prick.* When he tried speaking to Abigail about it, she just looked tired and said the cleaner was coming the next day – did it really matter?

The lack of discipline – especially as the boys got older – struck him as almost immoral, and once, after a rage, he'd sat there yelling at Rory while Rory explained to him in his slow, quiet barrister's way that families weren't brought up any more, they were run, which was why it was better to teach children how to win than how to be good, especially when success had so little to do with morality. Then Rory got up, sighing, and helped clear the table and stack the dishwasher, having given no indication whether he agreed with this theory or had simply come to the conclusion that it was the sensible option.

He thought about Rory walking slowly out of his study to the front door and slouching under the porch light – Tony only ever went to visit at Christmas, and whenever he thought of Rory he always saw the porch light shining above

him – ready to shake hands with him and talk about capital-
ism, heroism and teenage pregnancy. He thought about
Abigail with her overlarge earrings and shapeless clothes,
hollering for the boys to come downstairs and say 'hello'.
He thought about the large, shapeless, over-decorated family
Christmas he was about to walk into and picked up the telephone. Twenty minutes later, which was how long it had
taken him to convince Abigail he wasn't coming, he left the
holdall – still packed – on the sofa, and rang the doorbell
at No. 16 Pollards Close.

'Margo?'

She answered the door with a cigarette in her hand, and
he saw, behind her, the shopping still unpacked on the table.
'I think I will come tonight – if the invitation still stands?'

10

Valerie Kline answered the door in her yellow Littlehaven Free Church sweatshirt and stared at Dominique Saunders standing on her front doorstep.

'Hi,' Dominique said. It was the first time she'd ever knocked on the door of No. 10.

Valerie Kline stood smiling nervously at her, holding on to the door with both hands. There was food in her mouth – it looked like boiled egg – and a smell of vinegar hung happily round her.

'Sorry, I was having a late lunch.' She wiped her mouth then brushed some crumbs of yolk off her sweatshirt.

'I'm not interrupting you, am I?' The sound of a TV was clearly audible.

'No – I've finished.'

'Good. Well . . .' Dominique had come out without a coat and had to wrap her arms around herself to stop shaking.

'You want to come in?' Valerie said.

'Oh, no, I was just wondering if you were busy tonight?'

'Tonight?' She started to cough.

'It's just we're having a small Christmas Eve party and I was wondering if you wanted to come?' Looking past Valerie into the hallway, Dominique saw Brendan Kline's trench coat that Monica had been wearing that morning in the precinct hanging up on the banister. 'Brendan as well – I mean Brendan's invited as well.'

'Brendan? Brendan's out tonight.'

'Brendan's out?'

'Brendan does go out,' Valerie said, smiling, 'but thank you for the invitation – thank you anyway.'

For a minute Dominique thought Valerie Kline was going to shut the door on her. 'So – you'll come?'

'Oh, I don't know.'

'We're only having a buffet – nothing formal,' Dominique said. 'And just a few friends. Monica will be there,' she added.

'Monica?'

'Monica Duraty, my . . .' Dominique broke off, to see if the name had any effect on Valerie Kline. 'I think she and Brendan are doing some work together at Ciba?'

'I don't know.' Valerie shrugged. 'I've never heard him mention a Monica.'

'I just thought it would be nice for her, knowing somebody there tonight.'

'Sorry, but who is Monica?'

'Didn't I say? Monica's my, she's my . . . you know, she's my mother.'

Valerie, confused by Dominique's invitation, didn't know what to say. She'd been in the middle of watching *The Slipper and the Rose*, which was one of her favourite films, and had just got to the part where Richard Chamberlain was getting himself dressed for the ball that evening when the doorbell rang.

'What time is it?' she said.

'What – now?'

'No – the party – tonight.'

'Tonight? Oh, around eight?' Dominique was staring intently at Valerie Kline, noticing for the first time the tension in her face and the way the sides were drawn down towards her chin.

Valerie turned away, trying to pick up the sound of the TV, convinced that Richard Chamberlain's father had finished singing 'Find a mate, dear boy, find a mate', which meant that the scene where him and his parents discussed marriage prospects was nearly over, which meant that the scene leading up to the ball was about to begin.

'And like I said – if Brendan wants to come, he's more than welcome,' Dominique said, now convinced that Valerie was trying to get rid of her.

'Brendan's going out – didn't I already say?'

'Well, if he changes his mind.'

'I'll let him know.' Valerie Kline shut the door and went back into the lounge, sitting down in the armchair she'd been sitting in all afternoon, with her legs folded under her, watching Richard Chamberlain make his way round the extras in the ballroom, bored, until he turned round and saw Gemma Craven walk in, then his whole face changed. For Valerie, this was the climax of the film and she didn't care what happened afterwards. The tears had just started to roll when she heard the doorbell go again.

4

Dominique stood there for a moment trying to work out if her invitation had been accepted or not.

Brendan Kline was all she'd thought about on the way back from town that morning and throughout lunch, which was sliced pineapple because Mick said he was putting all his energies into the meal that night and didn't have any left over for lunch. Stephanie wouldn't sit still because of her new lightsaber, Delta was preoccupied and Mick had ranted to himself about pineapples and how these hothouse wonders of the Victorian high table had been so degraded in their own era. He went on to say that he was going to set up a charity to protect the pineapple's exoticism and make it a legal offence to put it on pizzas or allow people like Linda Palmer to get their hands on them. She'd sat and listened, unable to get the image of Monica and Brendan Kline walking through the crowded precinct, laughing together, out of her mind. There was no sign of Monica at lunch – were she and Brendan having lunch together as well?

Then she rang the bell again.

The door opened and there was Valerie Kline.

'Yes?'

Dominique wasn't sure, but it looked as though Valerie Kline had been crying. Her eyes were shining and her cheeks were blotchy. 'Sorry, I wasn't sure – are you coming tonight or aren't you?'

'I'll be there,' Valerie nodded, then shut the door again.

Dominique stood in the doorway to the spare room and watched as Monica, sitting on the edge of the bed, put her make-up on.

'Are you standing in the doorway for a reason, Dominique?'

Did she need a reason? It was her house, after all – but then she'd always needed a reason or proof of a reason for Monica to spend time with her.

When she was growing up, Monica would come home any time between seven and nine – sometimes later if she was in the middle of an experiment or had a function to go to. If Dominique had been clever, Monica would have taken her with her, but she wasn't so she stayed at home. After Marcia, the last au pair, had left, Dominique would let herself into the empty Barnes flat after school and remember how they used to go out to an American burger bar round the corner, telling herself how she and Marcia used to have good times together and that she missed Marcia. She even wrote her a letter once, and Marcia's mother wrote back saying that Marcia had become a tour rep for a holiday company in Greece. There was no one else after Marcia, who was last in a long line of underage, under-qualified girls, disinclined to be surrogate mothers to Dominique. After Marcia, she was given keys to the flat. She taught herself to prepare three-course meals for her and Monica – meals Monica never commented on because she was too busy telling Dominique the crockery

216

or cutlery wasn't quite right or that she'd made a mess of the kitchen.

Dominique's interest in cooking, which flared up out of necessity at the age of fifteen, died away to nothing that summer after driving down through France with Monica's boyfriend at the time, Daniel. The gourmet trip – as Daniel referred to it – consisted of the three of them in a Renault in varying degrees of heat with Dominique in the back and the Michelin guide for whatever region they were passing through on her lap. Unable to make the connection between the coloured lines on the map and the countryside passing the window, Daniel had mocked her map-reading skills continually, until Monica told him to shut up – not in defence of Dominique, but because the constant taunting and mockery bored her. They only stopped the Renault to eat. At lunch they all ate together and in the evening they'd check into whatever hotel had rooms free. Monica and Daniel then went out to have a gourmet expcrience, and Dominique was left in the hotel. She'd been forever hungry on that trip, and the hunger made everything seem strange – including the almost supernatural fear of burglars she acquired after spending a night staring at a poster warning of burglary on the back of a door in a hotel just outside Lyon. Something happened in Lyon – and she and Monica returned to England alone.

That September the meals for two recommenced in the evenings in the flat in Barnes until they became unbearable and Monica told her she'd get something at work or on the way home and Dominique should sort herself out. So she started to subsist on instant soup, donuts, chocolate and bubble gum, drifting around the flat between coming home from school in the afternoon and going out to school the next morning, watching the weather through the window as if the rain and sun had nothing to do with her. The TV was on all the time – something she'd got used to when Marcia was there and had watched it constantly, when she wasn't either dyeing her hair in the bath or using the bathroom with her boyfriend, who'd been stationed down in Dover with the army.

So she became fat – and learnt how to be really alone. She grew so fat, in fact, that she was nearly six months pregnant before Monica even noticed. When she did notice, Monica stood there screaming incomplete sentences at her that sounded more like tabloid headlines than anything: daughter of world-famous food-dye scientist pregnant at fifteen . . . too late to abort. How had it happened? It was only thinking about it now that Dominique realised how strange it was that Monica had never asked her who the father was.

A month later, when Monica was able to walk into the flat without screaming at Dominique, she came in with a bag of maternity clothes she'd bought at a charity shop and emptied them onto the bed: flesh-coloured maternity tights, denim pinafores, smock tops and a couple of felted oversize jumpers. The maternity clothes were the only things she ever remembered Monica buying for her. There must have been other things – when she was a child – but these were all she remembered.

The school only put her in for five O Levels and she had to sit those in an isolation room. A week after the final one her waters broke at three in the morning. Monica rang for an ambulance and helped get her dressed, and it wasn't until the ambulance men rang at the door that Dominique noticed Monica wasn't dressed. Monica was still in her nightdress. Monica wasn't coming with her.

She never knew what arrangements Monica had made in the months leading up to her departure from the Barnes flat in the early hours of the morning to give birth – to what? She didn't even know if it was a boy or a girl. All she remembered was Monica, in the later stages of the pregnancy, bringing papers home for her to sign, and that it was only after signing that she fully realised what the documents and the interviews with adoption services meant. It meant two weeks on a postnatal ward without a baby and not finding a single person on the hospital staff who would tell her whether it was a boy or a girl. Monica turned up at the end of the two weeks when they discharged her, and when they got home from hospital she talked about a research programme that was starting up in Canada, and jobs – not careers, but jobs – that Dominique should start thinking about. Which was Monica's way of saying she should think about making some money and maybe looking for a place of her own. The exam results came through. The only one she passed was Home Economics – which she got an 'A' in.

Later that night, when she told Monica, Monica just laughed and said that if she'd realised how stupid – how truly stupid – Dominique was, she would have let her keep the baby because then at least she would have had something to do. Dominique had stood in front of her as she said that, and realised that, whatever people said, it was possible to kill another human being – and maybe even to enjoy doing it – and at that point she had to leave the room. She hadn't said anything to Monica then, and now – watching her finish her mascara – she still didn't know what to say because all she actually wanted to do was ask Monica whether Brendan Kline was the child she was forced to give up for adoption because that was what she'd been thinking ever since she saw them walking through the precinct together. She'd never walked through a crowded shopping precinct with Monica, laughing, like Brendan Kline had.

'I invited Valerie and Brendan Kline tonight.'

219

'Brendan Kline?' Monica looked up at her standing in the doorway.

'Brendan Kline,' Dominique said again. 'From Ciba?'

Monica started putting her lip-liner on. 'I didn't think you knew Brendan Kline.'

'I don't.'

Distracted by her daughter's tone, Monica looked up at her.

'But you do,' Dominique said.

'I do – yes.'

Dominique stared at her and didn't say anything.

'It's sweet of you to invite him for my sake.'

'For your sake?'

'I presume that's why you're inviting him – if you don't know him.'

'He can't come anyway.'

'That's a shame,' Monica said, still distracted. 'I've only really started corresponding with him at Ciba over the past three months when our respective research paths crossed. I tried to get him to come out to Canada, but he couldn't. I came back from Montréal to see him, in fact.'

'And us.'

'What?'

'And us – you came to see us as well.'

'Of course,' Monica said.

'You must have been surprised when you found out where he lived.'

Monica shrugged, picking up her lipstick. 'Littlehaven's small, and I don't believe in coincidence – you know that. You wouldn't think they're related – the Klines,' she added.

'They're not,' Dominique said. 'Brendan's adopted.'

Monica didn't flinch; Monica didn't even look up from her reflection in the mirror. 'Really? I didn't know.'

8

'Which ones?' Linda said, turning to Joe, a different earring in each ear.

'The pearls.'

She turned back to the mirror, unsure. She would have chosen the pearls herself until Joe said, and now she wasn't sure. Anyway, he was sitting on the side of the bed reading one of his water-feature brochures – how could he even see the pearls from there?

'Aren't you wearing your new polo shirt?'

'Which one's that, then?' he said, without looking up.

'The one we got in Debenhams.'

'When was that?'

'Back end of November – the same day I bought my dress.'

'What dress is that?'

'The one I wore when we had the Niemans round to dinner.'

'When was that?'

She stared at his back for a while. 'Have you got any memory – any whatsoever – of the Saturday we spent down in Brighton together?'

'When was that?'

'The day we bought your new polo shirt – the one that's still in the bloody carrier-bag – and the day I bought the dress I wore when the bloody Niemans came round.'

'All right, Linda, all right.'

She turned away from him back to the mirror. 'For Christ's sake, Joe.'

Sighing, he put the brochure down. 'What?'

'Nothing.' She put a third layer of lipstick on her lips, wondering why it was that lipstick seemed to vanish when you argued.

Joe was looking at her now, thinking how he'd walked into the bedroom after his shower and how it had smelt of the perfume she'd just sprayed on; how expectant she'd looked and how he'd stood there holding the towel round his waist, rapidly trying to track the source of her expectancy. The top she was wearing; he hadn't seen the top before, which meant it must be new, only he didn't say anything because he didn't like the top – especially the butterfly appliqué on it. He had been so busy standing there trying not to say anything about the top and succeeding, that now he realised (while fingering through his water-feature brochure) that she thought he hadn't noticed at all.

4

Monica and Mick were in the kitchen making blinis and doing something complicated to salmon without the aid of a book, and Dominique was making her way pointlessly between the kitchen and the lounge where Stephanie and Delta were trying to lay the table.

'Can I take the angels I made off the tree and put them on the table?' Stephanie asked.

'Of course you can.'

'And the tinsel?'

'There's tinsel in the bag in the cupboard.'

She went into the hallway where Mick pushed past her, carrying a stack of crockery. She was still standing there when he made his way back to the kitchen and he put his hands round her waist, pressing his thumbs into the small of her back. She leant back against him for a moment then he disappeared into the kitchen again, saying something to Monica that made her laugh.

Dominique went into the lounge. 'What are you going to do with the tinsel?'

'Put it round the edge of the table.'

'That's a good idea,' Dominique said, drifting back into

223

the hallway where she nearly walked into Monica, who was taking the cutlery through. 'Here, take this,' she said, pushing her daughter back towards the lounge where Delta and Stephanie were arguing over whether Bagpuss was male or female in a continuing purge that Stephanie had been carrying out all afternoon on all her former heroes in an attempt to uncover further transvestism.

'Is anyone watching that?' Dominique said, looking at the TV, which was still on.

Neither Stephanie nor Delta heard her.

'I said is anyone watching that?' she yelled.

The girls looked up; Delta shook her head.

'Well, I'll turn it off then.' She went over to the TV, knocking her leg on the corner of the glass coffee table. 'Stephanie, will you clear these marbles away now,' she shouted, suddenly infuriated by the sight of the small glass balls rolling backwards and forwards across the heating vent. When she looked round, Mick was standing in the doorway watching her. From behind the dining table Delta and Stephanie were doing the same thing.

'Everything okay?' Mick asked, slowly drying his hands on the tea towel he was holding, then slinging it over his shoulder.

'I'm fine,' Dominique said.

Mick nodded, but stayed in the doorway watching her. 'Want to come and make sour cream?' he said after a while, still watching her.

'No.' She stayed by the TV, pushing the marbles she'd just asked Stephanie to move up and down the heating vent with the toe of her shoe.

'Want to come and watch me make sour cream?'

She looked up at him.

'Come on.' He stood there, waiting, knowing that soon she was going to turn round and walk slowly towards him so that he could lead her into the kitchen and lift her onto a bar stool, not caring if Monica saw or what Monica thought about this. Then he'd go back to making the sour cream, with Dominique on the stool watching him. They both knew this was how it would be; even Delta and Stephanie knew, which was why they'd gone back to work on the dining table, putting so many decorations on it there wasn't room left for any food.

'Monica says you've invited Valerie Kline tonight?' he said once she was sitting on the bar stool and he was squeezing lemon juice into a bowl of cream.

'I did – nobody ever invites her to anything.'

'But it's not as if we've invited everyone in the Close apart from her, is it? Why Valerie Kline?'

Dominique didn't say anything.

Why had she suddenly taken it into her head to invite Valerie Kline? Committing acts of charity wasn't like her. 'Why not the Youngs next door?'

'They've taken out a lawsuit against us.'

'They have?' Mick said, as if he was hearing this for the first time.

'You know about this, Mick,' Dominique replied, irritated. 'We were in France and the fencing people came to put up the new fence in the back garden – the one that came down in the storm? Only they accidentally put it up an inch too far to the left,' she paused, 'or the right, depending on which way you're looking at it. Anyway, the Youngs lost an inch of their garden and you refused to have the fence taken down and put up again and . . .'

'I did?'

'And now they're suing us. You know all this.'

'Our neighbours are suing us?'

'The fence is the reason why we don't get a Christmas card from them,' Dominique said, ignoring him. 'The fence

225

is the reason we don't speak when we see them out on the drive. The fence is the reason why they complain when we barbecue in the summer. It was the Youngs who blocked our planning permission for that conservatory we wanted.'

'When did we want a conservatory? We never wanted a conservatory, did we? Thank God for the Youngs,' Mick said, 'I feel like writing them a thank you letter.' He opened the freezer, got the vodka out and went through to the lounge with it.

A minute later he opened the hatch in the wall and Dominique could see through to the dining room and the table the girls had decorated. She watched through the hatch as Mick lined up the wine glasses and Monica arranged the salmon on the serving plate, taking a tissue out of her sleeve and wiping her fingers while saying something to Delta. Dominique watched them talking together and thought about how she was giving Monica the family Monica had never given her, and that this was what she came here for – to be part of a family; to stand there talking to Delta while letting Stephanie put tinsel in her hair.

Dominique sat staring through the hatch thinking that Monica had no right to any of it.

Monica instinctively turned to look back through the hatch at her daughter, and knew, from her face, exactly what she was thinking.

Linda stood over the heating vent in the black and silver jumpsuit she'd changed into just before leaving the house when she realised that Joe didn't like the appliqué top. Kicking a couple of marbles out of the way, she wondered why she'd made the mistake of asking Monica Duraty what she'd done to the salmon. She only wanted her to iden- tify the green stuff on the side of it, but was now standing there listening to Monica's opinion on the fishing industry

226

in Scotland and the North Atlantic, and the difficulty she'd had sourcing wild salmon from the Orkney islands. She even had an opinion on smoking techniques. Linda, who hadn't dreamt of uncovering a passion on this scale, was just wondering if she dared change the subject when Monica moved off to speak to Valerie Kline – why had Dominique invited her, and why did everybody in the room apart from her and Joe already know about Greenfields Phase IV?

She stood there long enough to overhear Monica asking Valerie how her feet were before crossing the room towards Daphne Nieman, who was standing talking to Sandra Nassam, smiling with the knowledge that the Quantum Kitchens/Nieman double-glazing offer was proving even more successful than she'd anticipated. In fact, her smile was so lopsided at the thought of this that Daphne Nieman, watching her approach, thought she was either drunk or beginning to show early signs of cerebral palsy.

Linda made her way across the parquet towards them, enjoying the sound of her heels on the wooden floor. 'Have either of you got any idea what Valerie Kline's doing here?' she said, coming to a halt and trying to put her drink-free hand in her pocket until she remembered that the jump-suit didn't have pockets and that Joe had made a crude joke about why that was when she bought it three years ago, which meant that as little as three years ago Joe was still making crude jokes with her, which meant that as little as three years ago, Joe was still thinking crudely of her.

'We're talking business,' Daphne said flatly, ignoring the Valerie Kline question.

Linda smiled hopefully, thinking that it had to be better than the North Atlantic fishing industry.

'I'm looking for new premises,' Daphne was saying.

Linda turned round. 'Winke's expanding?'

'Winke's not expanding, no, but Nieman double glazing is, and that's why we're looking for new premises.'

'You help out at the company?'

'For a year now,' Daphne said, yelling 'More vodka' in Mick's direction. Then turning back to Linda, 'And I don't help out – I run the company.'

'I had no idea,' Linda said, wondering how on earth Daphne had managed to run Nieman double glazing for a year now without her knowing anything about it. Mick came round and poured more vodka.

'But – what does Winke think about you running the company?'

'Firstly, Winke doesn't think,' Daphne said, 'and secondly, who would give a fuck if he did?' She paused. 'Poor Winke.'

Linda tried to laugh, but ended up choking and fingering the zip at the top of her jumpsuit.

'I've put years into Nieman glazing, setting it up then building it up – I'm thinking of selling up. Come on, admit it – how much sweat have you put into Quantum Kitchens?'

'Quantum is all Joe's,' Linda insisted.

'Well,' Daphne said, unconvinced, 'I'm getting tired of watching the world through double glazing. I think it might be time to hear it again, you know? Touch it . . . smell it. Winke is about as much use as a fishing rod in the desert, and I'm sick of wiping his arse for him, you know? Really sick.'

Linda stood there nodding and trying to ignore the fact that the Niemans' marriage had just been hung, drawn and quartered by Daphne – and the whole thing had only taken as long as the Slade song on the stereo. The conversation with Daphne Nieman left her so drained that all she was capable of right then was a parting smile and a slow walk across parquet, out of the lounge and up the hallway to the downstairs toilet, whose door was locked and whose occupant had to shout out twice before she realised.

'You can go upstairs,' Mick yelled from the other end of the hall.

Linda went up to the bathroom, trying to remember if she'd ever been upstairs at the Saunders' before. The family bathroom was at the top of the stairs like it was in their house, only the Saunders had kept the original lilac tiles and bathroom suite that had been one of the first things she and Joe had ripped out when they moved into No. 8. For some reason the lilac didn't look so bad in the Saunders' house – maybe because nobody cared.

After poking through the make-up on the windowsill – which she guessed was Delta's – she went back into the hallway. The door to Stephanie's room had been left open and a dull red light was shining through it. The door to Delta's room was shut, but she could hear music coming from in there and it sounded like The Doors – were they having a revival already? Then, as quietly as she could, she pushed open the door to Dominique and Mick's room, taking in the sex safari theme that started with black carpet and animal skins on the floor and ended in the zebra-stripe duvet covering the bed. On the wall there were photographs of flowers – only they didn't look like flowers.

Linda thought of the master bedroom at No. 8 with its reproduction Georgian furniture and floral wallpaper and knew that it would never be the same again. Then she thought of how much happiness the mahogany and floral prints had given her and how she would go home tonight and despise them for not being black or having zebra stripes. Was life always this relentless? Did you always end up having to despise the things that made you happy? How dare the Saunders do this to her – and why not just have photographs of flowers on your walls rather than flowers that looked like genitalia? Did Dominique and Mick mind Stephanie seeing this? Weren't mahogany and real flowers

229

better for children? Linda would rather Jessica associated her and Joe with mahogany and floral prints, but then Jessica still hated her, so if mahogany and floral prints didn't account for anything when bringing up a child – and she'd got that wrong as well as everything else – then what did? She felt suddenly so exhausted she could have fallen asleep on the Saunders' sheepskin rug. She seemed to be continually tired at the moment. The nausea she'd been experiencing over the past month had been replaced by a tiredness that overcame her so suddenly that she'd fallen asleep on the bathroom floor the other day, still wearing the rubber gloves she'd been cleaning the loo with.

Trying to keep herself awake now, she stood there thumping lightly on the doorframe while looking down at the sheepskin rug, wondering if the creature she could see moving through one of Dominique's discarded bras was a mouse.

Then she turned round and there was Delta standing in the hallway, watching her.

'I was looking for the bathroom,' Linda said, slowly removing her hand from the doorframe.

'It's there at the top of the stairs.' Delta pointed behind her. 'I guess it's the same in your house because all the houses are the same. Laing have made everybody exactly the same so nobody ever needs to get lost.'

'Well, I'm lost,' Linda said, looking at Delta and thinking how like Mick she was.

4

Paul Nieman was sitting on Delta's bedroom floor, his back and neck resting against the bed. A copy of *The Waste Land* was open on his lap and he was meant to be choosing a passage from it for Delta to paint onto the wall, but the only part of *The Waste Land* he liked was the clerk peeing in the stairwell after leaving the secretary's flat. Delta seemed to think he knew it by heart and, like everybody else, was under the impression that he'd taken on the editorship of the school magazine of his own free will, when in fact it was his form tutor who'd persuaded him, saying that he needed an extracurricular activity with weight to talk about at university interviews. Girls in particular, he noted, seemed to presume he edited the school magazine because he was clever; or that he was clever and therefore edited the school magazine. Even his form tutor had forgotten that it was she who gave him the idea, and now the drama department were begging him to write a play and he had to keep putting them off with excuses of heavy commitments elsewhere. He'd even started believing the heavy commitment thing himself and had taken to slouching along the corridors between lessons, sighing, and people would come up

231

to him – people he'd never even spoken to before – and squeeze his shoulder in sympathy. Paul Nieman was the school's dauphin.

'Did you copy it?' he said to Delta, looking at the matador painted on the wall opposite.

'No, I saw it.'

'You saw it?'

'It's meant to be Morente. The bull he's fighting weighs I don't know how many pounds and the suit Morente is wearing weighs nearly half the weight of the bull. He died just after making the move he's making in my mural.'

'The bull?'

'Morente.'

Paul nodded, but he wasn't really listening. The bull unsettled him and made him think of how he'd masturbated about Linda Palmer again that afternoon. How he'd stood naked in front of his bedroom mirror with the lightsaber he'd bought from Goodies that morning, in his mind defending Linda Palmer from being raped by something only half human.

'We were in Spain,' Delta was saying, 'and Dad took me for my birthday. I can't remember how old I was – nine, ten?'

'I don't agree with that.'

'With what?'

'Taking a child to blood sports.'

'I was the one who wanted to go.'

'It doesn't make any difference,' Paul said. 'To me, that's wrong. You were only nine and your dad took you to see someone die – to see another human being die.'

'But he didn't know Morente was going to die.'

'So what did he do when he realised?'

'He watched – we watched – everyone watched.'

Paul didn't say anything. He had been mistaken about Delta Saunders. All along those slow gliding movements of hers had concealed an appetite for death.

232

'Have you found the passage you were looking for?' she asked, pointing to the book.

'I need to pee,' he said, getting up.

He went into the bathroom, and after washing his hands automatically opened some mouthwash and filled his mouth with it to get rid of the taste and smell of bull's blood.

Back in the bedroom the matador was still on the wall making the last move he'd ever make and the bull was still bleeding to death. The Doors were still playing, the rainbow incense was still smoking, and Delta was still sitting loosely on the bed with *The Waste Land*, waiting for him. It was all too intense – he suddenly wanted more than anything to be in his own bedroom looking at pornography.

'I bet you know it off by heart,' she said, smiling at him as if she'd uncovered something about him nobody else knew, or managed to penetrate him in some way.

Paul smiled back, bored. 'D'you want to go downstairs?'

Delta sat up. 'Downstairs? Why?'

He shrugged.

'What – and see our parents drunk?'

Paul shrugged again. 'Do you want a drink?'

'Maybe,' Delta said, smiling again as if she'd been momentarily confused but was getting the point now. 'I think there might be some Bacardi – wait,' she broke off, 'there's someone outside.' She opened the bedroom door, thinking it might be Stephanie, and there was Linda Palmer standing with her back to them in a jumpsuit that made her look like a low-budget alien from *Star Trek*, her hand on the door to the master bedroom.

Delta knew for a fact that Linda wasn't standing there looking at the Mapplethorpe prints.

Paul stood staring past Delta in her layers of skirt and purple T-shirt to where Linda Palmer was framed against black carpet and white walls, and after a while the room ceased to have anything to do with the Saunders. It was as if it had been created solely for Linda Palmer to move through in her black and silver jumpsuit, her sandal heels leaving polka-dot prints across the carpet. Something inside him suddenly stopped as he realised that he'd spend the rest of his erotic life inside that black and white room. The realisation affected him so profoundly that he had to go and lie down on the bed, and when Delta came back in and said, 'That woman was looking in my parents' room, can you fucking believe it?' he didn't say anything. Then when she tried to pick up where they'd left off by sitting next to him and opening the book again, he said, 'Fuck *The Waste Land*.'

'Really?' Delta said, worried that she hadn't been offbeat enough and that there was something she was missing about Paul Nieman.

4

Linda, unaware that she'd had such a profound effect on the destiny of another human being, went back downstairs and joined the circle of people standing round Valerie Kline, wondering how it was that sixteen stones' worth of sandal-wearing, *Dr Kildare*-watching recluse could suddenly be so alluring – especially when most of the people in the Saunders' lounge had outgrown the myth that she'd murdered her husband and buried him at the end of the garden. The myth really did turn out to be a myth when Daphne Nieman, who was standing next to her, tugged her sleeve and told her that Mr Kline had in fact gone to Tibet. 'All that time you all thought he was at the end of the garden, he was in Tibet,' she whispered to Linda.

'Tibet?'

'Mr Kline joined the Free Tibet Campaign.'

'From what?'

'I don't know what he was before – a lawyer or something.'

'I mean free Tibet from what?' Linda hissed.

'The Chinese,' Daphne said, staring at her. 'You do know

that the Chinese walked into Tibet and the Dalai Lama had to go to India?'

'I forgot,' Linda said, pushing her left hand through hair thick with spray and trying to ignore the fact that Daphne was still staring at her like she was the only person in the room who didn't know the exact whereabouts of the Dalai Lama – it was the second time today someone had mentioned him. The future seemed suddenly bleak; a future with no more mahogany furniture or floral wallpaper to sink your dreams into, only black and white rooms and nuclear weapons that might or might not go off, the Dalai Lama constantly on the move and people at parties expecting you to know what his latest grid reference was as well as having an opinion about the Chinese invasion of Tibet.

'He works voluntarily in a school there – no running water, electricity or anything – at an altitude of God knows how many thousand feet above sea level.' Daphne was panting at this litany of high-altitude deprivation, and it left Linda wondering which part of his not-for-profit lifestyle it was that Daphne found so appealing.

'Can you imagine Winke ever doing something like that?' she said, as though working voluntarily in a school in Tibet was the antithesis of double glazing.

Like most of the people there, Linda was looking at Valerie Kline properly for the first time as she stood there fanning herself, trying to resist the urge to grab hold of Valerie's fat shoulders and ask her how she survived her husband walking out on her; how she managed to carry on when Mr Kline had left the house one morning for Tibet without saying a word.

'Hot?' Daphne said, watching Linda fan herself.

'What?'

'I started getting hot flushes about three years ago – it's the menopause.'

236

'It's not the menopause,' Linda said.

'The hot flushes up here aren't so bad,' Daphne said, stroking her cheeks, 'but the ones down there,' she carried on, smiling, 'are terrible. I only had to smell a man . . .' She shook her head. 'I would have paid for it.'

'Paid for it?'

Daphne nodded. 'I don't know about Joe, but Winke – he's like Frankenstein's monster before Frankenstein got round to applying the electricity. Don't you ever wonder what it would be like to get fucked rather than having to do all the fucking yourself? Women on top – when aren't they? Apart from Dominique,' Daphne added.

'It's not the menopause,' Linda said again, trying to drown Daphne out.

'You just have to get used to it – it gets worse. The only way through is HRT pills. You'd think there might be another way, but there isn't. I would get hold of the medication as fast as I could, if I were you. In fact, I've got some Meno-lite in the cabinet at home – I'll post some through your door.'

'It's PMT,' Linda shouted.

'My God, if you think it's PMT, you really are menopausal. And by the way,' Daphne carried on, interested, 'I never knew Joe had a tattoo.'

Linda turned round and looked at Joe, who was standing next to Dominique. He'd taken his sweatshirt off and there on his right arm, for the whole Close to see, was a tattoo he'd had done years ago at a place that used to be in one of the archways under the promenade at Brighton. No matter how many kitchens Joe fitted, or how many bedrooms they had, that tattoo would always be there.

She was just starting to move away from Daphne, towards Joe, when she was distracted by something running down the side of the pot the Swiss cheese plant was in and onto the parquet. 'Joe might have a tattoo,' Linda said, rounding triumphantly on Daphne, 'but at least we don't have mice.'

People turned round; she wanted them to turn round because she was convinced that they'd all been looking at Joe's tattoo, and she wanted them to stop. The Saunders might have floral genitalia on their walls and zebra stripes on their bed and fuck all night long in their black hole of a bedroom, but they also had mice. Was Dominique at long last being punished for her inability to make her house a decent place, and for daring to think that life would be sweet in a mahogany-free world? Linda couldn't stop smiling as word spread and people's eyes followed the progress of the mouse, who was now running along the skirting board, driven senseless by mouse fears, which probably weren't all that different, Linda thought, watching it, to human fears.

'Stephanie's hamster,' Mick shouted.

'They're not mice?' Linda said, disappointed.

'Hamster,' Mick said, 'it's Stephanie's hamster. We bought her two for Christmas.' Then, 'You used the plural?'

'I what?'

'The plural – you said mice – you saw more than one?'

'There was another one upstairs.'

'Where upstairs?'

'The bedroom,' Linda said without thinking.

'The bedroom?'

'I mean the bathroom.'

'Is the bedroom door shut?' Dominique said later that night, turning to face Mick, her hair caught between her cheek and the pillow.

'You saw me shut it, Dom,' he replied, leaning over her and kissing her, but her eyes closed down on him, which meant he wasn't getting anywhere tonight. 'Do you want me to check again?'

238

When she didn't say anything he got up and rattled the bedroom door a few times to convince her. 'And I checked every crevice in here and the bathroom, and the other hamster – wherever it's still at large – isn't still at large in here,' he said, getting back into bed.

'But what will Steph think when she only gets one tomorrow?'

'She was only ever expecting one.'

'And what if the other one turns up?'

Then, before he got a chance to reassure her or make something up, she said, 'What's that noise?'

'It's the other hamster.'

'I know that,' she said, impatient, 'but it's making a strange noise – not like the one it was making before.'

Mick lay there listening to it for a while, not just to placate her, but because he was genuinely curious. 'It's pining,' he said after a while. 'Let's hope he doesn't die of a broken heart in the night.'

'How do you know it's a he?' Dominique said.

'I just do.'

'What if he escapes again?' she said, readily accepting Mick's gender diagnosis.

'He can't, Dom. The catch was loose on the cage before – I mustn't have closed it properly when I gave them their food earlier.'

She didn't say anything after this, and he thought she must have gone to sleep until she turned over to face him again. 'What did you think of Valerie Kline?'

'I don't know – did you believe all that stuff about Mr Kline teaching in Tibet?'

'Why shouldn't I?' She paused. 'Did you?'

'I don't know.' He waited, but she didn't ask him any more questions and after a while she fell asleep. He pulled the duvet up over her shoulders and pushed her hair back across her cheek, wondering what was preoccupying her so much at the moment and why she'd gone to such lengths to invite Valerie Kline tonight. With his thumb, he started stroking the mole on her right ear thinking that nobody knew her like he did; how nobody knew she could have led an army and their elephants across the Alps if the times had called for it. He'd known that about her the first time they met and he remembered thinking what a terrible mother Monica was for never having revealed to her daughter what she had inside her, but then he fell in love with her and kept as silent about the elephants and the army as Monica had, because he was terrified that once Dominique knew, she'd leave him.

8

Between the hamster being found in the study and leaving the Saunders' Christmas Eve party, Linda had drunk too much vodka – as well as something else she couldn't remember because the vodka ran out. Now she was standing in her own kitchen, watching Joe look for the vodka in their drinks' cabinet.

'Didn't there used to be something up here?' he said, feeling with his hand along the top of the cabinet. 'Some ornament or trinket – or something?'

'I lost it.'

'Lost what?'

'The gazelle.'

'What gazelle?'

'The one that used to stand up there – the one you made me, Joe. My gazelle?'

Joe straightened up, the bottle of vodka in his hand. 'What gazelle, Linda? I don't remember any gazelle.'

'The one you made me when we were at Whateley Road. You were so proud of it.' Linda wasn't sure what else to say. 'Well – I lost it.'

Joe shrugged and poured them both a glass of vodka.

241

'You enjoyed yourself tonight,' she said, watching him.

'I did? Yeah, I did.' He smiled.

'Did you know Daphne has been as good as running Nieman double glazing?'

'Daphne? No.'

'She's been running it for a year now – that's what she said. And the stuff she was saying about Winke and her . . .' Linda stopped suddenly. This was too close to home. 'The Niemans will be the first to sell up and move onto Phase IV – we'll be overlooking them in one of the new five-bedroom Tudor houses. Joe?' She paused. 'Joe?'

'What?'

'What are we going to do about Phase IV?'

'Do we have to do anything?'

'Well, we should at least go and look at the show home.'

'We can't even afford the mortgage on this – you're thinking of moving?'

'Well, that's what everybody else will be doing.'

'Will they?'

'Things move, Joe. The things that don't get left behind.'

'Then let's get left behind.' He handed her the glass of vodka.

Linda started to drink, wondering if this was the moment to just let it all go, and stop. She waited as Joe came up close and started stroking her arm – aware of how much she needed to know he was still capable of coming close – when Jessica came thumping down the stairs and running into the kitchen.

'Why haven't I seen this?' she shouted.

'Seen what?' Linda immediately yelled back.

'This – this note.' Jessica waved the note that had come through the door yesterday. 'It was addressed to me,' she said, jabbing her hand into her chest bone. 'It was addressed to me – why did you open it? It was a letter – addressed to me,' Jessica screamed at Linda.

'Well, hardly a letter. We didn't know who it was from – your dad and me – so we thought we'd better open it for you.' This wasn't true – she'd opened it before Joe came home – she just wanted to deflect some of Jessica's hatred, which was homing in on her with weapon precision, by implicating Joe.

'"Dad and I", it's "dad and I",' Jessica screamed, tears starting to run as she left the kitchen and thumped her way back upstairs, the note crackling in her hand.

'What was all that about?' Joe said.

'You heard what it was about,' Linda yelled. 'I just want to know what she was doing in our bedroom – the note was in my vanity unit – what was she doing there?' Without waiting for a response from Joe she went to the foot of the stairs. 'Jessica? What the hell were you doing in our bedroom? Jessica!' she called out again when there was no reply. Her hand went out for the banister but it wasn't where she thought it was, and she had to put her hand on the wall to stop herself from falling over. 'You've got no right to go in our bedroom.'

The door upstairs opened.

'I don't give a fuck about your rights.'

'Jessica!' Linda screamed, but she didn't go up; she stayed in the hallway with her foot on the first stair and her hand on the wall. Jessica had never said that to her before, and she realised, looking down, that her right leg was shaking.

It was still shaking as she tried to walk back into the kitchen. 'Did you hear that?' she said to Joe. 'Did you hear what she said to me?'

'She's going to be upset, Linda – it was addressed to her,' he said, wavering and falling against the drinks' cabinet.

'Did you hear her, Joe? Are you going to stand there and let her get away with talking to me like that?'

'Just calm down, love.'

'I am calm, and will you stop calling me "love" when you don't mean it, I can't stand it,' she yelled.

They stood looking at each other, aware, in the silence that followed, of the TV playing in the lounge, which either meant that Belle was still up or had fallen asleep watching it.

'She thinks the note's from Mr Browne,' Linda said. 'She thinks it's a love letter.'

'I know,' Joe said, watching her. 'You should speak to her.'

'After what she said to me? Where the fuck are you going?' she yelled as he left the kitchen, the glass of vodka still in his hand. 'Joe?'

'Upstairs – to see Jess.'

'But I need you down here – we need to talk about this – I need you, Joe. Joe?' She followed him out into the hallway as the door to the lounge opened and there was Belle, a bottle of Pale Cream Sherry in her hand.

'Heard enough?' Linda hissed.

'I was just going into the kitchen,' Belle sniffed, 'looking for a glass.' She paused. 'Want one?'

Linda looked at the bottle then at Belle as mother and daughter stared at each other. Then the moment passed.

Jessica was lying face down on the bed with her fingers in her ears when Joe walked into the room.

'Jess? Jess?' He shook her.

'What?' She rolled onto her back and he saw she'd been crying. 'I didn't hear you come in – had my fingers in my ears.'

'Why's that?'

'You were arguing. Even with my fingers in my ears I could still hear you – it just sounded like you were doing it underwater.'

244

'Mum's upset.'

'She's always upset – or hysterical – about something. I'm leaving home,' she added as Joe sat down on the bed beside her.

'What – tonight?'

'No – tomorrow; first thing tomorrow.'

'You don't want to do that,' Joe said, taking a sip of the vodka. 'It's Christmas Day tomorrow – there won't be any trains.'

Neither of them said anything for a while.

'She hates me,' Jessica said.

'Who does?'

'Mum.'

'She doesn't hate you,' Joe said, realising – even through the vodka – that he'd given Linda the same empty reassurance – when was it? When she'd been talking about Jessica. 'You're just so similar, that's all.'

Jessica sat up. 'We are?'

Joe wasn't entirely sure what he'd just said, but he nodded anyway.

'That's pretty fucking depressing, Dad.'

'Jess –'

'She said you both opened the letter,' Jessica carried on, pulling it out from under her pillow. 'But I know it was her.'

'I can't remember.' Joe was beginning to wonder if he had the stomach for this, aware that it was too late now.

He watched her reading it again, saw what happened to her face as she read and how tiny she suddenly seemed; how in need of protection.

'Are you going to ask me who it's from?' she said, looking up at him, not even bothering to conceal her excitement. Then, without waiting for an answer, 'Mr Browne.'

'Mr Browne? Really?' Should he tell her? Why should

245

he be the one to tell her? Why was she talking to him about all of this anyway? Because – he suddenly realised – she had no one else to talk to.

How long ago was it that he made that swing for Jessica – the one that used to hang from the apple tree in the back garden at Whateley Road?

He remembered the garden there so clearly. It backed onto the railway line and it wasn't much of a garden, but there was the apple tree and the swing he put up the summer she was five. He wore shorts all that summer and the long grass near the railway line gave his legs a rash. Everything lost its colour that year and English people who didn't know better were dying on foreign beaches in the midday heat. That's all you heard about. He remembered the afternoon in July when he was busy staking out the ground for a small fishpond, and hearing Jessica scream, 'Look – look!' When he did look up, she was standing on the swing pointing at the grass.

He bent over the patch in front of the swing. 'Looks like a grass snake,' he said, unsure, wiping his face with the bottom of his T-shirt. He picked up an old piece of wood with some nails sticking out of the underside that had been balanced against the back of the house and, crouching in the grass, tried to entice the snake to crawl onto it. 'It's not even a snake,' he said after a while, straightening up. 'It's a slow worm – it's only a slow worm.'

'I don't care,' Jessica sobbed.

'Come on, Jess,' Joe had snapped, suddenly reminded of the heat. Everything looked the same washed-out yellow – even the horizon. 'I'm getting rid of it, so will you just stop crying.' He managed to encourage the worm onto the wood again and was poised, ready to fling it into the trees, but he was too impatient – lifting the wood before enough of the worm was on it. 'Will you just shut up,' he yelled at Jessica, who was still crying.

246

'Kill it,' she screamed.

'It's only a bloody worm.'

'Just kill it.'

Hunched over, the wood still in his hand, he started hitting the worm with the flat side, but no matter how hard he hit, it wouldn't stop moving. The worm's movements were no longer fluid, but there was still life in the jerking way the creature tried to contract and make less of itself. He turned the wood over to the side with the nails in and started hitting it that way, but the nails kept getting stuck in the hard earth and Jessica was still crying. Then he started hitting whichever part of the worm seemed to be moving until he realised that the movements were an inanimate object's reaction to the force of being hit – they were no longer spontaneous. The worm was dead.

Behind him, Jessica had stopped crying and the only sound was the sound of the swing as the chains rubbed the bough.

The slow worm was a brown and green mess on the bald patch of grass and a column of ants was already making its way towards it.

He looked up at her, angry with her for the first time in her life, and had to throw the piece of wood away into the brambles because he was afraid he would start hitting her with it.

They stared at each other – Jessica as triumphant as she was terrified of what she'd made him do, and unsure how much further either of them wanted to take this experiment in love. If murder lay at the beginning, what lay at the end?

The slow worm took a fortnight to decompose and when all traces of it had finally disappeared, Joe went out with the watering can at night when Jessica was asleep, watering the bald patch of lawn and trying to make the grass grow back. Then the rain came and a thick dark green clump grew back almost overnight. He thought Jessica didn't use the swing any more either until Linda told him she only went on it while he was out at work.

'When I was downstairs with Nan earlier, I looked out the window and saw his lights on.'

'Whose lights?' Joe tried to take a step away from the vodka and the memories and concentrate on the young woman in front of him.

'Mr Browne's,' Jessica said, losing patience. 'He said he was going away for Christmas, but there were lights on in his house. D'you know what that means? D'you know what that means, Dad?'

Joe shook his head. 'He forgot to turn them off?'

'No,' Jessica laughed, thinking he was as caught up in all this as her. 'It means he's still there. Wherever it was he was meant to be going – he decided not to go.' She paused. 'I think he's waiting for me to write back.'

'Jessica –'

She let out another laugh.

His heart lurched as he realised he wasn't going to say anything because she'd find out soon enough – then he started laughing with her.

He was still laughing when he walked into the bedroom where Linda was busy stripping the bed. 'Linda – what are you doing?' he said, watching her, still in her jumpsuit and sandals, scuttling along the perimeter of the bed and dragging off the linen.

'I'm doing a white load, Joe.'

'What – now?'

'Yes, now.'

'It's Christmas Eve,' he said as she pushed him out of the way.

She turned round and stared at him then started stripping the pillowcases.

248

'You're not seriously going to do that now, are you?' Joe said, sitting down on the mattress.

'You don't seriously think I can just go to bed as if nothing's happened, do you?'

'What's happened?'

'What's happened, Joe? Let's start with this morning. This morning when I was out shopping I was accosted by an evangelical, in public and in broad daylight, telling me he used to be an alcoholic, and if it hadn't been for Paul Nieman . . .'

'Paul Nieman?'

'. . . I don't know what would have happened.' She exhaled. 'More recently, Jessica swore at me. She swore at me in a way she's never done before.' Linda inhaled and waited for some sort of reaction from Joe. 'But I suppose that's what you've been talking to her about. Is she ready to apologise?'

'She's –'

'Forget it, just forget it.' She hurled the pillows at the bed head. 'We've got Tudor mansions growing in the field behind our house – I had Daphne Nieman telling me I'm menopausal and that her marriage is on the rocks; I've had other people's mothers going on about depleted salmon stocks in the North Atlantic, like I'm meant to give a shit, and . . .'

Joe cut in. 'What the fuck are you talking about? Why does it always have to fucking be like this? I've had enough – I've had enough of it,' he shouted, throwing the empty vodka glass he was still holding across the room.

Linda stopped – suddenly – her mouth still open. 'Don't leave,' she said, without thinking.

'I can't do this any more, Linda.'

They stood there looking at each other, Linda trying to stop crying, and Joe trying to start.

'Please don't leave,' she said again.

'I'm not leaving,' he said quietly, disappearing into the en suite.

She stayed where she was, watching the door to the en suite close, then went over to the vanity unit and picked up the broken glass. Still on her knees, she listened for sounds from the bathroom, but there weren't any.

Joe put the loo seat down and sat on it, his elbows on his knees, staring at Linda's cork Hanson scales. He didn't care that he'd just broken a glass – he'd done it without thinking, in a moment of – what? Anger? Now the anger was gone; now he was sitting on the loo behind a locked door, staring at a pair of scales, feeling nothing. The only thing he was really aware of – and this was only a vague idea – was that he wanted Linda to stop, but stop what? If she'd asked him, he would have said, 'All of this.' But what did he mean by that? He didn't know – and the strange thing was, essentially he was happy with his life. He picked up the brochure on water features that he'd put in the basket by the loo earlier and started to flick through it, suddenly remembering the gazelle. He *did* remember the gazelle; he remembered working on it in the kitchen at Whateley Road before Linda got up. He made her the gazelle because she'd had a thing about them when they went to visit that cousin of his in South Africa, only he knew from her face – the morning he gave it to her – that she'd forgotten ever having a thing about gazelles. So – he thought, triumphantly – she'd stopped remembering before he ever had. They'd made love that morning – he was sure they had.

Staring at a cotton-wool bud with nail varnish on it that hadn't quite made it to the bin under the sink, he pulled violently away from the memory of Whateley Road, thinking instead of the underwear he'd bought Linda at Leroy's. Then he thought of the Christmas present he'd found at the back of the cupboard a month ago – *The Guide to Corporate Entertainment* – and felt sorry for himself. In fact, he didn't know which of them he felt more sorry for.

How long ago was it that he used to fumble with the keys at the front door because he couldn't get them into the lock quick enough?

There had been love once; so much love it had seemed limitless.

28 FEBRUARY 1984

8

Linda was cycling on the flat, waiting for the bike to tell her she'd done seven miles. 'There's no reason why Daphne should get more than a five per cent discount – don't let her talk you into anything else.'

'I won't,' Joe said, sitting on the side of the bed and staring at himself in the vanity-unit mirror as he did up his tie. 'I'm only going through the plans with her and trying to get an idea of what sort of surfaces she's thinking of for the units. We haven't got round to talking about price yet.'

'The Niemans can afford whatever the Niemans want to afford.' Linda broke off to breathe. 'What range did she choose?'

'The Chichester,' Joe said.

'The Chichester?'

'That's what Steve said.' Joe finished his tie and carried on sitting there.

'You should drive up to the Niemans'.'

'Linda – they only live two doors up – why would I want to drive?'

'Because this is business and parking outside the Niemans' will put you in the right frame of mind.'

Joe, who didn't have frames of mind, just nodded.

She got off the exercise bike and opened the bedroom blinds. 'And when you go in, don't put your briefcase on the floor so that you have to kneel down to get out the sample cards – put it straight on the dining table.' She thought about this as Joe nodded again and went downstairs without another word.

'Joe,' Linda said, walking onto the landing. 'Joe?' She waited until he appeared at the foot of the stairs. 'Just walk in and put your briefcase straight on the dining table. Don't forget.'

'I won't.'

She stood on the landing, looking through Jessica's bedroom window at the field behind the house, which was full of cranes and bulldozers whose droning was already part of the day's background noise. There were four Portakabins just the other side of the fence, beneath the tree, and the yellow Laing flag that had been flying at full mast since the day the Portakabins arrived could be seen from every window at the back of every house on the Palmers' side of the Close. The site manager, who she'd seen while out walking Ferdie the other day, said they were hoping to have the show home up within the next two months.

He'd stood in his site boots under the tree she wanted cut down, trampling snowdrops round the trunk as the rain started, light at first then getting heavier until it was running off his hard hat as they stood there talking and her eyes picked out Ferdie trying to squat. Then the site manager asked her if she wanted an umbrella and she stayed under the tree and watched as he made his way back to one of the Portakabins, disappearing inside. Meanwhile, Ferdie pushed out one turd after another until there was a small pile under the tree on the spot where the site manager had been standing. Pulling on his lead she dragged him towards the Portakabin.

'You're sure?' she called out at the sight of the large white umbrella.

'If there's one thing we've got an excess of, it's umbrellas,' he said, laughing. 'Keep it – if you don't want it, drop it back round when you're next out walking the dog. I'm here most days,' he added.

The white umbrella with Lone Star Investment Funds written across it was in the downstairs loo in the corner by the sink – Joe hadn't even noticed it yet.

She heard the front door slam. 'Joe?' There was no answer. 'Joe?' She went into the spare bedroom and watched through the window as he walked up the street to the Niemans'.

When she got to the Methodist Church the hall was locked, and twenty minutes later – when most of the aerobics class was standing outside and it was still locked – an elderly woman with a surgical dressing over her right eye emerged from the church and told them there wouldn't be any aerobics that morning.

'Nobody told us anything,' Linda said.

'Well, no . . . it's all been quite sudden.' The woman paused. 'There probably won't be a class next week either.'

Linda thought she recognised her – wasn't it Jessica's old Tawny Owl? Her hair had been badly permed then badly dyed auburn. It looked, in fact, like a more catastrophic version of Izzy's, who took the class, and for a moment Linda thought this might be Izzy's mother and that something awful had happened to Izzy. Then they'd have to stand outside the locked church hall when they were all cold and the wind was getting up, and pretend to care.

People started drifting back to their cars.

The woman's left eye was going red. 'It's the minister,'

she said at last, 'Minister Macaulay – he's gone.' She stood staring blankly at no one in particular.

In the car park, car engines were starting up and people were leaving. After a while, Linda was the only one left and she had to put her hand over her nose to block out the smell the wind brought round of meat frying in Mr Li's Chinese takeaway, whose ventilation shaft was on a wall by the side of the church.

'He's gone – he's just gone,' the woman said, wiping her nose with her hand. 'I'm meant to do the flowers this morning – for Sunday.'

Her grief was repetitive and Linda, who was cold now, said, 'But what about Izzy? Where's Izzy?'

'I don't know,' the woman said, 'that's what I'm trying to say – I don't know where either of them have gone.'

Linda, who had been rattling her car keys against the palm of her hand, suddenly held them still. 'What – Izzy and Minister Macaulay? You mean they've gone together? Eloped?'

'Eloped,' the woman said, nodding and starting to cry again, waiting for the slightest whiff of compassion from Linda. She would have done anything to cry on a stranger's shoulder right then and would have let Linda take her in her arms and hold her if grief had been something Linda believed in.

Linda took in the navy blue sweatshirt with prints of all the different nautical knots. 'Are you Izzy's mother?' she said after a while.

The woman stared blankly at her. 'Izzy's mother? Why would I be Izzy's mother? I'm Mrs Macaulay.'

'Mrs Macaulay?'

'Minister Macaulay's wife.'

Linda didn't say anything.

'A girl from an airline rang about a week ago to confirm

258

tickets to Delhi and I told her she'd made a mistake, even when she said the booking had been made by a Mr Macaulay.'

'Delhi? They've gone to Delhi?' Linda paused. 'Where's Delhi?'

'India,' Mrs Macaulay said, subsiding into another ecstasy of grief.

Linda could picture Izzy in somewhere like Miami, but India? Why India? Why Minister Macaulay? Then she tried picturing them on the plane together – an impenetrable aura of passion surrounding them.

'The girl who phoned was from Imperial Airlines – are they any good? I don't know anything about airlines – I've never flown before. John was always trying to get me on a plane, but I've got this fear of flying – I can't help it. I think it's unnatural, don't you?'

Linda stood staring at her through the fumes from Mr Li's extractor fan. Was she referring to infidelity or flight?

'I thought the girl on the phone must have made a mistake because things just carried on as normal. On the Tuesday of last week I went to hospital to have a cataract removed from my right eye and John came with me. He goes to his Early Music group Wednesdays and he went this Wednesday,' she said. 'I phoned Cyril who plays viola da gamba and he said John was definitely there.' She paused. 'He just never came home.'

Linda shivered.

'The only thing he had with him when he left the house at seven on Wednesday was his oboe. The next day,' she said, lowering her voice, 'I went through the wardrobe and his drawers. His socks, underpants and aftershave were still there. Everything he needs was still there,' she repeated, as if these were things she'd always believed he was unable to live without and whose continued presence seemed to

259

mystify her more than John Macaulay's absence. 'Could he really have gone out Wednesday evening, spent two hours rehearsing Handel then driven to Gatwick and flown to India – with nothing apart from his oboe? Do you know anyone who would do that?' she asked Linda hopefully.

'Well . . .' Linda pretended to think about it. 'No.'

'I tried phoning the girl back at Imperial Airlines and couldn't get hold of her, but I spoke to one of her colleagues and they said there's only one flight to Delhi a day. The flight they were booked on was a Thursday morning flight. Yesterday's flight,' she said, helplessness creeping back into her voice.

'They probably spent Wednesday night at one of the airport hotels,' Linda said, impatient to get back to Pollards Close and tell Dominique that there would be no more aerobics with Izzy because Izzy had eloped to India with Minister Macaulay. Then, seeing the woman put her hand over her mouth, she realised too late what she'd just said. 'Sorry – I'm sorry.'

'Oh God,' Mrs Macaulay said, 'oh, God.'

'Look,' Linda said, digging in her mind for the right cliché – one that would console and also enable her to extract herself.

'The new stained-glass window was only put in Wednesday. I had my cataract done on Tuesday and the altar window was put in Wednesday. It took John three years to raise the money for that window. I just don't understand how he could leave it like that.' She looked at Linda with her one good eye, expecting her to say something. 'Would you like to see the new glass?' she said, sniffing and leading Linda into the church in the same unconscious way she'd just led her through a thirty-year marriage that had culminated in adultery and elopement to India, to show her the new stained-glass window above the altar.

'Nice. It's nice,' Linda said.

'He was passionate about it – stained glass was a passion of his,' Mrs Macaulay said sharply. 'I just don't understand how he could leave it.' She sat down in one of the front pews. 'We've got the Guides and Brownies doing church parade on Sunday and they're sending another minister for that – but nobody's phoned me. The minister they're sending hasn't phoned me. People haven't been kind . . . people just haven't been kind,' she said to herself, her voice getting lower and lower.

Linda drifted to the back of the church.

Mrs Macaulay, sitting in the pew staring up at the stained glass her husband had designed himself, was trying to make some sort of connection between their marriage in Portsmouth, John's passion for stained glass, an aerobics teacher with bleached hair and a girl from Imperial Airlines who had phoned to confirm a reservation on yesterday's flight to Delhi. 'By the way,' she said suddenly, 'your little girl used to come to Brownies. I'll never forget how upset she was when she didn't get her First Aid badge. You look very similar,' she added, turning round, but Linda was gone.

12

Daphne answered the door with bare feet – Joe didn't know why this struck him particularly, but it did. Her toenails, which were painted burgundy, looked stark against the beige carpet in the hallway.

'Joe – come in,' she said. 'I was just on the phone.'

Inside the Niemans' house it was warm – almost too warm – and it smelt of oranges.

'Coffee?'

'If you're making some.'

Joe put his briefcase on the floor and knelt down, hauling out the sample cards for worktops and flooring. 'Is it okay if I lay these out here?' he said, standing up and putting the cards on the dining table.

'Go ahead.'

In her own house Daphne was much more reserved than when she was out in company, and it had the effect of making her seem much more capable of intimacy.

'You've been to the showroom?' Joe asked, watching her make the coffee.

'About a fortnight ago. You weren't there, but – what's his name?'

'Steve.'

'Steve – that's right. He took me around.' She brought the coffee over to the table, poured it then sat down, gently pulling a couple of worktop samples towards her. 'I also talked with your secretary on the telephone. I'm guessing she's worked with you for a while?'

'Maureen? Forever.'

Daphne nodded, smiling. 'I'm also guessing that when she first started working for you she seriously thought about falling in love with you.'

Joe laughed nervously and focused on the sample cards. 'Steve said you'd pretty much decided on the Chichester range of units?'

'Pretty much – as long as they come in white. I want white; all of this white,' she said, moving her arm across the Laing kitchen.

'And the flooring?'

Daphne nodded. 'And the flooring.' She turned over a sample card with a bright pink square of melamine on it. 'Has anyone ever asked you for this?' She looked up at him. 'Would you remember?'

'I'd remember – no, not yet.'

'Not yet – you sound hopeful.'

Joe shrugged. 'It takes all sorts to make the world go round.'

'Your mother used to say that?'

'She did.'

'It would be bad for business as well – if we were all the same.'

Joe looked down at the samples spread across the table.

Daphne sat back in her chair, taking sips of coffee. 'The bathroom needs doing as well – you don't do bathrooms, do you?'

Joe shook his head. 'I've drawn up three different sets of plans – based on the Chichester range.'

'Three different sets? For a kitchen two by three?' Daphne looked at him. 'That's impressive, Joe.'

He laid down the first set of plans.

'Have you thought about work surfaces?' he said, scanning them. 'We've got a new range of tiled surfaces – in white.'

'Tiles? Tiles would be a nightmare to clean – all that grouting.' She shook her head. 'Definitely no tiles – don't try and sell me tiles.' The phone started ringing. 'Will you excuse me?'

She disappeared upstairs and left Joe staring protectively at all the things that belonged to him on the Niemans' dining table. He picked up the block of tile samples and was about to put them on the dining chair next to him when he saw a copy of the magazine his mum had been reading the day he went over to see her before Christmas. Joe, his head stuck in *Hunks of Humankind*, failed to hear footsteps coming back downstairs.

'See anything you like?' Daphne said from the doorway.

'Sorry,' he said, putting it down.

'No – it's fine,' she smiled. '*Hunks* is a catalogue for an . . .'

'Escort agency, I know. It's okay.'

'You don't look like it's okay, and it's not an escort agency. They provide a much fuller service than that.'

Joe's hand went out for a biro lying on the table in front of him.

'Linda's lucky,' he heard Daphne saying. 'I mean – she's married to someone who likes women; not all women are. *Hunks* is an option for women who don't want to disrupt their daily lives – and most women don't. We just want to make them more bearable. We've got used to paying for so much – why not sex as well? It's cheaper than marriage counselling.'

Joe rolled the biro backwards and forwards across the table.

'Winke doesn't like women,' Daphne said. 'But you like women, don't you, Joe?'

Joe looked up at her, still standing in the doorway, and it struck him for the first time how sad her face was. 'I love women,' he said without thinking, wondering how he was going to make the leap from this back to the plans for Daphne's fitted kitchen.

8

Linda left the Methodist Church and Mrs Macaulay, jumping two sets of lights as she drove home, exhilarated at the thought of Macaulay and Izzy's elopement to India. She took the corner into Pollards Close at such a speed that her tyres left skid marks on the road outside the Youngs', whose house was the first in the Close. Then she saw Joe doing a U-turn and pulled up beside him, the Quantum Ford and white Toyota facing in opposite directions and blocking the road. They wound their windows down.

'It went fine,' Joe said. 'Daphne didn't ask for a discount.'

Linda stared across the passenger seat and through the open window at him, trying to work out why he was telling her about Daphne and discounts when so much had happened since then.

Joe looked down at the clock on his dashboard. 'Aren't you meant to be at aerobics still?'

'It was cancelled.'

'Was it?' he said, uninterested.

'You'll never guess why?'

'Why?'

'Minister Macaulay – the minister at the Methodist Church? He's run away – eloped – with Izzy.'

'Who's Izzy?' Joe said, confused.

'The aerobics teacher.'

'Where did they go?'

'India.'

Joe let out a short laugh, preoccupied.

The urgency with which Linda had driven home – Mrs Macaulay's story so tangible it was like having the minister and Izzy fucking on the back seat of her car as she jumped the lights – disappeared. At the sound of Joe's short laugh the desperation to tell everyone that a Methodist minister had eloped to India with an aerobics teacher left her – the idea of a place like India even existing seemed suddenly ridiculous.

Joe had no interest in the minister and Izzy; he'd just remembered what it was he needed to ask Linda. 'I meant to say this morning – Al rang yesterday – you remember Al?'

'Al?'

'National Auricula and Primula Society Al? He rang to say he's got some alpine auriculas for Mum's pot. Flame-coloured – that's how he described them.'

Linda didn't say anything; she couldn't get the picture of the post-coital lovers leaving on a plane for India out of her mind.

'I just wanted to check it with you,' she heard Joe saying.

'Check what?'

'That you don't mind if I go round to Al's after work to pick up the alpine auriculas? I could even take them straight over to Mum's tonight, I suppose.'

Linda woke up. 'Tonight? You're going down to Brighton tonight?'

'I could do – Al's at Partridge Green – that's nearly halfway there anyway.'

'But I thought we were keeping the urn.'

'Since when?'

'Don't you remember me saying how nice it would look planted with daffs outside the front door?'

'Well – I can get us another one.'

'But the urn's in the shed – you put the urn in the shed on Christmas Eve.'

Joe turned his engine off. 'It was in the shed. It's in my office now – over by the filing cabinet.'

Linda didn't know what to say; the thought of Audrey's urn leaving the shed without her knowledge or permission made her panic. It was unlike Joe. 'Why can't you take it Saturday?'

'I thought you wanted me to paint the garage door Saturday?'

He was right, she'd already planned his weekend. 'Well, in that case, maybe I'll go out tonight,' she said, meaning to threaten him.

'So it's okay if I go down to Brighton?'

'I could go to the cinema or something.'

'That's a good idea – you could take Jessica.'

Since when had she ever gone to the cinema – let alone with Jessica? She wouldn't go. They both knew she wouldn't go.

'Unless we all went,' Joe said, relenting.

'To the cinema?'

'No – to Brighton. I could drop you off at Belle's and Jess could come to Mum's with me and the alpine auriculas.'

'I don't want Jessica going to Cassidy Street with your dad there – I told you that.'

'Mum's been asking after Jess, Linda.'

'If she wants to see her that badly she'll have to come to see her here.'

'We never invite her and she doesn't drive anyway.'

'Well then she should do something about your dad.'

'That's not fair, Linda.' Joe turned the engine on again. 'I've got to go. I'll be back around nine – nine to nine thirty.'

Linda watched him go without responding to this. The white Toyota stayed parked in the middle of the Close with the engine running while she watched through the rearview mirror until Joe disappeared. Then she put the car into gear and parked on the drive.

Without going into the house, she crossed the road to No. 4. Brian Young, who was retired, was out in the road with a bucket and scrubbing brush, angrily trying to wash the skid marks she'd left earlier, outside No. 2, off the road's tarmac surface. Ignoring him, she jogged across the Saunders' front garden and rang the bell.

Dominique answered the door. 'Linda – aren't you meant to be at aerobics?'

'It was cancelled,' she said, waiting for Dominique to invite her in, but she didn't.

Dominique stood in the doorway staring at the broken branches of pampas grass behind Linda, preoccupied.

'I didn't see you there,' she said.

'No.'

She waited.

'So,' Dominique said at last, 'do you want to come in?'

'Just for a minute.'

Dominique stood in the doorway for a second longer then walked off down the hallway leaving Linda to shut the front door.

'Izzy wasn't there,' Linda said, following her into the kitchen. 'You'll never guess why.'

'Why?' Dominique said in exactly the same way Joe had. 'Tea? Coffee?'

'Coffee,' Linda said, pulling herself up onto one of the bar stools. What was wrong with everyone today? 'Instant's

269

fine,' she added as Dominique started to pour water into the filter machine.

'We don't have instant.'

'Okay – well,' Linda paused, waiting to retrieve her thread, when Valerie Kline walked into the kitchen in her peach and turquoise tracksuit.

'Do you want something to drink?' Dominique asked her.

'Sorry – I didn't realise you had someone here,' Linda said, shocked.

'There's coffee,' Dominique was saying to Valerie as she turned the filter machine on, 'or I can do tea.'

'Coffee's fine,' Valerie said from the kitchen doorway.

'What were you saying about Izzy?' Dominique said, turning to face Linda again.

'Why weren't you at aerobics?'

'Valerie's here.'

'But it's Friday – Friday's aerobics.'

'Brendan's in hospital,' Dominique said, 'and I'm trying to persuade Valerie to let me drive her to visit him.'

'I can get the bus,' Valerie said, her piebald tracksuit filling the Saunders' kitchen doorframe.

'You're not getting the bus,' Dominique insisted, 'I'm driving you.'

'I got the bus yesterday.'

'I didn't know Brendan was in hospital yesterday.'

'I'm getting the bus,' Valerie mumbled.

'You're not getting the bus – you've got verrucas; you can barely walk.'

Linda stared at Dominique; she'd never seen her like this before.

'Brendan was attacked in the lab at Ciba on Wednesday night,' Dominique said. 'Animal rights activists – that's right, isn't it?'

Valerie nodded.

'Izzy's gone,' Linda yelled suddenly.

Dominique stopped what she was doing and turned to face her. 'Gone? Gone where?'

'India – she's gone to India with Minister Macaulay from the church.'

Valerie lurched slowly into the kitchen. 'Poor Judith.'

'Who the hell is Judith?' Linda shouted.

'Judith Macaulay.'

'What – you know her?'

'India?' Dominique said, switching the coffee machine off.

'India, Dominique – they've gone to India.'

'But what will they do in India?' Dominique said after a while.

'Who cares.'

'I overheard her at class a couple of weeks ago saying she was getting interested in Yvengar yoga.' Dominique broke off. 'The coffee's ready.'

'They've gone,' Linda said again, frustrated by the fact that Dominique just didn't seem to be getting the point – she was more interested in Valerie Kline than she was in getting the point about Izzy and Minister Macaulay. 'They just left. I mean – they did it – they just left.'

Dominique was staring, preoccupied, at the light on the base of the filter machine.

'Left what?'

'This,' Linda screamed.

The three women were silent.

'I should go,' Valerie said, 'I want to be at the hospital by twelve thirty.'

'But we haven't had coffee yet – the coffee's ready. We'll drink this then I'll drive you to the hospital.'

'I've got to go,' Valerie said, walking out of the kitchen.

Linda sat on the bar stool and watched Dominique follow

her out then turned her attention to the coffee machine that was blinking and telling her it was ready. Why did nobody give a fuck about the fact that a Methodist minister had just walked out on his wife at the age of fifty-whatever and left for India with an aerobics teacher? They'd gone to India, where they'd never grow old but fuck each other to death instead – and nobody was interested.

A phone started ringing somewhere in the silent house.

Linda listened to it for a few seconds, still breathing heavily, then went to the front door and saw Valerie Kline standing on the pavement outside No. 4 and Dominique halfway up the garden.

'Shall I get that?' she called out. Dominique turned and stared at her like she'd never seen her before. 'The telephone – it's ringing.'

'It's in the study,' Dominique said.

Linda went back indoors, but by the time she got to the study, the caller – whoever it was – had rung off. She stood in the middle of the room, taking in the wall-to-wall bookcases. She'd never seen so many books before – when did Mick and Dominique get the time to read all these?

Then she moved over to the desk, and there on top of a brochure for Beaufort Viticulture was the gazelle – her gazelle; the gazelle Joe made her. She sat down in the chair and picked it up, suddenly exhausted. She was still holding it when Dominique walked in.

4

Dominique followed Valerie up the hallway.

'I'm fine – I can see myself out.'

'Let me drive you,' Dominique said. They were in the front garden now. 'Just let me drive you.'

Valerie stopped at the top of the garden and looked back at Dominique standing by the front door, smiling wildly. 'Why?' she said.

'Why what?'

'Why do you want to come to the hospital?'

'To see Brendan.'

'You don't know Brendan. You don't know anything about Brendan.'

Then Linda Palmer appeared in the doorway. 'Shall I get that?' she called out.

Dominique turned slowly round.

'The telephone – it's ringing.'

'It's in the study,' Dominique said.

Linda disappeared back indoors and Dominique started walking up the garden towards Valerie. 'You can tell me.'

'Tell you what?'

'About Brendan.'

'There's nothing to tell about Brendan.'

'Tell me about Brendan,' Dominique was shouting now. 'Just tell me about Brendan.'

'Mind your own bloody business,' Valerie snapped, slipping off the kerb in her sandals and onto the road. Not a day had gone by since Christmas Eve when Dominique Saunders hadn't knocked on her door. In the past few months she'd missed countless episodes of series she'd been following for years and she found Dominique's inexplicable interest in her and Brendan exhausting.

Dominique stood on the manhole cover in the lawn and watched Valerie Kline disappear into her house. Then she turned round to go back indoors, remembering that Linda was still inside, and saw Mr Young from next door standing in the middle of the road next to a bucket, staring at her.

'Who was it?' she said, walking into the study and seeing Linda sitting at the desk with the gazelle in her hand.

'They rang off.'

Dominique was suddenly furious with Linda for turning up when she did to tell her some irrelevant piece of news about somebody eloping to India. Valerie Kline was ready to be driven to the hospital. If it hadn't been for Linda, she and Valerie would be in the car on their way to see Brendan. This thought consumed her and left her with no intention of trying to explain Mick's theft to Linda right then. 'Mick bought it in Kenya,' she said. 'The wooden deer – he bought it when he was in Kenya.'

'It's a gazelle,' Linda said.

'I wouldn't know,' Dominique shrugged. 'It's one of Mick's knick-knacks.' Then, because she found lying easy and needed to punish Linda for distracting her from Valerie Kline, 'He got it at one of those roadside stalls where you pull over, get out of the car and then realise it's all a load of

274

junk but end up buying something anyway.' Dominique paused, but there was something in the way Linda was holding the gazelle that filled her with so much rage, she added, 'I keep meaning to throw it away, but somehow it always escapes – next time.'

'It's my gazelle.'

Dominique didn't say anything.

'It's my gazelle,' Linda said again.

'Linda –' Dominique tried to laugh. 'Mick picked it up in Kenya.'

'Joe carved this for me. I thought it was lost.'

'Linda –'

Linda didn't say anything because she knew that they both knew it was her gazelle.

Then the phone started ringing again and Dominique went to answer it. 'Hello?'

8

Linda left the Saunders' house clutching the gazelle. Joe
and Dominique Saunders – why hadn't she realised? The
way Joe had been behaving lately suddenly made sense.
The way he pretended not to remember the gazelle when
they'd had that row on Christmas Eve. She ran up the
garden and across the road. But why this? Why had Joe
given Dominique the gazelle? When she got indoors she
made straight for the phone and dialled the number for
Quantum Kitchens.

'Maureen – is Joe on the line?'

'Linda – you all right?'

'Joe – is Joe on the line?'

'I don't think so – he's just this minute walked in. Wait
– it's flashing at me.'

'What's flashing?'

'The button – Joe's button.' Maureen broke off. 'You sure
you're all right?'

'I'm fine – is Joe on the line?'

'Well, the button's flashing – d'you want me to go in?
Has something happened?'

'Nothing's happened.' Linda slammed the phone down.

Joe was on the line to Dominique. Dominique was taking a call from Joe; it was Joe who'd been trying to call when Linda didn't pick up in time. Had they met that morning – thinking they had time between Joe's meeting with Daphne Nieman and the end of aerobics class? Images of Izzy and the Reverend Macaulay got confused with images of Dominique and Joe in the Saunders' safari set of a bedroom. Had Joe even gone to Daphne's?

She was looking for the Niemans' number in the address book when the phone started ringing and she nearly pulled it off the wall. 'Yes?'

'It's me – Maureen. D'you want me to get him to ring you when he comes off?'

Joe got to Quantum and went straight into his office, putting the bag of donuts he'd bought on the desk and picking up the phone. He dialled the Cassidy Street number so that he could tell Audrey he was dropping by later with the alpine auriculas, only he hadn't anticipated Derek answering and nearly hung up. When was the last time they'd spoken? They'd had a row about a year ago.

'Hi, Dad.'

'Who's that?'

'It's me – Joe.'

Silence.

'I can't talk now.'

'That's fine,' Joe said quickly.

'I'm taking the windmills over to the garden centre. I'm busy loading up the car – I can't talk now.'

'That's fine,' Joe said again.

'Did you want to talk to Mum?'

'If she's there.'

'She isn't – she went out. There's no one here at the moment.' He paused. 'Don't forget to wrap up warm. I've just been out to the car and it's colder than it looks out there – so you wrap up.'

'Okay. I will do.'

Derek didn't say anything after this, but Joe could hear him rasping on the other end of the phone. The rasping carried on for another minute then the line went dead.

He took one of the donuts out of the bag and ate it while watching through the window as the couple Steve had been showing round got back into their car. Then Maureen walked into his office without knocking.

'Linda just rang.'

'Linda?'

'Everything all right?' Maureen said.

Without answering, Joe turned the bag of donuts round to face her.

Maureen took one and immediately started eating it.

'Does she want me to call her back?'

'I don't know – she didn't say.' She stood there wiping the sugar away from her mouth. 'Thanks for the donut,' she said, then left the office.

Joe sat swinging from side to side in his chair, finishing his donut and not really thinking of anything, then left his office and went into the showroom to find Steve, who was rearranging the natural stone floor samples. 'I went to see Mrs Nieman.'

'Mrs Nieman?' Steve said.

'Pollards Close, Mrs Nieman,' Joe said. 'I saw her this morning – she's definitely going for the Chichester range and she said she wants white.'

'Joe,' Maureen yelled, her mouth full of donut, 'Joe, it's that woman again.'

'What woman?'

'The one who rang this morning and wouldn't leave her name.'

'So, who is she?'

'You want me to ask?'

'It doesn't matter – put her through.' He went back into his office.

'Hello – Quantum Kitchens?'

'Hello Quantum Kitchens.'

'Who is this?'

There was a pause. 'It's Lenny Pope – Belle's hairdresser, Lenny?'

'Lenny. Right. Lenny.' Joe sat up and leant forward over his desk, picking up a biro and starting to press the tip down onto the fake leather surface, forming a random chain of dots. 'Maureen said you phoned this morning, but wouldn't leave a message.'

'Maureen?'

'Our secretary.'

'You don't mind me calling?'

'No.'

'You're not busy?'

'I'm busy, but it's fine. It's fine. How did you get the number?'

'Yellow Pages.'

He waited.

'Listen – I was phoning for some advice. You're sure you're not too busy for this?'

'It's fine – honestly, it's fine.'

'I'm about to take out a lease on some premises and I wanted your advice. I don't know anyone else who's been down this road – and you said I could ring, so I'm ringing.'

Joe carried on pressing his biro into the desk top, turning the random dots into a tree. 'Where are the premises?'

'Baxter Street.'

'Down near the bus station?'

'That's right – the lease includes shop premises and a flat above.'

'D'you need the flat above?'

Lenny paused. 'Yes.'

There was a brief silence.

'I've got to let the agent know by next Wednesday.'

'Next Wednesday? So . . .'

'What?'

'D'you want me to come down?'

'If you've got time, I mean, you don't have to. It was just an idea.'

'I'm thinking. I've got some plants I was going to drop off at Mum's – I'm going down to Brighton tonight anyway. I could come and see the premises then.'

'Tonight? Is that okay?'

'Have you got keys?'

'I can pick up a set from the agent – are you sure?'

'Course I'm sure.' He was sure; he hadn't been, but now he was. 'Is around seven too late?'

'Seven's good. D'you want to meet me there?'

'Give me the address again.'

'Sixteen Baxter Street – it's the only empty shop down there.' She paused. 'That's sixteen Baxter Street.'

Joe put the phone down, trying to remember what time he told Linda he'd be home.

4

Dominique picked up the phone as Linda stood up, still clutching the gazelle, suddenly relieved that it was going. She waited until she heard the front door slam then turned back to the phone. 'Hello?'

'It's me – Monica.'

'Where are you?' This was always her first question whenever she heard Monica's voice.

'Here – Littlehaven.' She paused.

'I didn't know you were in the country.'

'No – look, you couldn't pick me up, could you?'

'What's that?'

'I said I was wondering if you could come and pick me up?'

'What – now?'

'Is that okay?'

'Where are you – Ciba?'

'I'm at the hospital.'

'The hospital?'

'I've been to see Brendan – Brendan Kline?'

'You flew from Montréal to see Brendan Kline?'

'A friend at Ciba phoned to tell me about the break-in.'

'You flew from Montréal just to see Brendan Kline?'

'Yes.'

Neither of them said anything.

Dominique stood holding the phone. 'Why?' she said at last. 'You have to tell me why.'

'I'll tell you over lunch – where do you want to go?'

'I don't know.'

'There must be somewhere.'

'There's a place in the precinct.'

'I'll have a think. When should I expect you – in fifteen minutes? I'll be waiting outside the hospital.'

The phone went dead.

Dominique half thought of staying at home and leaving Monica waiting outside the hospital, because now, after all these years, Monica was about to start talking and, despite her relentless pursuit of Valerie Kline over the past two months, Dominique wasn't sure she wanted to hear. Indecision kept her rooted to the study floor staring through the window at the garden fence. Then she changed her mind again and became suddenly terrified of arriving at the hospital and Monica not being there; of Monica and Brendan Kline disappearing suddenly without a trace so that she'd never hear the truth.

She ran upstairs into Stephanie's room and packed her ballet things while trying to ignore the scuffling sounds the hamster was making in the corner. Stephanie had ballet straight after school on Fridays and she might not have time to pick the things up later. She carried the pink case down-stairs, her hands sticky from the resin on the soles of the ballet shoes.

She left the house and got into the car just as it started to rain. The rain slowed the traffic down and it took her over twenty minutes to get to the hospital, but Monica was there waiting outside like she said she would be, under-neath a Macmillan Cancer Relief umbrella.

Dominique pulled up right in front of her in an Ambulance Only bay and wound the window down, keeping the engine running.

Monica stayed on the pavement staring blankly into the car, and it took her at least ten seconds to recognise that it was her daughter in the driver's seat staring back at her. She put the umbrella down and automatically got into the back of the car as if it was a taxi.

'Gatwick Manor,' she said to the face in the rear-view mirror.

Dominique turned round to look at her. 'Gatwick Manor?'

'I booked us a table there. I'm sorry, Dominique, but I really couldn't stand the idea of prawn cocktail in a precinct café. We'd be bothered by young girls in strange uniforms walking around with wet J-cloths looking for surfaces to wipe – I just know we would.'

Dominique, who had spent most of the twenty-minute drive imagining the reunion with Brendan and how it would take place round his bed on the ward, was suddenly no longer able to imagine anything with Monica in the back of the car.

'Aren't we going up?'

'Up where?' Monica asked, irritation biting at her words.

'Onto the ward – to see Brendan.'

'I've seen Brendan – Brendan's fine.'

'But I haven't.'

Monica pushed her wet umbrella along the floor. 'Why would Brendan want to see you? Come on – drive. The table's booked. How long do you have?'

'For what?'

'Lunch.'

'I have to pick Stephanie up from school at three thirty,' Dominique said, thinking she should warn Monica in advance that time – for her – wasn't limitless and that even

283

a reunion she'd waited twenty years for wasn't immune from routine. At some point routine always interfered, driving away anything greater than itself that it wasn't able to accommodate or absorb, and it was more difficult for women, being guardians of the quotidian, to accommodate the extraordinary – especially when accommodating it meant that daily lives had to carry on being the same afterwards when actual lives would never be the same again. There wasn't any guarantee, either, that after opening a rift in the fabric of daily life, you'd ever be able to close it again. Then what? All she knew was that whatever happened next, she had to be at the school gates by three thirty so that Stephanie could be taken to ballet – because it was a Friday like any other Friday.

'Can't someone else pick her up?' Monica was saying. The idea of Dominique having other commitments right then irritated her. 'What about Mick?'

Dominique shook her head. 'Mick's on a course.'

Monica wasn't interested in Mick's course. 'Well it's only twelve thirty now. We've got plenty of time.'

'As long as I'm back for three thirty,' Dominique said again, and saying it made her feel worthy; as if she was standing on superior moral ground to Monica.

'This country's ridiculous,' Monica said as they pulled away, passing a sign that had opening times on it for the Accident and Emergency unit. 'An Accident and Emergency unit that only works nine to five? How exactly are you meant to time an act of fate so that it happens during working hours? It's ridiculous – the whole system's ridiculous. I had to fill up Brendan's water jug when I got there this morning and every time you ask anybody a simple question – like why weren't the water jugs refilled or why hasn't the saline solution been replaced – they look at you as if you, personally, are preventing them from saving the lives of those who

284

are dying elsewhere in the hospital. How can they possibly make you feel guilty simply for asking a question?'

Dominique watched Monica in the mirror as she sat looking out the window, and it struck her suddenly that Monica was nervous, that her attack on the NHS was nothing more than an attack of nerves. As they drove out of Littlehaven towards the bypass, Dominique was trying to work out if she'd ever seen Monica nervous before. She hadn't – this was the first time.

'Can't Brendan go privately?'

'He doesn't believe in that.'

Dominique didn't say anything. If Monica knew what Brendan did and didn't believe in then she knew Brendan Kline well.

Their eyes met in the rear-view mirror and Monica was the first to look away.

The rain was getting worse and even with the windscreen wipers on full it was only just possible to see the road ahead. The last time she drove along this road was before Christmas on her way to pick up Mick from the airport and she thought it had looked beautiful. Today it wasn't beautiful, it was brown and grey and felt small and relentless. Suddenly Mick's suggestion of New Zealand didn't seem so bad.

The car carried on through heavy rain, both women silent under the climactic drumming on the roof that nothing could break the rhythm of. In order to stay calm Dominique drove faster and faster until they were virtually aquaplaning along the waterlogged road.

By the time they turned into Gatwick Manor the day had become so dark with rain that the lights lining the drive had been turned on. Dominique parked where she'd parked with Mick when he'd taken her to lunch, only now the topiary Father Christmas had gone. She turned the engine off and they sat there locked into the rhythm of the rain on the car roof until, suddenly desperate to get out, they made a move for the doors at the same time.

Dominique pushed herself quickly out of the car and slammed the door shut then realised that the child locks were still on in the back.

She stared at Monica through the rain, trapped in the back of the car, banging on the window, and wondered what it would be like to walk away from her; to carry on walking all the way to the airport where she could sit and watch the planes. Then she remembered Stephanie, who needed picking up from school; who had a ballet lesson and who then had to be driven home from ballet, fed, watered and changed ready for the junior swimming competition at The Haven later that evening – where they were meeting Delta. Daily life made abandoning Monica and walking to the airport to watch the planes impossible.

'Dominique! Dominique – can you just open the bloody door,' Monica yelled.

If you break that you can pay for it, you bitch, Dominique thought, watching her mother inside the car, thumping at the window.

She opened the driver's door and released the child lock.

'For Christ's sake, Dominique,' Monica said as the door swung open and she hauled herself and her umbrella out of the car. She put it up and went running into the hotel.

Dominique was left standing in the rain looking at the car and the two open doors. She stood there for so long that when she finally went inside, the receptionist – the same one who'd been on the day she and Mick were last there – told her there were towels in the lobby restroom. Seeing Monica's wet Cancer Relief umbrella in the stand, she ignored the receptionist and automatically walked through to the restaurant, which was much busier than it

286

had been the last time: more waiters, more diners, more food. Monica was in there somewhere as well.

'Your colleague is on that table there,' a waiter said, then disappeared.

Dominique saw a hand raised, waving at her. Monica was sitting at a table in the centre of the room.

'Isn't there somewhere more private?' Dominique said, sitting down and seeing that there wasn't, but somehow expecting Monica to fix it.

'They're fully booked,' Monica said. 'A conference for prosthetic limb manufacturers and distributors.' She leant forwards. 'You wouldn't think to look at them that these people were the distributors of prosthetic limbs, would you? Do you think any of them have direct experience of their product?'

Dominique stared at her. This was Monica in public; the Monica who belonged to other people – people she worked with; people at conferences – all the different men who'd been part of her life over the years. This was everyone else's Monica – not the Monica she used to sit alone in the flat in Barnes waiting for.

A waiter came over and put a glass of champagne in front of Monica.

'You're drinking champagne?' Dominique asked her.

'Another glass,' Monica said, turning to the waiter.

'Not for me.'

'Another glass,' Monica insisted.

'A mineral water,' Dominique said to the waiter. Then to Monica, 'I've got to get Stephanie at three thirty.' She paused – 'Remember?' – then lit a cigarette.

'Do you have to?'

'I have to. She has ballet straight after school then we're going home and doing a quick turnaround before going back out to The Haven for the junior swimming competition.

Stephanie's competing in the twenty-five metres front crawl.'
She sat smoking, watching Monica drink her champagne
and read the menu. 'I'm busy,' she added.

'There's no fish,' Monica was saying to herself. 'How
strange.'

It occurred to Dominique, watching her, that she was
happy – grouchy because of the jetlag, but happy. The overlarge umbrella, the rain and the car journey had temporarily
obscured this from her but now she turned her full attention to the fact that Monica was happy.

The waiter reappeared with Dominique's mineral water
and Monica's second glass of champagne, and took their
order. While they waited for their starters at least six people
approached their table, taking them for conference delegates.

'Your face,' Dominique said when they had their table to
themselves again.

'What about my face?' Monica finished the first champagne and sat holding the empty glass, twisting it in her
fingers. 'I had surgery. I flew down to Caracas and had cut-
price surgery done to my eyes and my chin.'

'You had plastic surgery?' Dominique stared at her,
wondering whether she was telling the truth or laughing
at her, or telling the truth and laughing at her. 'I don't
believe it.'

'I'm getting vain in my old age.'

'I can't believe you flew down to Caracas and had plastic
surgery.'

A basket of bread arrived and Monica started to make
her way through this and the second glass of champagne.
'I'm thinking of going back – having something done to my
thighs and stomach.'

Dominique lit her second cigarette.

'The surgeon was Iranian, I think.'

Their starters arrived.

288

'Did you really go to Caracas?'

'Of course I did – I can give you the Iranian's contact details if you want. God, what is that you're eating?'

'Soup – I ordered soup.'

'I've never understood how people can order soup in a restaurant.'

Dominique tried to enjoy the rest of it but in the end put the spoon down and gave up. No longer preoccupied by trying to eat her soup, she couldn't take her eyes off Monica's face as she made her way through a salad, thinking that this was the woman who had thrown Dominique's make-up bag away when she was fifteen, telling her she had to concentrate less on her face and more on her work. Now, twenty-six years later, she was telling her she'd lain in a room somewhere in Caracas and allowed a stranger to make incisions on her face because she'd grown vain in her old age. How old was she anyway? Dominique didn't know. 'When did you have it done?'

'January,' Monica said, wiping her mouth.

'Was it okay to make a long-haul flight so soon?'

Monica shrugged. 'Something's happened – quite recently – that's made me want to buy back a bit of time. Not much – I'd settle for as little as five years.' She paused. 'Think how much living can be done in five years.'

Dominique looked across the restaurant, which was beginning to empty. Outside it was still raining. She imagined the Iranian working with his scalpel, trying to retrieve the five years Monica had asked for from fatty tissue. Maybe she'd asked him to cut away remorse as well because surely you only got to be as happy as Monica was at her age if you had no remorse.

'I just wanted to buy myself some time,' Monica said again, only this time it was said with intent, and Dominique couldn't avoid her gaze.

She sat there thinking, Now we're coming to it – trying not to breathe in the smell of beef and boiled carrots she knew she wouldn't be able to eat from the plate the waiter had just put under her nose.

Looking up, she saw that Monica was about to speak and suddenly couldn't bear the thought of hearing what it was she had to say. She stared across the restaurant at the table in the window that she and Mick had sat at, and it was as if they were still sitting there.

'Dominique . . .'

'Mick's stopped flying,' she said loudly in order to stop Monica saying whatever it was she was about to say. 'His last flight – to Florida – was just before Christmas.'

'His last flight? You didn't say anything – I knew Laker was in trouble, but Mick . . . why didn't you say anything at Christmas?'

'I don't know – he'd only just found out.'

'Did Laker make him redundant?'

Dominique nodded.

'Is the package good?'

'The package? I don't know – I suppose so. Mick's got ideas . . .'

'He'll fly with another airline?'

'I don't think so.'

'I can't believe he won't fly again.'

'He's talking about New Zealand.'

'New Zealand? New Zealand's a long way away.'

'From where?'

They stared blankly at each other.

After a while, Monica said, 'How is Mick? Is he coping with all this?'

'Mick doesn't cope with things, he just is – I mean he doesn't talk about it. If he wanted to carry on flying, he would, so I suppose he doesn't . . .' Dominique shrugged.

'He says he wants a vineyard and that he's thinking about New Zealand – that's all he's really said.'

They looked down at their plates and slowly picked up their cutlery.

A woman in a beige suit with beige hair walked into the restaurant and announced that the afternoon seminar for the prosthetic-limb conference was starting in ten minutes. The room started to empty until Monica and Dominique were the only ones left and the woman in beige came over to them and wanted to know why they were still on their main course. Monica put her fork down and told her they weren't conference delegates and went on to say that she wasn't sure how she felt about being mistaken for one.

Then she and Dominique looked at each other and laughed.

Once the woman had moved away, still not entirely convinced, Monica said, 'I can see you all in New Zealand.'

Dominique didn't know whether Monica meant it or whether she was just being generous about Mick's redundancy. She didn't know why they were talking about New Zealand when Mick had never mentioned it again since the night of the Palmers' dinner party. She just wasn't ready to hear what Monica had to say, and she'd never realised before how much lying really was a veritable alternative to telling the truth, and how much more seriously Monica took her when she was lying. It almost felt as if Monica was treating her like an adult.

'Mick's got shares in a vineyard in France through a company called Beaufort Viticulture – we're thinking of going over to spend a month there this summer. Maybe we'll do a reconnaissance trip to New Zealand over Christmas.'

Monica nodded and checked her watch. 'Listen – Dominique.'

'Aren't you jetlagged?' Dominique said desperately, still not ready to hear Monica out.

'Not yet. I think people make too much of a thing out of jetlag – anticipating it before they've made the journey. Dominique . . .'

Apart from running out of the restaurant, Dominique didn't know what else to do. They'd been through prosthetic limbs, the menu, Mick's redundancy, New Zealand and – briefly – jetlag. She had no other deterrents to hand. Out of the corner of her eye she was sure she recognised the Argentinian waiter who had served her and Mick that day, but she couldn't remember his name, and what could he do anyway – save her? She wasn't even sure what it was she wanted him to save her from.

'Dominique – I've got something I really do need to tell you before I fly back.'

'You're flying back?'

'In two days' time. There are some things I need to sort out here. Slimshake, who use our Blue Dye No. 1 in one of their diet shakes, are about to issue a product recall – then I'm flying back.'

'To Canada?'

'Where else would I be flying back to?' Monica said. Then, looking at Dominique, she said, 'I'm in love.'

She stared at her daughter for a long time after she said it then sat back in her chair, as a waiter – not the one they'd had before but a different one – asked them if they wanted dessert.

'I'll take a look at the menu,' Monica said. 'Dominique? What are you having?'

'What am I having?'

'That's what I said – what are you having?' Monica said again.

They scanned the menu in silence, Dominique unable to

292

make any sense of it no matter how many times she read it – including the two times she read it upside down. She looked up at Monica, who read out, 'Pineapple cheesecake – what do you think that will be like? I don't think I've ever had pineapple cheesecake. I'm not sure – I think I'm going off the idea and I really don't think I could face fruit crumble.'

'Are you seriously contemplating what to eat?'

'Of course.' She paused. 'I think I'll just have coffee. Are you having anything? Are you having anything else to eat, Dominique, or do you just want coffee? Two coffees,' she said to the waiter when Dominique didn't say anything. 'And I'll have a brandy as well.'

They waited in silence for the two coffees and brandy and it was the only silence between them that Dominique had ever been in control of.

Once the drinks were on the table, she looked across at Monica and said, 'Is that what you had to tell me? Is that why we had lunch?' She was shaking her head. 'I can't believe this – I can't believe I'm sitting here listening to this. When you rang this morning – when you were standing waiting for me outside the hospital in the rain – when we drove here – is this what you wanted to tell me? Is this all you wanted to tell me? You phoned me up this morning and we drove here so that you could tell me you're in love and now you sit there drinking your coffee expecting me to give a fuck about it – expecting me to give a fuck about any of it.'

'I thought – well, I thought you might have realised.'

'How could I possibly have realised?'

'The way you were talking on the phone this morning.'

'About what?'

'About Brendan – Brendan Kline. I'm in love with Brendan Kline, Dominique. It's Brendan I keep making the

293

flights between Montréal and Gatwick for. Why do you think I was on the plane last night as soon as I found out what happened at Ciba? Why do you think I've spent the morning in hospital with him? Why do you think we're waiting for the doctors to give him the all clear before he flies out to Montréal to join me?' Monica put her coffee down. 'I thought you might have guessed.'

'But I saw you together, and . . .'

'You've seen us together?'

'Christmas Eve. I was in the precinct on Christmas Eve and I looked through the window of Fontana's and I saw you walking with Brendan Kline,' Dominique said, starting to cry. 'You had all this shopping, both of you; you were carrying this shopping and laughing together and I watched you until you went through to the car park. You were out shopping together,' Dominique broke off. 'I thought . . . it just suddenly all made sense.'

'What made sense?'

'I thought . . .'

'What did you think?' Monica said, losing patience.

'I thought you were related. I saw you together and I thought he might be your grandson.'

'You think Brendan Kline's my grandson?' Monica cut in. 'What are you talking about?'

'You're twice his age.'

'Yes, I'm twice his age, and no, he doesn't love me – not in the way I love him. Is there anything else you need to know?'

'I don't want to know anything. This isn't about you – I'm not talking about you. I'm talking about spending two weeks in hospital after a Caesarean section – on a postnatal ward without a baby. Have you got any idea what that's like? You never came to see me – not once.'

'Didn't I? Delta wasn't delivered by Caesarean, was she?'

'I'm not talking about Delta – or Stephanie. I'm talking about the first baby. You let me go in that ambulance alone and I saw the door to the flat shut before they even got round to closing the ambulance doors.'

Monica was looking at her, taking sips now from her brandy. 'Do you still think about that?' she said after a while.

'Every day. I think about it every day.'

'It seems ages ago,' she said, staring at her daughter.

Dominique stood up, knocking the table and spilling her coffee, which hadn't been touched.

'Sit down,' Monica said sharply.

In the background they heard the waiters making a joke among themselves and laughing.

Realising that Dominique wasn't going to sit down, she said, 'You've got Mick now – and Delta and Stephanie. You've got a wonderful family, Dominique.'

'Why are you telling me this?'

'Both the girls – they're wonderful.'

'Why are you telling me this now?'

'Because you've got two wonderful daughters.'

'But I don't love them,' Dominique sobbed. 'I don't love Mick. I want to, but I can't – I don't know how to.'

The waiters were still laughing and outside it was still raining. The woman in beige walked into the restaurant again looking for someone, then walked out. 'You might have a form of autism,' Monica said after a while. 'I often thought that when you were a child. There were a few things you were obsessed with and other than those you didn't really seem to care about anything else. There was that cupboard you used to sit in most evenings and week-ends as well – it was almost impossible to get you out. Then there was the difficulty in relating to other people – espe-cially me.' Monica tried to suppress a yawn. 'I suppose I should have taken you to see someone, but there was forever

295

something going on at work, especially then. Wasn't that when I was trying to get that triphenylmethane blue dye through regulations – Blue Dye No. 1, that was it; the one we're having all the trouble with again now – and at home I was on my own. I was always so tired, Dominique. I don't remember ever not being tired, and the tiredness was . . . debilitating. But what you're describing,' she said, yawning, 'does sound like a form of autism – has Mick ever commented on it? I thought I might be autistic myself, but then . . . I've been alone my entire life. This is the first real thing that's ever happened to me – more real than my work even, and I was never expecting it. I never expected this.'

'What about me?'

'This is different.'

Dominique looked away. 'Mick loves me,' she said slowly, suddenly feeling as though she was talking to someone much younger who had no means of understanding her and it was making what she said sound trivial. 'He knows me – and he knows that for the past twenty years of marriage I've been trying to love him back, but I'm tired. I'm tired of this; it's been going on for twenty years now and I just want it to stop.'

'You should see someone,' Monica said again, beginning to look round her to make sure that – apart from waiters – they had the restaurant to themselves still.

'You did this to me,' Dominique yelled at her. 'You did this to me when you put me in the ambulance by myself at three o'clock in the morning – I was sixteen years old.'

Monica coughed. She started coughing then she couldn't stop.

'For fuck's sake, Monica – you never even asked me who the father was.'

'You never asked me who yours was,' Monica retorted. She finished her brandy, looking around for a waiter, suddenly angry. 'I tried to stay on top of things, but I didn't

296

know what was going on with you. You weren't the easiest of children, Dominique.'

'Do you want to know?' Dominique asked.

'Not really. Where have all the waiters gone?'

'You know who it was, don't you? You knew as soon as I told you I was pregnant. Daniel – gourmet Daniel. The last night of the gourmet trip – in Lyon. You went out on your own to meet somebody you'd done some work with and left me in the hotel alone with Daniel. Daniel – whose appetite clearly extended beyond his palate. Adults should learn how to be alone – children have to.'

'Dominique!'

'Did you see it coming? Did you ever think that there might have been something you could have said or done to warn me? I would never have expected you to protect me, but you could have warned me.' She broke off. 'How long did it take you to work out what had happened? Maybe you realised that night when you got back to the hotel. I remember leaving pretty quickly the next morning.'

'I don't remember.'

'And we certainly never saw Daniel in Barnes again.'

'I don't remember.'

'You have to remember Lyon,' Dominique yelled.

Monica bent down and picked up her handbag as the waiter who served them first put the bill down on the table.

'I don't even know if it was a boy or a girl – nobody ever told me.'

'What makes you think I do?'

'You sorted out the adoption.'

'Of course I did – you were only sixteen.'

'You were only sixteen when you had me,' Dominique said, watching her.

'And you've got no idea what I was trying to save you from.'

297

'Save me from? You regretted me?'

'Of course I regretted you.' Monica looked up at her. 'What? What is it?'

'There has to be something more – you can't leave it at that.'

'You want more?'

'Of course I want more – I've always wanted more. There was never enough of anything.'

Monica stood up. 'I wish you'd never been born.'

Dominique stood there staring at her mother for several seconds more then ran out of the restaurant, her face wet with grief, the same grief that was hauling her shoulders up and down and making it difficult for her to fit the key into the car's ignition.

She got to Springfield Park School five minutes early and was somehow able to stand under Sandra Nassam's umbrella and listen to her talking about the Summer Fete while she waited for Stephanie.

Monica watched Dominique run from the restaurant and made no move to follow her. Then she sat back down, looking at the door her daughter had run through, and signalled the waiter over. 'Excuse me,' she said, waving the bill and yawning. 'Is service included?'

8

Linda put the phone down on Maureen and stood watching
Ferdie, who was out in the back garden, looking up every
now and then to stare at her face in the kitchen window
then going back to nosing along the line of shrubs. He was
pining for Belle – he'd been pining for her ever since she
left on 27 December – and Linda was half thinking of giving
him to her because it was no fun living with a dog who
spent most days wishing you were someone else. She
watched him turn round and check the kitchen window
again, then, aware that she was hungry, she overrode her
Slimshake regime, went to the freezer and picked out a
pack of twelve fish fingers. There were eight left. She put
them in the toaster and ate them all then went upstairs
to change. She needed to change before driving to Quantum
Kitchens to see Joe and tell him that she knew. That she'd
found the gazelle he made her at the Saunders', and now
she knew.

Dropping the gazelle on the bed, she went over to the
bedroom window. Dominique's car wasn't on the drive. Where
was Dominique? Linda took off her coat, leotard and tights
and pulled open the drawer to look for clean underwear, and

299

the first thing she saw were the bra and pants Joe bought her for Christmas, which she'd had on once.

She stood there remembering how they'd kept the light on for as long as they could that night, pretending they wanted to see each other. It had taken so long, with Linda moving less and less the longer it took and Joe moving more and more, until she was lying still as though she was asleep, willing him to come as his stomach slid up and down over her because of the sweat he'd worked up. There was so much sweat, and they'd persevered until he came and she was able to rip the underwear off. She should throw them out, she thought, changing into a pair of white jeans and a black silk blouse then sitting back down on the bed, looking at herself in the vanity-unit mirror. There was no sign on her face that a migraine was beginning somewhere at the back of her skull; no sign on her face of the pain she was in. The pain was making her sleepy, but she couldn't sleep now – she had to drive to Quantum. She thought briefly of Judith Macaulay standing outside the Methodist Church that morning, the tears running down her cheek from under the dressing covering the cataract eye, then lay down on the bed, taking hold of the gazelle.

If she could just shut her eyes for ten or fifteen minutes then she'd feel better. Lying on the bed with her eyes shut, it occurred to her that she was waiting for something, and five minutes later she realised that she was waiting to cry, but had fallen asleep before she got round to it. While she was sleeping, she dreamt that the bomb had gone off and that in the aftermath Jessica was driving one of the bull-dozers from Phase IV, trying to build a house for Minister Macaulay and Izzy, who kept giving birth to baby gazelles.

She woke up later, dry-eyed and with an intense migraine. The radio clock said 4:46. She'd been asleep for almost four hours – where was Jessica? She listened but the house was silent. Then she remembered why she'd fallen asleep and it was as if her body suffered an instant weight gain, suddenly sinking deeper and deeper into the bed until it took all her strength to haul herself into an upright position. Avoiding looking at herself in the vanity-unit mirror, she got up and went onto the landing. The migraine was now so bad it was affecting her balance and she had to keep her hand on the wall to stop herself from falling over. She stood there for a while with her eyes closed, then went into Jessica's room.

Jessica's school uniform was hanging on the back of her chair – she must have come home, changed and gone back out again and Linda hadn't heard a thing. Standing there, the grief and anger she'd been waiting to feel ever since laying eyes on the gazelle in the Saunders' study suddenly took hold of her and she started sobbing, the migraine getting worse and worse, as she took in the bed with its seashell duvet cover, the rag doll and a glove puppet of Sooty.

She walked over to Jessica's desk and picked up her rain-soaked school pullover from the back of the chair, burying her head in it. It smelt strongly of Jessica, and in between sobs she breathed in her daughter.

Then, still clutching the pullover, she looked around the bedroom – for what? She knew about the suffering – what Jessica endured every day going into school – she was looking now for some sign that Jessica enjoyed life. She scanned the room twice, but didn't see anything. 'Oh God,' she said, burying her head in the pullover again. 'Oh God, Jessica, I'm so sorry, I'm so sorry.'

She carried on standing by Jessica's bedroom window well into dark, the grief and anger over Joe replaced by a sense of regret so absolute that she would have been happy to die of it right then.

*　　*　　*

301

Jessica cycled home from school through the rain with the farmhouse eggs she'd made in home economics that afternoon, trying to keep the bike steady and avoid the pot-holes so that the cream sauce didn't leak through the bike basket. Miss Davies told them that after heating the eggs through they should sprinkle fresh parsley over the top then serve them immediately.

She parked her bike in the garage and went into the house through the kitchen door, her mind still on parsley. She knew they wouldn't have any fresh parsley, but maybe they had dried. After carefully making room for the farmhouse eggs in the fridge, she checked the spice rack, but couldn't see any.

'Mum?' she called out, going upstairs to change. 'Mum?' There was no reply and she couldn't remember if Linda's car had been parked outside or not. Grabbing a navy blue towel from the bathroom, she went into her bedroom, stripped off her soaking school uniform and dried herself, the towel leaving bits of navy fluff all over her body. Then she got dressed as quickly as she could because she couldn't stand being naked. She couldn't even stand her feet being naked, which was why she never wore sandals in the summer. While drying her hair, she checked to see if Linda was in the garden. Linda wasn't, but Ferdie was. She opened the window and whistled at him and he stopped treading his circle to look up at her on the off-chance that she might be Belle.

She put the first few chapters of *How to Survive a Nuclear War* into a rucksack – along with some notes she had made in art that afternoon on terrorism while the rest of the class locked Miss Percy in the art cupboard – then went into the bathroom and spent the next ten minutes carefully dabbing at a few scabs on her chin with the spot concealer until she realised that the concealer made it look worse because it had been formulated for someone who spent at least two weeks a year on the Costa del Sol. She washed the concealer off and seriously thought about putting a plaster over her chin and telling Mr Browne that she'd fallen off her bike, but in the end she left it. She went back into the bedroom and picked up the rucksack and Joe's old denim jacket that she'd acquired because she liked wearing Joe's old things. When she left the bedroom, she saw through the open door to her parents' room, Linda's feet at the end of the bed.

Despite the fact that she hated Linda more than anyone on the planet – even Reagan – even Thatcher – she had an underlying fear that one day she'd come home and find her either dead or gone. 'Mum?'

Linda was lying on the bed asleep, holding what looked like some kind of wooden figure. Jessica couldn't remember her mother ever sleeping during the day before and, not entirely sure she wasn't dead, crouched down by the side of the bed on a level with Linda's face.

There was a white line of dried saliva running out of the corner of her mouth and she was still breathing. Linda was alive. Jessica stood up, relieved, then reminded herself that her mother's life was so densely packed with trivia that she had trouble working out why evolution had allowed her to prevail – and that was why she hated her. She checked the radio clock by the side of the bed. It was 4.15 – she was meant to be meeting Mr Browne at 4.30. She went running downstairs with her rucksack and out of the front door, heading through the rain towards No. 14.

She rang the doorbell but there was no answer. There were no lights on in the house either – she was sure he'd said 4.30. She turned to look back down the Close, hoping to see him driving up the street, parking his car, getting hurriedly out and apologising for being late, but the road was empty. She rang again in case he was in the garden –

even though it was pouring with rain – and this time the door to No. 16 opened instead.

'Hi.' It was Peter Klusczynski, dressed almost exactly the same as her.

'I was ringing for Mr Browne.'

'I saw – through the window,' he said.

'But he's not in.' Jessica looked down at the dwarf conifers between the houses. 'I was meant to meet him at 4.30.'

Peter Klusczynski was looking at her rucksack. 'You can come and wait in here if you want.'

'No, I'm fine – thanks.'

'Okay.'

He went back indoors and Jessica carried on waiting outside No. 14. The continual rain made the afternoon feel still – more like a Sunday than a Friday – and it made the Close smell of all the raw materials it was built of: the tarmac and cheap brick and hastily laid turf. It was one of the most depressing smells in the world. She was aware of the denim jacket she was wearing becoming heavier and heavier as it absorbed more and more rainwater. Then she thought of Mr Browne's light beige carpet and how when he did show up – because he was bound to show up soon – he'd be revolted by her dripping water all over his carpet, especially given the two spots on her chin.

The front door to No. 16 opened again.

'It's pissing down,' Peter said, 'come and wait inside – come on.'

Jessica hesitated. There was no sign of Mr Browne; she couldn't stand out in the rain waiting for much longer, and she couldn't bear the thought of going home and finding Linda still stretched out on the bed in her domino outfit and there being no lights on in the house. So she followed Peter Klusczynski into No. 16.

They went through to the kitchen and she stood there

looking around thinking that she'd never seen a kitchen in such a state before. In the Palmers' kitchen there was virtually no trace of human activity. No visiting alien would think for a minute that it was a place where food was prepared and eaten. In this kitchen there'd been too much human activity, and as much as Jessica hated herself for the reaction she had, she couldn't help feeling that there was something inappropriate about such extreme chaos.

Peter looked at her, momentarily confused, unable to believe that Jessica Palmer was standing in their kitchen. 'Coffee?'

'I don't drink coffee.'

'You don't?'

'I mean – I've never had it before.'

'Shit – it's not like I'm offering you smack or anything.'

She held on to her rucksack and didn't say anything.

'Well, d'you want to try some?'

She shrugged and watched him search through the debris on the benches for the things he needed.

'Sit down. Take your coat off, if you want – it looks wet. Put it on that chair by the radiator, it might dry off.'

She took off the coat, hanging it on the back of the chair, and as it started to warm up the denim let off vapours that smelt of Joe.

Peter didn't move so much as lunge with precision round the kitchen, making sense of the chaos without disturbing it.

'Where's your mum?' Jessica said.

'Out shopping. Sugar,' he said to himself, 'we need sugar.'

He stood there for a moment, located it, then brought it smoothly to the table along with two cups of coffee. He watched as she took her first sip. 'More sugar?'

'No – it's fine. It tastes fine.'

'We could go into the other room,' he said.

305

Leaving her rucksack on the kitchen table, they went through to the lounge, which had a wood-burning stove in it. Jessica had never seen one before – she didn't know people had things like this in their houses. The walls were covered in books – mostly science fiction – and there was a painting on the chimney breast of a winter landscape with a rutted road and no travellers.

They were about to sit down on the green sofa opposite the stove when they realised that was exactly what adults would do, so they sat down on the floor instead, nursing their coffee and not sure what to say to each other because nothing they could think of would reflect the intimacy of the moment.

'What's the time?' Jessica said after a while. Her face was hot but the rest of her was cold from standing out in the rain for so long.

'Four forty-five – what time were you meant to be meeting Browne?'

'Four thirty.'

'That's not like him – was it to work on the book?'

'How d'you know about the book?'

'I didn't know it was meant to be a secret.'

'It isn't,' she said, suddenly angry. 'I just didn't think anybody knew about it. I didn't think you knew Mr Browne.' Jessica stood up.

'Wait,' he said, 'I didn't mean it – whatever I said, I didn't mean it.'

'You didn't say anything – you're smirking.'

'I'm not smirking, I'm smiling: at you.'

'You think it's funny?'

'What's funny?'

'Nuclear war – you think it's funny?'

'Is that what you talk about – you and Browne?'

'People need to know. Putting aside the governments of

the world there's enough information on loan in your average library on how to design a nuclear bomb; the materials for its manufacture can be bought on the open market for not very much money, and as for the nuclear material itself – small discrepancies happen all the time. In fact, you don't even need to make a bomb, you could just disperse a cloud of radioactive particles into the air. Anyone who retained even twelve milligrams in their lungs could die within days. All it takes is the will of an individual – and it doesn't have to be Reagan; it doesn't have to be anyone who's even heard of Reagan.'

Peter got to his feet. 'So this book you're writing – it's like the ultimate British DIY survival manual or something?'

Jessica left the room. A minute later she was in the doorway wearing her wet denim jacket and hugging her rucksack to her.

Peter was going to kiss her; he was going to kiss her without asking and without warning because he'd been overwhelmed by Jessica Palmer for as long as he could remember.

'You're going to die,' she said, staring at him. 'You're smirking and you're going to die.'

Peter stayed where he was. 'I'm not smirking – I'm smiling – and eventually I will die, yes.'

'I'm going to survive. Mr Browne and me – Mr Browne and I intend to survive,' she corrected herself.

'Well, great . . . only you should try to sound less cultish about it – I'd hate Browne to disappoint you. I mean, he's already forgotten his meeting with you. You know why?'

Jessica shook her head, suddenly afraid.

'Because right now he's cruising the aisles of Tesco with a trolley, debating how many cans of tomato soup to buy. The rough draft of your DIY manual doesn't stand a chance against canned soup. You only have to stand in one of Tesco's brightly lit aisles and hold a can of soup in your hand and

307

the nightmares all vanish – didn't anybody ever tell you that?'

'How do you know?'

'How do I know what?'

'How do you know Mr Browne is in Tesco's?'

'Because he went with my mum.'

'Why would they go shopping together?'

'They fuck together so why not shop together,' he said loudly, watching her. 'You didn't know?'

She shook her head, trying not to cry.

'You're not fucking him as well, are you?'

'No,' she yelled.

'But you want to?'

'It's not like that.'

'What is it – the ex-army thing? The aura of control and domination?'

Outside a car door slammed, but neither of them heard it. There was laughter as well.

'It's not like that – it's not like that,' Jessica kept saying.

'It is like that – you're just a fucking cliché, Jessica. You're no different to anyone else.'

'I do not want to fuck Mr Browne,' she screamed as the front door opened and Mr Browne walked into the lounge, carrier-bags full of shopping crackling against the walls.

All Jessica remembered next was trying to get out of the house, but every doorway and exit route was blocked by Mr Browne and Mrs Klusczynski and all their shopping. The bags just seemed to carry on multiplying until she was walking over shopping that cracked and split and burst and she had to hold on to the walls because her feet were getting caught in the debris, until at last she made it to the front door and out into the rain.

Linda went back into the bedroom, re-did her hair and

make-up then went downstairs and had a raspberry Slimshake (with the now habitual dash of Campari) to cancel out the eight fish fingers she'd had earlier. She went into the garage to see if Jessica's bike was there and saw that Jessica had left the garage door up. Irritated, she went to shut it when a car made its way into the Close and for a moment she thought it was Dominique, but it wasn't; it was Sandra Nassam, who'd just picked Jamie and Leila up from the same school Stephanie Saunders went to. Through the car window, she saw Leila's head underneath a straw boater and thought how much she would have liked to have seen Jessica in a uniform like that, then wondered if she would have loved Jessica more as a child if she'd worn a straw boater with a gingham ribbon round it.

Then Dominique's car did turn into the Close and Linda walked out of the garage and into the rain. She crossed the road and the garden at No. 4, nearly slipping on the wet grass until she found her feet on the manhole cover by the pampas grass.

Linda's car was pulling away from outside No. 8 and Jessica went running towards it screaming, 'Mum – Mum.'

The car stopped and the window was wound down. 'I've got to go out – I'll be back soon.'

'Mum!'

Linda gave a wave, the gears making a deep splintering sound as the car went screeching off through the rain, round the corner and out of the Close.

'Come back,' Jessica yelled after the retreating white Toyota. 'Come back you bitch, you fucking bitch, you fucking, fucking bitch . . .'

4

Dominique, who was opening the back door of the car for Stephanie, turned round to see Linda standing on the manhole cover in the garden.

'Linda,' she said, putting an umbrella up over her and Stephanie, but Linda didn't say anything, she just stood there staring at her.

Stephanie got out the car in her ballet leotard and tights.

Dominique took in the fluorescent pink stain running down the front of Linda's blouse where the chemicals in the Slimshake had reacted with the chemicals in the fabric.

'Going out tonight?' Linda asked her.

'In about forty-five minutes' time – Stephanie's got a swimming competition at The Haven at six.' She paused because Linda laughed. 'Was there something you needed?'

Linda carried on laughing.

'I've got a stomachache,' Stephanie said, bending over.

'How bad?' Dominique turned back to Linda. 'Was there something you needed?' she said again. 'I've got to go.'

'I know,' Linda said slowly, her eyes fixed on her. 'That's all I'm saying for now – I know.'

Dominique stood underneath the umbrella and watched

Linda slipping her way back up the garden, her blouse so wet from the rain that you could see the outline of her bra. Something was wrong.

They went indoors. Stephanie lay down on one of the sofas in the lounge and Dominique went into the kitchen, leant against the cooker and rested her face in her hands, rubbing her eyes.

Then Stephanie appeared in the doorway, offering to show her the highlights of her ballet lesson.

'I thought you were lying down – you said you had a stomachache.'

'It keeps coming and going – can I show you my demi-plié?'

'I'll just put the kettle on then you can show me.'

'Mrs Miller said there was a tape of all the Grade One music that we should buy so we can practise at home. Can we buy the tape?'

'Of course.' Dominique leant over the sink and yawned.

'I'm ready to start,' Stephanie was saying.

Through the kitchen window she saw Linda's car stop outside and Jessica, in black, running down the street towards it. Then the car pulled away, screeching past the house and out of the Close, and Jessica was standing there yelling something.

'I said I'm ready to start,' Stephanie said again.

'Okay.' Dominique tried to finish her second yawn before turning round to see Stephanie standing with her feet in first and her hands in port de bras, staring straight ahead of her and counting.

It struck her for the first time how like Monica Stephanie was.

8

Linda got to Quantum at five o'clock and there was Maureen on the steps, locking up the showroom.

'You've just missed him,' she said, turning round.

'When did he go?'

'About five minutes ago.'

Linda stood there, thinking. She was now convinced that Joe was meeting Dominique tonight – but where? Then she remembered Joe telling her he was going to take the pot down to his mum's tonight. Brighton. Dominique and Joe were meeting in Brighton. 'I need to use the phone,' she said.

'The phone?'

'Just quickly.' She broke her face into a smile.

Maureen hesitated. She was unsettled by the fluorescent pink stain down the front of Linda's blouse – this wasn't like Linda. In all the years she'd known her, she'd never once seen her with so much as a mark on her and here she was with a fluorescent streak running from breast to waist. 'I've got to get home,' she said.

'I won't be long,' Linda replied, staring at her and wondering what it was a fifty-three-year-old widow had to get home for.

'I've got Gareth staying with me this week.'

'Gareth?'

'My son, Gareth, he's home from Geneva.'

'What's he doing in Geneva?'

'Studying conducting.'

'Conducting what?'

'Well – an orchestra.'

This was too much for Linda. 'Just open the door for me, Maureen – I'll be two minutes.'

Sighing, Maureen opened the door to the showroom she'd just locked and unset the alarm then stood in her coat by the door.

Linda went into Joe's office and shut the door then rang Cassidy Street. It was Derek who picked up. 'Derek – it's me, Linda – Joe's wife. Has Joe phoned today?'

'Joe?'

'Your son – Joe – he's meant to be dropping a pot off at yours tonight.' Silence. 'Is Audrey there? Can I speak to Audrey?'

Silence again, then, after a while, 'Audrey's gone out. I hope she wrapped up – it's colder out there than you think.' He paused. 'Don't forget to wrap up warm, and don't forget to . . .'

Linda slammed the receiver down, inhaled, then dialled the number for The Haven. It rang and rang but no one answered – all that bullshit of Dominique's about Stephanie having a swimming competition. Through the blinds she could see Maureen waiting, immobile.

This was where Joe phoned her during the day. This was where Joe phoned Dominique – he'd phoned her this morning when Linda had been at No. 4. She opened his drawers and found nothing but a donut and a set of sticky marker pens, and it suddenly struck her how easy it would be – if she were Joe – to conduct an affair from here. He

313

could phone any time he wanted and he was forever in and out of the office.

Dominique was home all day and both girls were at school. The possibilities for secrecy seemed suddenly limitless and it amazed her to think just how much of their marriage so far had been speculated on trust – what kind of an investment was that?

Maureen had moved; she was just outside the office, tapping on the window.

'Just a minute,' Linda called out, picking up the phone and dialling The Haven again. This time someone answered.

'The swimming competition . . .'

'Yes?'

'Tonight's swimming competition?'

'Yes?'

'There is one?' Linda shouted.

'Yes.' The voice paused. 'The junior swimming competition begins at six.'

Linda slammed the phone down and stood up.

Maureen had taken up her position of vigilance by the showroom door and didn't bother to hide her relief when she saw Linda emerge from Joe's office. 'Everything all right? You look –'

'What?'

'Well – hungry.'

Why was this all anyone seemed to say to her. She left Maureen to lock up the showroom and reset the alarm, when it occurred to her that she ought to start being more pleasant to Maureen because Maureen had access to daytime Joe.

'Do you want a lift?' she said.

Maureen shook her head. 'I've got some things to pick up on the way home.'

'Well –' Linda made her way back to the car. 'Give my regards to Gavin.'

314

'Gareth,' Maureen corrected her. 'It's Gareth.'

'Gavin-Gareth.' Linda smiled and got into her car, slamming the door shut. She stared through the windscreen at the Littlehaven rush-hour traffic on the Foundry Lane Industrial Estate roundabout and realised that Dominique might in fact only be telling a white lie – maybe Stephanie was going to compete in the junior swimming competition at The Haven – maybe Joe was meeting them there? How would that work? Her mind went momentarily blank as she realised how hungry she was and how tired she was of being hungry.

She clicked the key in the ignition so that she could switch on the wipers then drove to a roadside café on the road to The Haven – that they all used to joke about when Jessica was small because of the smell as you drove past and the fact that it was used by bikers.

She pulled up in the lay-by and ordered a bacon sandwich then carried the greasy white paper bag back to the car, slamming the door and starting to eat so fast she was making grunting sounds. Grease was running out of the sandwich across her wrists and when she'd finished she scrunched up the bag and threw it on the floor then quickly wiped her hands across the carpet on the inside of the door. She looked for the travel wipes she kept in the glove compartment, but they weren't there and the fact that the travel wipes weren't there suddenly sent her into a rage of self-revulsion, which consisted of her slamming the door to the glove compartment over and over again while thumping on the steering wheel with her greasy fist. She carried on doing this until the hinges of the compartment broke and she sat there breathing heavily, the taste of fried bacon in her mouth, realising with relief just how much she'd come to hate Dominique Saunders over the past two years. How much she hated her parquet flooring; how much she hated the photographs on the walls of the Saunders' bedroom; how much she hated the children; how much she hated Mick; how much she hated the whole of No. 4 Pollards Close and the myth that was the Saunders. What interest could Dominique Saunders possibly have in fucking Joe Palmer, and why – while she was fucking him – did the myth that was the Saunders still look so perfect? The Saunders didn't shout at their children and they never had rows – still. Their lives moved slowly and quietly towards what, nobody knew, but the Saunders were happy – still.

She must have dozed off because the sound of three motorbikes pulling into the lay-by woke her up. The clock on the dashboard said 6.30. She'd had four hours' sleep that afternoon – what was she doing falling asleep again? She was constantly tired at the moment and the tiredness came on her so suddenly that she was often asleep before she even realised. It was like someone knocking her over the back of the head – all she could remember was regaining consciousness afterwards – never losing it. Putting the car into gear she drove back onto the road. The feel of the wheel sliding beneath greasy fingers irritated her and the migraine was still there. She drove into The Haven at 6.45 beneath a banner advertising the Junior Swimming Competition that night, and double-parked, blocking in a yellow Porsche. The car park was the fullest it had ever been. Starting at the far side, she began checking each of the parking bays overlooking the wall that kept the forest out, looking for Dominique's car. She wound her way through the entire car park, bay by bay, until she was standing beneath the banner strung between the two slate gateposts at the entrance to The Haven. On this side a Celebrity Golf Charity Event was being advertised.

She stood looking out at the road for a while. A car drove past, but it didn't turn in – maybe it had been going to, but

316

then saw the rain-drenched woman standing under the banner, staring out into the road, and had just driven past instead. How could she blame them – she knew from experience that affluence stays well clear of madness because affluence has no contingency plans – nothing to fall back on. She walked slowly back into the car park, looking over her shoulder every time she heard a car. Then she went into reception, making her way over to the pool entrance and pressing against the glass to the side of the automatic doors. A shot was fired inside the pool and a row of young girls who'd been poised on the starting blocks all dived into the water and started doing the butterfly stroke up the pool. Linda watched, briefly distracted by the fact that they knew what to do: they knew how to dive, how to do butterfly stroke, how to turn under water. The winner – a girl in a yellow cap – even knew how to be the winner. Who were these people?

She looked along the bank of spectators, but couldn't see either Dominique or Joe. Scanning the wet and dry girls and boys sitting on benches along the side of the pool, she couldn't make out Stephanie either. She stood there a second longer then went into the ladies just outside the Mahogany Bar and washed her hands, sniffing them as she came out to make sure there were no traces of bacon left, and nearly walked into Delta Saunders.

'Where's your fucking mother?' Linda said.

'Linda?' Delta stood back. 'Linda?' she said again.

The sound of applause echoed from inside the pool, and over Delta's shoulders Linda saw the bank of spectators clapping. 'You heard me – where's your mother?' She slammed her hand down on the unmanned reception desk.

Outside, wind rushed suddenly through the tops of the trees.

'I don't know – are you looking for her?'

Linda laughed.

'I was meant to meet her here. Stephanie was competing in the twenty-five-metre front crawl, but I haven't been able to find them – and Stephanie didn't compete,' she added.

'Of course she didn't.'

'Maybe I got it wrong,' Delta said.

Linda stood blinking rapidly while taking in Delta Saunders. She thought of the joke Delta had played on her the night of her dinner party with the Niemans – the soufflé joke – and how she'd stood in the doorway of No. 4 in her dressing gown with wet nail varnish, and wondered if Delta knew. Lovers needed accomplices; people they could trust when they couldn't trust themselves. Delta might not be the only accomplice – maybe there were others. Was anybody above suspicion? She thought back to the dinner party in December. It was possible that the Niemans knew, and that all of them had spent the whole evening sitting round the dining table eating gazpacho and laughing at her. They'd all gone home still laughing; laughed themselves to sleep and woken up laughing the next morning. The whole world knew – the whole world apart from her.

'You and your parquet flooring and your cheese soufflés and your silk kimonos . . . living in your perfect home with your perfect parents where everything's always just so perfect you think there's nothing to trip you up,' she shouted, saying all the things to Delta she'd meant to say to Dominique.

Delta heard the words 'parquet' and 'soufflé' and couldn't work out why Linda was yelling at her when all she wanted to know was where her mother was.

'Well, I know now so you can stop laughing.'

The swimming competition had ended and people were starting to leave the pool, walking through the automatic doors with their wet children, who ran shivering towards the changing rooms. Delta and Linda were suddenly in the middle of a flood of human traffic.

'You can stop laughing,' Linda screamed at Delta and the adults and children surrounding them in reception. 'You can all stop laughing now.'

Joe got to Al's for five thirty. *Sunnymeade* was a modern bungalow on the main road running out of the village and the front garden's immaculate lawn was surrounded by borders full of rose bushes that had been pruned back nearly to rootstock.

Joe parked on the drive and Al appeared before he'd even had time to switch off the car engine.

'Lovely garden,' Joe said as they walked to the front door.

'Well, me and Cissie – we've got the time. Hopefully this year we'll get the weather as well – not today, mind. Come in.'

The interior of the bungalow was as immaculate as the front garden. Joe heard someone busy in the kitchen as he passed, but Al led him straight through to the conservatory at the back.

'Here, take a seat, Joe. Cissie'll be here in a minute. You all right, Ciss?' he called out.

There was no response and Al tapped his right ear, smiling. 'She only wears her hearing aid for the TV,' he said.

The conservatory smelt of the retriever lying across the doorway and something sweet he couldn't identify. It also smelt of the elderliness of Al and Cissie.

Joe sat down. 'You've got a great view here.'

Al smiled again and the two men stared out through the conservatory windows across the garden and the fields beyond, to where an even heavier bank of cloud was rolling in off the Channel and over the Downs towards *Sunnymeade*.

'We only got the conservatory put in last year,' Al said.

319

'It was an anniversary present from our daughter, Jane – you might remember Jane?'

Joe didn't, but he nodded anyway.

'It's been a godsend for Cissie, who hasn't been well – hasn't been so mobile these last few years.'

'What's that he's saying about me?' Cissie said, walking in with a tray twice the size of her.

'Here,' Joe said, standing up and trying to take the tray from her.

'You sit down – I've got this.' She put it on the bamboo coffee table with the glass top. 'The teapot,' she said, turning to Al, 'that's the only thing I couldn't get on the tray.'

'You shouldn't have gone to so much effort,' Joe said, watching her unload the stack of bone china.

'It's no effort.'

'I thought I was just stopping by to pick up the auriculas.'

'Well, now you're here you can have some tea. Doesn't he look the spit of Derek?' she said as Al walked back in with the teapot.

'That's what I said to him when I saw him that day.'

'The spit,' Cissie said, shaking her head as if it pleased her but was also unnatural all at the same time.

In the distance, the Downs disappeared into cloud as they sat eating cheese and onion pie, tinned salmon sandwiches, Victoria sponge and rock buns, listening to the rain on the conservatory.

'Another bit of cake?' Cissie said.

'I couldn't.' Joe still had his mouth full. 'I'll finish this then I'm done – I really am stuffed.'

'You don't need to eat for a week after one of Cissie's teas,' Al said, looking sideways at his wife. He cleared away the dishes, refusing help from Joe, and disappeared into the kitchen to make more tea.

320

Joe, who thought Cissie had dozed off, took a quick look at his watch.

'Got somewhere to be?' she said, her head turned towards him and her eyes wide open now.

'In a bit.' They could hear Al in the kitchen. 'You shouldn't have gone to so much effort.'

'Oh, I should. I like to.'

'Al said you haven't been well.'

'It's my legs – an old snakebite I got when I was in Africa. When it's damp like today the ache sends me half mad. I don't know why the rain in England should make me suffer for a snakebite I got seventy years ago in Kenya, but it does – doesn't make sense, does it?'

Al came in with more tea.

'I'll go and plant up the auriculas,' he said.

'Don't bother.' Joe stood up. 'I'll take them as they are.'

'But you said you bought a pot for them.'

'I did, but I can plant them up.'

'It won't take two seconds.'

'It's raining.'

'I'll put the garage roof up and do it under there.'

Joe stood up. 'I'll come and help you with the urn – it's a stone urn I bought for them. You'll need help lifting it.'

'Says who?'

'Al –'

'He won't need help. He spent most of the war digging ditches – it's where he met your dad – digging ditches. That's right, isn't it?' Cissie looked up at her husband for confirmation.

Al was nodding. 'We spent a fortnight in Lewes prison.'

'Dad did?'

Al carried on nodding. 'Then they let us out to dig ditches. That's what they did with conscientious objectors in the war. Right – I'll just be outside.'

Joe poured more tea then sat back down and listened to Cissie talking about growing up in Africa and the long journeys they used to make for weeks on end across the bush.

He left *Sunnymeade* – after a tour of Al's greenhouse – with the auriculas all potted up in the back of the car and Cissie waving from the front door. Turning onto the main road, he was out of sight before they went in.

He drove on down to Brighton, belching all the way because of the tinned salmon and, despite the rain, took the road over Devil's Dyke rather than the bypass. He was stuck behind a tractor for a while by Poynings, but didn't care – and got to Brighton early enough to go to Cassidy Street first before meeting Lenny.

He left the urn in the car and ran through the rain to ring on the doorbell, unsure what to do about the fact that if his dad was up and about there was a fifty per cent chance of him answering the door.

He rang the bell again, the rain beating down on the corrugated plastic porch roof. A couple of the windmills that had been on the dining table the last time he was there were now outside, and he wondered whether it was Audrey or Derek who put them there. Still no answer – were they out?

Looking back at the car, he thought of Al potting up the auriculas – maybe they'd gone into Brighton for a meal together. There was that Italian place, just off Baxter Street in fact, that he remembered them going to – Etna's, that was it. He remembered because his dad used to tease his mum about the crush the proprietor had on her, and when they came back from a meal his mum would walk into the front room, take off her coat and stand there, accusing the room of spinning round. Later, if he and Darren hadn't fallen asleep, they'd hear laughter coming from the other bedroom.

He rang for a third time, and after a few minutes his mum answered the door – in a dressing gown.

'Joe,' she said.

'You're in,' he said, his eyes on the dressing gown. 'Nobody answered – I thought you might be out or something.' He paused. 'Were you in the bath?'

She shook her head. 'No – no, I wasn't in the bath. Your dad's out,' she said, quickly looking over her shoulder into the house.

'You're all right, aren't you?' Joe asked, watching her.

'I'm fine – I was just having forty winks, that's all.' She was standing behind the door, which was only partially open, looking at him like he was a door-to-door salesman. 'What are you doing here, Joe?'

Joe laughed. 'Am I coming in, then?'

'I don't know – now's not a good time.'

From behind her in the house there was a chinking sound. 'Are you sure you're all right, Mum?'

'I'm fine, Joe, it's just – I wasn't expecting you.'

'I got something for you – well, you and Dad.'

'Have you?' she said, preoccupied.

'Something to replace the old chimney pots them blokes bought off you.'

'Joe . . .'

'I bumped into Al – you remember Al? I bought a new pot and he planted it up for me – something to put a bit of colour in your front garden.'

Audrey was standing there nodding, but not really listening.

'D'you want me to get the pot out of the car?'

'No, I don't!' she suddenly shouted. 'It's good of you, Joe – it's sweet – it's just like you, but I don't want you unloading any bloody pot right now because I'm busy.'

'I thought you said you were taking forty winks?'

'It's none of your bloody business what I'm doing, only if I stand here talking to you much longer I won't be doing anything cause your dad'll be back in an hour's time.'

'But Al's planted you up some auriculas – flame-red alpines.' He saw shadows in the house over Audrey's shoulder. 'Are you sure you're all right, Mum?' he said, the dressing gown bothering him even more now he'd seen the shadows. 'D'you want me to come in? We can talk – I'll get the auriculas out in a minute.'

'For fuck's sake, Joe,' she hissed, 'I don't want to talk – and your bloody dad's home in under an hour.'

Joe stepped back, out from under the porch so that he was standing in the rain. 'What's going on, Mum?'

'I love you, Joe – I love you for thinking of me and for the auriculas, what were they again?'

'Alpines,' he said automatically. 'Flame red.'

'Lovely,' she nodded. 'If you come back another time with your flame-red alpine auriculas I'll love you for it, but right now you've got to piss off.'

'Everything all right?' a man's voice said just behind her. 'Only I heard shouting.'

'Everything's fine, Ray.'

Joe stood in the front garden of No. 24 Cassidy Street, his mother and him staring at each other through the torrential rain.

'Who's in there with you?'

She carried on staring at him and didn't say anything.

Joe stood there in the rain thinking, his mother knew Ray; Ray who'd been buying harnesses with Lenny in Leroy's that afternoon. He tried not to think of the harnesses – he was about to make a gift of Al's three prize alpine auriculas to his mum in the stone urn he'd bought from Capability Brown's before Christmas – and the only thing his mum was interested in was Ray.

324

'Don't look at me like that, Joe. Don't think you can live without it – don't ever think that – because you can't, and don't expect anyone else to either, so stop looking at me like that and piss off now, love, or you'll catch your death standing there.'

Joe blinked to get the rainwater out of his eyes and wiped his face with his hands.

'You're paying for it?'

'Make sure you take those wet clothes off when you get home,' she said, then shut the door.

She mustn't have closed it properly because a second later it shut with a bang.

Joe stared at the front door for a while, thinking about ringing it again, then took a few steps back until he was standing by the gate looking up at the house. Then he got back in the car, turned the engine on and drove slowly away from No. 24 Cassidy Street, an ice-cream van clearly visible in the rear-view mirror until he turned the corner and it disappeared.

Fifteen minutes later he parked the car outside No. 16 Baxter Street where he was meant to be meeting Lenny, suddenly furious with her, without knowing why.

Linda ran down the steps, laughter ringing in her ears as she ran through people and umbrellas, through the car park and carried on running until she reached the golf course, cutting across the top end of it on the diagonal and reaching the lane on the other side. Once her feet hit tarmac, she stopped for a while and, bending over with her hands on her knees, waited to get her breath back. When she did, she started walking. She didn't know where she was walking to, but she knew what she was looking for – Dominique Saunders' car parked somewhere up this lane. Dominique telling her she was taking Stephanie to the swimming competition when she wasn't; Joe telling her he was taking the stone urn down to his mum's in Brighton when he wasn't . . . it all added up to this: the Saunders' car parked somewhere up this lane, and Dominique and Joe . . .

She walked to the brow of the hill where the Forestry Commission car park was – for people who wanted to visit the iron-age hammer ponds – and, feeling suddenly sick, vomited. Watching it soak into the ground, she wondered what the fluorescent pink was then remembered the raspberry Slimshake she'd had between the fish fingers and the bacon sandwich. When she looked up, she saw Paul Nieman's campervan parked under the trees directly ahead of her. Of course. If everyone in Pollards Close was complicit, why not Paul Nieman? Is that how they managed it? Did he lend them his campervan?

The ground feeling about as steady as her stomach, she just about made it to one of the beech trees in the Forestry Commission car park before vomiting up the rest of the fish fingers. She wiped her mouth, stalking through mud and leaves towards the campervan, knowing that once she slid the side door open everything would fall into place and the laughter would stop ringing in her ears. Ignoring the rain and the fact that the world felt suddenly, unbearably dark and the trees hostile – especially since she'd left fluorescent-streaked vomit down the trunk of the beech – she reached the van, pulling hard on the door.

'Joe!' she said, stumbling even though she'd anticipated the two naked bodies being there. 'Joe,' she said again, crashing into the cupboard opposite the door and knocking over a vase of plastic roses.

'What the fuck is this?' a man's voice said – and it wasn't Joe's.

'It's the police – the English police,' another voice kept saying, and she recognised this voice – it was Winke Nieman's.

326

Linda, who'd fallen onto her side, swung her head slowly round, noticing that there was a distinctly shitty smell inside the campervan. Then she saw that the two bodies were in fact Winke Nieman crouching over Steve – Quantum Steve – splayed out on the van's lino floor. Winke was tottering backwards on his knees, trying to work out what was going on.

Somebody yelled as the heel of her boot caught their shin.

'Mrs Palmer?' Steve said in disbelief, raising himself up on his elbows and trying to see beyond the bulk of Winke.

Steve and Winke Nieman – were they in on this too? How vast was this conspiracy – did it have any limits? It had started with Minister Macaulay's wife this morning – then the gazelle – then Maureen at Quantum – then Delta Saunders – and now Steve and Winke Nieman. She stood up, knocking her head against the roof of the campervan and started to laugh above the sound of the rain banging down on the roof. 'You expect me to believe this?' she yelled. 'You expect me to believe any of this?'

Winke Nieman and Steve in Paul's campervan was a good decoy, but she wasn't being put off the trail now. She stood looking out at the rain in the forest through the door she'd left open, then jumped out of the van and ran back through the trees towards the lane leading to The Haven.

'Wait – Mrs Palmer!'

She turned round and saw Winke Nieman, naked, running after her. Even through the rain she could hear the hollow slapping sound his stomach made as he ran after her and the soles of his feet against the layers of wet leaves on the forest floor.

'Mrs Palmer – please!'

She got to the edge of the Forestry Commission car park and turned round to see Winke pick his way across the rocks in the car park, his arms outstretched for balance.

The last thing she saw was Winke giving up the chase and sitting down on a rock, checking his watch.

'Don't think you get to have the last laugh,' she yelled at him, then jogged back down the lane and across the golf course to The Haven. Getting back into her car, she slammed the door shut, reversed then pressed down so hard on the accelerator that the car skidded violently across the road as she drove at high speed through the gateposts and out across the main road.

Even with the headlights on full she could hardly see through the rain. Her hands were so wet it was affecting her grip on the steering wheel, but she carried on driving fast, the taste of vomit still in her mouth, aware of a thudding sound that wasn't the rain. She couldn't see anything on the road ahead, but turning to look through the rain-streaked side window, thought there was something moving through the trees at the same speed as the car, galloping alongside the car – and it looked like a gazelle.

Joe waited for ten minutes then got out of the car and rattled on the letterbox of No. 16 Baxter Street, even though he could see that there were no lights on anywhere inside. **KEITH'S UNISEX HAIRDRESSER'S** was written in gold lettering across the front of the shop. Underneath this there was a sign saying *No Appointment Necessary*. An old man and a group of students passed before he saw Lenny walking up the pavement towards him, coming from the direction of the bus station.

She had her head down, under her umbrella, and didn't see him standing there until she was nearly in front of him. Then she looked up, surprised – as if she'd expected him to change his mind since the phone call that morning.

'Have you been here long? I didn't know whether you'd come or not.'

'I said I was coming.'

'You found it okay, then?'

'It wasn't difficult.'

'Did your mum get her auriculas?'

Joe didn't say anything.

'What?' she said, watching him.

'Nothing.'

'You're wet.'

'It's raining.'

'I mean you're really wet – and angry.'

He nodded, his hands in his pockets, and stared down the street in the direction she'd just come from, half thinking of getting back in his car and driving home.

'What?' Lenny said again.

He turned back to face her. 'My mum's seeing Ray – your friend Ray.'

'I know.'

'You know?' he shouted.

Lenny didn't say anything.

'I've just come from there. I went round to give her some auriculas – I bought her this stone urn and Al planted them up with some alpine auriculas. I drove straight to Cassidy Street and I couldn't believe it – my mum's paying Ray – and you knew?'

'Ray's a good man,' Lenny said carefully.

'I couldn't believe it. My mum, I mean . . .'

'Ray's a good man,' Lenny said again. Then, her eyes still on him, 'You're crying.'

'Course I'm not fucking crying.'

'You're going now, then?'

'I couldn't believe it,' he said.

'People do what they have to – to get through,' Lenny said. 'This is what your mum's worked out.'

'What's she worked out – Ray?'

Lenny paused then backed away from him and put a key in the lock in the shop door. 'Why are you angry with me?'

'I don't know,' he said.

'You're coming in?' Her hand was on the key.

He stared at her in the doorway.

'You want to talk some more?'

'No,' he said and paused.

Lenny turned the key in the lock, and after another moment's pause they walked into Keith's, which smelt of other people's heads and cheap shampoo. The walls were hung with black and white photos of people who had probably never had their hair cut by Keith and the three empty barber's chairs were all swung round to different positions.

He watched as she picked up the junk mail from behind the door and put it on one of the chairs, swinging it round to a new position.

'It was a hairdresser's before?' he said.

'You don't have to change the subject.'

'I want to.'

She nodded. 'There's no nasty story – the man who owned it retired, that's all; a stroke or something.'

'You've already decided to take it, haven't you?' he said, taking in the heavily varnished tongue-and-groove covering the walls and the three mirrors, which were the cleanest things there.

'I could double the capacity,' she said after a while. 'This side of the shop could be used as well.'

'Would you still do unisex?'

'I'm speaking to a Chinese bloke who works with me at the moment – he's interested.'

They looked at each other in the mirror for a minute then Joe walked over to the window, tracing his fingers over the lettering **KEITH'S UNISEX HAIRDRESSER'S**.

'What would you call your hairdresser's?'

'Evita's,' she said, as if it was a joke he was meant to get.

'Evita's?'

'It's personal.'

'Are you speaking to someone about a loan?'

'I'm speaking to Midland, but they haven't approved anything yet.'

'Don't let them persuade you to take out anything bigger than you've asked for – whatever they say about rates. Just stick to the amount you've calculated.' He paused. 'If they're unsure you can tell whoever you're speaking to at Midland that Quantum Kitchens is prepared to make an investment.'

He'd been looking out the window when he said this, but when she didn't say anything he turned round.

She still didn't say anything.

'I'm offering to make an investment – if you go ahead with the whole thing.'

'I know – I know that. I'm just not sure how I feel about it.'

'Neither am I,' Joe said.

He took a quick look at his watch. He'd told Linda he'd be back for nine thirty.

'Got somewhere to be?' Lenny said.

'Yes.'

She nodded and went to the back of the shop where there was a doorway hung with beads. After getting briefly caught up in it, Joe followed her through and found himself in a kitchen that must have been part of the original house before it was turned into business premises. Joe looked around him, taking in the bulbous old fridge with its clasp handle, and on the wall above it a This England calendar, turned to October. The picture was Christchurch Meadows grey with frost – that's what the caption read – he didn't know, he'd never been to Christchurch Meadows. 'Keith wasn't exactly profit-orientated, was he?'

Lenny shrugged. 'He made enough of a living to keep this going till he died.'

'Making a living's not enough any more. Is that the flat up there?' he said, pointing to the staircase.

'It's included with the lease.'

'Would you live there?'

'To start with.'

She paused for a minute then opened the door at the bottom of the staircase leading up to the flat.

'You want to see it? Have you got time?'

He looked at his watch again. 'No.'

'You should see everything included in the lease if you're thinking of making an investment.'

He followed her up the lino-covered stairs and at the top she took the set of keys out of her bag again, opening the door to the flat then closing it after them.

The flat was illuminated by a fish tank three feet by five, and Lenny didn't bother to switch any lights on. The air was close and smelt of cigarette smoke and algae. There was a brown velveteen sofa, a drop-leaf table and a couple of stools. The coffee table was covered in ashtrays and copies of *Chat* as well as a dying house plant with a pink bow still wrapped round the pot.

'All this shit was just here – left like this,' she said.

'Even the fish?'

'Even the fish. It's some poor sod from the agent's job to come and feed the fish every morning and check the water because some of them are meant to be rare and worth a lot of money.'

'They are,' Joe said, looking in the tank.

'You like fish?' she asked, watching him. 'Doesn't mean anything to me.'

Joe turned round to look at her. 'What are you thinking?'

'I'm thinking – can I picture myself living here?' She shook her head. 'I don't know.'

'You'll be fine,' he said, wanting to go up to her. 'Can I use your loo?'

'It's not mine, but it's through there,' she replied, pointing to a door in the corner of the room.

The door led through to a bedroom where there was an immaculately made bed with a row of teddy bears lined up on the pillow. There were more ashtrays on the bedside table. Another smaller door led off from the bedroom to a cold, damp bathroom where the sound of seagulls on the window ledge outside made him nervous.

'Does the flush work?' he called out.

'Just give it a tug.'

The cistern came to life then shuddered its way to silence again.

After looking briefly at himself in the mirror he went back through to the other room, leaning against the door-frame and watching Lenny bent over the tank. The watery light catching at her face and arms made them look softer than they had all evening.

She looked across at him in the doorway, trying to make up his mind whether to stay or go.

'Seen enough?' she said.

He nodded, walking quickly over to where she was standing, near the fish tank, her arms folded.

'You're cold,' he said, taking hold of her and not even thinking about it; kissing her forehead then kissing her properly, their arms getting caught up as they reached out for each other.

'Wait,' Lenny said, holding tightly onto him. 'I've got to tell you something.'

'What?' Joe was helping her out of her jacket and pulling at the neck of the jumper she had on.

'Whatever's about to happen – I won't feel guilty about

it. I'm never going to stand next to you, sit next to you or lie down next to you and listen to you talking about guilt. We're never going to have one of those conversations.'

Joe stood back for a moment, confused. 'Fine,' he said after a while. 'That's fine.'

He forced his knee between her legs, edging her back towards the brown velveteen sofa. They took off their own shoes and each other's trousers.

'No guilt,' Lenny said, breathless now.

Joe nodded and pushed her sideways onto the sofa and didn't care about the position or what angle she was lying at or whether he was crushing her or what their arms and legs were doing; he just needed to be inside her.

He didn't notice anything after that – apart from the fact that he was sweating – until after he came.

'Joe – I can't breathe, Joe,' she said, easing him off her.

He knelt in the corner of the sofa and Lenny sat up slightly, both of them semi-naked. Their thighs had cigarette ash stuck to them from the sofa, and looking down he saw that there was ash from Keith's cigarettes in his pubic hair.

The light from the fish tank made their bodies seem restless still.

Lenny was aware of him staring at her. 'What?'

He put his elbow back on the arm rest. 'Nothing.'

After a while she got up and he watched her put on her jeans and throw him his.

'Come here,' he said as she was about to do up the flies. She crossed the room and he passed his hand over her stomach, which was still wet with his come, and round her waist.

'I'm going to the loo,' she said, leaving the jeans undone.

He heard her pee, then the cistern going. The sound of the cistern filled the flat and made it sound as if there was water running down the walls until Joe had convinced himself that it was raining indoors and that he could feel it falling on his head, shoulders and thighs and that the sofa, when he felt along it, was wet.

Then Lenny walked back into the room, stopping in the doorway and leaning her head against the frame, looking at him kneeling there without his trousers. 'Feeling guilty?'

'No. I was thinking how easy it was, and I was wondering if wars start in the same way.'

Lenny stood there banging her body gently against the doorframe. 'People are different, but human beings – they're all the same. You will feel guilt – maybe not now, but you will,' she said.

'You didn't want this to happen?'

'I wanted this to happen . . . I wanted this to happen since I first saw you at Belle's. I don't give a fuck about your wife or your daughter.'

Neither did Joe right then. He didn't give a fuck about Linda or Jessica or anything that had happened in his life so far. He walked over to where she was standing in the doorway and started kissing her again.

'I want a cigarette.'

'Where are they?'

'Over there – by the fish.'

Joe watched the fish dart around, thinking he was going to feed them, then picked up the packet and gave it to her, starting to kiss her neck.

'No,' she said, pushing him away. 'I'm dressed now.'

'Then get undressed.'

'No.' She lit a cigarette and blew smoke out over his hair.

'Please,' he said, pulling at her and rubbing himself against her.

She ignored him, feeling the sweat on his forehead as he pressed it against her collarbone.

335

When she'd finished the cigarette she threw the stub onto Keith's immaculate bed then put her left leg up on the opposite side of the doorframe so that Joe could rest against it.

He kept his head buried in her chest and she brought him off with her right hand.

'Are you happy now?'

'Yes – fuck, yes,' he said as he came.

After a while she went and sat on the sofa and watched him get dressed.

The right leg of her jeans was wet from him and she was cold. She reached over for another cigarette and sat turning the packet over and over in her hands.

'What are you thinking about?' Joe asked, watching her.

'The people I've killed.'

'You've killed people?'

She nodded.

'When?'

'The Falklands. I wasn't even meant to see active combat.'

Joe finished dressing back into his sodden clothes and realised that he wasn't surprised. Somehow he'd known this about her from the first moment he'd seen her standing in the entrance hall at Belle's with the scissors in her hand.

'How many?'

'Five people – men. It doesn't sound like a lot, but it is. One is a lot.'

'Is that meant to make a difference?'

'It could do.'

'Well,' he said, looking round to make sure he'd put everything back on that he'd taken off. 'It doesn't.'

'What about later? Later on?'

'It doesn't mean anything to me,' he said, standing over her. 'Come on.' He didn't know why he said that – they had nowhere to go; he just knew that he couldn't leave without her. 'Come on,' he said again.

'I want to sit here for a while.'

'I've got to go.'

'So go. I'm staying here.'

He stared at her. 'I can't leave you here.'

'Why not?' she said, laughing.

'Lenny . . .'

The laughter stopped. 'Just go.'

He stood there watching the light from the fish tank move over her and thought about going, but nothing happened. He stood there for another moment then walked past the fish tank to the door.

She turned to look at him.

'Nobody's ever made me this unhappy before,' he said, 'you know that, don't you?'

'You were happy a minute ago.'

'Now I'm unhappy. I've been unhappy ever since I saw you.'

She didn't say anything.

'I didn't ask for this – I never expected anything like this.'

'So what are you going to do?'

'I'm going.'

'Where are you going?'

'Home,' he said, without thinking.

She nodded, staring at him.

'But I'll be back soon – you know that, don't you?'

She nodded again.

One of the larger fish in the tank started nosing at the gravel in the bottom of the tank, then Joe let himself out of **KEITH'S UNISEX HAIRDRESSER'S** and got into the car. He switched the light on and saw that it was nearly ten o'clock.

2

Linda took the corner into Pollards Close even faster than she'd taken it that morning, slamming the brakes on hard outside the Saunders' house and turning the wheel until the car was positioned at the top of the drive. Dominique's car wasn't there and, looking across the Close, she saw that Joe's wasn't either. Where were they? Where did they go?

Putting the car into first, she pressed her foot down hard on the accelerator and drove into the Saunders' garage door, unable to avoid banging her head off the steering wheel even though she'd braced herself. She sat there breathing heavily, the Saunders' garage door just the other side of her windscreen, then put the car into first.

The outside light at No. 2 went on and Brian Young opened his front door.

'What the hell was that?' he yelled into the rain.

Linda got out of the car, saw him recognise her and saw him hesitate.

Then he left his front porch and walked out onto the Saunders' drive and they both stared at the garage door where it had buckled just below the handle. 'Are you okay?'

'I don't know what happened,' she said, giving the roof of her car a few light drums, oblivious to the rain now.

The streetlight on the pavement began to flicker.

'Just a minute.' Brian Young disappeared back inside his house, reappearing with a golf umbrella. 'Do you want to stand under this?'

'I'm fine,' she said, smiling even though it was probably a waste of time smiling because he wouldn't be able to see it through the rain.

He came over to look at the front of the car. 'Your right headlamp's smashed,' he said, crouching down. 'The bulb's smashed as well.' He straightened up. 'The rain makes the tarmac greasy.' He looked at the road, whose surface was unsteady beneath the rain and the flickering streetlight, then turned to stare at her, not entirely convinced, adding, 'You were lucky.'

She didn't say anything. There was the taste of warm saliva in her mouth again and she tried to think of something to stop her vomiting.

Brian Young looked down at the front of her car again, the headlamp illuminating his thighs, crotch and midriff. 'We were watching television and we heard this noise.' He shook his head. 'We just heard this really loud noise.'

'Where's Dominique?'

'What? Oh, she had to take Stephanie into hospital.'

'Hospital?'

'She had this really bad stomachache – Dominique thought it might have been an appendicitis.'

Linda stared at him. Was Brian Young in on this too? Was he just another of their stooges? If she rang the hospital to check, would they back up Brian Young's story? What if not only Brian Young but all the staff at the hospital were in on it too?

'I did offer to drive them,' he was saying. 'I know relations aren't . . .' he shrugged '. . . smooth between us, but I did offer to drive them.' He looked up at her. 'Dominique was worried about Delta – she was meant to be meeting them at The Haven. There was some sort of swimming competition going on. I thought she might be home by now.'

'Dominique?'

He shook his head. 'Delta. We heard the car coming down the drive and thought it might be her.'

Linda wasn't interested in Delta. 'So – Stephanie's got an appendicitis?' she said, smiling.

'What?' he said, distracted by the fact that there was a dog wandering up the Close. 'That's what Dominique thinks – I didn't see Stephanie; she was in the back of the car when Dominique rang, but from what she said that's what it sounded like anyway. They left for hospital at about six, and they're still not back . . . so.' He turned round to look at the garage door again. 'You really were lucky. You're sure you're okay?'

Linda drummed on the roof of the car a couple more times. Her face, her hair, her clothes were all saturated, and the rain kept falling, and the streetlight carried on flickering, and Brian Young carried on standing there under his umbrella, and No. 4 Pollards Close remained in the dark.

Linda shook her head and laughed, hair getting stuck to her cheeks. Then she got back into her car.

'What shall I tell Dominique – when she gets back?'

Linda laughed again, slammed the door shut and reversed to the top of the drive.

*   *   *

Brian Young stood under his company umbrella, his shoes and trouser hems now soaked. He looked to see if the stray dog was still in the Close, but he couldn't see it. Then his attention switched to the Saunders' drive and the flickering streetlight he'd already phoned the council about twice – he'd have to phone them again.

8

Linda sat at the top of the drive, the engine running with intent, and watched Brian Young go back to his own front porch. He waved at her then shook out the umbrella, wiped his feet on the mat, dusted a cobweb from the Victorian lamp by the front door then went back inside. She turned the wheel, reversed the car into the street and hit the accelerator as something ran out from behind the pampas grass in the Saunders' front garden. She didn't have time to stop, and felt the wheels on the left-hand side of the car rise up and down. Parking the car, she got out and walked quickly back onto the road. It was a dog she'd run over – a small dog.

It was Ferdie.

Crouching over him, she looked up to see if there were any witnesses, but the street was empty. Not knowing what else to do and not wanting to get caught in anyone's headlights, she realised that she had to get Ferdie off the road – and this wasn't going to be easy given that Ferdie wasn't dead, he was dying. His head and most of his body was a mess, but irritatingly there was a quiver still in his lower left flank. She never knew how to deal with inconclusive things like this and really didn't have time for Ferdie's death right then. Going back down their drive, she opened the garage door and tried looking for some bin-liners. There weren't any. Joe must have something somewhere in the whole garage, surely, for picking up a dead dog from the road. Not wanting to turn the garage light on, it was impossible to find anything so in the end she gave up, opening the tumble drier instead and pulling out three of Joe's shirts that had been in there. She tried to remember which one he'd had the longest then went back up the drive and onto the road.

She tried pulling Ferdie off the tarmac and onto Joe's shirt only she'd never pulled a dying dog off a road in the rain at night before. Irritated, she discovered that bits of Ferdie were sticking to the road's surface where the tyres of her car had driven over him. It was impossible to pull him off clean and his left flank was still quivering and now her nerves were completely fractured.

'If you make a sound – a single sound, you little fuck,' she muttered, pulling, scraping and picking until she managed to get most of Ferdie off the road, standing up and rubbing the patches that were left into the road's surface. This was the kind of thing they made look easy on TV when in fact you needed a tool bag to do it properly. Holding Ferdie, wrapped in Joe's shirt, as far away from her coat as possible, she ran back down the drive, pulled the garage door shut and turned on the light.

Without daring to see if Ferdie's flank was still quivering, she opened up the chest freezer and put him inside on top of some potato waffles, and as she shut the lid it suddenly dawned on her that Brian Young might be telling the truth: what if Stephanie really did have an appendicitis? What if Joe really was in Brighton? For the first time it occurred to her that the gazelle – her gazelle – had been in the Saunders'

343

study. If Joe had given Dominique the gazelle, why would she keep it in the study? It didn't make sense. What if it wasn't Dominique Joe was having an affair with? Why did Joe need to be having an affair at all – with anyone? Staring at the bloody handprints on the lid of the chest freezer, she realised that this was just about the only thing she was convinced about – that Joe was having an affair. Was it with someone she knew? Would this make it worse than someone she didn't know? She went into the house through the door to the kitchen and washed her hands. After she'd done this, she picked up a cloth and some Dettol and went back into the garage to wash the blood off the lid of the chest freezer.

Once she'd done this, she went back into the kitchen and squeezed out the cloth and it was then that she had her idea: she was going to pretend that nothing at all was happening other than what she wanted to happen. Joe didn't know she knew: it was up to her to decide what was and what wasn't happening – not Joe.

She went into the hallway and saw Joe's denim jacket hanging up – soaking wet from the rain – and thought for a moment that he'd come home, even though his car wasn't outside. Maybe something had happened to the car and he'd left it in Brighton and got the train home. Then she remembered that it was Joe's old jacket, and that Jessica wore it now.

She went upstairs into Jessica's room.

Jessica was lying on her bed with her headphones on. She took them off and sat up when Linda walked in. 'Where've you been?'

'The Haven – I went up to The Haven.'

Jessica pressed the soles of her feet together, holding the headphones between her legs. 'I didn't know where you were.'

Linda was staring at her. 'Have you been crying?'

Jessica shook her head.

Linda was about to say something else but in the end asked if she wanted a hot chocolate.

'Can you make it with cream?'

'I haven't got cream.' Linda paused. 'There might be some marshmallows – I could put those on top.'

Jessica nodded. 'Where's Dad?'

'Oh – he's out.'

Jessica waited until Linda had left the room before putting her headphones on again and lying back down.

Linda went downstairs to make the hot chocolate – and saw the farmhouse eggs Jessica had made at school that day in the fridge. She went back upstairs.

'I saw the farmhouse eggs, Jess – I'm sorry.' She turned round, but Jessica was asleep. She stood there for a moment with the hot chocolate in her hand, feeling suddenly over-whelmed by her own heroism, then put it down on the desk and went over to the bed. 'Jessica?'

Jessica's right arm jerked as she ran her hand quickly under her nose and said something, but she did it in her sleep.

Linda took the headphones off then pulled the duvet over her. The only time they were usually this close was when they were yelling at each other, and it occurred to her that the last time she'd really looked at Jessica she'd been about eight. Then, with a longing that knocked the wind out of her so that she had to steady herself by gripping onto the bed's headboard until she thought the skin on her knuckles would split, she thought: Why isn't she eight any more? She'll never be eight again and I missed it – I missed every-thing.

The clock by Jessica's bed said 9.35. She had a shower then went downstairs and thought about making something so that the house was full of the smell of baking when Joe got back – because Joe would get back. What did she make that Joe liked? What had she ever made that he liked? There was something – the night the Niemans came to dinner he asked her to make something. What was it? He'd whispered in her ear; she'd felt him close behind her, close enough for his hair to brush her ear – and she'd refused him? Now, thinking about his hair and how close he'd been standing to her, she found this hard to believe.

Rapping her knuckles on the kitchen bench, she remembered: treacle pudding. He had asked for treacle pudding – told her he loved her treacle pudding. Linda closed her eyes for a moment: Joe loved her treacle pudding.

She started rapidly going through the cupboards. The Atora suet was out of date, but she got the box out anyway. The oven would kill whatever it was in the flour that was making it shift in the jar and look turbulent. The only thing she didn't have was the eggs. She thought she had eggs and tried looking for them, but there were no eggs anywhere in the kitchen. For a moment she stopped and nearly gave up, but what kind of woman – no, what kind of wife – would let a chicken, a fucking chicken, prevent her from satisfying her husband? She didn't need eggs.

Putting on an apron that she tied as tightly as she could round her waist, she started talking herself through the creation of the treacle pudding. By 10.30 the pudding was on the boil so she put a white load on and stood watching the cycle until she was sure she heard a car. It wasn't a car – it was the washing machine playing tricks. An hour later she really did hear the sound of a car and turned round just as the headlights juddered through the frosted glass in the front door. She waited for the car to park and the engine to eventually cut out then opened the front door and stood there smiling under the porch light.

*   *   *

346

Turning into Pollards Close Joe saw lights on in the hallway and the master bedroom of No. 8. He pulled up outside the house, parked in the street and kept the engine running. They'd moved in the day Argentina invaded the Falklands – 2 April 1982 – and he remembered Linda thinking at the time that what was happening on an island over eight thousand miles away in the South Atlantic would make the removal lorry late or, worse, that it wouldn't turn up at all. What was happening in the South Atlantic made her worry that it would rain and that the removal men – if they turned up – would drop the cream and beige sofas; it made her worry that Ferdie, who was only six months old at the time, would work out how to pick the lock of the dog basket he was shaking and crapping in and escape; it made her worry that Jessica, who'd just started wearing black in April 1982, was reading too much and would never make friends and that she'd become a loner – making her, Linda, into the mother of a loner. She was worried about all these things because she'd read the headlines that day and was suddenly reminded of all sorts of things she didn't have time for right then, like Argentinians, the South Atlantic, and war.

Linda and Jessica had driven ahead with the van and he'd sorted out what was left to sort out at Whateley Road. When he'd arrived at Pollards Close later that morning he'd done exactly what he'd done just now, pulling up outside the house and leaving the engine running. He remembered seeing Jessica's head through the back window of Linda's white Toyota, parked in front of the removal van. He remembered getting out of his car and tapping on the window where Jessica, slumped in the back, was trying to look glum and dishevelled while feeling nostalgic about Whateley Road. He gave her a small wave through the window and pointed to the locks, which were pressed down on both doors. She leant forwards and unlocked the door with hands that were sticky from a drink she'd spilt earlier that made her smell of oranges.

'You okay?'

'No. We moved house today, in case you hadn't noticed. Mum just keeps going on about how we've got no furniture and how we're all going to be rattling around in there we've got so much space – like it's the Taj Mahal or something – and the man with sideburns is creepy.'

In the kitchen among the boxes, Joe had found Linda unpacking a wooden animal – what was it? A deer or something – no, the gazelle, it was the gazelle. He'd always thought she didn't like it and remembered being touched that she hadn't taken it to the municipal tip; touched that she hadn't heard him come in; touched that she provoked all these thoughts in him when he didn't even love her. He'd wanted to wrap his arms around her and protect her from his lack of love for her. Only she turned round then and looked up at him – frowning instead of smiling.

He turned the engine off and looked across at the house and there was Linda, standing at the front door under the porch light, wearing an apron. Was she waving at him?

As Joe got out of the car she even managed a small wave, and this was while noticing that the tyres on the back of the car were much flatter than the ones at the front, which meant that the auriculas were still in the boot. If she walked up to the car and opened the boot she'd see a stone urn potted up with auriculas because Joe hadn't been to Cassidy Street, but she wasn't going to say anything – she was going to stay on the porch, smiling.

It was 11.30.

She waited.

He got out of the car and walked towards her. He looked exhausted, but she could see he had things to tell her; she

348

could feel them beginning to lap at her toes already and the only thing she had to do was ensure that he didn't tell her – that he never told her. As long as they were untold, she could control them, and she could control Joe if whatever it was he was doing, whatever other life it was he thought he was leading, was never given the chance to breathe; to become reality. She mustn't give the other Joe oxygen; oxygen was what she was going to starve him of.

'Linda . . .' he said, coming to a halt in front of her.

She could see him building himself up to say whatever it was he needed to say and he needed to say it so badly he wasn't even going to wait until they were indoors; he was going to do it right here by the front door under the porch light. The only reason he hadn't said anything yet was because her smile was confusing him so, still smiling, she pulled him indoors, saying, 'Come inside – it's freezing out there,' ignoring the fact that Joe smelt of smoke.

She got him into the hallway, but he became motionless again once she shut the door.

'Linda . . .'

She had to keep him moving. 'Through here,' she said, leading him into the kitchen. 'Guess what?'

'What?' he said.

'I made something.'

'You did?'

She nodded. 'Your favourite.'

Joe rubbed his hands quickly over his face. 'What's my favourite?'

'Treacle pudding – do you want some?'

He didn't respond.

'Why don't you make custard, and I'll sort the pudding out.' She turned ecstatically towards the pan she'd boiled the pudding in and lifted the basin out, standing it on the surface and taking the tinfoil off the top; swinging her face backwards and forwards across the steam. 'Did you smell it when you came in?'

It was essential that she got Joe to move; her entire future depended on keeping him moving, so she handed him the saucepan she had ready, with half a pint of milk measured into it, and told him to put it on the boil.

He moved over to the cooker then came to a halt again.

Linda started to get plates out, ignoring the fact that Joe was standing in the middle of the kitchen, motionless. She counted to sixty, knowing that if he hadn't moved by then she'd have to come up with something else. Then on the beat of sixty he jerked to life and walked slowly over to the cooker.

He switched on the hob and turned round, staring at her.

She flashed him a quick smile.

'Linda . . .'

'The custard powder's in the jug – just there,' she said through her smile.

'What?'

'We need custard – to go with the pudding – the powder's in the jug there, ready.'

'We're having custard?'

'Of course – look, the milk's about to boil.'

He stood there for a moment, overwhelmed, before turning off the gas and pouring the milk into the jug that Linda pushed across the surface towards him.

His right arm and face disappeared in steam then he turned round again. 'Linda, look . . .'

'Treacle pudding!'

'It's nearly midnight.'

'It's a treacle pudding without eggs – no eggs in it whatsoever,' she said, turning it onto a plate and lifting the basin off. The pudding was just about set.

He shook his head.

'What – you don't believe me?'

'I don't want pudding.'

'You don't want treacle pudding?'

'No, I don't want treacle pudding.'

'Well, I'm having some.' She turned her back on him and cut herself a piece, somehow managing to eat it. 'Egg free,' she said. 'The sponge is entirely egg free. I didn't think it would work.' She brushed her hands over the jumper she'd put on after her shower, walked quickly past him, and grabbed the jug of custard.

'Linda . . .'

'Come and try some.' She filled her plate with custard then dug the spoon in.

'Linda!'

'Try some – it's your favourite. Come on, Joe,' she implored him, 'you know it's your favourite.' Turning towards him, she pushed the spoon into his mouth, suddenly taken with the idea of force-feeding him treacle pudding . . . of maybe even killing him with treacle pudding.

'For Christ's sake,' he mumbled, trying to swallow.

'More?'

'It's fucking midnight,' he said, banging on the table and making the kettle jump. He opened out his hands, imploring her to embrace this fact – any fact. The facts were crowding in on him now.

'You're right. Here,' she broke off, 'your tea.'

'Linda . . .'

'I'm off to bed – come on.' She yawned then walked upstairs, waiting until she got halfway up before turning round to look over her shoulder. She heard Joe hesitate then follow her. By the time she'd reassured herself that it was his tread she heard on the stairs, she'd almost ripped the banister off the wall. She got him into the bedroom, shutting the door behind them. They moved around each

351

other, passed each other on the way to and from the en suite and performed all the other minutiae of ritual that took them from dressed to undressed until Linda was lying in bed in the dark next to Joe.

She waited for him to fall asleep first before falling asleep herself. She slept lightly for about five hours; five hours full of bad dreams.

1 MARCH – 11 OCTOBER 1984

8

Linda woke at six, and knew exactly what it was she had to do. She had to remove the stone urn, planted up with auriculas, from the back of Joe's car; she had to remove anything that would trigger in him an impulse to confess – including his tongue, if it came to it. She dressed in the clothes she'd dropped on the floor the night before – as quietly as she could – then went into Jessica's room. The heating hadn't come on yet and the house was freezing cold.

'Jessica,' she hissed. 'Jessica.' She knelt down next to the bed and gave her a light shake. 'Jess!' she said again, gripping onto the headboard.

Jessica woke up suddenly, terrified. Someone was kneeling beside her bed. Then she recognised her mother, and for a moment she thought Linda had come to kill her – that all their rows had culminated in this.

'What? What is it?' Linda said hoarsely, looking down at Jessica's terrified face.

Jessica lay there, managing to turn onto her side and press the back of her body against the bedroom wall. 'You're going to kill me, aren't you?' she said.

'I'm what?'

355

'You're going to kill me.'

Linda stared at her. 'What the hell are you talking about – I just wanted your help with something, that's all.'

'What – now?'

'Right now.'

'What time is it?'

'I don't know – early. There's something we need to get out of the boot of Dad's car.'

'Why can't Dad do it?'

'He's asleep.'

'Why can't he do it when he wakes up?'

'I want to do it before he wakes up.'

Linda stood there and waited as Jessica got out of bed.

'I'm already dressed,' she said, confused.

'You fell asleep – last night.'

'Last night?'

'I brought you up a hot chocolate, but you were already asleep. I didn't want to disturb you.'

Jessica looked over Linda's shoulder at the mug of hot chocolate on the desk where it had been left the night before.

'I put marshmallows in it. You asked for marshmallows.'

Jessica stared at her. She couldn't remember Linda ever making her a hot chocolate before – why would she have made her one last night? 'Marshmallows?'

Linda nodded. 'You need shoes,' she said, looking down at her daughter's bare feet.

'I'm sorry about the hot chocolate.'

'It's fine – just put some shoes on.'

'Where are we going?'

'There's a pot in the back of Dad's car with plants in it. He bought them for Nan Palmer and she didn't want them – he's really upset about it,' Linda said, off-hand, not daring to look at Jessica. 'I thought we'd take them out of the car and put them at the end of the garden so he doesn't have to think about them any more – doesn't have to get upset any more,' she said.

They went downstairs.

'It smells funny,' Jessica said when they got to the kitchen.

'Funny?'

'It smells like – have you been baking or something?' She stared at the apron thrown across the breakfast bar and the two bowls with the remains of treacle pudding and custard in them.

'Last night.'

'What did you make?'

'It doesn't matter now,' Linda said. 'Go through and open the garage door and the door to the garden as well, but do it quietly – I don't want Dad waking up.'

She quickly cleared the remains of last night's midnight feast into the sink then took the spare set of keys off the rack by the front door and went out to where Joe's car was parked. The world outside was silent and frost-ridden and Linda slipped crossing the pavement. Behind her she heard Jessica opening the garage door. She knew it would be easier if she reversed her car out and drove Joe's in because then they wouldn't have to carry the pot so far, but that was more likely to wake up Joe, and Joe mustn't be woken. She unlocked the boot and there was the stone urn full of wilted alpine auriculas. Joe had been to Al's for the auriculas – he must have been meaning to go to Cassidy Street, but never got round to it.

'We can't carry that pot,' Jessica said, coming up behind her and looking into the boot. She was shivering with the cold.

'We have to.'

'We won't even be able to lift it – it's stone, Mum.'

'You get that side and I'll get this.'

'Circles don't have sides.'

357

'What?'

'The pot's circular – circles don't have sides.'

'Not now, Jessica,' Linda warned her. 'Right – have you got your hands under it?'

'We'll never do it.'

'I'm pushing it your way.' Linda pushed. 'Come on, Jess.'

'I can't.'

'Come on!'

They hauled it out of the boot, balancing it for a moment on the bumper before lowering it onto the grass verge at the side of the road.

'Mind your feet,' Linda said.

'We did it,' Jessica replied, pleased.

They stood there, panting, both of them looking down at the pot.

'They look dead,' Jessica said. 'What are they?'

'They're – I don't know.' Linda shrugged. 'Something specialist.'

She took hold of the rim and started to roll it over the pavement towards their front garden, leaving a white trail across the tarmac. It rolled easily down the lawn, but took a while to get through the garage past Linda's car, and the bottom got chipped when they lifted it over the doorstep into the garden.

'Where's it going?' Jessica stood up straight, breathing heavily.

Linda looked around the garden at the lawn covered in leaves that had been erratically scraped into piles over the winter months and were now rotting. 'Behind the shed.'

Jessica followed Linda's instructions without hesitation now.

They got the pot behind the shed where Linda had once planted a clematis and forgotten about it, and stood there looking down at the auriculas Al had nurtured and planted

358

up for Joe. Then they looked at each other and started to laugh. The laughter became hysterical and soon Jessica was bent over with it and Linda was clutching the back of the shed.

After a while she staggered into the garage and there was Joe, standing in the kitchen doorway in the three-quarter-length striped terry towelling dressing gown she'd bought to make him look like Roger Moore.

'I came down to make tea,' he said, as if coming down-stairs was something he needed permission to do. 'I saw you and Jess in the garden – d'you want tea?'

Linda nodded, her mouth loose and her face relaxed, staring at him.

'D'you want me to make breakfast?' he said. 'I could do waffles.'

'I think we've got waffles.' She went to the freezer and lifted the lid. In the kitchen, Joe was filling the kettle with water. Picking up Ferdie – who was now frozen, his lips pulled back as if he'd been sharing her and Jessica's joke – she found the box of waffles and started laughing again.

Joe reappeared in the kitchen doorway, his toes spread out over the step. 'What?' he said, staring at her standing by the chest freezer, cradling what looked like Ferdie in one hand and a box of waffles in the other.

'Nothing,' she said, shaking her head, too hysterical now to say anything else. 'Nothing.'

The only thing Joe found reassuring about the whole scene was the Birds Eye logo on the box of waffles.

Following the February crisis and Ferdie's untimely death, Linda and Joe Palmer had never got along better. Everybody in Pollards Close commented on it – even the newlyweds who bought No. 14 when Mr Browne sold up to move in next door with Mrs Klusczynski.

359

During this time, Linda took her cue for reality from other people's opinions of them – which was that they had never got along better – and in this way successfully managed to ignore the fact that Joe was now going down to Brighton at least three times a month. Once – only once – did Linda give in and phone Belle when Joe said that's where he was going.

'That you, Linda?' Belle said, picking up the phone.

'Can I speak to Joe, Mum?'

'Joe? Is he meant to be here?' Belle said.

'Don't worry – I've got my nights muddled. I don't know what I'm doing ringing you – he's out playing golf.'

Silence on the line.

Then Linda saying again, 'He's out playing golf.'

Sometimes he *was* out playing golf, but not that time. That time he was out getting his hair cut because he came home with it cut in a new style, which meant that someone other than her now had control over Joe's hair – only she couldn't say anything because as long as they didn't talk about it, Joe's hair remained cut in the same style he'd always worn it.

Life carried on; a life created by Linda for Linda.

The strain of living like this meant that there were moments when reality became corrupted by possibility as all three Palmers started looking for a way out.

One Saturday afternoon in early summer, Linda was cleaning the grouting in the en suite shower cubicle while Joe was downstairs in the garage, putting up some new shelves. Even above the sound of the extractor fan she could hear the high-pitched grinding of the drill going into breeze blocks. She'd bought a new cleaning product for the grouting from Robert Dyas and stood with her hands on her hips and her face frowning with satisfaction, comparing the wall she'd cleaned to the one she hadn't – pleased at the obvious difference – when it occurred to her that she couldn't hear Joe's drill any more. She waited for it to start up again, but it didn't. When had it stopped? She became suddenly convinced that Joe wasn't drilling holes for new shelves at all, but had been putting hooks into the garage ceiling that he was going to tie rope to before climbing up the old stepladder, kicking it away and hanging himself.

That Joe should attempt suicide seemed a vivid possibility – wasn't that the squeaking sound the old ladder made when it was opened? The rope was already up and now she could hear the deeper squeaking the ladder made when it bore the weight of Joe climbing it.

'Joe,' she screamed, running out of the en suite. 'Joe,' she screamed again when she got to the kitchen, still in her rubber gloves, the J-cloth with pink grouting cleaner on it, in her hands.

Through the open door she could see Joe holding his spirit level against the garage wall and making marks with his carpenter's pencil. When he'd finished, he turned round to look at her. 'What?'

There was another moment about a month after this when temperatures were in the high twenties and she was out in the back garden mowing the lawn in shorts and a bikini top. Joe had bought her a spaniel pup – Horatio – to replace Ferdie who, as she explained to both Joe and Jessica, must have jumped into the chest freezer when she wasn't looking – and frozen to death. Horatio veered between two behavioural extremes: hysteria and catatonia. That morning he'd been yelping round the house nonstop with his eyes and tongue rolling, as if anticipating being gang-raped by a pack of dogs. Then by 11 o'clock, when Linda plugged the lead for the Flymo into the garage socket, he was lying in the centre of the lawn, inert.

She lit a cigarette. Whenever Joe came home from

Brighton he always smelt of smoke, so she had to take it up again. She went out into the garden and started up the Flymo, moving it over the patchy lawn and wondering where all the red ants' nests had come from. Even the sound of the Flymo didn't get a flicker out of Horatio, and his inertia made her suddenly, unaccountably furious. She tipped her head back, blowing out the smoke and looking straight up at the sun in the sky. With the cigarette still in her right hand, the Flymo in her left and moving red sunspots all over the garden, she dragged the lawnmower across the lawn and over Horatio's tail and back legs in one sweeping movement. As the dog started screaming she took another drag of her cigarette, the Flymo still running. She felt better – much better.

Linda wasn't the only one affected by the strain of it all – Joe had his moments as well. There was the weekend he was in the shed cleaning all the cracks and crevices in Jessica's old dolls' house with a carton of ear buds, when he became suddenly aware of somebody standing in the doorway, blocking out the light.

In a panic, he staggered to his feet. The ear buds spilt out onto the shed floor and he banged his head off the emergency lantern hanging from a nail in the roof.

'Linda – don't!' he shouted, instinctively turning round with his hands held protectively in front of him.

'What?' she said, staring back at him. 'I just came to ask you where you kept the spare amps?'

Another night, he was watching *Lawrence of Arabia* on TV with the patio doors open because of the heat when he heard a bang coming from upstairs. He went out into the garden, looking up at the back of the house. 'Jess?' he called up at her open window.

No reply.

He went running back indoors, suddenly convinced that

Linda was upstairs trying to murder Jessica. He pictured Jessica lying on her bed listening to music and Linda pressing a pillow over her face, suffocating her.

'Jess!' he yelled, trying to take the stairs two at a time, 'Jess!'

The bedroom door was ajar. He stumbled in and there was Linda standing in front of Jessica's wardrobe while Jessica knelt on the floor among a pile of LPs that had fallen out of the cabinet.

'Dad?' Jessica looked round and saw him stooped over, panting for breath.

'You should take more exercise, Joe,' Linda said, without turning round. 'We were just having a clear-out up here.'

In August that year, Linda persuaded Joe to have an advertisement made for Quantum Kitchens that would play in the cinema at Littlehaven's new Arts Centre. One of the best adverts showing at the time was for Starr Shoes and had a denim-clad man wearing new boots, running through a quarry while being chased by a Jeep with four men in it who looked Colombian – where did the director get Colombians from locally, Linda wondered? The men in the Jeep start shooting at the man in denim and are just drawing level with him, revolvers raised, when the Jeep breaks down. With smoke pouring from the engine, all the Jeep doors open simultaneously and the four men get out then look down and realise that they've got no shoes on. Meanwhile the denim-clad hero has scaled the side of the quarry in his new boots from Starr Shoes. He waves at the barefoot Colombians standing in the quarry below by the broken-down Jeep. After smiling at the camera, he holds up a sign: *Starr Shoes – make it your choice*. The barefoot Colombians in the quarry try shooting at the sign, but the bullets don't reach. The sign starts growing, getting bigger and bigger until it fills the screen.

As soon as Linda saw the Starr Shoes advert she knew that Terry King was the director she wanted for the Quantum advert.

'The best advertisements aren't just a string of images,' Terry said over coffee during an informal meeting with Linda at Quantum offices. 'The best adverts have plots.'

'Like the one for Starr Shoes,' Linda put in.

'Like the one for Starr Shoes,' Terry agreed.

Linda was as impressed with Terry as she'd anticipated being – especially given the fact that he was only in his late twenties.

The opening shot for the Quantum advert would show a newlywed couple in their first home with the bride in tears over the state of the kitchen and the young man tearing his hair out trying to comfort her. It would then cut to the Quantum Kitchens showroom, where Steve – who turned out to work well on camera – would give the young couple a guided tour, save the day and – by implication – the marriage. Terry wanted the final scene to show the newlyweds back home in their new Quantum kitchen, opening a bottle of champagne and starting to kiss – at which point Steve's head and torso would appear, wagging a finger at the couple, before pulling a blind down across the screen. The blind would have **Quantum Kitchens – Affordable Dreams** written across it. The slogan was Linda's idea and the backing track they jointly decided on in the end was Olivia Newton-John's *Xanadu*, which would start up as the young couple walked through the showroom doors.

At the same time that filming was taking place at Quantum Kitchens, Jessica and Mr Browne's manual, *How to Survive a Nuclear War*, had been accepted by small independent publisher, T(he) R(ight) T(o) K(now) – TRTK. Jessica went up to London with Mr Browne and Mrs Klusczynski to meet TRTK's editor, who was also a dentist at the Whitechapel Hospital. The meeting took place in a room in the hospital during which the dentist/editor forgot to take off her surgical gloves. TRTK published books on third-world poverty, biographies of revolutionaries, and women's rights – they were looking to expand their nuclear section. Jessica had been back up to London twice on her own since then for further meetings while Mr Browne and Mrs Klusczynski were somewhere in Greece on holiday.

Jessica brought the TRTK catalogue home to show Linda. Linda was touched, but couldn't work out why a dentist would also publish books – who read these books anyway? And where was this world Jessica went to on a train from Littlehaven where female dentists ran political presses in their free time?

Linda spoke to Trevor Jameson at the *County Times*, who'd already run an article in July on Jessica sitting her A Levels early, to tell him about the publication of *How to Survive a Nuclear War*. After suggesting that his daughter Martine and her husband play the role of the newlyweds in the Quantum advert, Trevor promised to make Jessica's book front-page news, even though he didn't like the title. Friday's edition of the paper was about to go to print when the news came in that Judith Macaulay, wife of Minister Macaulay who disappeared in February, had committed suicide in the Methodist Church by hanging herself from the balcony. She was found by Brownie patrol leader Hannah Greene, who was first to turn up for Church Parade on the Sunday.

The suicide made Linda feel guilty without really knowing why and she got sick of looking at the picture on the front of that Friday's *County Times* of Judith Macaulay crouching with a pair of open secateurs in her shrubbery during happier times, laughing.

The Friday after – the first Friday in September – Trevor ran the article on Jessica. The headline read 'LOCAL GIRL GETS BOOK PUBLISHED'. The photograph printed underneath had been taken in the back garden of No. 16 with

Jessica in the centre and Mr Browne and Mrs Klusczynski on either side. Linda didn't like the photo – which looked unsettlingly like a family snapshot with the three of them standing underneath the cherry tree and Mrs Klusczynski's hand on Jessica's shoulder.

A week after the article was published filming started on the Quantum advert. Joe didn't get involved. Even when they were shooting in the showroom, he just sat in his office as normal.

The advert was due to be released at the cinema in October and Linda decided to organise a screening before that on the 11 October at No. 8 Pollards Close.

Joe woke on the morning of the eleventh to hear Linda telling him that it was a perfect autumn day. She said it another three times – laying a lot of stress on the word 'perfect' – before he even got round to opening his eyes.

When he did open them, vaguely aware of a bluish light in the room, he saw her slipping out of her dressing gown and feeding her legs into a leotard, pulling the stretch cotton up over her ribcage and breasts. This took her approximately three seconds, which meant that his wife had been naked for three seconds and he hadn't been conscious of it. He'd seen her arse, he'd seen something darker as she bent over, and he'd seen her breasts, and the sum total of all these parts – before the stretch cotton got to them – was that Linda had been naked and he hadn't even noticed. Still only semi-awake, he'd watched his wife undressing in front of him and noted the aniseed smell she let off as she bent over with the irresponsible curiosity of a passer-by – only he wasn't passing by.

Then he realised that she was watching him watch her and thought about how she'd paused before stepping into her leotard so she must have been aware of him watching her since then. She'd paused because – unlike him – she was aware that she was naked. Now, dressed in the leotard with her hip bones jutting out, she paused, waiting. She carried on waiting until he yawned and rolled over before getting slowly out of bed.

'What's that?' he said through a second yawn.

'I said, it's a perfect day out there – a perfect autumn day.'

'It is?'

He couldn't remember why the weather needed to be perfect today, he only knew from her tone that it did, and that it was something she felt she had temporary control over, which was why she'd paused provocatively – she had paused provocatively – before stepping into the leotard.

'The screening tonight, Joe,' she said, watching him through the mirror as he scratched at his stomach beneath the pyjama waistband. 'It's a perfect autumn day – and we've got the screening tonight. The Quantum advert screening.'

Joe carried on staring at her, trying to make a connection between the weather and the screening – the screening was taking place indoors after dark, so what did it matter? 'Great,' he said after a while.

She kept her eyes on him as he went over to the window and looked out – something he never used to do – then got onto the bike.

Joe disappeared into the en suite and reappeared ten minutes later looking exactly the same. He laid out everything he was going to wear that day on the bed, aware of the constant movement out of the corner of his eye that was Linda.

Unable to believe that he was about to get dressed in the clothes he'd just laid out, he picked up the shirt and put it on, mildly amazed that it still fitted. He was about to leave the bedroom when Linda said, breathless, 'Change the tie.'

Joe stood there, suddenly aware that it was Linda who seemed to be emitting the blue light. 'The what?'

'Your tie – you need to change your tie. You never wear that tie with that shirt.'

He went over to the vanity unit, watching himself in the mirror as he undid the tie, then opened the wardrobe and pulled out another one, pushing it in his trouser pocket.

He paused by the bedroom door, half expecting Linda to ask which one he'd chosen, but she didn't.

'I put the bread out near the toaster – and there's eggs as well – somewhere.'

'You're not eating?'

'I already had breakfast.'

'You ate something or you drank something?'

'I had a shake.'

'I thought you stopped the diet.'

'I did stop the diet – I started it again a week ago.'

The reason the diet had been stopped and restarted was the pack of antidepressants that came with the starter pack.

Joe kept hold of the tie in his trouser pocket. 'Does Jessica need breakfast?'

'I don't know – what's the time?'

'Eight.'

'Hasn't she already left for school?'

'I don't know,' Joe said, leaving the bedroom and going downstairs into the kitchen where there was the smell of toast – and where Jessica was standing.

'We didn't know whether you'd left for school or not,' he said.

'Why would I have left for school – it's only eight.'

'What time do you usually leave?'

Jessica hooked two slices of toast out of the machine and turned round to look at him. 'Eight fifteen,' she said.

'Eight fifteen,' Joe repeated.

She stood staring out the kitchen window, eating her toast in silence.

'Mum said there were eggs,' Joe said.

'She always says that – there never are.' Jessica shrugged, without turning round.

Joe wanted some breakfast, but was afraid to go over to the toaster while Jessica was standing there, so he stayed where he was, wondering when exactly he'd become so afraid of his daughter and whether you always ended up becoming afraid of people you lied to – whether not telling the truth was even the same thing as lying. After a while he went into the lounge and stared through the patio doors at the same view Jessica was staring at next door in the kitchen. The Laing flag on the other side of the fence was barely moving, but the mast was leaning over to one side, pointing skywards at an angle. When had that happened? He was full of a sudden, overriding hunger he was unable to satisfy because he was afraid of going into the kitchen where his daughter was, and he didn't know what to say to her any more. Since when hadn't he known what to say to Jessica? Since about three months ago.

Out the window the flag was now almost completely still.

Suddenly angry, he went back into the kitchen and walked aggressively over to the toaster, pulling two slices of Mighty White out of the bag.

'What's wrong?' Jessica said after a while.

He looked up. 'Nothing.'

'You were staring at the bag of bread, like . . . I don't know.'

'What is this?' he said, picking up the Mighty White bag and staring intently at the picture of a boy on the side.

'Bread – like it says.'

'But when did we start getting it?' he said, in a panic because the packaging seemed suddenly intensely unfamiliar.

'We've been getting it forever,' she replied, finishing her

369

toast and putting the plate on the draining board next to the blue-streaked glass Linda's shake had been in. 'It looks like white bread, but it's got the nutritious value of brown.' She paused. 'It's for people who can't make up their minds.'

His toast popped up and, ignoring Jessica's comments, he reached for the Blue Ribbon margarine. The packaging for this seemed just as unfamiliar as the packaging for the bread, only he decided not to mention it. 'What?' he said, seeing Jessica's face.

'The noise.'

'What noise?'

'The way you're eating – you're making a noise,' she said, disgusted by his appetite right then.

He wiped his mouth. 'I'm sorry about the noise, Jessica. I'm sorry if it's breakfast-time and I'm hungry.'

'I didn't mean that.'

'Do you want me to go and eat somewhere else so the noise doesn't bother you?' He threw his plate with the half-eaten toast on it into the sink, and left the room.

'Dad – where are you going?' she called out after him.

'To work,' he said, 'if that's okay with you.'

'But you're coming home for the screening tonight?'

'Of course I'm coming home for the screening,' he said, his hand on the door chain.

'Mum's put a lot of effort into it.'

'And I've said I'll be there.' He felt suddenly exhausted – like he'd done a day's work already, and it was only eight fifteen in the morning.

'We've got the Saunders, the Niemans and the Nassams coming – and Steve and Maureen from the office as well.'

Joe swung round. This was exactly what Linda would have said if she'd been standing there.

'And I'm doing fondue,' she added.

He stared at her standing in the kitchen doorway, trying

370

to persuade him to come home that night with the promise of fondue – whatever that was. When they used to talk, Jessica would spend hours trying to convince him that if he could just open his mind to the possibilities in the relationship between space and time, it would only take a small leap of faith to believe in the existence of parallel universes; even if they couldn't be seen yet. Now the only thing she was trying to convince him of was that it was worth coming home tonight because she was making fondue, and he didn't know whether this made him or her the child still.

'I'm doing cheese,' Jessica said, 'but I could do a chocolate one instead – if you want.'

'A chocolate what?'

'A chocolate fondue – I could do fruit and things, and we could have a chocolate one instead.'

Chocolate, cheese, it didn't matter, Joe thought, because he'd already sacrificed Jessica; he'd sacrificed his daughter – to what? To Lenny? To the future? – and now he had an even greater responsibility for her than he'd had when she was just his daughter because now she was also his victim. The door chain slipped out of his fingers and rattled against the frame. 'Cheese is fine,' he said, 'I'll see you later.'

He walked out of the house and got into his car without turning round to look back, because out of the corner of his eye he was sure he saw movement and didn't want to see Jessica standing at the front door in her school uniform trying to wave him off to work because, beyond her belief in parallel universes, she had a whole host of notions left over from childhood about what wives should do. She was trying to cover up what she perceived to be Linda's below-average performance by stepping into Linda's shoes – only she was too young to behave like this; she was too old as well.

He was tired of women; he didn't understand them.

Joe was almost at Foundry Lane Industrial Estate by the time he realised he hadn't even said goodbye to Linda, and once he'd parked the car at Quantum Kitchens she only featured in his mind in the abstract – as a vague blue presence.

4

Dominique opened her eyes, took in sunshine on the other side of the curtains, and knew she wouldn't be able to get up. The black dogs had come for her in the night. She rolled over to face Mick.

'It's eight o'clock,' he said, yawning.

She stared at his nipples and the moles on his chest and didn't say anything.

He yawned again then swung himself quickly out of bed into an upright position.

'Come on, Dom.' He patted the curve of her hip. 'We're running late.'

She watched him disappear into the en suite, his feet slapping loudly against the cork tiles in there. Then there was the sound of water – peeing, flushing, washing – which was the sound of the day beginning, and it was all too much for Dominique.

Mick came stalking back into the bedroom smelling of cologne – one she'd bought him that he said he liked and that she'd liked when she bought it, only now she wasn't so sure.

'Come on, Dom,' Mick said, rapidly going through his drawers.

'I'm coming,' she replied, watching the bottom of the curtains blowing in and out in a draught that was coming through the window.

Mick went through to Steph's room.

'I can't tie my shoelaces,' Steph's voice said.

'You can tie your own laces,' Mick said, 'so tie them and get downstairs – and you're not taking your rag into school today, Steph – you'll only give Mrs Howard the satisfaction of confiscating it.'

'I can keep it secret,' Steph said.

'You can't keep anything secret,' Mick responded.

'Where's Mum?'

'Coming. Steph – downstairs now.'

Dominique listened to the footsteps on the stairs and it felt as though the day ahead was a labyrinth they were walking into, and that she didn't have the energy to follow them.

She lay there listening to bags slamming on tables, crockery being unstacked and kettles being filled with water, and the whole thing exhausted her and left her short of breath. She just wanted to sleep; she just wanted not to have opened her eyes – however long ago it was that she'd opened her eyes – and seen sunshine on the other side of the curtains.

She heard Mick's voice coming up through the floor. 'I'm frying eggs.'

'I'm on a diet.' That was Delta.

'We don't do diets in this house, Delta, you know how I feel about dieting.'

'But I'm going to Spain with Liz next summer – I've got to shift this stuff off my hips.'

'We need to talk about Spain, and this Liz person – who is Liz?'

'A friend.'

'Well, we need to talk about Spain and the friend – Liz – and you're perfect so eat up. Steph – are you ready? You've got piano today, so don't forget your music. It's in the hallway – there – just by the umbrella stand. There!' Mick said, raising his voice for the first time. 'Use your eyes, Steph.'

Steph walked back into the kitchen with her music case. 'Mrs Nassam says love's the best fat burner ever.'

'What does Sandra Nassam know about love?' Delta said, disgusted.

'More to the point,' Mick warned her, 'what is it you think you know about Sandra Nassam? Never presume to know anything about other people – anything.'

'Why haven't you got a boyfriend?' Steph asked.

'Who wants a boyfriend,' Delta said. 'I want a lover.'

'You need to get married first,' Mick said through a mouthful of food, 'then you can take a lover.'

'I'm never going to get married,' Delta said.

'Never?' Stephanie paused, amazed, then said, 'Where's Mum?'

'Mum's coming.' Mick's voice, off-hand, reassuring.

'I bet you I'll never get married,' Delta insisted.

'How much?' Mick said. Then, before she had time to answer, 'Right, we're off – Delta, you need to move your car off the drive.'

'Aren't we cleaning our teeth?' Stephanie asked.

'No time.'

'But you have to clean your teeth.'

'Okay, okay. Steph, upstairs – go on – you've got three seconds. Delta, move your car.'

How did Mick do it? Dominique wondered, lying upstairs, listening to her family getting ready for the day. She knew why he did it, she'd always known that, she just didn't know how he found the energy.

She listened to Stephanie climb the stairs, but she didn't

hear her go into the bathroom. Instead it went silent and Dominique, who was lying with her back to the door, knew that if she rolled over she'd see Stephanie standing in the bedroom doorway, watching her – and she didn't want to see Stephanie or deal with Stephanie right then, so she shut her eyes and lay very still.

She heard Stephanie tread softly towards the bed, whispering, 'Mum . . . Mum?' and it was as if she knew Dominique was only pretending to sleep, and needed to uncover her pretence before going to school.

Dominique became aware, lying there trying to keep her eyelids still and her breathing regular, that she was afraid; afraid of Stephanie and the brushing of her soles as she crossed the sheepskin rug. Dominique lay there barely breathing, certain Stephanie had reached the side of the bed and that the clacking sound she could hear was Stephanie's knee joints as she bent down until her face drew level.

Then Mick's voice came yelling from downstairs, 'We're going – come on, Steph!'

Dominique waited, but all she could hear was the sound of Mick's feet on the first few stairs. 'Steph!' he yelled, even louder this time. 'Downstairs – now – come on!'

'I'm coming,' Steph yelled back. Her face must only have been centimetres away; close enough to almost smell the freckles on it and feel the loose hair from her fringe as her knee joints clacked again and she stood up.

'Steph!!!'

Dominique, whose lungs were at breaking point, didn't think she could hold her breath any longer when she felt Stephanie's hair on her face again.

'I know you're awake,' Stephanie whispered in her ear, before leaving the bedroom and running back downstairs.

Dominique, gasping for air, heard Mick's voice at the foot

of the stairs. 'What were you doing up there? It doesn't matter – get in the car – I'll be out in a minute.'

Outside she heard a car door open, followed by Mick's heavy tread on the stairs.

'Dom? Are you awake, Dom?'

She rolled slowly over and stared at him, standing in the bedroom doorway, the car keys in his hand.

'I'm taking Steph to school now,' he said.

'Okay.'

'There's tea in the pot downstairs.'

'Okay,' she said again.

He waited another few seconds then went back downstairs, calling out, 'I won't be long.'

She didn't respond. The front door banged shut and she heard the car start up. The house was silent, and she couldn't remember the last time she'd felt so depressed. She'd been ready for an attack of depression when Delta started art college in Brighton at the beginning of October, but Delta was still living at home – this year anyway – and she knew herself well enough to know that there rarely was a reason for the attacks. The black dogs just came running out of nowhere and got hold of her and she couldn't explain it.

With the depression came fear and panic as well as a tiredness that was narcoleptic. Now there was nobody left in the house, the fear and panic had gone and she thought about getting up and going downstairs for a cup of tea then coming back up and having a shower. She lay there and deliberately imagined herself doing these things. She ran through the whole going downstairs, getting a cup of tea, having a shower scenario, but the thought of actually doing it overwhelmed her. So she lay in bed, listening to the pack of black dogs chasing round the bedroom, staring forlornly through the open door onto the landing where the rest of the house and the outside world lay, as if she was looking into another dimension. How was she going to do today? How was she going to do tomorrow? When Mick was still flying and she had days like this she had to manage, but Mick wasn't flying any more and she no longer had to manage.

They had two estate agents coming to look at the house before lunch and that evening Linda was having people round to watch the advertisement they had made for Quantum Kitchens, and Dominique didn't know how she was going to manage any of it when she couldn't even make up her mind whether to lie on her right side or her left. Why were the estate agents coming again? She had to stop forgetting these things – Mick kept telling her. They were putting the house on the market because they were moving to New Zealand, only none of them had ever set foot in New Zealand before, which meant that they were about to exchange reality for an idea. She hadn't brought Mick to a halt yet and he hadn't brought her to one either; they were both just going ahead with this idea of New Zealand, but what if the only reason Mick was moving them to the other side of the world was in the expectation that he'd find her there; that she'd be waiting for him – homestead style – with open arms? How was it that somebody could go looking for someone they already had by their side?

She was starting to become afraid again when the phone rang in the study downstairs. It rang twice then whoever it was called off. She lay staring at the curtains for about another fifteen minutes then, vaguely aware that she was hungry, managed to get out of bed and make it to the bedroom door, where she was sure the kimono Mick had brought back from Kyoto should be hanging, before remembering that Delta had it now.

The absence of the kimono almost defeated Dominique and she half thought of going back to bed, but she didn't.

She made it to the en suite where her terry towelling bathrobe was and put that on instead, suddenly glad of it because it was cold in the house.

Ignoring the breakfast debris in the kitchen and Stephanie's music case that had been left on the dining table, she poured herself a cup of tea and was hovering in the hallway beside the coat rack, trying to decide whether to go into the lounge or back upstairs, when the phone started ringing again.

She walked through to the study, sipping at her tea, and picked it up. 'Hello?' She stared through the window at the row of pots with hydrangea cuttings in them that Brian Young had given her in September – as a peace offering, she guessed; to let her know that the war of the fence was over between them. 'Hello?' she said again. Was there anybody on the line?

'Hi,' a woman's voice said.

Dominique paused. Was it Delta phoning from Brighton? Delta wouldn't be in Brighton yet, and anyway, Delta wasn't a woman, she was a girl.

'Hello?' How many times had she said that now? She needed a cigarette. She could see the open pack and a red lighter on the bookshelves, nestling against the spine of *Adolf Hitler – A Life*.

'It's – er – Laura – here.'

'Laura?' She walked across the study, but the phone line, even stretched, didn't reach. Did they know a Laura? 'Excuse me for one minute,' she said, putting the phone down on the desk, walking over to the shelves and lighting a cigarette. She picked up the phone again, but it was silent on the other end. Then she heard a sigh – and remembered who Laura was. 'Laura?' she said again, remembering her exactly now from the day she went to pick up Mick at the airport before Christmas, and how Laura had stood under airport strip lighting with her new short haircut that had defined her cheekbones, and how, despite the streamlined look, she'd smelt almost docile, and the combination had made men look at her. Dominique must have noticed, standing there talking to her that day, men looking.

'Is that you, Dominique?'

'Speaking.' Why had she just said that? She never said that.

She'd gone ice-skating with Laura once at the Rockefeller Center during a New York stay-over. Laura had worn a red scarf and laughed a lot, and they thought they might be friends, and Dominique had been touched by Laura's persistence because women didn't usually bother with her. It was as if they could smell a potential for immorality on her; a courtesan-like quality that she herself wasn't aware of, but Laura, laughing Laura, persisted, and for a while they had been friends, friends enough to ice-skate together, but it hadn't lasted.

Other women loved Laura, they welcomed her among them, cosseted her and protected her from the men she seemed to provoke abusive behaviour in. Laura used to have a flat near Gatwick – maybe she still did – overlooking the tracks and platforms of Horley Station, and one of her boyfriends had dangled her out of the window in front of a crowd of commuters waiting for the 7.52 to London Victoria. Despite this Laura had somehow managed to remain intact – in a way that Dominique, who had never suffered at the hands of men, only women, hadn't.

She stood looking at the hydrangea cuttings, smoking and waiting for Laura to speak, aware that Laura hadn't expected her to pick up the phone. Laura had phoned expecting Mick to pick up. Laura had phoned before nine o'clock in the morning because at that time it should have been safe; at that time it should have been Mick who answered. Laura wanted to speak to Mick; Laura needed to speak to Mick – Dominique could hear it in her voice – and they both knew, she and Laura, that Laura shouldn't be phoning.

'Is Mick there?' Laura hesitated, then said again, 'Is he there?'

Dominique didn't respond. She let her thoughts unwind like tentacles around her until she could see them all laid out. She knew now what it was that had bothered her that day when they met at Gatwick – there had been something triumphant about Laura because Laura knew what it meant to have Mick inside her. This was why Laura was phoning, and Dominique was trying to work out what she should feel about all of this because she really should feel something, only the black dogs were yapping round her ankles and when they were doing that she found it difficult to feel anything other than tiredness. She tried to feel shock, but that didn't work. Then she tried grief, and lastly anger, but nothing shifted inside her. The front of her mouth went dry, and at the back of her throat an acid saliva collected and she thought – she hoped – she might vomit, but it didn't amount to anything. The pane of glass that stood between her and the rest of the world – that had been there for as long as she could remember and stopped her from touching things or holding them in her arms – was still there. Even speaking to the woman Mick must have been having an affair with – for how long? – didn't shatter it. Nothing seemed real – not even this. She could understand where Laura was coming from, but Mick? What was Mick doing?

The line was silent, but it wasn't dead. She was more angry with herself than she'd ever be with Laura, whose behaviour was at least natural, whereas she – she was standing in her dressing gown staring at a row of hydrangea

381

cuttings and stubbing out a cigarette, waiting to feel some-thing. It was unnatural; she was unnatural.

'Was he meant to be?'

'What's that?' Laura's voice said.

'Was he meant to be here?'

Laura hesitated again. 'I don't know. Dominique . . .'

'He's taking Stephanie to school. I wasn't well this morning, so he took Steph.' She paused – this was becoming a conversation. 'Shall I tell him you rang?'

'No,' Laura said quickly. 'It's fine. Forget I rang, Dominique – just forget I rang.'

'How can I do that?'

'I'm sorry, look . . . we're not having an affair or anything. It's nothing like that.' She cleared her throat. 'It only happened once – Barbados – in Barbados.'

Dominique put the phone down because it was her right to do so, but primarily because she couldn't be bothered to speak to Laura right then.

She opened the study window and lit a second cigarette. Sheila Young was talking to her dog, Bix, in the garden next door, and she must have had her patio doors open because Dominique heard the phone ringing inside No. 2 and for a moment thought it was Laura phoning the Youngs next door – but why on earth would she do that?

She listened to Sheila pick up the phone and sound pleased to hear from whoever it was on the other end, then she shut the window and went back upstairs to the unmade bed, where she lay waiting for Mick. Looking at the radio alarm clock, the numbers on the LED panel told her that her husband had been gone thirty minutes. It was a fifty-minute round trip to Springfield Park School. She rolled onto her back, then onto her side again, and at some point must have fallen asleep because when she came to, she could hear sounds coming from the kitchen below and a few minutes later Mick walked into the bedroom.

Blearily, she watched him cross the room.

'You awake?'

'Just,' she said.

He stayed where he was at the foot of the bed, watching her.

'How was Steph?'

'Fine – we just got there in time.' He paused. 'She wants a horse.'

Dominique yawned. 'Steph does? She's never ridden one, has she?'

Mick shrugged. 'She wants to start lessons – there are a couple of stables we could phone.' He broke off. 'Are you okay?'

'I'm okay.'

'I'm making coffee – do you want some?'

'Not just yet.'

'Is it your head – have you got a headache?'

'I'm fine – I'll come down and get a coffee.'

Mick sat down, taking hold of her feet and studying her toes. 'It's the black dogs, isn't it?' he said after a while. 'They came in the night.'

'They came in the night,' she agreed.

He thought about this. 'What are we going to do about these black dogs?'

'I don't know.'

He nodded, still studying her toes. 'Is it something I've done – or not done?'

'It's nothing – it's me,' she reassured him, pushing his fringe off his forehead and managing to smile.

'What's bothering you?' He tried again, running the knuckle of his forefinger down her throat.

'Nothing.' She kissed his finger.

383

He kept his finger near her mouth in the way he did when he wanted her to bite on it.

She bit on it now, distracted, thinking about how she'd picked up the phone earlier and heard Laura's voice and not been surprised. All she had to do to bring everything crashing down was mention Laura, and part of her felt excited at the thought of a crash; of bringing an end to things. Why was she forever hankering after an ending – did she expect something to be uncovered or revealed to her at the end? There was nothing fraudulent or deceitful about her life; not even Laura managed to bring an element of fraudulence into things – like she would have done in any other marriage.

Dominique was so preoccupied by this that, looking down, she was surprised to find herself staring at her own breasts splayed out across her chest and, further down, her navel – where at some point in her existence she'd been attached to Monica. The sight of her navel – and of her children's – always overwhelmed her; there was something almost obscenely fundamental about them.

Mick had undressed her. The dressing gown lay thickly open, his leg was hooked over her and he was sucking on her nipples. He'd also undone his trousers because the cold metal buckle was flopping onto her belly.

'No,' she said.

Mick smiled at her.

'Mick – no,' she said, forcefully this time.

He quickly pulled back and stood by the side of the bed.

'What – what is it?'

She pulled the dressing gown back round her, breathing hard, telling herself it was because of Laura, but she wasn't so sure. 'We've got the estate agent coming,' she said.

'Fuck the estate agent,' Mick replied.

She lay looking at the closed curtains. The sun was still

shining through them; outside the day was still perfect. She heard Mick doing up his flies and his belt, and sitting down on the other side of the bed.

'I'm sorry,' he said softly, then, 'I love you,' leaning over and kissing her ears.

She knew he was sorry; she knew he loved her; she didn't know why Laura had to go and phone this morning or why the black dogs wouldn't leave her alone and stop prowling round the bed. She just wanted to be happy like other people – like Mick – like Linda Palmer; she didn't want to be like this forevermore.

'Can I get you anything?'

'I'm fine. I'll get up soon.'

'Do you want to cancel tonight?'

'What's happening tonight?'

'We're going to No. 8 to see the Quantum advertisement.'

Dominique rolled over to look at him. 'That's right – no, I'll be fine.'

'You're sure?'

'I'm sure.'

They looked at each other and Mick was about to say something when the doorbell rang.

'That can't be the estate agent already, can it?'

'I suppose I should go and answer it.' He paused then stood up again and left the bedroom, closing the door carefully behind him. She heard him go downstairs then a loud, cheerful young man's voice filled the house, and the voice was saying 'nice' a lot before she started to drift, until she was back in Gatwick airport before Christmas, standing in front of Laura, who'd just come back from – where was it again? It didn't matter. What did matter was Barbados, and Dominique remembered Barbados because this had been Laura's most triumphant moment during the whole conversation. She'd relished Barbados in a way Dominique hadn't consciously understood at the time. What was it she'd said? That Dominique, who'd never been before, should go. Laura had been on Mick's cabin crew on the Barbados flight a month earlier, which was when it had happened, and she found it easier to imagine it happening in a hot climate because that would require less effort on Mick's part. The light through the curtains made her feel as though she was underwater; as if their entire world had sunk beneath the sea. Laura was in love with Mick. She'd been full of it, bursting with it that day; barely able to stop herself from telling Dominique.

Through the bedroom door she heard the loud young voice commenting on the bull painted on Delta's wall and Mick explaining, and the loud young voice sounding interested.

The black dogs had fled, suddenly, and it had something to do with Laura phoning. With a sudden burst of energy, she got out of bed and went to find Mick, who was still talking to the estate agent in Delta's room.

'She said you only did it once.'

'Dom –' Mick stared at her, his eyes wide, worried.

The estate agent, who hadn't thought there was anybody else in the house, looked startled.

'You only fucked once – apparently – in Barbados.'

'Dom –'

'Is it true?'

The estate agent looked away. There wasn't a great deal to look at, but he kept finding new, ever more absorbing things, while waiting for the woman in the terry towelling robe – who he presumed was Mrs Saunders – to move out of the doorway and clear his escape route.

'What are you talking about?' Mick stayed where he was, not attempting to get any closer.

'Laura. You and Laura. She phoned this morning to speak to you and ended up speaking to me – about Barbados.'

Mick's eyes grew wider, taut. 'Ah – Barbados.'

'Ah – Barbados,' she mimicked him, not unkindly. She didn't want to put her hands to her face to check, but she might even have been smiling. 'Was that the only time it happened?'

'The first and the last,' he said, without trying to reassure her, expecting her to believe him.

'Why Barbados?'

'I don't know – why at all?'

'Do you want me to ask you why you did it?'

'Do you want to ask me?'

Smiling, Dominique bit her lip. 'I don't know – no.' She paused. 'Do you need to talk about it?'

'Do *I* need to talk about it?' Mick's eyes grew even tauter, as he stood there ready to protect her from herself.

'Well – clearly you needed to fuck Laura, so there must be some element of our lives that you need to talk about. Some element that I don't. I mean, after all, Mick, it's not like I need to fuck *him* or anything,' she said, pointing to the estate agent, who'd run out of things to look at. 'Was it good?' Dominique turned back to Mick.

'I don't remember.'

'Remember.'

Mick stood there, his mind full of Dominique, trying to work out whether the fact she'd found out about Laura terrified or released him in some way – and why was she smiling?

'It was different.' He paused. 'She wasn't you. There's nobody apart from you.'

'Is that why you did it – to find that out? Was it experimental?' Without giving him time to answer, she went on, 'Were you drunk?'

'Yes.'

'Was she drunk?'

'Yes.'

The estate agent sat down on Delta's bed, his hands on his knees, noting with relief that there was a Rubik's Cube wedged between the pillow and the headboard.

'Is Laura the only one you've ever committed adultery with?'

'Adultery?'

'That's what it was.'

Mick shook his head. 'That wasn't what it felt like.'

'So what's adultery meant to feel like?'

'I suppose – a place you recognise when you find yourself there; a place you want to go back to. I didn't find anything – with Laura – that I wanted to go back to.'

'Do you regret it?'

Mick hesitated, and right then he regretted that more than anything else.

'I think it meant a lot to her – Laura – probably more than anything else in her life so far,' Dominique continued.

'That much?'

She nodded. 'That much.'

Mick started to take a step towards her then stopped. 'What do you want me to do?'

'Nothing. I don't need you to do anything.'

The estate agent, who'd tried to stifle a rising cough but failed, started to choke.

Mick turned round. 'Are you okay?'

'Can I get a glass of water?' the young man asked, getting to his feet and choking uncontrollably now. He pushed past Dominique, and she and Mick stayed where they were, listening to the estate agent run down the stairs and out of the house. The front door banged shut.

'You're not perfect,' Dominique said, breaking the silence.

'I never said I was.'

Then, carefully, 'I think I'm falling in love with you.'

388

'You think?'

She stood there, holding her arms out towards him, waiting to see if he stepped into them; waiting to see if what she had become in the past half an hour fitted into Mick's future plans for them.

8

Joe looked up from the catalogue on his desk to see Maureen peering at him through the glass panel to the side of his office door, before knocking on it. This was unlike Maureen, and as she walked in he had a sudden premonition that she'd come to hand in her notice.

'Everything all right?' he said.

'Well . . .' She put her hand on the chair in front of his desk.

'Sit down,' he said.

'I'm fine.' She paused. 'It's just this, Joe.'

'What?' He put his pen down then picked it up again.

'I'm not coming tonight.'

'Tonight?'

'To the Quantum screening – at your house.'

'Right.' Joe nodded, relieved. Maureen wasn't handing in her notice.

'It's not that I don't want to,' she carried on.

'No?'

'No, it's not that.'

He stared at her fingers, which looked red and chapped, gripping onto the back of the chair, and noticed for the first

390

time the Tipp-Ex marks on the fabric – he'd have to get Maureen to do something about those because he was pretty sure now that she wasn't handing in her notice.

'It's not that I don't want to come,' she said again.

Joe didn't try to speed things up by prompting her, because he'd become suddenly aware, staring at her permed grey hair and the wrinkles emerging from the dark cleft between her breasts, of just how much he respected Maureen – and that he was afraid of her.

'It's not that I can't – I just don't feel I should.'

She was watching him carefully; Joe could feel her even though he had his eyes fixed on his pen. 'Well,' he mumbled, 'it'll be a shame not to see you, but if you're busy.'

'Oh, I'm not busy,' she said quickly.

He looked up then looked straight back down.

'It's just I'd find it difficult with Linda. I mean, I've known Linda for a long time – I've known you and Linda for a long time,' she added.

Joe managed to lean back in his chair and look up, without looking at Maureen. 'Well, yes . . . it's a shame about tonight. You're sure you can't come?'

Maureen sighed and stood up straight. 'What's going on, Joe?'

'What's going on? Nothing.'

'What's going on, Joe?' she said again.

He dropped the pen and watched it roll off the catalogue onto the desk, then roll across the desk and over the edge onto the floor. Neither of them made a move to pick it up. 'I don't know.'

She nodded, running her hand across the top of the filing cabinet and checking her palm for dust. 'I put calls through from this Lenny woman nearly every day, Joe, and that's why I can't come to your house tonight, and why I can't see Linda.'

Joe didn't know what to say.

'You're hearing me, aren't you, Joe? You know what it is I'm saying, don't you?'

Joe nodded.

Maureen sighed again, but her face had softened and lost the hardness it had when she first walked into the office.

'It makes me feel uncomfortable – complicit – putting the calls through. I don't want to do that any more. I don't want to take calls from her. Tell her not to phone here.'

'Maureen –'

'I mean it, Joe. I'm not putting her calls through any more.'

They stared at each other.

'You'll have to conduct your business elsewhere.'

'It's not business.'

'Whatever it is – what is it?'

Joe stood up. 'You won't change your mind about tonight? I'd like you to. You've been here since the beginning, Maureen.'

'Don't change the subject, Joe. Sooner or later you're going to have to make a choice, and I know you haven't heard this from anybody else, but you're hearing it from me – and you know it anyway.'

Joe pushed the trade catalogue he'd been reading round his desk, wondering what he could say to acknowledge Maureen's courage in speaking to him, but before he got a chance, she said, 'Give her up, Joe.'

'I can't.' He looked at Maureen properly for the first time since she'd stepped into the room. He was ready to tell her everything, and Maureen, who thought this was what she wanted, suddenly worried that she wouldn't be able to bear the weight – what with Gareth being in Geneva and everything – and pulled back at the last moment, opening the office door, her eyes sad and her mouth tight.

Joe saw all this. 'It's good to talk, anyway,' he said.

'We're not talking,' Maureen replied, and left the office, the light bouncing off her shiny peach blouse, the line of the shoulder pads clearly visible.

Instead of judging him, she'd left nothing more than a vague air of disapproval behind her that was only too familiar to Joe.

He sat back down at his desk, the palm of his hand flat against the catalogue, then, suddenly angry, he picked up the phone and dialled the number for Evita's, which was where Lenny would be at this time.

'Hello – is Lenny there?'

'She's busy cutting right now.' The voice paused. 'Is that you, Joe?'

'Look, it doesn't matter.'

'You're sure? I can call her over.'

'No, leave it.'

'D'you want me to tell her you called?'

Joe thought about this for a second, hearing hairdryers and laughter down the line. 'If you want.'

He put the phone down and left his office, walking straight past Maureen – who looked up but didn't say a word – and out of the Quantum showroom.

He got in the car and drove into town, parking in the new multi-storey behind Marks and Spencer. Five minutes later, cold because he'd left his coat on the back of his office door, he walked into Wakefield Jewellers. After ignoring offers of help from two assistants, he stopped in front of a revolving glass case that juddered at the end of each revolution. The handyman in him knew exactly what was wrong with the motor in the base of the display case, but customers in jewellery shops weren't meant to offer to mend faulty motors – Joe knew that now. It was the kind of thing he would have done without hesitation, as a young man, but

393

Linda had taught him to know better. Behaviour like that only made people suspicious because kindness wasn't to be trusted – and that was the way it was.

So, trying hard to ignore the faulty motor, he focused on looking for a present for Lenny because it was her birthday today. They'd had the scene where he broke the news that he wouldn't be able to spend it with her, and it had become a scene because he cared more about his absence than she did; it was him who wanted the argument – not her. All she'd said was, 'I don't go in for birthdays much anyway.' Then, 'This is starting to get complicated, isn't it?' She hadn't sounded happy or sad as she said it, she just said it because it was true; things *were* getting more complicated. It was a fact, and Lenny was good with facts – only sometimes Joe wished she wasn't.

His nose was almost touching the glass. Why was he looking at crucifixes? He didn't know, but he was suddenly sure that that's what he was getting Lenny for her birthday – the most expensive one. He'd never bought Lenny jewellery before. With Linda he never seemed to get it right – apart from the watch he'd bought her for one of their anniversaries, and a bracelet when they'd been in Devon one summer that she wore all the time for a whole year, then never wore again. Maybe she'd lost it – he'd never seen it on her since.

Distracted by the logistics of how to get the crucifix to Lenny, and aware that he wanted to get it to her as soon as possible, but that they hadn't arranged to meet until the following Friday, he didn't notice Mr Wakefield, who owned the shop, standing next to him until he heard somebody speaking.

'What's that?' he said, looking round.

'A confirmation gift?'

'What?'

'You're looking for a confirmation gift?'

Joe stared at the old man's eyes. 'No,' he said, 'no, I'm not.' He paused. 'But I'll take that one there,' he added, turning back to the display case, because if he carried on looking at Mr Wakefield's eyes for much longer he'd end up telling him the whole story from the beginning. He had to tell someone.

Linda parked her Toyota in the multi-storey, on Level 2, surprised at how full the car park was.

She put her sunglasses on as soon as she got out of the car because beyond the concrete walls there was sunshine. Dropping the car keys in her handbag, she was almost at the exit to the lifts when she realised she'd just walked past the Quantum car. She stopped in her tracks, turned round and went back to Bay 33 where she'd passed it.

How many Quantum Fords were there? One. So why was she looking at it like it might not be Joe's? She walked round the side and peered through the windscreen. What was Joe doing in town at this time of the day? There was a troll with pink hair that Jessica had given Joe for his birthday one year, standing on the dashboard smiling frantically at her, as well as an apple with a bite taken out of it that was only just going brown. She stood up, suddenly struck by the fact that the car knew more than she did – this was the car Joe drove down to Brighton in.

Walking back over to the exit, she went into the precinct and made her way to Boots, convinced that people were staring at her. She wasn't imagining things; people were definitely staring. What? She wanted to scream. What now? The woman at the pharmacy counter couldn't take her eyes off her when Linda asked for some of the HRT pills Daphne Nieman had given her.

She checked the shelves. 'No, we don't stock those.'

'You don't stock them? A friend gave me a pack – I've already taken one course – are you trying to tell me they don't exist?'

The woman checked the stock list, then a pharmaceutical catalogue. 'They exist,' she said, 'we just don't stock them.'

'So where should I go?'

'Abroad – looking at this.'

'Abroad?' Linda shouted.

'You won't get Meno-lite in this country,' the woman insisted. 'It hasn't passed UK regulations.'

'Well, when will it pass regulations?'

The pharmacist appeared at the counter. 'Everything okay?' he said, aware that Linda's voice was getting louder and louder.

Linda rounded on him. 'I've been told I can't get Meno-lite in this country.'

'You've taken Meno-lite?' he asked.

'One course.' Now the pharmacist was staring at her – what was it today?

'I'd advise you against taking any more.'

'Why's that?'

'There are potential links between Meno-lite and sepsis, which increases gastrointestinal permeability by destroying digestive-tract tissue.'

Linda nodded.

'Nothing's been proven – clinically – but until it is safe, Meno-lite won't be available over the counter in this country.' He paused. 'Are you okay? I mean – do you feel okay?'

'I feel fine.'

'How long ago was it that you finished the course of Meno-lite?'

'I don't know – about five months ago?'

'Five months? Any side effects?'

'Side effects? Like what – like what sort of side effects?'

'Nausea, vomiting – stomach cramps?'

Linda had a sudden image of herself knee deep in mud and leaves, staring at fluorescent pink vomit down the trunk of a beech tree. She shook her head. 'No – nothing.' She felt nauseous now, but that was because she'd just walked past the Quantum Ford parked in the multi-storey in the middle of the day when it wasn't supposed to be there. 'I wasn't even taking it then,' she said out loud, thinking of the night in the woods when she'd gone looking for Joe. 'I mean, it was the fish fingers that night – I ate too many.'

The pharmacist was still looking at her, one hand hooked in the pocket of his white coat. His nametag said 'Mervin', and that was the strangest name she'd heard of for a long time – especially for a pharmacist. But then, what should a pharmacist be called?

'What?' she said. 'Did I say something?'

'Who's your doctor?' the pharmacist asked.

'Who's my doctor?'

The pharmacist nodded, taking in the woman on the other side of the counter, whose veins had become so pronounced that her skin was more like tracing paper – with such a visible network of blue beneath it, she was giving off a blue light.

Linda walked away, too preoccupied by her failure to obtain more Meno-lite to concentrate either on the pharmacist or the beer-making kit she wanted to buy Joe. Dominique had bought Mick one and now there was a vat of the stuff fermenting in the airing cupboard at No. 4. Soon everybody in the Close – apart from them – would be making their own beer.

Still preoccupied, she walked straight out of Boots, and into Joe.

'Linda,' he said, staring at her as if she was a long way away – at the end of a pier or standing on top of a mountain.

Only she wasn't. They were standing so close their faces were almost touching, which only increased – for Linda – the sense of strangeness and unfamiliarity she was experiencing looking at him this close up.

They took a step back from each other, and Linda saw the small Wakefield Jewellers bag in his hand.

Realising what it was she was looking at, he looked down at it himself, but didn't say anything.

'Are you okay?' he asked.

'Of course I'm okay,' she said, fiddling with the strap on her handbag and wondering whether to mention the Wakefield bag or not. 'Why?'

'You look cold,' Joe said after a while.

'I'm not cold.'

The people passing them in either direction were all staring at her.

'You were in Boots?'

'What's that?' she asked, distracted.

'I said – you were in Boots?'

'Boots? Yes – look, I've got to go,' she said, suddenly wanting to put as much distance between her and the Wakefield bag as she could.

An old man sitting on a bench nearby belched.

'Where are you parked?' Joe asked.

'The multi-storey.' She paused. 'What about you?'

'Oh . . .' Joe swung his body away from her then back to face her again. 'Just behind Sainsbury's.'

She nodded. He was lying, but she was relieved because she didn't think she could bear the walk back through the precinct to the multi-storey with him – and clearly Joe couldn't either. Since when had a short walk together through a crowded precinct seemed so unbearable?

398

'You're sure you're okay?' he asked again. 'It's just you don't look well – I'm worried about you.'

She felt the cynical laugh filling up her throat, but cynicism admitted knowledge of things she'd chosen not to acknowledge, and after fighting a quick battle with herself she managed to swallow the laugh.

'I'm fine – honestly.' She smiled at him. 'See you later,' she added, starting to walk off, before stopping a couple of feet away and turning round. 'Don't be late tonight,' she warned him.

'I won't.'

She left him standing there and didn't turn round again because every time she did the Wakefield bag just kept on getting bigger and bigger.

She drove home fast – as if she had something she needed to get back to – and when she got stuck behind an ice-cream van she became so furious with the ice-cream man's optimism in driving his van around in October that she nearly broke her horn, she was leaning on it so hard.

The house, when she got home, was silent. There was no reason why it shouldn't be, only this afternoon the silence had an emptiness to it that made her anxious, so she switched on the kettle and radio, filling the house with noise and steam. Standing beside Joe in the precinct, she'd suffered a mild attack of agoraphobia, and felt the sudden need to be home. Now she was home, she felt anxious and was about to go back out and sit in the car because she didn't know what else to do, when the local radio station she was listening to announced a product recall on all Slimshake powders. The DJ made the announcement again then put a Van Morrison track on.

Linda stood in the middle of the kitchen, the car keys in her hand, stopped by the brief memory of enjoying the song – a boyfriend she'd had before Joe used to play it all the time. She couldn't remember his name, but she did remember him climbing up the drainpipe at the back of the Lynton Hotel and trying to get into her bedroom. At the time, he'd frightened her, but now – thinking back – how many people were you likely to come across in life willing to scale three-storeys' worth of drainpipe to get to you? Had he been in love with her? He'd gone to one of the Greek islands and married a woman there. She was going to cry; no, she wasn't going to cry. She spun round and went straight to the cupboard, getting out the Slimshake box to look for the customer helpline number.

She phoned and got someone called Haley on the other end, who she tried talking to about the product recall, but all Haley was interested in was the Slimshake newsletter, and whether Linda had a personal success story she wanted to share with other subscribers. Did Linda want to join their miracle-makers club for women over twenty stone?

Linda put the phone down and went into the downstairs loo, balancing the car keys between the hot and cold taps before looking at herself in the mirror. 'Fuck,' she said when she saw what it was people had been staring at.

Her veins were so visible beneath her skin that they dominated all the exposed body parts. Afraid, she lifted her jumper and saw that they were visible on her stomach as well. Her body's entire network of veins was rising to the surface and even the no-man's land of skin between the veins was turning blue. What was going on? She let her jumper drop and ran back into the kitchen, redialling the Slimshake helpline number. 'Haley? Is that Haley?'

'This is Haley – how can I help?'

'I'm blue – I'm turning blue.'

'Who is this please?'

'I'm fucking blue,' Linda said, losing patience.

She could hear Haley digesting this then the line went dead.

Linda stared at the phone in disbelief then dialled again. 'I'm fucking blue,' she yelled. 'Did you fucking cut me off? You have to help me.' This time the line went dead before she'd even finished yelling.

She spent the next thirty minutes jamming the Slimshake helpline at head office in Basingstoke, and Haley kept cutting her off. Then she phoned the surgery and tried to get an appointment with Dr Nassam, her GP, but Dr Nassam was out on call and there was no slot available with any of the other doctors for another two days. She nearly gave in and cancelled the Quantum screening, but after a few minutes' hysterical contemplation, decided to call next door at the Nassams' – on the off-chance that either Dr Nassam was home or she would be able to arrange to see him before the evening.

She rang the doorbell at No. 6 and it was Sandra who eventually answered.

'Linda?'

'Hi.'

'My God,' Sandra said after a while, taking her in. The effect of the blue was entirely undiminished in the clarity of the perfect autumn day.

'Sorry to bother you, but I don't suppose Osman's in, is he?' Linda tried to hide her desperation, but the way Sandra was looking at her was only making it more acute.

'He's out on a call.'

'Will he be in later?'

'We're coming to yours later – for the screening?'

'I mean later before the screening.'

'I don't know.' The effect of the blue was wearing off on Sandra, who was never preoccupied by other people's problems for long. 'He's taking Jamie to tennis.'

401

'I just need to see him – even if it's only for five minutes. I wouldn't ask, but as you can see . . .'

Linda's desperation, which came suddenly searing through the afternoon, began to irritate Sandra, who had problems of her own.

'Look.' She held her hands out in the way she did when she returned faulty goods to shops and the assistants didn't jump to give her a refund. 'I can see that you need to see – someone – but you're just going to have to phone the surgery, Linda. I'm completely – completely – stressed out at the moment. I was made Events Organiser on the Springfield Park PTA this year and I'm up to my eyes trying to organise the Autumn Fair. The balloon people need their deposit by Tuesday and the falconer isn't confirming till Friday – I mean how busy does a falconer's diary get, for Christ's sake? And if it rains – if it rains – God.' She paused, thinking. 'I meant to ask you – this director who filmed the Quantum ad for you – does he do videos of school productions?' she asked, her mind moving rapidly now. 'A professional video of a school production that could go on sale for parents to buy – how much would he charge for something like that? Has he ever done anything like that? I really need to get my hands on a professional.'

'I think he filmed *Worzel Gummidge* at Greenway School,' Linda said when she finally caught up with what Sandra was saying.

'*Worzel Gummidge*? I don't know *Worzel Gummidge*.'

'The scarecrow? The talking scarecrow?'

Sandra stared at her. 'Well, our Christmas show this year is *Peter Pan*.' She leant against the doorframe. 'God – I hope it doesn't rain,' she said, her mind switching back to the school's Autumn Fair. 'What I really need to get hold of is a machine that makes the sky blue. The Soviets have one.'

Linda was watching her in silence now.

402

'I don't suppose you know any Soviets?' Sandra asked.

'Sandra?'

'You do?' Sandra stood up straight, suddenly attentive as Linda leant towards her.

'I'm turning fucking blue,' she yelled in her face.

Sandra, who was now confronted with Linda's open mouth, saw that not only her tongue but even her tonsils were blue. 'It suits you.' She couldn't think of anything else to say.

Then Linda was gone.

Sandra watched her run down the drive and disappear back inside No. 8. Now what? Were they still invited to the screening that night, or not?

By the time Linda got home she'd decided that her only option was fake tan – and she spent the next two hours in front of the vanity unit in the bedroom applying Bronze Age over skin that was rapidly turning a definitive blue.

By the time Joe got home, Linda was orange – and there was no sign of the Wakefield bag.

By six o'clock that evening the lounge at No. 8 Pollards Close was set up with every spare chair in the house, including garden furniture.

Linda, who'd managed to temporarily tame the blue of her skin with Bronze Age, went through to the kitchen to help Jessica with the fondue. She'd read somewhere that the Swiss drank *glühwein* with fondue and what finally made her decide to go ahead with this was that it could be made in advance and reheated at the last moment. She stood at the sink filling a pan with wine, watching Joe in the floodlit garden, pacing round the perimeter of the fishpond. Something was wrong. She knocked on the kitchen window, but Joe didn't hear.

'What is it?' Jessica said, turning round.

'I don't know – something.'

They both stood and watched Joe in the garden.

'It's his fish,' Jessica said.

'I can see that.'

'I was only saying.'

'Don't start, Jessica – not tonight.'

Jessica threw the tea towel she was holding onto the draining board, and Linda watched her join Joe – the two of them standing staring into the fishpond. She leant over the sink and opened the kitchen window.

'What is it?' she called out, irritated. She needed to get Joe into the shower before people started to arrive in an hour's time.

Jessica and Joe swung round and looked at her then turned back to the fishpond.

'What the hell is it?' she yelled again.

Jessica walked slowly over to the open kitchen window.

'Has one of the fish died?' Linda asked.

Jessica shook her head. 'They're all dead.'

'What – all of them?'

'The ones that are left. There's no water in the pond – it's all gone.'

'Where?'

Jessica shrugged. 'Looks like it drained away.'

'How's that?'

Linda shut the window and Jessica appeared in the kitchen doorway.

'You start to get the fondue sorted – I'll take over.'

'He's fine, Mum.'

'He's not fine – I can see he's not fine.'

'He's upset, that's all – just leave it.'

They stood facing each other, suddenly aware of the cold from outside, then Linda saw the Eiffel Tower brooch pinned to Jessica's T-shirt, just above 'Kontagion'.

'Where did you get that?'

Jessica stared down at where Linda was pointing and saw the brooch. 'Nan gave it to me at Christmas,' she said, holding on to it. 'Remember? She got it in Paris.'

'Paris?'

'When she was younger, she was in love with a man who had an apartment in Paris and he gave it to her. They're real diamonds,' Jessica said, still unconvinced, relaying to Linda the information Belle had told her, but now feeling the need for them to be real.

'Paris?' Linda said again, staring at her daughter. Then she began to laugh. 'Paris? She told you she had a mystery lover with an apartment in Paris and you believed her?'

'She told me a love story,' Jessica said. 'A love story.'

Linda stood there, laughing. 'And when did this love story happen? She left home to marry Eric, then Eric died and she married Jim – and I can tell you now, there's no love story there.'

'She wasn't talking about Eric – or Jim. She was talking about someone else.'

'There wasn't anybody else. She's making it up.' Linda broke off. 'Paris? The closest to Paris Nan ever got was the registry office down at Portslade. Within a month of marriage, Jim was making his way through Brighton's cheaper ranks of professionals.'

Something in the way Jessica was looking at her, either not quite believing her or not quite understanding, made her feel suddenly destructive. She was going to destroy this love story Jessica thought she had hold of – wipe it out of existence. 'Jim screwed himself to death at a rate of . . .' she made a quick exasperated gesture with her hands, 'however many shillings an hour, an hour a week, fifty-two weeks a year over . . .' she made the same gesture with her hands again, 'however many years.'

Jessica stared at her, still giving no sign of having understood a word of what she was saying.

'Apart from manning the hotel bar in the evening, Jim did fuck all. Nan ran Lynton Hotel single-handed and when Jim died he repaid her by leaving the whole fucking thing to Brighton Cricket Club. She probably told you he died of a heart attack playing cricket one Saturday afternoon.'

'This isn't about Jim,' Jessica said.

'You want to know how Jim died? Where he died?'

'This isn't about Jim,' Jessica said again. Then, 'Nan didn't tell you about Paris, did she?' Her voice was triumphant now. 'She never told you – did she?'

'There's nothing to tell. There never was any Paris. You don't know anything,' Linda said suddenly. 'You don't know how lucky you are.'

'Lucky – you think I'm lucky? What – because we live in a four-bedroom house and have two cars? Am I supposed to be grateful for that?'

'Yes you fucking are,' Linda yelled back. 'We fought for this – me and your dad – we worked so hard . . . when you were a baby, I used to take you with me, cleaning.'

'Oh, spare me the sob story.'

'You've got no idea how hard we worked.'

'For what? For your chest freezer and your washing machine?'

'For you.'

'I don't need these things.'

'How do you know?'

'I see you poring over your Ice Man catalogue, making your lists and – and that's your life – and none of it matters because we're on the verge of World War Three and people like you don't even know it.'

'People like me?' Linda shouted. 'You and your politics, Jessica . . . you and your Third World War and your bombs . . . they're like possessions to you; luxury goods, that's all they are, luxury goods, and you can only afford them because we pay for them. You've never been cold or hungry or seen things you weren't meant to. It's us – your dad and me – who've made your world comfortable enough for you to dream about nuclear bombs – so go ahead, take us for granted, but don't you ever dare despise us.' Linda broke off. 'You're nothing but a fucking liberal.'

'And what *is* a liberal, Mum? How exactly would you define a liberal?'

'Someone who's never had to make a choice – I was cleaning rooms at your age.'

Jessica rolled her eyes, but her hands were shaking.

'I had the keys to every door in the hotel – every door. Nobody was interested in protecting me, Jessica, and I can't even begin to tell you the things I saw, having keys to all the rooms in a hotel in Brighton during high season – I can't even begin to tell you. All I know is,' she said, looking up, 'I would have done anything to be you at your age – to know as much as you do . . . to know as little.'

Linda pushed past her out into the garden then saw what the floodlights did to her skin. She stepped back towards the garage door.

'Joe!'

Joe turned round and stared at her for a moment then walked over.

'The water's gone,' he said.

'Maybe it's the lining.' Linda was still trying to calm down after her argument with Jessica and talking about pond lining helped; almost made her feel as though they had a connection, her and Joe, out here in the floodlit garden.

'I built that myself – it's not the lining.'

'What is it then?'

'I don't know.' He pushed past her into the garage and turned out the floodlights.

It went dark in the garden, which, with its puddles of light that windows threw out onto the grass, suddenly looked like everyone else's garden.

'Why did you do that?' Linda followed Joe into the garage.

'Well, there's no point keeping the lights on, is there?'

'Where are you going? Joe? Where are you going?'

'To phone Al.'

'What – now?'

'He might know.'

'What would Al know?'

'Where the water's gone.'

Linda needed to get Joe over this moment and didn't have the energy right then to work out how, because she'd spent all afternoon getting her skin to look flesh-coloured. Resisting the temptation to turn the floodlights back on because she knew that would provoke him, she crossed the dark garden towards the fishpond and knelt down, her hand anticipating water, despite what Joe and Jessica had said. She brought her outstretched palm lower and lower until it touched the dead fish. She knew it was a dead fish, but the sensation of touching something dead in the dark was so livid, the dead fish could have been anything – it could have been a dead baby for all she knew – and at the end of the day, what did she know? She remembered, briefly, trying to breastfeed Jessica in the first forty-eight hours after birth, looking down and seeing nothing but maggots pouring out of her nipples, and screaming the ward down to get help. They kept her in hospital for two months after that and put her on antidepressants, and by the time she got home Belle and Joe had got Jessica into a routine that worked for them and meant nothing to her.

She rubbed her hands backwards and forwards across the

grass, then sniffed them, but there was no smell. The fish couldn't have been dead for long. Turning her head, she looked up at the back of the house and saw Joe on the phone, so he must have got hold of Al. He put down the phone and leant on the breakfast bar and suddenly Jessica was standing next to him, crying, then she was leaning against him and he was stroking her hair. So she'd made Jessica cry again – that's all she ever seemed to do. Linda remained crouching on the lawn until she saw Jessica stand up straight again, which meant she must have stopped crying. While she watched, Joe and Jessica started talking together, but then they'd always known how to do that.

Her knees were saturated with dew now, and when she tried to stand up she felt dizzy and became immediately overwhelmed by the sensation she'd often had recently that the earth really was round; even the Turkey oak seemed to be leaning away from her, its branches scraping across the sky. She stood up straight and looked more carefully. The tree really did seem to be leaning over – luckily it was leaning away from No. 8 in the direction of one of the new houses on the other side of the fence. Linda turned her head between the back of her house and the new houses on Hill View and realised how hemmed-in she felt. She'd call the council tomorrow and get that man – what was his name again? – Wayne – Wayne Spalding to come out and look at it.

She spun round suddenly, the soles of her shoes happy to lose their grip on the wet grass, and strode back towards the house, shouting, 'Joe – you're going to have to go out.'

'What – now?' He turned to face her, his hands still on the breakfast bar.

Jessica wasn't in the kitchen.

'Osman doesn't drink – I forgot.'

'Osman? Osman drinks.'

She could see him staring at the wet patches on her knees,

trying to work them out – did they signify something that would help them all get through this moment?

'He's a Muslin, Joe – Muslins don't drink. What? What are you looking at me like that for?'

'Muslim; he's a Muslim.'

'What did I say?'

'Muslin,' Joe replied.

'Muslin, Muslim, whatever, he doesn't drink and I've got nothing to offer him.'

'The garage is full of orange juice.'

'That's for the buck's fizz.'

'I thought we were having *glühwein*?'

'The *glühwein*'s to go with the fondue – I'm giving people buck's fizz when they arrive.'

Joe stood by the breakfast bar, the overhead light giving his thick black hair shine, and thought about this. 'Why?'

'To celebrate – because we've got so much to celebrate,' she said, trying not to sound frantic. 'Ten years of Quantum! We're having a party, Joe!' She paused.

They stood staring at each other. It was the first time they'd come close to an argument since February – they'd fallen out of practice.

'Will you just go out and get me some mineral water.'

'Where do I get mineral water from?'

'I don't know – Tesco's? I'm sure Tesco's is still open.'

Joe pulled his car keys off the rack, then left the house without saying another word, slamming the door behind him.

Linda went over to the hob and gave the *glühwein* a stir, thinking that it was going to stain the pan and that maybe she should have asked Joe to get some more sachets – this was all she had. What if it went down well?

She went to the front door and opened it, but he'd already left – the tail lights of the Quantum Ford were disappearing round the corner of the Close. Linda carried on standing there, wondering if she'd done the right thing. Then she went back inside and made the buck's fizz, arranging the glasses in rows on the tray.

Terry King, the director, was the first to arrive at seven, in time to set up his equipment.

The Niemans arrived next – without Winke, who thought he might be coming down with flu – and while Daphne talked to Linda about the kitchen Quantum had fitted in the spring, Linda waited for the right moment in the conversation to slip in a request for more of the HRT pills from wherever it was Daphne had got them from, but she never got round to it because the Saunders and Nassams, arriving together, rang on the doorbell just then.

'Sandra tells me you called earlier?' Osman said, squeezing her hand and peering at her.

'I did?' Linda pretended to remember. 'Oh – that. It was nothing,' she laughed. 'Nothing,' she repeated, turning to Sandra this time.

Everyone, including Osman, was given buck's fizz. Linda looked at her watch. It was 7.45 – how could it take Joe over an hour to drive to Tesco and pick up some mineral water?

Not knowing what to do with people now everyone was here, she tried to get them into the lounge. Terry had set up, but there was no sign of him. She went over to the patio doors and was about to draw the curtains when Mick Saunders asked where Joe was.

'I sent him out on an errand,' Linda said, trying to sound languid.

Mick said something she didn't catch.

'He'll be back soon,' she said loudly. Then again, 'He'll be back soon.' She went into the kitchen and stared at Jessica standing next to the fondue on the breakfast bar.

411

'This is nearly done.'

Linda didn't say anything, she was too busy staring at Peter Klusczynski, who was standing beside Jessica, his arm slung loosely round her waist. 'Where did you come from?'

Peter turned quickly round, his arm dropping to his side, a smile still on his face. 'Number sixteen.' He looked quickly at Jessica, who just smiled back at him.

'I mean,' Linda said, impatient that Jessica was choosing tonight of all nights to fall in love in the kitchen – over fondue, which, like the advert, was one of the evening's major features, 'how did you get in?'

'Through the front door.'

'I didn't see you come in,' Linda said, getting impatient with herself now. Then, suddenly flicking her head up. 'Are you laughing at me?'

'No, Mrs Palmer – no.'

'Mum – the fondue's ready,' Jessica said again, trying to distract her.

Linda took a step towards Peter Klusczynski. 'Just don't go having one of your fits, that's all I ask – tonight's a big night for us.'

She went over to the sink and poured herself a glass of water. Jessica had invited an epileptic to the screening, and where the fuck was Joe?

Turning round, she nearly walked into Osman, who was standing peering into the pan on the hob.

'What's this?'

'*Glühwein* – to go with the fondue,' she said, adding, 'It's got alcohol in it.'

'D'you want me to start putting plates out?' Jessica asked.

'You do that – I'll get everyone back in here.' Linda went into the lounge where people had been shunted after arriving. 'The fondue's ready,' she yelled.

Mick and Osman were standing near the door talking

about Osman's plans to open his own surgery on the Hill View Estate – one that would be fully equipped for small operations. Linda overheard Osman wondering whether Edwina Curry would come to unveil the commemorative plaque.

Sandra Nassam was talking to Dominique about the Autumn Fair.

'I don't know how you get the time,' Dominique said as Sandra promised her that this year's Fair was going to be spectacular.

Since the incident with the Saunders' garage door, Dominique and Linda hadn't seen a great deal of each other, but Linda needed to speak to her now because she was sure she'd seen somebody who looked like an estate agent going into the house that morning.

'The only thing we need is the weather,' Sandra was saying. 'A day like today would be perfect. I was saying to somebody earlier – all we need is one of those machines the Soviets use on their May Day parades – the one that disperses clouds so that they can guarantee blue skies.' Sandra smiled, starting to bite her nails.

'There's a machine that disperses clouds?' Dominique laughed. 'What's it called? The Cloud Buster? The May Day machine?' She laughed again.

'I'm serious,' Sandra insisted. Then, leaning forward, 'The other night Osman said to me either he goes or the PTA goes – he thinks it's taking over my life.' She paused, looking around the room for Osman. 'I know which one I'm choosing.'

'The fondue's ready!' Linda shouted. 'Will everyone *please* make their way to the dining room!'

'Fondue?' Dominique said. 'What – now?'

Daphne Nieman, who was sitting on the sofa alone, got up obediently and made her way through to the dining room.

'Where's Paul?' Linda asked.

'Isn't he upstairs with Jessica?' Daphne said.

'Jessica's downstairs – with Peter.'

'Downstairs?' Daphne had lost interest in the where-abouts of her son and shrugged. 'Are you okay?' she said to Linda.

'Of course I'm okay.'

'You just look a little nauseous, that's all. You're not feeling sick or anything?'

Linda managed a breezy laugh. 'Of course not.' She paused. 'Is it just me or is it hot in here?' She walked quickly away from Daphne Nieman and ran upstairs to the en suite bathroom. Amazed to find the door locked, she started rattling on it, thinking it was Joe in there – and that he must have returned from Tesco without her noticing.

The door opened and a bloodshot Terry King stood there, grinning.

'What the hell are you doing?' she shouted, pushing past him into the bathroom. She was about to pick up the bottle of fake tan from behind the fern when she realised that Terry was still there – laughing.

'What the fuck's going on here?'

'Shut the door – I'm not quite finished,' he said, then wiped his nose and made his way over to her so that they were standing at the sink together.

Linda looked down at the rift of powder on Joe's shaving mirror. 'You're taking cocaine? In my bathroom?'

'I think you're fucking amazing,' Terry said. 'Don't you?' He collapsed onto the loo, in hysterics now.

Somebody rattled on the door.

'Just a minute,' she managed to call out cheerfully, while staring at the parts of her body clothes didn't conceal. Beneath the fake tan the blue was becoming more intense, which meant that her skin was taking on a greenish hue.

414

Glancing at Terry, who was slumped against the toilet cistern, she worked in another layer of tan, then, without thinking, washed her hands and dried them. The towel was covered in brown smears and the back of her hands were virtually green.

'I don't fucking believe it,' she muttered, pulling at the towel and dropping it into the laundry basket, whose lid was lying on the floor. She reapplied fake tan to the back of her hands then turned round and kicked Terry in the shins. 'Wake up – people are eating fondue at the moment and we need to start the film straight after that.'

'There's fondue? You made fondue?' he said, trying to sit up straight and finally giving in to his erection.

'You haven't got time for fondue – you need to get the film set up.'

'Aren't we waiting for Joe?' Terry asked.

'Joe's gone,' she said without thinking.

After that she let out a couple of deep breaths and managed to walk back into the hallway, smiling.

Once Linda had left, Terry staggered over to the bath and pulled back the shower curtain. Paul Nieman was standing there, a pair of Linda's white lace knickers in his hands, staring at Terry.

Joe sat in the Quantum Ford in Tesco's car park, smoking the ganny Audrey gave him before Christmas that he'd only just found – by accident – in the glove compartment. He'd been sitting there since 6.45, and it was now 8.15. He'd known, as soon as he parked the car, that he had no intention of going back to No. 8 Pollards Close, so there was no point buying any mineral water. Instead, he sat in the car smoking, watching the new superstore close for the night, convinced that Jessica – aged two – was pounding across

415

the bonnet of his car, pot-bellied and laughing, looking as if she was being blown along by a great force. He sat watching her, laughing with her, until the pounding stopped and she just seemed to vanish.

With the ghost of Jessica gone from the bonnet of his car, he became suddenly aware of the cries coming from the new floodlit football pitch at the other end of the car park. He would have liked a son, he thought, listening to the game.

Switching the engine back on, he drove slowly out of the car park and round the mini roundabout, taking the turning for the A23 to Brighton.

By 8.45, Linda was still trying to get people back into the lounge with their *glühwein*, ready for the film to start.

'What's that you're drinking?' she said as Osman Nassam filed past.

'I don't know.' Osman held up his glass for her to inspect, confused.

'You're drinking *glühwein*?'

'I don't know – it came from the pan. This is *glühwein*?' He paused. 'Sandra,' he called out across the room, 'we're drinking *glühwein*. We drank it while we were in Switzerland,' he said, turning back to Linda. 'Sandra loves *glühwein* – real *glühwein*, I mean. Not the stuff you get in sachets over here that you just add wine to.'

Linda stood staring at Osman Nassam, wondering if she'd remembered to hook the sachets out of the pan. Mick Saunders was pushing through the doorway past her, smiling to himself. He must have heard.

'Where are you going?' she said, instinctively grabbing his arm.

'The kitchen – to get some water.' Mick pulled his arm gently out of her grasp.

416

'Why d'you want water? I made *glühwein*.'

He turned on her. 'It's because of the *glühwein* that I need the water,' he hissed, disappearing in the direction of the kitchen.

'I thought you didn't drink,' she said, rounding on Osman.

'I drink – socially.'

'I sent Joe out to get mineral water because you don't drink.'

'I do drink.'

'But you're Muslim.'

'Lax.'

'Lax,' Linda repeated. 'Joe's out there,' she shouted, pointing to the office blinds in the front window that were now shut, 'he's out there because of you – because you're not supposed to be drinking. I sent him to Tesco's to get mineral water for you.' She pushed her finger between the lapels of Osman's sports jacket. 'If it wasn't for you, he'd be here now; if it wasn't for you . . .'

Just then Terry came into the lounge, tripping over wires and feet and chair legs and finally making it to the projector where he got the reels moving. Osman made the most of this distraction to edge away from Linda, who remained standing by the dimmer switch on the wall.

'Where's Joe?' Daphne said suddenly.

'Yes – where is Joe?' Dominique echoed.

'Aren't we waiting for Joe?' somebody else said.

'Where's Joe?' Daphne said again.

'I don't know,' Linda yelled, drunk, hungry and full of fear, 'and anyway, Daphne, the question you should be asking is – where's Winke?'

'He's coming down with the flu.'

'Coming down with the flu?' Linda jerked her head rapidly up and down, spittle running across her chin. 'I'll tell you where he is.'

'He's at home,' Daphne said, her hand on her new Ethiopian necklace.

'How much d'you want to bet?' Linda leered at her.

'I don't gamble,' Daphne said quietly.

'What's that?' Linda yelled across the lounge at her.

'I said I don't gamble.'

'Every day of your life's a gamble, Daphne, and you know it.'

'I know that Winke's at home, with the flu,' Daphne said, frightened now.

'And I know that the moment you walked through my front door, Winke went running out to Paul's campervan and drove it to the Forestry Commission car park behind the Golf Club.'

The room was silent now.

'Why would Winke take Paul's van?' Daphne asked, at the mercy of her curiosity – her voice so small now it sounded as though she was standing at the end of a long tunnel.

'Because,' Linda started yelling again, 'the van's got the space for Winke to lubricate his fist and shove it up Steve's arse.' She wiped the spittle off her chin.

'Who's Steve?' Daphne asked after a while.

Osman started choking on his *glühwein*.

'Joe's business manager.' Linda turned to Osman. 'Will you shut up! So – now we all know where Winke is, does everybody want to know about Joe? Joe's busy fucking somebody somewhere in Brighton. I presume it's a woman,' she said, looking at Daphne. Then, to Dominique, 'For a while I thought it was you, and that pissed me off so much, I drove my car into your garage.' She broke off. 'It's not Delta, is it?'

'Delta?' Dominique stood up.

Linda stared at her for a moment longer then went

418

running out of the front door and across the street, straight into two Mormons standing outside No. 4. They turned round, in their matching macs, carrying matching briefcases, and stared at her. Then the front door opened and there was Delta.

'Hi,' the Mormons said, 'is your mummy home?'

'Are you fucking Joe?' Linda screamed over their heads.

Delta, who had been standing against the doorframe, stood up. 'What the hell are you talking about?' she yelled back at her.

The Mormons tried to back off, but Linda was blocking the way.

'It came to me just now – you started Art School in Brighton in September – that means you're in Brighton during the week.'

'You're fucking mad.'

'Maybe,' Linda conceded.

The Mormons shuffled away from the front door along the wall, straight into Dominique. 'Delta?' she called out. 'Are you okay?' Then, to Linda, 'Just go home.'

Linda took one last look at mother and daughter then stalked back across the road.

She was still panting, short of breath, when she walked into the lounge again at No. 8. The only people left were Daphne, who hadn't moved an inch – not even her eyes – since Linda's revelation, and the Nassams – who hadn't had such a good night out in ages.

'Amazing . . . just amazing,' Terry said, from behind the projector.

'Just shut up and start the fucking film,' she commanded as she dimmed the lights and watched the Quantum Kitchens showroom come onto the screen with the familiar Ford Escort Joe had driven away in at 6.30 that evening parked outside. What had she done? He hadn't even wanted to go.

The camera panned the showroom and there at the back was the door to Joe's office. Joe had been inside when Terry was filming. You couldn't see Joe on film, but he was there behind that closed office door.

Linda kept her eyes on the moving image of the Quantum showroom while to either side the lounge seemed to slope off into a curve and she was momentarily amazed that they all managed to stay attached to its surface and not slip off.

Somewhere in the background *Xanadu* was playing, and Linda was leaving the screening, walking automatically towards the garage.

The marijuana fumes were thick in there, and both Peter Klusczynski – who was sitting on her chest freezer – and Jessica – who was squeezed between his legs – were smoking. Mick Saunders was standing next to them, drinking Beefeater gin out of the bottle.

'I read your book,' Mick was saying to Jessica.

'You did?' She looked up to see Linda standing in the doorway.

'Everybody happy?' Linda walked straight past them.

'We were going to smoke in the garden, Mrs Palmer, but it was too cold.'

Ignoring him, Linda opened the garage door.

All was quiet in Pollards Close.

'Mum – I'm sorry about the smoking,' Jessica said.

'Quite frankly, Jessica, I don't give a fuck what you and your Polish friend get up to.' She unlocked the white Toyota.

'He's not.'

'What?'

'Polish.'

'My parents are,' Peter said. 'I was born here.'

'So what does that make you?' Linda opened her car door. 'Half Polish and fully epileptic?'

'Mum? Where are you going?'

420

'To look for Joe.'

'Where's Dad? Where's he gone?' Jessica said, walking over to the car.

'I don't know.' Linda cast her eye over her daughter. 'I sent him to Tesco's – to get mineral water – and he never came back.'

'Mum?' Jessica ran over to where Linda was standing in the doorway, starting to sob and trying to nestle into her.

Jessica's hair, which she never washed and which was thick with grease, was directly below Linda's nostrils. Suddenly revolted by her offspring, she pushed Jessica away from her, but Jessica clung on, and the hands clinging to her jumper had biro equations scribbled over them – equations that meant nothing to Linda.

'Get off me,' Linda yelled.

Jessica tried to get back to Linda's warm, drunk body.

'Get off me – get away from me,' Linda screamed, finally managing to pull her daughter off her.

They stood facing each other.

'Where's Dad?' Jessica screamed back at her.

'I don't know, Jess. I've done everything I can . . .' Linda stopped and, turning round, saw Mick Saunders standing there, the gin bottle still in his hand.

'Look – is there anything I can do?'

She stood watching him. 'Are you laughing at me?'

'I'm not laughing at you, Linda, I just want to know if there's anything I can do to help.'

Linda looked away. She didn't want kindness right then; kindness would destroy her.

'Joe's a good man,' Mick said.

Linda didn't respond to this. 'You could stay here with Jessica – would you do that? I don't know how long I'll be.' She got into the car, started up the engine and accelerated up the drive.

'Mum? Where are you going?' Jessica shouted, running after the car. 'Where are you going?'

She watched the white Toyota disappear round the corner then walked back through the garage into the house.

The advert had come to an end. Daphne Nieman was still sitting immobile in the armchair next to the patio doors; the Nassams were kissing each other heavily and Terry King was watching them.

'You want me to run it again?' he said when Jessica walked into the room, followed by Peter Klusczynski – and Mick.

'Could you all just fuck off home, please – the party's over.'

The Nassams pulled apart, stood up and made a begrudging exit.

Daphne didn't move.

'Dad's not coming back,' Jessica said to Mick.

'What makes you say that?'

'I was down in Brighton at the end of the summer holidays and I saw him there – with this woman.'

'That doesn't mean anything.'

'I saw him – I saw them,' Jessica said, staring at Mick. 'I saw them,' she said again. 'And they were together. I mean – they were together.'

'How do you know?'

'Anyone could tell. I saw them.'

'What were they doing?'

'Nothing.'

'Nothing?'

'They were standing outside a greengrocer's shop – nothing.' She paused.

Mick turned the lights up.

Daphne still didn't move.

'I watched Dad pick up an orange, smell it, then put it

back down again. The woman was holding his arm, watching him.'

'What did you do?' Mick said after a while.

'I walked away – I didn't want him to see me. If you'd seen them,' Jessica trailed off. 'She was youngish – blondish – I don't know,' she said quietly. 'Mum's gone to Brighton to look for him. I know you wouldn't think it to look at her – to look at them,' Jessica said, starting to cry again, 'but she's always loved him, and when I saw him that day, I realised . . .'

'What?'

Jessica shook her head. 'Even if she does find him – what's the point? I saw the way Dad was looking at that woman that day. I knew it was only a matter of time. Sometimes you can't bring people back, can you?' she said, staring at Mick.

'Tonight's weird,' Peter said, taking hold of her, tighter and tighter, until they were gripping on to each other.

Mick turned away from them and went through to the kitchen, where he picked up the phone and dialled his home number. Looking at Linda's gazelle, which had been returned to the sideboard, he listened to the phone ringing at No. 4 and was just about to put it down when he heard Dominique's voice on the other end.

'Were you asleep?' he said.

'Kind of.'

'How's everything over there?'

'Okay – now. It took me a while to calm Delta down.'

'What's wrong with Delta?'

'Linda came over here and accused her of fucking Joe.' He heard Dominique rubbing at her face. 'What's the time?'

'Just on midnight,' he said, peering at the cooker clock.

'How is Linda?'

'Hysterical – she just drove off in her car. Jessica thinks

she's gone to Brighton to look for Joe. Joe's seeing another woman.' Mick exhaled.

'I know – she told everyone.'

'Are you okay?'

'I'm fine. I think.'

The receiver was moist from his breath and Mick could smell Linda's perfume on it. He imagined Linda's hands, with their viciously painted nails, holding on to it as she tried to make some sense of her world, set it straight in some way. That's all most people spent their time doing – why did he have to hold it against them? They were only protecting themselves from loss because between the beginning and the end of life everybody lost something.

There was silence on the line. Then Dominique said, 'We should put the house on the market.'

'We are going to put the house on the market,' Mick said.

'Then we should go to New Zealand,' Dominique's voice said.

'We are going to New Zealand,' Mick reassured her. Then he said, 'I want to see you. I'm coming over.' He put the phone down and went outside onto the Palmers' porch, watching as the front door to No. 4 opened and Dominique appeared and started to cross the front garden.

'Who was that on the phone? Was it Mum?'

Turning round, he saw Jessica and Peter standing in the hallway. Jessica was trying to tuck her hair behind her ears while staring expectantly at him.

'I'm going up to Peter's – I don't want to be here right now.' She was about to step outside when, suddenly terrified, she said, 'I'm going to fall.'

The next minute, not only Jessica but the whole of No. 8 Pollards Close started to slide down the hill. They carried on sliding until they came to rest on the virtually intact remains of a Roman road. The rest of the houses on that side of the Close, along with the new houses on Hill View and the cranes, diggers and other contractors' vehicles, had fallen into the old chalk quarries on either side of the ancient road that had been hastily backfilled two centuries ago, and that torrential rain had finally destabilised.

Mick, who had been pushed back into the hallway, had an image of Dominique leaving No. 4 and crossing the front garden, then he lost consciousness.

Linda drove down the A23 towards Brighton, still drunk, past the cricket ground and new pavilion that Jim's death had paid for, through the town towards the sea. Finding a parking spot right outside Lynton Flats, she turned the engine off and sat in the car, staring up at the sheltered accommodation that used to be a hotel and wondering how Belle could still live there – why she hadn't moved as far away as she could. As soon as she got to Brighton, she knew she was going to sec Belle because Belle had been there at the beginning when she and Joe first met, and there was something she needed to know that only Belle had the answer to. Belle might even know where Joe was. She didn't know why she thought this, but she did.

Sitting outside the flats, she had a sudden memory of Jim in his immaculately pressed trousers and Argyll jumper. Jim was particular about things like creases in his trousers and thought that being particular gave him weight inside the home and flair outside it. Jim being particular meant that the hotel ran like clockwork and the flat at the top, under the roof, where they all lived, also ran like clockwork. Creases were ironed into exactly the right place on each piece of clothing (including underwear), cupboards never ran dry and meals were always served on time, and she never heard Jim – or Belle, for that matter – complain, and because she'd lived with it since she was six years old, Linda used to think that the marriage she was living with was how marriage was.

Sometimes Jim, staring through the window opposite the kitchen table, would comment on the flight of the birds. Migratory patterns were something he knew a lot about. In all Linda's memories of him, Jim was stationary: sitting at the dining table; sitting in his armchair; watching snooker on the TV; standing in front of the bathroom mirror, carefully shaving; standing in the small front garden that used to be outside Lynton Hotel, leaning on his hoe and staring out across the road and beach to sea, but never actually hoeing. He was lean for such a motionless man – too lean – and his leanness made people distrustful of him, although he was popular with younger women.

Belle was a blur compared to Jim's statue-like existence. Linda was much older before she realised that Belle made herself into a blur around Jim to stop herself from killing him, which would have been easy, he was so still. She also realised that Jim stayed still in order to tempt Belle. What Linda had mistaken – when she was younger – for a terse sort of harmony, was in fact a prolonged battle. They were fighting all the time; they'd been fighting for so long they didn't even have to speak to each other any more when they fought. Belle stayed silent out of hatred and Jim stayed silent because somehow he'd got the upper hand in the arrangement they'd made all those years ago when they first met.

She got out of the car, her back to the sea, and stared up at the town, electricity mapping it out against the hump of the Downs – Joe was in there somewhere, among all that electricity – then she walked up the steps to the front door, looking briefly at the hotel's old fanlight. She rarely came back to Brighton – Joe was always the one who drove down to see Belle or pick her up, and Belle was always saying that the other residents thought Joe was her son and not her son-in-law.

Linda buzzed for the warden and waited. It was nearly eleven o'clock. She buzzed again.

'Yes?' A voice came through the intercom, irritated, unfriendly.

'I'm here to see Belle Higgins.'

'Have you rung her bell?'

'I thought we were meant to press for the warden after ten.'

A sigh. 'Is she expecting you?' The voice was muffled because the speaker was turned away, watching the TV. 'Who are you?'

'It's Linda – her daughter.'

A second later, without any further questions, the door opened.

She walked in and went straight upstairs, her hand running up the banister Joe and his dad came to repair all those years ago. She knocked on the wrong door – sure Belle was in Flat Four – and the woman who answered told her it was number three she wanted, then stood in the doorway watching Linda as she started banging on the door to Flat Three.

'Mum? It's me – Linda.' She leant her forehead against the door, the migraine that had started on the A23 now moving from the back of her head round the sides towards the front.

At last the door opened and there was Belle, in the track-suit Linda had bought her for her birthday.

'What the bloody hell do you want?' she said when she saw her daughter.

Without answering, Linda pushed past her into the lounge.

Belle shut the front door, but stayed standing near it. 'You're wet,' she said.

'It's raining outside.' Looking around, Linda noticed an empty sherry bottle on the carpet where it had rolled against one of the coffee-table legs.

'There's no need to look like that,' Belle snapped. 'Just you try getting pissed on a state pension.'

'You're drunk.'

'So are you – and you don't look well. What are you doing down in Brighton, Linda? It's gone eleven.'

Ignoring her, Linda sat down on the sofa, and after a while Belle walked slowly over to the armchair and slid into it, her swollen ankles stuck out straight in front of her.

'Do you want a drink? There's another bottle of sherry in the kitchen.'

Linda stood up. 'Haven't you got anything other than sherry?'

'Like what?'

'Like wine – anything?'

'Wine's an acquired taste I never acquired – I like things sweet and simple. I like sherry – especially cheap sherry. The expensive stuff tastes too complicated.'

Linda brought the sherry in and poured Belle a glass.

'Aren't you having any? Go on, have a glass with me.'

'All right – all right.' Linda got a second glass then sat down and poured herself one, even though the migraine was throbbing just behind her temple now, and the pain was beginning to affect her muscle co-ordination.

'What's that you've got?'

'Where?'

'On your jumper – there.'

Looking down, Linda saw the Eiffel Tower brooch Jessica had been wearing earlier that was now caught on her jumper, hanging open by the pin. She pulled it off, holding it up to the light before putting it on the coffee table.

Belle didn't make a move to pick up the brooch, they both just sat there staring at it.

After a while, Linda looked away, scanning the photographs on the sideboard. 'Why did you never put any photos of Dad up? There's plenty of you and Jim – who you hated – but none of Dad.'

Belle jolted her shoulders up and down, which was as close to a shrug as her arthritic body could manage. 'Don't know what happened to the photos of Eric.'

'But what about the wedding photo?' Linda asked, suddenly insistent on this.

'I don't know – I suppose there would have been one. I really don't remember, Linda.'

'Did you hate him as well?'

'Eric? You couldn't hate Eric. Why are we talking about Eric, anyway? There were times I wanted to talk to you about him, but you weren't having any of it. Why now?' Belle sighed. 'Eric was content with his lot in life – and that's a much rarer thing than you might think. He believed in happiness – most people don't; whatever they say. Before he joined the army, he used to work on the buses. He got up at six, walked to work, spent the day on the buses and came home in time for tea – a pretty piss boring day, but Eric was so happy he could of lived the same day over and over again for the rest of his life.'

'Why did you marry him?' Linda asked, realising that she was still in her coat.

'I don't know – I suppose he had no real inclination to fall in love; he just didn't have a need for it, and I'd been in love before Eric – once – and it got to me badly. I didn't want it to happen again.'

'This?' Linda held up the Eiffel Tower brooch.

Belle nodded.

'Jessica told me – I didn't believe her.'

429

Belle shrugged. 'I don't want to talk about it – I still don't want to talk about it.' She shrugged again. 'Eric wanted to be happy – that was all. He reminds me of Joe,' Belle said. 'That's who you want to talk about, isn't it?'

They looked at each other.

'Joe's a happy man,' she added.

Linda tilted the empty sherry glass and watched the last trickle make its way nearly to the rim before putting it straight again so that the trickle ran down to the bottom of the glass.

'Do you remember that job Joe did for his cousin in Portsmouth when you first met – when he lived with him for three weeks to save on petrol? Me and Jim couldn't believe the state you got yourself into over him being away. You were pining like an animal, you were actually pining – taking to your bed like that. You spent the whole three weeks buried under a blanket, running a temperature, hardly eating and not washing. I'd never seen anything like it before – you were a right state, and he was only gone for three weeks. Do you remember Jim dragging you to the bath-room and forcing you to take a wash – do you remember that?'

Linda smiled. 'I was lovesick.'

'He was only gone three weeks,' Belle said again.

'I suppose three weeks when you're eighteen – it's like . . .' Linda looked down at her feet, noticing that the leather was wet on the toes of her shoes, and didn't want to be thinking any of these things, but this was how her mind worked these days. She looked up at Belle. 'I don't know what it's like.'

The clock on the mantelpiece, which used to be in the dining room when it was a hotel, struck eleven thirty. Belle pulled herself to the front of the chair, edging as far forward as she could and wondering if she could manage to lever herself up without asking Linda for help. 'What are you doing here, Linda? Why aren't you at home with Joe and Jessica?'

Linda stood up, knocking her leg against the coffee table. What was she doing standing in the middle of her mother's flat at nearly midnight?

'Here,' Belle said after a while, 'help me up.'

Linda lifted her mother out of her chair, suddenly frightened at how light she was.

Belle walked slowly with her stick into the kitchenette and Linda stayed standing in the middle of the lounge. She heard Belle get the tin with the crackers in out of the cupboard. 'I'm not staying,' she said.

Belle appeared in the doorway. 'What's going on here, Linda?'

'It's Joe.'

'What's wrong with Joe?' Belle said, watching her daughter start to cry, suddenly aware that she didn't want to know what was wrong with Joe. She didn't want to know anything about any of them; she wanted to be sat in her armchair alone, eating her crackers and cheese, so she stayed in the doorway and watched as Linda wept. Neither of them made a move towards each other.

'I don't know,' Linda was saying through tears. 'I don't know what's wrong with Joe. I don't think he's very happy at the moment.'

'Why not?'

'I don't know – he's just not happy.'

'But he's always been happy with you.'

'That's what I'm trying to say – what I've been trying to say – he's not with me. Joe's not with me.'

'Well . . .' Belle carried on standing there, but Linda showed no sign of stopping crying.

'And I wanted to ask you – he was with me, at the

431

beginning, wasn't he, Mum? There was a time when he was there?'

'Why are you asking me?'

'Because you were there,' Linda yelled, starting to sob again.

Belle shuffled back into the kitchenette and, leaning on the bench, banged at the strip lighting with her stick to stop it flickering. 'I know who Joe's with,' she said to the lump of Red Leicester on the bench.

Linda was in the doorway. 'You what?'

'I said – I know who Joe's with.'

'Do I know her?'

Belle shook her head.

'How long have you known for?'

'Since about twenty minutes ago when you knocked on my door. I'm not hoarding anybody's secrets, Linda. The flat's too small and I haven't got many years left, thank God. I can tell you where they are, but I don't think it'll do any good.'

Linda was crying again.

Belle turned away from her. The light in the kitchen was steady now and, satisfied, she started to cut up her Red Leicester, trying to ignore the sobbing coming from the lounge. The light started flickering again and this time she banged it so hard she nearly cracked the bulb. She put the biscuit tin back in the cupboard and took a breather, feeling an inordinate amount of pleasure at the sight of the orange cheese on the white cracker. Linda had tried to get her onto Ryvita once, but she liked her Jacob's Cream Crackers. She listened. The crying had stopped. Relieved, she put the crackers onto a plate and left it on the side, because she had a feeling Linda would see them and want some. Then she walked through to the lounge.

Linda had gone, leaving behind her a blue light.

432

Belle went back through to the kitchenette and picked up the plate with the crackers on, going into the lounge and sitting down in her armchair. She let out a fart and laughed. 'That's the cheese,' she said to herself, starting to doze off before she'd even finished the last mouthful.

The warden was sure she'd heard the front door go. Grunting with irritation, she hauled herself out of the chair and away from the TV and went into the entrance hall. Then she remembered letting in a woman earlier, claiming to be Belle's daughter when she was pretty sure it was a son Belle had – maybe she had a daughter as well. She should go upstairs and check to make sure Belle hadn't been bludgeoned to death and had all her worldly goods stolen, which was something the *Advertiser* had reported as having happened last week in another residential home in Hove.

She climbed the stairs, hating Belle for being her responsibility, and thought wearily of the phone calls she'd have to make and interviews she'd have to conduct and paperwork to be filled in if Belle had been bludgeoned to death.

She knocked on the door five times until Mrs Jenkins along the corridor stuck her head out, wanting to know what was going on, and she said, 'Nothing', waiting until Mrs Jenkins had gone back inside before using her master keys to open the door.

The warden went into Belle's flat. There was no sign of the woman she'd let in earlier, but everything seemed to be there that should be. Then she saw Belle in the armchair, asleep, and was suddenly revolted by the sight of her and the way the crackers and Red Leicester cheese had fallen onto the floor. She turned away, and there on the coffee table was the Eiffel Tower brooch Linda had left behind.

She picked it up and held it to the light. They looked like diamonds – not that she knew anything about jewellery.

They were probably paste diamonds – the brooch didn't feel very heavy. She hesitated, then the strip lighting in the kitchenette started to flicker and the crackling sound made her panic so she left the flat with the brooch in her hand, and went back downstairs.

Linda sat in the car with the window wound down, listening to the sea and not feeling particularly moved by the sound, but aware that she'd grown up with it. The air coming through the open window was cold and wet with spray, tightening the skin on her face. A couple passed by on the pavement and she couldn't tell which of them was more drunk. She sat there listening to the woman's heels until she couldn't hear them any more. What was she waiting for? If she didn't leave Brighton now, she'd find herself back in Lynton Flats, running up the stairs and screaming at Belle for the address. She wound the window up and patted her face dry, able to see in the streetlight the tan smears on the tissue. Then she put the car into gear and, leaving Joe behind her somewhere in Brighton, drove onto the A23 towards home and what? Jessica. She needed Jessica, but she didn't feel well. She didn't feel well enough to drive, but she had to drive to get to Jessica.

Twenty-five minutes later, she took the corner into Pollards Close in a much wider arc than she needed to, and there were so many lights and they all seemed so bright that she thought dawn must have already happened some-where between Brighton and Littlehaven, only she'd missed it and now it was daylight. Her house was meant to be straight ahead along with everyone else's, but she couldn't see any houses – there was nothing apart from sky, which was as good as nothing.

Joe was lying in bed in Brighton, next to Lenny. Three hours later they were still there. They'd moved the fish tank into the bedroom because Lenny was afraid of the dark and Joe couldn't sleep with the light on so the fish tank was a compromise. He was just watching her face and the way the watery light caught at it, thinking that lying next to her always made him feel as if she'd just fallen from a great height and he'd been there to catch her, when there was a boom that came, not from above like thunder, but sideways. Then there was the sound of something exhaling and inhaling simultaneously.

He got out of bed and went through to the lounge to look out the window, expecting to see something different, but outside the night sky was still the same colour it always was. Then the view became distorted as cracks ran in a frenzy across the panes of glass. A second later there was another bang, more muffled, and the cracked glass fell in shards onto the carpet. The jagged remains left in the frame were the most violent things he had ever seen. He automatically dropped to the floor with the second bang, looking at his watch. It was 2.59 a.m. Then he looked down at his shirt sleeves, which were covered in dust blown through the open windows. There was orange in the sky now, but the silence continued.

He got dressed in the clothes he'd put on after his shower at No. 8 Pollards Close earlier and left the flat. Outside, people were emerging from buildings along the length of Baxter Street, in search of other people. The night was full of smoke and dust and, suddenly, the sirens that civilisation produces in times of crisis.

Joe made his way towards the seafront, along with everyone else, following the direction of the sirens. When they reached the promenade, crowds of people in evening dress were disappearing into and emerging from the dust that was much thicker here. Some of them were still carrying drinks.

435

Policemen were unstacking deckchairs and placing them along the promenade, instinctively facing the sea as if it were high noon in high season.

The road along the seafront had already been cordoned off, and Joe saw a BBC camera lifted on someone's shoulder.

'What's happening?' he asked a man in a black bomber jacket.

'A bomb in the Grand. Wait till the dust shifts,' the man said, not looking at Joe.

The dust didn't shift, but after a while Joe made out the hotel's white front with its black railings. The top half had collapsed into the bottom.

'Who was it?'

'IRA, I'm guessing.'

'Did they get Thatcher?'

The cameraman shrugged, turning his attention back to the dust and flames, waiting to turn conjecture into fact.

There were people in evening dress going down onto the beach, stumbling across pebbles, heading nowhere.

After another five minutes, Joe turned away, walking slowly back to Evita's.

The flat was freezing. He went and shut the curtains so that he didn't have to think about the broken window, then went into the bedroom. The fish tank had survived the explosion, intact.

'Where've you been?' Lenny said, only half awake.

'There was a bomb.'

She let out a low laugh before turning over and falling back to sleep.

Joe started to get undressed again then stopped and went through to the lounge, sitting down on the sofa and trying to pull the phone across the coffee table without knocking the ashtray off. It was freezing in the lounge. He dialled his home number, but the line was dead. Thinking he might have dialled it wrong because his fingers were stiff with cold, he dialled again but the line was still dead. He dialled a third time before giving up and calling the operator.

'I can't get through to my home number.'

'What's the number please?'

For a moment he couldn't remember, even though he'd only just dialled it.

'The number you were trying to dial, please.'

At last Joe remembered and then the operator's line went dead. She kept him waiting for three minutes.

'Sorry to keep you,' she apologised as her voice came back onto the line. 'There's been an incident in the area.'

'What sort of incident?'

'I'm afraid that I'm unable to confirm the nature of the incident at the moment.'

'Well – when will the lines be back up?'

'We should be able to confirm this in due course.'

'In due course?' Joe put the phone down without thinking and, looking up, saw Lenny standing in the bedroom door. 'I thought you were asleep.'

'I was.' She leant her head against the doorframe, watching him.

'There was a bomb.'

'I thought you were joking.'

'At the Grand.'

Her eyes were on his shoes. 'You went out?' She broke off. 'Did they get Thatcher?'

'I don't know. I don't think so.'

He stared at the crucifix round her neck that he'd put on her when he'd arrived the night before.

'We lost a window?' she said, staring at the jagged remains in the frame and the way the curtains blew into the room. 'Who were you on the phone to?' she asked after a while.

'The operator.'

437

'Who were you on the phone to before that?'

'You know who I was on the phone to.'

'Why were you phoning them?'

'Because of the bomb.'

'But the bomb happened here. Look – we lost a window.'

'I just had this feeling I should phone.'

'What – because of the bomb?'

'I don't know.' He paused. 'The lines are down – the operator says there's been an incident.'

'What sort of incident?'

'They don't know at the moment.'

Lenny nodded and yawned. 'The incident's here.'

'What?'

'I said the incident's here – there's been a bomb in the Grand and our lines aren't down.'

'You think I'm lying?' he said, watching her.

'No – I don't think you're lying.' She stared back at him. 'Are you leaving?'

Joe sat looking at her for a long time then shook his head. 'No – I'm not leaving.'

'You're staying?'

'I'm going, but I'm not leaving.' He stared down at the ashtray on the coffee table, and the stubs from the night before. 'I've got this feeling, Lenny. I need to see Jessica – and Linda,' he added.

Lenny, waiting in the open doorway, watched him cross the room to the front door. 'So – what's going to happen next, Joe?'

He stopped and turned round. 'I don't know. I don't want to know. Most people don't – whatever they say. If they did, fortune tellers would be the richest people in the world; and they're not.' He paused. 'I'll phone – later – I'll phone.'

Lenny nodded, and Joe left.

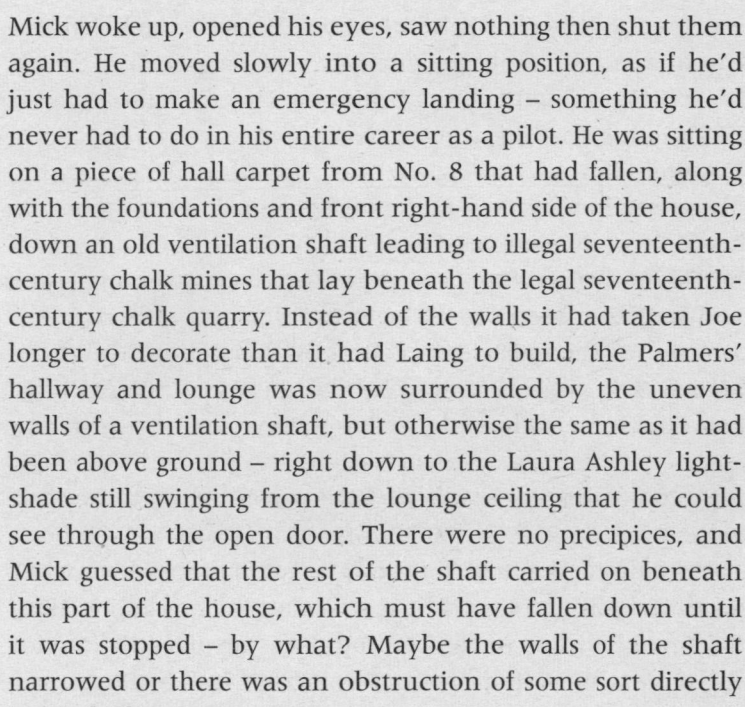

4

Mick woke up, opened his eyes, saw nothing then shut them again. He moved slowly into a sitting position, as if he'd just had to make an emergency landing – something he'd never had to do in his entire career as a pilot. He was sitting on a piece of hall carpet from No. 8 that had fallen, along with the foundations and front right-hand side of the house, down an old ventilation shaft leading to illegal seventeenth-century chalk mines that lay beneath the legal seventeenth-century chalk quarry. Instead of the walls it had taken Joe longer to decorate than it had Laing to build, the Palmers' hallway and lounge was now surrounded by the uneven walls of a ventilation shaft, but otherwise the same as it had been above ground – right down to the Laura Ashley light-shade still swinging from the lounge ceiling that he could see through the open door. There were no precipices, and Mick guessed that the rest of the shaft carried on beneath this part of the house, which must have fallen down until it was stopped – by what? Maybe the walls of the shaft narrowed or there was an obstruction of some sort directly beneath them.

Crawling through into the lounge, he made out the

439

Palmers' smashed TV and intact TV cabinet, which was about the same size as a sarcophagus. He sat there looking at the inside of the TV, trying to work out where the light was coming from. There wasn't much, but there was some – enough for his eyes to adjust to. Then he remembered Jessica and Peter standing by the front door. There was no longer any front door, just a hole looking out onto the walls of the ventilation shaft.

'Jessica?' he called out, expecting his voice to echo, but it didn't. The deep pile carpet and wet walls of the ventilation shaft quickly soaked up her name.

He hadn't been hurt by the fall, but he'd lost consciousness at some point and now he was getting stiff because it was cold. Where was Dominique? He was sure he'd been speaking to Dominique when it had happened – they'd been talking about New Zealand. The thought of New Zealand made him feel tired – who was it he'd been talking to about New Zealand just the other day? It was a she, because when he told her, she'd got mad at him, only he couldn't remember her name, all he could remember was her short blonde hair and that she'd been wearing jeans and had bare feet when she started to yell at him. What was her name and why had he hurt her so much? Whose idea was it to go to New Zealand anyway? It must have been his; he was the only one who ever came up with any ideas – apart from Steph. It might have been Steph who came up with the whole New Zealand thing. Then his mind went back to the blonde woman in jeans who'd been standing by a window somewhere telling him he couldn't go to New Zealand, and he'd said that he was going. Why did he want to go to New Zealand to start over again with the same woman and the same children? He wasn't a young man any more – did he have the energy? Who was the woman with the blonde hair yelling that she loved him and that he was everything to her and that they couldn't carry on like this?

Hadn't she opened the window? He'd listened to a Tannoy making announcements for a London train and they must have been high up because he'd seen the roof of a railway station and platform awnings, and microscopic people moving just over her shoulder. Then the woman who wasn't Dominique had screamed that she was going to jump and he hadn't believed her, but the way she'd gone to the window and the way her arms held on to it and the way her T-shirt had been raised up over her jeans waistband revealing her navel had made him change his mind. She *was* going to jump – she loved him but he didn't love her back, and once he remembered all this he remembered that her name was Laura, who wouldn't stop calling or writing to him because of one night in Barbados. Why had he fucked Laura in Barbados? To make her fall in love with him because he'd wanted to know what it was like to be loved like that. Only he couldn't work out how to make Laura stop – and in the end he'd had to go and see her in her flat. They'd talked about New Zealand and she'd threatened to jump. He had such a clear image of Laura standing on the windowsill, her bare toes pressing down into a layer of pigeon shit, before he'd lunged forward and pulled her back into the room, knocking his knee on the radiator and falling into a post-coital position on the carpet that lovers the world over assumed – only they hadn't just fucked and would never fuck again.

They lay there against each other, breathing heavily, knowing this. Laura didn't say anything, and by the time he left the flat she still hadn't spoken. He left her lying on the floor in silence. The last thing she'd ever say to him was, 'I'm going to jump.'

It was just as he remembered this that half the Palmers'

441

lounge ceiling fell in, covering the TV and his feet, and he sat there staring up through the hole at the Snoopy poster on Jessica's bedroom wall that he'd been looking at earlier. Then it occurred to him that it was only a matter of time before the rest of the ceiling collapsed and that there was nowhere to run to. Getting to his feet, he had some vague notion of pulling himself up into Jessica's room, climbing into the loft and getting onto the roof of No. 8, but he didn't know how far underground he was. Then the rest of the ceiling started to buckle, Jessica's bed slid down into the lounge and he found himself suddenly on eye level with the Laura Ashley lightshade.

He ran instinctively back into the hallway and stared at the wall of a ventilation shaft where the front door should have been, and the darkness that was an offspring of the adrenalin his body was producing started to rapidly fill his muscles as it occurred to him that he was about to die – and that it was about to happen here in the Palmers' lounge. He'd never felt so irrelevant in his entire life before. A combination of desperation, frustration and humiliation made him start kicking against the wall of the shaft, and it was then that he discovered the knee-high entrance to a tunnel that was small, but not too small. It would protect him – it might even lead somewhere. Slamming himself onto his belly, he used his elbow and hips to pull himself into the tunnel's entrance just as the rest of the ceiling collapsed and Jessica's bedroom fell down into the lounge.

He tried turning his head, but couldn't because the tunnel was too narrow. Choking on cement dust, he crawled forwards for about a metre to see if the tunnel opened up, but it didn't. If anything, it seemed to get smaller, so small that he felt as though the tunnel had hold of him. The pressure round his shoulders and ribcage was uncomfortably restricting and he started to panic. Movement is a natural

442

reaction to panic, and Mick tried moving backwards, but the tunnel was blocked by debris from Laing construction and Linda's décor. He couldn't move forwards and he couldn't move backwards, and his eyes were never going to get used to the dark because the darkness didn't need his eyes. The length of tunnel he was lying in belonged to a primordial world where there were no binary opposites. Just beyond the soles of his shoes there was a Laura Ashley lightshade, a TV and a piece of deep pile carpet that he now tried to picture in all their meaningless catalogue glory because right then they gave him a comfort he'd never sought for above ground.

Then he started to cry, and he cried because the Palmers' Laura Ashley lightshade was becoming dislodged from his mind in the knowledge that the darkness he found himself in was absolute and had no need of anything – not even his death. This knowledge was replaced by a nagging suspicion that it was more difficult to die down here than he'd thought and that immortality might just become the most banal of all his achievements so far. Still crying, he tried to validate himself in a round of 'Mick Saunders versus the darkness' and threw at it an aerial shot imprinted on his mind of the Great Wall of China, one of man's great achievements that even the darkness of space had to acknowledge as a stiff line snaking across the surface of the earth, but the Great Wall of China and even flying itself seemed to have more to do with the darkness than Mick Saunders, so instead he tried to get hold of the image of the Palmers' Laura Ashley lightshade again, which gave him a warmth nothing else could have done right then – not even Dominique – because it was utterly disposable.

Dominique watched No. 8 Pollards Close split unevenly in half, the back sliding slowly down the hill. Through the open garage door she could now see lights in the sky above Gatwick airport. Mick was no longer in the hallway, and as she walked onto the road, the front of what was left of the house fell suddenly underground. Without waiting to see what would happen next, she walked across the Palmers' front garden to where the roof of the house now was, on ground level.

Jessica Palmer, who had been flung sideways through the open front door as the front of the house sank underground, was lying across the porch, face down.

'Jessica,' Dominique said, whispering without knowing why.

After a while Jessica rolled onto her back and put her hand over her face as if the sun was shining into her eyes. She stared at Dominique without saying anything then got slowly onto all fours before pulling herself up. 'The bomb?' she said after a while.

'The what?' Dominique stared at her.

'Was it the bomb?'

'What bomb?'

'*The* bomb?'

'There wasn't any bomb.'

Jessica nodded and looked at the roof of the house again. 'Did Mum come home?'

'Not yet.'

Jessica nodded again, her right hand gripping the edge of the porch. 'What should I do?'

'You should stay here.'

'You're going somewhere?'

'I'm going to find Mick.'

'Mick was here,' Jessica said.

'You stay here,' Dominique said, 'and call an ambulance or something.' As she climbed onto the roof of No. 8 and swung down into the loft, the last thing she saw was Jessica getting to her feet and calling out, 'Peter? Have you seen Peter anywhere? Peter?'

Dominique, who was now in the loft, didn't respond. She found herself briefly among bin liners full of old clothes, a baby bath and a deflated dinghy, then jumped down through the hatch onto the upstairs landing, stopping briefly to see if her weight made anything shift, and it was while she was on the landing checking this that the door to the Palmers' bedroom gave way and there was Paul Nieman, covered in plaster dust, naked but for a pair of knickers, which Dominique presumed were Linda's. 'You have to get up onto the roof,' she whispered.

Slowly, without saying anything, Paul walked over to where she was standing and they both waited to see if anything was going to give. Then Dominique put her hands together and signalled to Paul to put his foot there.

With her help he was able to haul himself up into the loft, where he waited again, crouching.

Dominique watched him climb through the hole in the roof she'd let herself down through and heard the soles of his feet picking their way over the roof tiles. As Paul jumped into the front garden the floor in Jessica's room gave way. She waited for the plaster dust to settle then started to call out Mick's name, something she hadn't done until then.

There was no answer.

Staring down, she saw Jessica's bed on the lounge floor, surrounded by ceiling debris – and no sign of Mick. Would jumping break up what was left of this part of the house? She sat there trying to think about something there was no point thinking about when all she could see in her mind was the way Mick had walked into the coffee bar at Gatwick when they were both only half the age they were now. She couldn't remember what time it had been, but it must have been late and she'd been on a flight from Rome that had just landed. Airports never really got completely empty, but Gatwick had been as empty as it ever got and without thinking she'd gone up to the boy wiping down the bar and asked if they were still open.

He'd stared at her for a while, they'd smiled at each other, and then, without replying, he'd switched the filter machine back on and made her a coffee as they started to talk. She was sitting at the bar drinking it when Mick, who'd been the pilot on the Rome flight, walked in. The coffee bar was opposite Arrivals. She hadn't seen him walk into the airport but he had seen her and he walked in like he'd been meaning to walk in on her like that for a long time. She thought he was going to walk right up to her and pull her off the bar stool she was sitting on so she held on tightly to the edge of the counter, but he didn't – he just stood in front of her holding his flight bag, breathing heavily.

'You were on my crew – just now – the Rome flight.'

She didn't say anything.

'You've been on my crew a lot lately, and . . .' he stopped, catching his breath, then turned sharply to the boy behind the counter. 'You can do me a coffee.'

'We're closed.'

'You can do me a coffee,' Mick said again, ignoring him, and that's what the boy did; he made him a coffee then carried on wiping down the counter as she and Mick moved instinctively to a table with a fake palm tree next to it, over-looking Arrivals.

'You were on my crew,' he said again as they sat down. The table, which hadn't been wiped, was covered in sugar. 'And that man you were talking to, the one making coffee,' he said, running straight on as if the two were connected in some way, 'was going to take you home and fuck you.'

'That's probably why I was talking to him,' Dominique

446

had said after a while. 'Maybe *I* was going to take *him* home and fuck *him*.'

She didn't know why she was talking to him like that, she only knew instinctively that he'd been wanting to talk to her for a long time and this gave her the confidence not to modify herself in any way, which made her feel like she was coming out into the open again for the first time in a lot of years. 'Maybe he was going to take me to a hotel.'

'He couldn't afford a hotel,' Mick said, looking over her shoulder.

'Can you?'

'I can.'

'So give him the money to take me to a hotel then.'

Mick smiled at her. 'I could do . . . but the thing is – he's gone.'

She turned round. The coffee-maker had gone and the only thing she wondered was when had the shutters gone down because she hadn't heard them go down.

'Anyway,' Mick said, 'he didn't look the hotel type.'

'There's a type?' she replied, turning back to face him. Then, without thinking: 'I used to be fat.'

She didn't know why she said that then – she still didn't – but after a moment's hesitation they both started laughing. The laughter filled the almost empty airport and made a couple of security guards lean out over the balcony they were standing on and look down at them. When they'd finished laughing, he said for a third time, 'You were on my crew.'

'I know – you keep saying that.'

'You've been on my crew a lot recently, and you never seem to go out with anyone.'

'Does it matter? Am I doing anyone any harm?'

'Oh, I think you could do a lot of harm.' That's what he said. Then he got up to go to the loo, leaving the flight bag

447

on the chair opposite. She spent what seemed like ages staring at the clasp on the bag, then got up and left before he came back because she knew he'd follow her. And he did.

When they saw each other again, five days after that on a flight to Boston, the first thing he said was, 'I've been trying to work out if there's anything you're afraid of.' She'd lived every day for the rest of her life since then terrified of losing him – and being terrified of losing someone was the same as loving them, didn't he know that? They'd been together for nearly two decades, but maybe she'd forgotten to tell him. Without thinking, she jumped down through the floor onto Jessica's bed, pointlessly gripping the end of it as the lounge slowly slid another metre down the shaft and she willed it to stop. It had to stop. It did stop, and looking up at the wall of the ventilation shaft once the dust had settled, she saw Mick's canvas shoes – the ones he wore to read and decorate in – jutting out from an opening in the wall just above her head.

Mick wasn't even sure whether his eyes were open or shut any more. Some lines of *Beowulf* that he must have learnt at school came into his head and he said them over and over again. Then he stopped and licked at his lower arm a couple of times. For some reason the segment of *Beowulf* he remembered led to a memory of Rod Stewart's 'We are Sailing' being played at top volume through open French windows and then all he could hear was Rod Stewart's voice and he knew that he would either die to 'We are Sailing' or hear it forevermore.

Dust filled the tunnel again, and when it settled he was aware of being able to move his lower legs, and once he started moving them there was a slight variation in the darkness, as if light was coming in from somewhere. Then he felt one of his shoes being pulled off and pressure round his ankle like somebody had hold of it and was checking for a pulse. Please let him still have a pulse. He tried moving his foot and the pressure left his ankle. 'I'm alive,' he screamed as loud as he could. This made the dust shift again. Maybe whoever had been holding his ankle thought the movement, which couldn't have been more than a twitch, signified a death rattle. 'I'm alive,' he screamed again.

With a sudden desolate sense that his body was now playing tricks on his mind, he became convinced that the pressure on his ankle was nothing more than an animal – a rat about to gnaw on his foot – but he'd definitely felt his shoe being taken off. Would a rat know how to untie shoelaces and take off a shoe? Is that something a hungry rat would bother to do? A second later he felt a tapping on the sole of his foot and a second after that he recognised a pattern, but the idea of the rat had overwhelmed his mind, which was in a place it had never been in before. He couldn't expel the rat from his mind, it just sat there filling it. Why would a rat talk to him before eating him, he thought. How would a rat know how to talk to him and – more importantly – talk to him in Morse? It wouldn't, because rats don't speak, animals don't speak, *ergo* there was no rat. His mind fought to deduce the rat out of existence as he realised that the word being tapped up through the sole of his foot in dyslexic Morse code was D-O-M-N-I-E-Q. Mick automatically corrected the spelling in his mind then lost consciousness.

When he came round he was aware of being pulled upwards. The air was getting fresher, and the soles of his feet were ringing with the things Dominique had said through them.

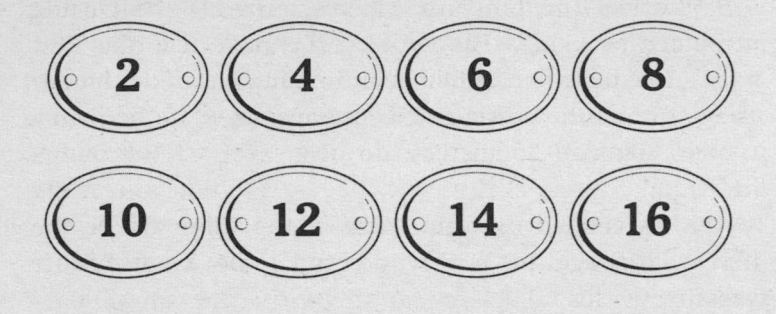

By three a.m. Emergency Services had evacuated the residents of Harvester's Way, Merrifield Drive and the half of Pollards Close that hadn't fallen down into the quarry. The houses that had fallen had first sunk into their own foundations then slid down the spine of chalk that formed the old Roman road into a quarry that had been backfilled, but was disturbed by groundwater because of illegal chalk mines which existed beneath the quarry that nobody had detected – not even the engineers using microgravity to identify voids and loosely compacted soil. Groundwater coming down the hill in a sudden rush disturbed the sand and gravel deposits beneath the quarry. The back of No. 8 was balanced on the spine of Roman road, but the front half had fallen into an old ventilation shaft leading down to the mines.

The four-hundred-year-old Turkey oak had reluctantly fallen, but not without a fight. Its branches were skewering the Laing show home and caught against its roots was a white Toyota. A man suspended on a wire from a police helicopter pronounced Linda Palmer, who was lying across the steering wheel with the palms of her hands pressed loosely against the shattered windscreen, dead, and gave instructions for the car and its dead driver to be taken up by the crane. 'One dead female down here,' he yelled through his radio.

By the time a medical professional got round to conducting an autopsy on Linda Palmer, he concluded that Blue Dye No. 1 (used in raspberry Slimshakes) had entered her bloodstream due to the erosion of digestive-tract tissue, inducing hypotension and an increase in acid levels in the body's fluids and tissues. This meant that by the time the white Toyota accelerated over the edge of the Close where the drive and garage to No. 8 was meant to be, Linda Palmer was already dead.

'One dead female,' the man suspended from the police wire yelled again, and paused. 'The dead female's blue, I'm telling you – she's blue.'

The camera crossed the police line at the entrance to Greenfields Estate, settling briefly on the people lining the pavements in the clothes they'd worn to bed after having been evacuated from their homes nearly an hour ago. A woman in pink pyjamas was arguing with a police sergeant. The camera recorded the ageing sergeant trying to pacify her then moved up Merrifield Drive until it reached the row of ambulances parked at the top near the railway line, stopping in front of the first ambulance, whose doors were open.

Inside was Paul Nieman, who had been in front of the Palmers' bedroom mirror wearing a pair of Linda Palmer's white lace knickers when No. 8 started to slide. The camera didn't know any of this, all it saw was an eighteen-year-old boy in female underwear in the back of an ambulance, having glass removed from his body.

It moved on up the row of ambulances to the only other one with its back doors open. There was a girl inside, filthy and scratched, but intact. She was holding hands with the

451

boy sitting next to her, and they were looking out on the world through the open ambulance doors like it meant everything and nothing to them. The camera had them framed.

'You were involved in the incident?' the reporter asked.

The camera closed in on Jessica looking down at her lap in a lopsided way before she looked up again and said, 'It's been a pretty heavy night – and it wasn't an incident, it was a landslide.' She broke off. 'I thought it was the bomb – you know, at first. I mean, I lost consciousness and then when I came to, I was so convinced it had happened – the bomb. I thought it was like the end of the world or something – I was so sure. I was just sitting there thinking, I'm still alive, and what does it mean – being alive still if the world's just ended?' Then she broke off again, starting to cry this time. Her hair was hanging down over her face, obscuring it. The camera, which had shifted slightly while Jessica was talking about the bomb, switched back to a head shot at the appearance of tears, but the morning's first express train to London, passing in sonic haste on the other side of the fence, drowned her out as she said, 'And my mum . . . I don't know where my mum is – if she came back, or . . . my dad – what happened to Dad? Nobody can tell me anything – nobody knows anything.' She stared straight into the lens before being pulled away by Peter Klusczynski. The camera backed off but framed Peter holding Jessica in his arms for a while before panning slowly around and moving round the corner into Pollards Close. Tony Browne's head passed across the left-hand side of the frame, moving in the opposite direction, towards the ambulances.

The garage door was up at No. 2, and inside, lit by storm lanterns and a couple of highly polished brass ships' lamps from the Youngs' nauticalia collection, was a trestle table with a white linen tablecloth over it and Sheila Young standing behind it, making tea. She was filmed making a fresh pot and pouring it into a row of Charles and Diana commemorative mugs that had been in the garage ever since the street party when they'd over-ordered. The camera chronicled Sheila Young's tea-making from the boiling of the kettle to the pouring of the last cup before she disappeared off-camera and back indoors to wash up used mugs and try not to calculate in her head how much the whole Blitz Spirit tea-making venture was costing them – if this was going to carry on all morning, when could she change out of her dressing gown and start charging for the tea?

The camera pulled away towards a man lying on a stretcher with a woman kneeling beside him. Mick only had one shoe on and Dominique was telling him something that made him laugh so the camera stayed where it was because it didn't want laughing survivors. Instead, it moved over to where a crane was setting down a white Toyota outside No. 4. Beyond the uniformed shoulders there was the smashed-up front of the car and the outline of a woman in the driver's seat. A woman sleeping? The lens followed the crumpled slope of bonnet and sensed how utterly defeated the car was. The woman was dead – the driver's door had been taken off and a fireman was pulling her out of the car onto the road. The camera moved round as fireman Rory Whyte ran his fingers instinctively over her face then checked them for traces of blue, only there weren't any. Blue wasn't something she was covered in, blue was what she was. The camera wanted dead, but it wasn't sure it wanted blue and dead. It paused, confused. Keeping the fireman in the frame next to Linda Palmer before moving back to the bonnet of the car and, briefly, the interior, whose glove compartment was disgorging used tissues and greaseproof paper, the camera finally pulled away as a helicopter passed overhead.

At the entrance to the estate a milk float was parked while the milkman, joined by the woman in pink pyjamas, argued with the ageing sergeant that he had rounds to deliver and that if he wasn't going to be allowed through he needed to talk to someone about compensation. He got back into his float yelling, 'As far as I'm concerned it's business as usual,' before driving through the tape.

The sergeant, who'd been running an anti-smoking campaign in schools for the past three years, stood there trying to decide whether to give chase, unsure whether outrunning a milk float was something he was capable of right then.

Following closely behind the milk float was a car with Quantum Kitchens written all over it.

The sergeant gave up.

In the aftermath of the Littlehaven landslide something of far greater national importance was happening just down the road and the news item was never broadcast. The only footage that made it to the screen was Linda Palmer being pulled from her white Toyota by fireman Rory Whyte, and this image exploded into the national consciousness a week later when Linda Palmer, dead, went national at the centre of one of the country's biggest disputes between Slimshakes Ltd and Ciba food-dye manufacturers.

Nobody saw Jessica and Peter Klusczynski holding hands in the back of the ambulance or Jessica in tears as the Quantum Ford drove slowly towards them; nobody saw Mick Saunders laughing and nobody had to edit out shots of Paul Nieman still in Linda Palmer's white knickers. Nobody saw Terry King digging in the rubble that was once the Palmers' back garden for Daphne Nieman; and nobody saw the corpse of Mr Kline – who had never made it to Tibet – being exhumed of its own accord from beneath the foundations of the shed in the back garden of No. 10.

As far as the rest of the world was concerned, none of this ever happened.